AFTER REALISM

After Realism

24 Stories for the 21st Century

EDITED BY

André Forget

Véhicule Press

Published with the generous assistance of the Canada Council for the Arts and the Canada Book Fund of the Department of Canadian Heritage.

 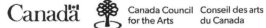

Cover design by David Drummond
Set in Minion and Filosofia by Simon Garamond

Dépôt légal, Library and Archives Canada and the Bibliothèque national du Québec, second trimester 2022

LIBRARY AND ARCHIVES CANADA CATALOGUING IN PUBLICATION

Title: After realism : 24 stories for the 21st century / edited by André Forget.
Names: Forget, André (Novelist), editor.
Identifiers: Canadiana (print) 20210377631 | Canadiana (ebook) 20210377658 | ISBN 9781550655964 (softcover) | ISBN 9781550656022 (HTML)
Subjects: CSH: Short stories, Canadian (English) | CSH: Canadian fiction (English)—21st century. | LCGFT: Short stories.
Classification: LCC PS8329.1 .A38 2022 | DDC C813/.0108110905—dc23

Published by Véhicule Press, Montréal, Québec, Canada
www.vehiculepress.com

Distribution in Canada by LitDistCo
www.litdistco.ca

Distribution in U.S. by Independent Publishers Group
www.ipgbook.com

Printed in Canada

Contents

Introduction

THE NARRATOR OF JESSICA JOHNS's story "Good Bones" has an unusual habit: she composes eulogies for the living. Some of these eulogies are written for people she knows and kept in colour-coded folders—blue for family, green for friends, orange for shitheads. Others she comes up with on the fly. Her mother and sister find this activity morbid, but Marv, a houseless man she hangs out with on her front step, sees the appeal. He even asks her to write one for him. This unusual pastime began when she heard a particularly touching eulogy at the funeral of a friend: it turned out to have been cribbed from a wiki article, which made her wonder "how many people could fit into the same template." Her own eulogies are flights of lyricism, with fantastical causes of death that include spaceships and poisonous fish.

"Good Bones" is a marvellous piece of writing, full of warmth and humour. But the story is also a parable about conventional realism— how its platitudes and clichés too often seduce us into thinking they are adequate to the things they describe. Realistic fiction, much like a standard eulogy, offers us a way of thinking about the world. In so doing, it places certain boundaries around what is imaginable. When we talk about realism in storytelling, we are never just talking about form or style. We are also referring to baseline moral and political truths, as well as certain laws of cause and effect, that readers can identify with. The eulogies in "Good Bones" are small acts of rebellion against those truths and laws. A eulogy that blandly lists someone's loyalty and kindness may not be incorrect, strictly speaking, but it obscures the singularity of life under a thick layer of cant. Johns's story is instead alive to the mystery of individuals and their private worlds. By using the charms of language, Johns's narrator uncovers the strangeness latent within the everyday. Her eulogies honour oddity.

As I prepared this anthology, I began to think of the other twenty-three stories as doing much the same thing. Whether it's the quiet intimacy of Tom Thor Buchanan's "Jamaica" or the paranoid horror of Gavin Thomson's "Beelzebub's Kiss," each of the pieces in *After Realism* pulls the curtain of reality back to reveal something stunning and bizarre. Together, they represent a collective attempt to grapple with a tradition dominated by the realist short story.

Realism is notoriously difficult to pin down. Instead of providing a definition, let me offer the first example that comes mind: the famous scene in Tolstoy's *War and Peace* when Pierre Bezukhov is taken out for execution. Awaiting what he believes will be his death, he watches a young man in front of him adjust the blindfold around his eyes for comfort moments before he is shot. Adjusting the blindfold is absurd under the circumstances, but it is also the most normal thing imaginable: its realism lies in the fact that it brings a moment of high tragedy down to earth. There's a humanity in the gesture we can all recognize.

If this is the essence of realism, I don't believe it will ever go out of style. But realism is also marked by far more pedestrian features: an emphasis on character development over plot, a straightforward or understated style, a preference for ordinary people and recognizable settings, a tendency toward introspection rather than action, and a rejection of the supernatural. This kind of realism operates as a convention. It depicts the world as we know it in terms that we are broadly familiar with. The Ontario that exists in an Alice Munro story, for example, is pretty similar to the Ontario you can visit today: the landscape is lovingly captured, and people act the way you expect them to act in real life. The Ontario that exists in an André Alexis story, on the other hand, is fundamentally different. Alexis might depict it using realist techniques—the place names are the same, as is the general texture of life—but just when you thought you knew what you were dealing with, someone gets eaten by their furniture. This is not to suggest that one approach is naturally superior to the other; but, if you've spent years reading stories about marriages failing in suburbia or the sterility of small-town life or grad students being miserable at parties, it can start to feel a bit predictable. When a writer introduces a talking cat, as Casey Plett does in "Portland, Oregon," or a girl whose soul can leave her body, as in Rudrapriya Rathore's "Girls Who Come in Threes," it can feel very refreshing.

Though the last hundred and fifty years have seen an explosion in literary forms and idioms—from high modernism to science fiction to magical realism—the realist short story has maintained a relatively stable place in the literary firmament, as anyone who has spent time reading submissions for a literary magazine can attest. This is in no small part because realist short stories are among the first things young writers are expected to produce. The realist story has been enshrined as a rite of passage, an exercise in style that must be mastered (or at least attempted) before moving on to novels, where the real action lies and where greater risks can be taken. This is particularly true in Canada, where university syllabi and short-fiction textbooks still tend to canonize realist stories as being exemplary of the form.

But the omnipresent weight of this tradition has tended to crowd out other stylistic options. In a 2015 essay for *Canadian Notes & Queries*, literary critic Alex Good argued that the generation who began their careers during the postwar boom—such as Munro, Mavis Gallant, and Alistair MacLeod—dominated the Canadian scene so thoroughly that their stories have today become a shorthand for CanLit. Younger writers like Tony Burgess, André Alexis, Heather O'Neill, and Zsuzsi Gartner have been fêted for their experiments with fairy tales and horror stories, but in the broader culture, the sixties generation—the "Monsters of CanLit," Good calls them—still embody a kind of mastery. While that mastery is one younger writers can, and often do, appreciate, the unquestioning worship of it by critics and academics has, Good believes, led to a literature gripped by stasis, nostalgia, and geriatric self-regard. "It's been a good half-century run for the Monsters of CanLit," he says in his conclusion, "but it's obvious now that their paths of glory led but to a common grave: dragging us down into the future, shackled to a corpse."

Six years later, it seems possible to offer a more hopeful literary prognosis. Ironically, this is because social and political circumstances have gotten much grimmer. The realism championed by Good's monsters now seems inadequate for depicting the post-Trump, post-Brexit world. Gentle musings about love, time, memory, and death from financially comfortable Baby Boomers stick in the craw of a generation for whom paying rent is an increasingly difficult proposition. The long decades of relative (if deceptive) economic and social stability Canada enjoyed in the late twentieth century have given way to a period of widespread angst. This has sparked a reaction as much aesthetic as political. To borrow a phrase from the Irish novelist Sally Rooney, realism tends to rely on the "continuous present," a world in which tomorrow is expected to be very similar to today. As COVID-19 has made clear, we no longer have the luxury of assuming present conditions will maintain indefinitely. The exhaustion with realism is not just a matter of taste but arises from a sense that a realist style can't cope with reality as we now experience it.

Looking back, it is clear that many of the most unusual short stories and collections published in Canada during the first years of the decade—Zsuzsi Gartner's *Better Living through Plastic Explosives*, André Alexis's *A*, Heather O'Neill's *Daydreams of Angels*, Spencer Gordon's *Cosmo*—were signposts in the woods, indicating a path forward for writers who wanted to renovate the realist tradition. The stories in this anthology borrow from myth, autofiction, sci-fi, fairy tale, documentary, and surrealism to chart a new course for the short story. As suggested by the title, the stories in *After Realism* are not so much post-realist as they are written with a conscious understanding that realism is one tradition among many. They are chronologically "after" the major boom of realist literature in the late twentieth and early twenty-first centuries. They are also "after" realism in the way a poem can be written "after" a certain poet. Some stories, like Sofia Mostaghimi's "Roxane and Julieta" and Michael LaPointe's "The Stunt," hew closely to the conventions of realism, while others, like Marcus Creaghan's "I'm Lonely Down Here" and Cody Klippenstein's "Minor Aberrations in Geologic Time," engage in a compressed form of fantasy world building.

The story of how this group of writers got to this point is itself an apt reflection of the time in which they are writing. Having come of age in the first decades of the twenty-first century, their artistic development has been marked by two existential struggles: one particular to the literary world, the other shared by most members of their generation.

Over the past thirty years, publishing in Canada and the US has been almost completely hollowed out, a process that began in the last decades of the twentieth century, as publishing and bookselling became more centralized, widening the chasm between professionals and amateurs, between those able to make a living off their work and those who must find other ways to pay the bills. As Elaine Dewar argues in her book *The Handover*, this process started with the rise of the book chain Chapters in the 1990s. Because it commanded such a large share of the market, Chapters had unprecedented power over book distribution. If books didn't sell within a set period of time, they were shipped back to the press, narrowing the window for marketing and reducing the chances that a book could become a slow-burn success. Major chains like Chapters were in turn consumed by Amazon, which operates on such a massive scale that it has a unique power to dictate terms to publishers. This has led to a cascading process of consolidation over the past decade, as established publishing houses merge and buy each other out in hopes that conglomeration will give them the leverage they need to negotiate with Amazon.

The result of this has been the creation of a near-monopoly in publishing. According to the *Financial Times*, one in four books sold worldwide are sold by the German multinational Bertelsmann, which owns Penguin Random House. As tends to happen in industries controlled by a few major players, this creates conditions in which authors and their agents have less power and fewer options. A handful of major publishers (namely, Penguin Random House, HarperCollins, and Simon & Schuster) can offer advances many times larger than indie presses can put on the table. But this makes them less likely to publish authors who won't provide a high return on investment. A successful writer needs to do more than just earn back their advance: they must be a revenue machine, a marketable commodity that can generate long-term profit for the company. The best way to do this is by building an enduring brand, remaining consistent to that brand, and writing the sort of book that can be conveniently adapted for film or television.

At the same time, newspapers and magazines have shrunk or shuttered, dramatically cutting into a source of secondary income many writers relied on. Book pages have been reduced; review sections have been decimated. Combined with rising rents and stagnant wages, these conditions have created a narrowing of horizons. You make it big, or you don't make it at all.

Much of this has been blamed on the internet. But the internet giveth even as it taketh away. Though conventional career paths are drying up, millennial writers have kick-started a golden age of little magazines. The low overhead involved in launching a digital publication has allowed people with limited resources to create influential journals and even publishing houses. Social media has made it easier for emerging writers to share their work than ever before, and because national borders can be transcended online, new distribution networks generate new networks of influence.

Traditional literary journals like *The Fiddlehead* or *The Malahat Review* publish work that can be read only by subscribers, and most of them are available only in print. If your local library doesn't stock them and you can't afford to buy your own copy, you're out of luck. Digital magazines are accessible to anyone with an internet connection, have considerably less overhead, and often reach far beyond their intended audience. A writer in Halifax, for example, can publish a story on a Vancouver-based website and then watch the story be retweeted by an author in California, who is followed by another writer in Scotland, who puts it on their Facebook page, where it is seen by a South African blogger—and so forth. During my time as editor-in-chief of *The Puritan*, a digital literary magazine, I was often surprised by the odd patterns of dissemination that emerged when I checked our social media feeds and Google Analytics. Though the magazine was firmly rooted in Toronto, the fact that our fiction editor, Noor Naga, spent part of her time in Egypt, and that we had published several Nigerian writers, meant that we developed odd pockets of readership around the globe. Some of these readers became contributors, furthering the publication's cosmopolitan sensibility. Over time, our output became defined less by our physical location, and more by the sensibilities and networks of our editors and contributors. Many of the stories in this anthology were originally published in online spaces like *Cosmonauts Avenue, Carte Blanche, OMEGA, Hazlitt,* and *The Puritan,* alongside fiction from across the English-speaking world.

Just as technology has made publishing and talking about literature in English an ever-more global phenomenon, political dynamics within Canada—in particular, the movement to recognize the territorial sovereignty of Indigenous nations—have caused some writers to question whether the Canadian state, and CanLit by extension, are morally justifiable projects. Literature in Canada has, of course, been a nation-building tool from the beginning and formally politicized as such since the 1950s, when the government invested in a series of funding bodies (such as the Canada Council) explicitly designed to encourage the development of a homegrown literature. Writers skeptical of Canadian nationalism understandably balk at the idea of contributing to a cultural undertaking framed in overtly jingoistic terms.

These factors have come together to create an emerging literary culture that is indifferent to nationalism, entrepreneurial, pessimistic about the odds of professional success, and open-minded on questions of form and style. CanLit *qua* CanLit has come to seem a parochial affair, predicated as it is on the notion that writers can or should be primarily defined by their citizenship. The structures that gave rise to and shaped this idea—universities, magazines, contests, and funding bodies—still hold significant sway, but this is mostly because they dispense money and provide (fitful) employment. Perhaps we should treat it as a sign of maturity that many younger writers in Canada define themselves more by transnational cultural movements and substantive formal and ethical questions than by geographic location or residence status.

In addition to the changes in the publishing industry, the writing in this book has also been shaped by seismic social and political shifts. A writer born in 1990 watched 9/11 before they were in middle school, finished high school under the shadow of the Great Recession, and graduated from university into a world of temporary, part-time, or contract-based jobs. Their twenties were marked by the Idle No More protests, Black Lives Matter, the Truth and Reconciliation Commission, the refugee crisis, and the main-streaming of far-right white nationalism. During this time, war abroad became a kind of background noise while political polarization at home reached a fever pitch.

If that young writer wasn't white or straight or didn't identify as a man, they would have had to contend with an establishment that

15

careened between a fetishistic desire to support them for "diversity" reasons and an active hostility should they refuse to affirm the bland liberal story that Canada is an essentially progressive and multicultural country. Black and Indigenous writers must pursue their work knowing that extrajudicial murder of their people is common. The scandals relating to alleged sexual abuse at creative writing programs at the University of British Columbia and Concordia University have led to a generational reckoning with the problem of harassment, sexual assault, and rape in the literary world. The increased visibility of trans writers—an important victory—has also led to a virulent backlash from right-wing media and academic figures who believe the movement for trans liberation is a threat to public order. The notion that history trends irrevocably toward progress has, for many millennial writers, been utterly discredited. Small wonder, then, that many of the stories in this anthology, like Paige Cooper's "Record of Working" and Camilla Grudova's "Madame Flora's," have a sinister and pessimistic edge.

Many of these problems are, of course, not unique to this generation. They have simply been heightened by rapid technological and economic changes. But, for many of the writers who appear in this collection, climate change is the unavoidable nemesis. Fiction is slow business. It takes years to turn a few sentences into a manuscript and a manuscript into a book, and it can take many more years for a book to be properly appreciated. The immediacy of the environmental threat, the inescapable sense that decisions made in the coming years will determine the fate of humanity, raises uncomfortable questions about the value of writing. It is a future-oriented activity, after all, and if the future is likely to be significantly shorter than the past, why go to all the trouble? Why not get involved in political agitation and direct action that could be of some use to the human race? Several of the stories in this anthology, including Cason Sharpe's "California Underwater," David Huebert's "Chemical Valley," and Christiane Vadnais's "Creaturæ," deal explicitly with the question of how we can meaningfully live in the face of a climate catastrophe that has already begun.

Given our anxious and paranoid time, it is not surprising that the contents of *After Realism* are intensely self-aware. Narrative itself is often the main subject. Characters engage in compulsive storytelling, try to rationalize the world around them or puncture its illusions, and the question of whether these stories can provide meaningful explanations is ever-present. One thinks of John Elizabeth Stintzi's "Going Toward Gadd," in which a Dungeons and Dragons game plays out alongside the self-exploration of the nonbinary narrator. In many of these pieces, a great deal of time is spent trying to figure out what is true and what isn't. For Paola Ferrante, Jean Marc Ah-Sen, and Eliza Robertson, style becomes the story as their protagonists use prose to defamiliarize the events taking place.

What I hope *After Realism* makes clear is that, while writers are influenced by other writers, they are also influenced by everything else around them. One can enjoy Kafka without knowing much about early twentieth-century Prague, but one cannot really understand Kafka without a passing familiarity with his world. Just as a reductively sociological approach sterilizes literature, a purely aesthetic one leaves it impoverished. By attending to the fact that these stories were produced by *these* people during *this* time, we learn to read them better.

Realism shaped how generations of Canadian writers understood their craft. As we find ourselves in a time when every orthodoxy is being questioned, perhaps this new generation, by moving beyond realism, can help us appreciate the aesthetic possibilities latent in the current period of crisis. These stories will not necessarily instruct, or edify. But, as acts of witness, as experiments in language, and as encounters with the sublime, they are heartening rejoinders to the flatness and cynicism rising like a tide around us.

Swiddenworld

Selected Correspondence with Tabatha Gotlieb-Ryder

JEAN MARC AH-SEN

Goldie's van Dongen

To SERGE MAYACOU, of HAMILTON

Serge,

I made some serious enquiries on your behalf about whether Goldie would be amenable to selling the Paul Kirchner and Peter van Dongen pieces. Kirchner is a definite no; with van Dongen, although he is rather attached to it, he did assure me somewhat indeterminately that this would not be the case forever. "This is *not* an 'anfractuous' enticement to entertain offers"—(his exact choice of words). I don't know that he has a firm number in mind; when he says something like that, it's usually to weigh up whether it's enough incentive to let it go. If it's too low, he may not counter-offer, just respond, "I'd rather just keep it" (as he has done before). Confidentially speaking however, I think I can tell you that no one—at least while I have been in his employ—has ever made an offer for it, much less expressed so much as an interest. I don't want to get your hopes up, but I think this bodes well. I know that he has been negotiating for years with a collector in Kalamazoo about an original Roy G. Krenkel. Goldie is under the impression that they are about to agree on a number (seven years onwards), but this wouldn't be the first time that he's over-estimated finances, or his bargaining power for that matter. Don't let appearances to the contrary fool you—though the studio is certainly spacious, well situated (opulent, some might even be accustomed to say)—Le Nid de Duc it is not. I have your contact information now, so I can advise you should the time come.

I enjoyed our conversation about Bruce Pennington and *Eschatus*. I am not aware of any publisher other than Paper Tiger ever having rights to publication through legitimate means, however. You are always welcome to stop by in the studio if you have any further questions, or simply want to look through what Goldie will be putting up for sale in the future—I would be more than happy to set anything (available) aside for you.

> – T. Gotlieb-Ryder

To T.G.R., of TORONTO

Tabatha,

Thank you for your note. I am touched by the gesture of consideration. I enjoyed making your acquaintance as well—if you could reach out should the van Dongen go to market, I would be in your happy debt. I would not hesitate to show my gratitude.

I looked through my *Galaxies* and could not believe you were able to reference the artist based on my inadequate methods of description. I can confirm it was Philippe Caza who did the cover in question.

> – S. Mayacou

To SERGE MAYACOU, of HAMILTON

Serge,

Movement on the Krenkel front imminent. If all goes as planned, the transaction will be finalized within a day or two. Privately, I can confirm Goldie is still taken with the van Dongen (it currently resides over his mantelpiece, next to the portraiture his wife, Marlana, made in his likeness). He will push lesser pieces on you to generate immediate funds for the Krenkel deal; additionally, he took note of your interest in Virgil Burnett and Howard Sherman (your taste does you credit) and has pieces in his possession to which he no longer bears an attachment. If you push past his resolve for the van Dongen, and make no allusions to possessing an awareness of privileged information, I know for a fact he will capitulate.

– T. Gotlieb-Ryder

To T.G.R., of TORONTO

Tabatha,

The van Dongen is at the framers now. If I am being perfectly honest, I am still shaking with disbelief at my good fortune of having come into contact with you. Not the crown jewel by any stretch, but a very good specimen of the man's untrammelled control of static movement, and a happy resident in any serious collection. What I find most appealing is how it is an example of his more oppressive and rough line work, uncluttered with the pretenses of Swartean flatness. I hope I am not being too forward in the hope of wanting you to see where it will be eventually situated at my residence. Please allow me to treat you to dinner one night as a show of my appreciation.

– S.

To SERGE MAYACOU, of HAMILTON

Serge,

That would be lovely. When will you next be in the city? I leave all particulars to you, and can be free most evenings after Goldie has closed the gallery. I thought it would be worth mentioning that he has recently made contact with a reputed former associate of Frank R. Paul who has a small stockpile of his artwork. The provenance is currently being assessed by someone in Teaneck. Interest is expected to be above average/crash-hot on account of renewed interest in his work; knowing Goldie's pricing, this will thin out the competition considerably. I can bring stats to dinner if you don't object.

– Tabby

To T.G.R., of TORONTO

My Little Fuckling,

You were a right saucy glitz-cunt last night. Nail on the ready, I could not wait to have you bucking and frisking like a hind in the wind. Your blithesome bunghole and its raucous puckerings hypnotized my mind to the Omega Point—glossolalic pronouncements, keeping perfect time with your intoxicated breathing, the echoing singsong of your colliding juddlies recalling me from the distant heavens of your tantra, the hint of a fetid musk wafting from your armpits. A more debauched ritornello has not been heard this side of midnight when I let my gasps unroll into moans.

When you began reciting the names of the assured masters—"Ray Feibush, Alex Schomburg, Virgil Finlay"—while engaged in unholy congress, I barely had the sense to blunder out myself into your mouth before it was too late. Even if I wanted to, I could not dispel the image of you soothingly anointing my gonads with my seed. My sweetest Tabby, tell me you will let me have you again, that you are not over-boyed (and with whom I must vie for your attentions). Barring such circumstances, that you will see me again in whatever capacity that allows me access to your naked splendour—cockservant, witness, figger, what have you. Let me be your nightstick, I have no hard limits. Old guard leather need not apply.

– The Joy Beaut Lover

To SERGE MAYACOU, of HAMILTON

Dearest Whorelet,

Did you think to have satisfied my ravening desires, O cockless wonder? Did I say you were finished with me? Did I give you permission to finish before I told you to? Your anointment was merely a prelude to your despoiliation. The sequelae of your actions will be tenfold. We will fructify your ten-a-penny cock yet, drudge. The acidulants in your jissom will smart and stain your body, your mouth, your anus—I can hardly wait to see how much further I can claw my finger up your gate and have you glimpse the storms in heaven. We will make a *swidden* out of you yet. Once we have finished laying the groundwork for your vitiation, I will sanctify your cockling with an appropriate and fitting ranking. I dub my quim Apeslayer: violator of all who kneel before my bilious heat. Fie, swoon and tremble before my blessed chalice, sate yourself on the quiniferous piquancy of my urticating clunge.

Do you know Julius LeBlanc Stewart's work? "Nymphs Hunting"? Our pairing brings it to life. Familiarize yourself with its sick-making majesty. I will brook no clanking irons. Does it bring you shame or pride that you fuck for profit? You are a grotty, foul, lop-sided cock-disaster who can't make up his mind about which hole you want to screw any more than you can decide which gets you hotter, the possibility that I might have an Ohrai or a Mark Harrison in the wings, hidden from Goldie's view. Poor, lamentable art lover, born too late to get in on the ground floor of Guido Crepax's reputation being pulled out of the rot-funk of the Italian gutter... You need me to derrick the vicissitudes of the art market so that I can maximize the length and breadth of your dollars like I maximize the length and breadth of your meat when I guide you inside me. I own you, therefore I can unmake you. You will need a shuftiscope when I am done with you, worm—skinfuls of foof,

> – Glitz Cunt

To T.G.R., of TORONTO

Tabby,

I read your letter with anticipation in the stockroom at work. I was already hard before my fingers found their way around my member. I frigged myself quickly and wiped myself on your letter before licking it dry. Your mention of Crepax occasioned my memory on the pages I had let slip all these years—Sterankos, Bodēs, Morrows. Why must you demean me so? Have I not been a percipient if tolerable servitor? What can I do to prove the fealty I swear unto you and your crimson cathedral of smut, bunt and disease? I could write a vexillology of your red minge and the congregants who advance behind it. The mild fragrance of sweat admixing with the sour sluices of your asshole awaken a dormant pathology inside me, the shit-stink of your soul are like embers that make your twat bawl out "Decretals of Minge!" in farting whimpers.

My waking reveries of your sour stockinged feet pressed against my nose while I nibble on the flaking skin of your heels prevents me from coordinating the movement of my legs when I am returning from the bar. Just the other night I sat drunk, transfixed on another woman's legs that reminded me of yours—they had the same bandiness, I swear I could perceive the same sweat stink of your armpits and the same contumelious smirk on your lips. I had a good frig with my thighs and had enough baby batter spilling down my ankles that I lost sense of myself and delighted in pouring my porter over my lap just so the barmaid could pat me down with her dirty dish rag.

I made my way home in a skronking stupor, vomited in the stairwell, and began to unbutton my shirt and trousers so that I could feel something warm on my chest and groin. I could not manage much more than half my normal size (it looked like a pufterlooner) but I smeared some vomitus up myself all the same and began to see the emblazoned image of your red, inflamed bunghole in my mind's eye, the raphe extending down your taint like Jacob's Ladder. When I had recomposed myself, I made my way into my apartment and called you on the telephone. We discussed Hannes Bok and Rowena Morrill briefly, but ended our conversation abruptly because you were feeling poorly. I regained my composure shortly afterwards and fell asleep while *Charlie Bubbles* was playing on the television.

– The Welland Canal

Insufflation Takes Two

To SERGE MAYACOU, of HAMILTON

Serge,

I have not heard from you for several weeks now; a third letter going unanswered is bordering on incivility, but I think I catch your meaning. I could forgive your remissness if I did not suspect an ulterior motive. Did I frighten you? I warned you that my sex was not for the meek and faint hearted. Did the insufflation of your nethers break you? Did you not like the feeling of being entered and roiled from within? Did the mere sight of blood make the measure of a man burrow up inside you? You'll have no bitter tears from I, worm-feeding cock-spastic. Never set foot in my place of business then; never write me, never phone me. I hope your van Dongen turns out to be a fake—knowing Goldie, the truth isn't that far off. No one will deign to engage you in transactions—your collecting days are finished. You'll bear the mark of a welch in our circle, which I can assure you, is as broad as my mouth. Good luck ever getting into anyone else's pants who knows who Bernard Sachs is. I hope you get gonorrhea in your throat and crust scabies in your taint, you hypospadic pup. Your necessaries smell like a leper colony. You were pissed up against a wall and hatched in the sun!

It's a cock sweetie, not a crumpled bill you're trying to squeeze into a vending slot. Fuck off and die you grostulating, rent-a-cock choirboy! The glitz-cunt is dead!

To T.G.R., of TORONTO

Tabatha,

I know full well that I am the last person you expected to hear from again, but I can only hope that if you are still reading these words, a morbid curiosity will give you the inclination to understand what I have to say.

Let me start by saying that I cannot apologize enough for my determined efforts to ignore you: yes, as I'm sure it will come as no surprise, I admit it freely. I was compelled to sever our relationship, such as I believe it was fast becoming, from outside influences I felt forced to succumb to. I will spare no detail, because I believe that an orderly mind still counts for something in these days of ease.

A few days after our last telephone conversation, I received a summons to Goldie's Trefann Court offices. He refused to elaborate on the nature of the visit, save to say that it would concern a matter of "renewable interest." I was met immediately by Goldie and two individuals approximately in their forties bearing the waxen demeanours of mortuary attendants. I believe you will know them to be Ms. Runthenthorpe and Mr. Freleng, celebrated art-scoundrel muckety-mucks and long-time associates of Goldie's. They had a proposition for me, which piqued my interest, knowing their reputation for implacable, purposeful acquisition.

Runthenthorpe had gathered that I was making moves to acquire several Murphy Anderson pieces as privately as possible and almost always through direct sales. Freleng, similarly, had become aware of the growing Howard Sherman collection I was amassing. This unsettled me to no end as I had taken considerable steps to remain anonymous and to never discuss the pieces publicly unless someone demonstrated the velleity to relinquish a piece. The more publicity these transactions had, the better chance potterers would come hunting for the sake of the muck and unsettle my own motivations of unspoiled, artistic contemplation, as we have discussed in days of yore.

Goldie and co. asked me in no uncertain terms if I would be willing to place bets at a coming auction they were holding. I professed that I did not quite grasp their meaning. Freleng and Runthenthorpe were in the process of downsizing their respective collections and were feeling anxious that they would not recoup their original expenditure, or that their pieces would not fetch the prices that in their estimation the broader marketplace could secure. It dawned on me that they were asking me to engage in shill bidding. I did not make any moral calculations on this front, but briefly considered the repercussions if caught. Goldie assured me that the only people who knew of the arrangement were present in the room, and that it had been the first time that any of them had attempted anything of the sort. A "chanson des mouches," Goldie had called it. He opined that though ants and bees were like communists, flies comprehended private enterprise consummately.

Before I could ask what would motivate me to assume the risk, Freleng and Runthenthorpe produced Anderson and Sherman originals from their respective collections. I was besotted with the Sherman in particular because I had assumed the majority of these pages had been destroyed at the production level long ago. Goldie assured me I could have one artwork on the spot, and the other at the end of the auction. If things went according to plan, they envisioned a time when I could call on them to perform the same service, ensuring a provident future. We shook on the agreement cordially, and then Runthenthorpe and Freleng took their leave of us, placing the Sherman on the escritoire by the entrance door for me to wrap up.

When we were alone, Goldie took the Sherman in his hands to appraise the detail with the assistance of a magnifying glass before asking me how I knew about the van Dongen. I feigned ignorance as to his meaning, for he still did not suspect the nature under which I acquired it. I don't need to tell you that van Dongen's work experienced a significant uptick in the months since Goldie off-loaded the page, essentially tripling in value in what memory assures me was virtually overnight. Goldie harboured some ill will on this front, but was more impressed than anything by my talents for prognostication. I attempted to disabuse him of this opinion, but he was fixated, especially since my interests overlapped with those of Runthenthorpe and Freleng. The matter was settled that he wanted me as a junior buyer and assistant. The suggestion was both attractive and dismaying— this was essentially the position you held with him. I balked at the offer as graciously as I could. He would not take "no" for an answer, however. He didn't care if I had heard of the Kupferstichkabinett or not; merely that I had produced results. He laid out exciting terms for my employment, but insisted that my focus could never attenuate or he would seek a replacement (a credo, as I would learn, he had lived by for years). Goldie found your focus recently to be lacking, and your oversight concerning the van Dongen was uncommonly galling to him. Of course, I am to be held accountable for the so-called lapses in your discernment.

It was inside the probable that your professional relationship with Goldie was now at an end. My intent was to continue seeing you and to work for Goldie, maximizing my wits and connections to more than make up for what had befallen you by my hand. It was my hope to buy you an original Pennington as a preliminary token of contrition. Your first letter had arrived asking why I had not responded to you, and though I drafted a version of the letter you now hold in your hands, I lost my nerve to send it. Goldie's disobliging work expectations occupied the best of me for a few days, and by then it was too late, for your last letter had arrived on my doorstep making the decision easy for me. I was soon filled with tremendous sorrow and regret—you seemed perfectly adamant (and within your right) to feel this way, and it did not appear to me becoming to pursue your attentions further. I did not always keep to this resolve, finding myself on the corner of your street on more than one occasion, watching outside your window for signs of suitors, or making cursory enquiries with your associates where you landed after Goldie sacked you.

You can imagine my happiness at learning that you are now the exclusive art representative of Thusnelda Baltuch. I can think of no one more deserving of this creditable position. I know there should be no reason for you to want any dealings with myself or Goldie, but I have been tasked by him personally to make whatever arrangements necessary to secure the best representations of Baltuch's work that you have available. There are no lengths that we will not go to acquire these pieces—no lengths. Goldie appreciates the history between the two of you, and has given me an impressive range from his collection with which to begin negotiations. A combination of selections from this grouping and cash value are also feasible (within reasonable limits). I cordially invite you to come to the gallery at your nearest convenience to discuss terms and selections, but know that Goldie would also be acquiescent to meeting at a more neutral location of your choosing. Please find enclosed some Stanislav Szukalski prints with Goldie's compliments. With apologies for the sprawling nature of this communication, and with sincere and affectionate apologies,
– Serge

To MR. MAYACOU, of TORONTO

Dear customer,

Thank you for your interest in Thusnelda Baltuch's work. At this time, we are not making her pieces available publicly. We will notify you should this change. Regards,
– T. Gotlieb-Ryder

To T.G.R., of TORONTO

Tabatha,

You can imagine Goldie's displeasure when the Baltuch pages went public without advance knowledge. The pieces he was interested in were no longer available by the time he had frantically approached one of your representatives at the opening reception of the Baltuch show. I would have been in for quite a hiding, I can assure you, had I not successfully moved a handful of Victor Moscoso pieces a few hours beforehand. Goldie was so blinded by rage that night that he hurled a bronze bust of his mother into the painting Marlana made in his likeness. The psychical implications of the act are, sadly, beyond me.

I saw you briefly by the Spitzweg painting—I did not know that you wore glasses. You looked radiant in crushed velvet, and your hair was very fetching in a chignon. Who was the gentleman who never left your side? Perhaps I overstep my bounds...

I have been authorized to offer two pieces as complimentary gifts, provided you and Baltuch agree to meet with Goldie at a location of your choosing: a Jack Cole *Betsy and Me* strip, which he recalls you admired on several occasions while in his employ, and a *Brenda Starr Reporter* strip by Ramona Fradon, which Baltuch has made no secret of admiring. I would never forgive myself if my neglectful behaviour in our relationship was somehow at the root of our inability to discuss business.

– S.

To T.G.R., of TORONTO

Tabby,

I am now hurriedly clearing the south wall of Goldie's lake home for the five Baltuch pieces he was able to secure from you at your La Castile meeting. Goldie and Marlana imparted to me in passing that some infelicitous things were mentioned at my expense (Marlana said she would elaborate when Goldie was asleep, but I can no longer tolerate being alone with that badger-legged woman after the sun has gone down. Bad enough she thinks we are married but not churched). I must admit that I find the experience of being brought so low at your hand extremely...stimulating. Your proviso that I must under no circumstances attend the meeting completed the enchantment. My mind is a boggle-de-botch; what must I do to obtain a response from you? After all, your will was my debasement (and can be again). Yours if you want it, a wife in watercolours, as it were,

> – Serge

Bespawler's Hanging Place

To MR. MAYACOU, of TORONTO

Bespawler,
> Cease all correspondence with me or face the consequences.
> – T. Gotlieb-Ryder

To SERGE MAYACOU, of TORONTO

Serge,
> I decided to break my silence after all these years because I heard the sad news of Goldie's passing. The community will undoubtedly be devastated. He was loud and brash, but he never laid a finger on me or treated me as anything less than an equal (except financially speaking of course). I had some fond memories while working for him, and our last meeting in the autumn to broker the Baltuch pieces was pleasant, painless. He spoke fondly of you at the dinner. He said you were like a son to him, and hoped you would take over the gallery after he retired and do your best not to run it into the ground. I suppose time has palliated my feelings of resentment for you to a degree. I appreciated you not writing me further after I insisted we break off communication. The world is a hanging place. Wishing you solace in this time of grieving,

> – T. Gotlieb Ryder

To T.G.R., of TORONTO

Tabby,

Thank you for your thoughtful message. I confess I had lost all hope of ever communicating with you, in person or otherwise. It was a lovely gesture that cut me to the quick because of the nature of our romantic history. I often think about how our lives might have been different had I availed myself of a more courageous line of action at a critical juncture in our lives. Surely the position I now hold was not incommensurate with whatever potential we may have shared as lovers. I am filled with regret but I realize the timing of a public disrobing of this nature is not entirely apropos.

The future of the gallery is uncertain. I want to continue on, but Marlana wants to unload the majority of the pieces to interested parties as soon as possible and sell the business; a few museums and private concerns have expressed interest in acquiring significant portions of Goldie's artwork en masse, sight unseen in some cases. If we entertain a liquidation, I would like to ensure the most deserving parties receive the most relevant pieces, which is to say, I do not want them collecting dust at a gallerist's warehouse because they are overpriced and deliberately out of reach, waiting for a Dominique de Menil to come nosing around like a truffle hog.

Marlana believes discrimination is unwarranted and wants to move to the south of France immediately. She wants us to be married at the moment it is (perceived) decent to do so. I am at cross purposes on that front, as it is compounding my stress over the funeral arrangements, of which I have (surprisingly) been charged with taking by the reins (where is Goldie and Marlana's daughter?!). I would be happy to return to you free of cost the Baltuch pieces—I understand Thusnelda has expressed regrets about letting those pieces go, and quite frankly, Marlana will not be aware of the minor financial loss. You are free to do with them as you wish; sell them again, keep them, et cetera. Think of it as token of my everlasting appetency for what we shared, once upon a time.

> – Serge

P.S. I further enclose the details of the funeral. You would be most welcome there, along with anyone you wish to bring.

To SERGE MAYACOU, of TORONTO

Serge,

I just wanted to write to let you know that the ceremony was tastefully done and in accordance with every law of propriety. It is exactly the way Goldie would have wanted it, barring of course the spectacle Marlana made of herself. On no less than four occasions I saw her fondling your genitals in full view of Goldie's family. I can tell you that his mother especially did not care for the flagrant disrespect conferred on the dearly departed. I make no judgments as to whom you share a bed with, but I would think that she could keep her hands to herself for a few blasted hours. Her behaviour was frankly indecorous and in shockingly bad taste.

I also want to ask about whose artwork hung above the casket. I have no recollection of the piece, so assume it is a new work, perhaps one you commissioned on Goldie's behalf? It bore a passage about a "day at the beach" or a "blank ballot" if I am not misremembering. And if I dare skirt the edges of shamelessness myself, can I ask if it is for sale? I know you are in mourning and I would not be surprised at a less than propitious response (if any), but it has been some time since I have been moved to enquire about a piece for my ownership. Apologies in advance for the indiscretion,

– Tabby

To T.G.R., of TORONTO

Tabby,

Apologies unnecessary. Your request was a happy intrusion into the sea of calamitous shit my life has become embroiled in. You are incorrect about the piece being from a new artist, but I cannot disclose at the moment whose hand was responsible. You will have to forgive this inflated need for secrecy, but the artist in question has asked that I not divulge their identity before they have completed the series to which it belongs. The pieces are rendered in a style considered a departure from their established credentials, and they have been wavering on the question of whether these shall ever be exhibited publicly or not. What I can tell you is that the inscription you have referred to is by Molavi, and reads as such:

X

Choosing the lesser evil
is choosing evil

Doing nothing
is always an option

But what kind of nothing, my friend

A blank ballot
A day at the beach

I thought it summed up Goldie's attitude toward political engagement rather well.

I will let the artist know that you have an interest in the work, and that you are also Baltuch's representative. Who knows? Perhaps I could have a good word with him about your talents for representation. Baltuch's profile has shot through the roof since she did those book-jacket designs for blewointment if I am not mistaken.

        – Serge

High Fantastic, High Drudgery

To SERGE MAYACOU, of TORONTO

Prannie-Mulch,

You may have succeeded in lowering my defences, but you still have many flights up the campanile to run. Do not presume that because I now entertain your personal company that the errors and follies of the past can be erased like a candle snuffed out in a parlour room; neither must you comprehend my small allowances with greasing your gut-stick in my presence for a passport to every home port at my disposal. You have merely entered the barbican, and must consider yourself a stateless person. Your whore's bath this morning was the beginning of your variegated humiliations, trials and excoriations. I will make

Giordano Bruno's sufferings look like a morning constitutional compared to what you will endure at my hands. You will *not* be moving to Lourmarin, and you will *not* be selling off Goldie's gallery. I will direct your every movement and stratagem with regard to Marlana. Am I understood, manfat? We will engineer the swift dissolution of whatever fishmongering commerce you were caught up in with Madame Pudge—no need to die on that hill. My list of demands shall be forthcoming. Scorf up the medicine now, little sissified itch-mite. Remember, this isn't high fantastic after all, this is high drudgery. The Glitz-Cunt is dead. Longlive the Glitz-Cunt.

    – T.G.R.

P.S. Press this letter to your nose and relive the fragrance of my putrescence. I had to see a star about a twinkle.

To SERGE MAYACOU, of TORONTO

Gash-Hound,

    Hilt and hair time will be further delayed. What follows are a list of my counter-value targets. Stand by for concurrence, leather stretching to follow.

    1. You will surrender all mid- to high-grade art in your possession to me at no later time than a week from receipt of this annexing letter. Supplemental to this requirement are all paper records and inventories pertaining to said collection.

    2. The forfeiture of these assets must occur on the lawn of Quail Pipe Manor, my place of residence, at the stroke of midnight on the night of the next blood moon (next Tuesday), wearing only a smile and after quaffing a vial of quebrachine, which I shall provide in preposterous quantities.

    3. For each article of art surrendered, you shall perform a short ritual of my devising, which I shall elucidate in detail. The ritual, hereinafter referred to as the SHUSH BAG, consists in the nibble and dribble of the scads of diamond-shaped bum oodles that are currently plaguing my nethers while you keep the census down. After each vitiation of seed, you

will be allowed a short respite for hydration (quebrachine or water only). No gel packs will be provided.

4. After this game of pebble dashing is concluded, you will undoubtedly need ample time for recovery. You will avail yourself of the amenities of Quail Pipe for no less than twenty-four hours, both to familiarize yourself in your new environs and become acquainted in the barracks with the other Sweetcorn Boys. There will be no quarter on this account. There will be no room for Marlana this night.

5. When sufficient mindfulness has returned to your faculties, you will convene in the sub-level man-pits for locally televised shew-combat. Report to Claude and Aldegonde for sanitation and oiling. Clinch holds are strongly encouraged.

6. Your future with me as Head Buggerclaw will depend entirely on this contest of wretches. I will not be undone by your pusillanimity again. Fight for your keepsakes as much as you fight for your Great Winnower. When and only when you have surpassed these requirements will my demands continue.

Assholes in retrograde,
   – The Great Winnower

To SERGE MAYACOU, of TORONTO

Gleetbag,

Your inventory is a shambles! I will have you consume more stramonium and Bynin Amara if you cannot be brought to heel. I know from memory that you had in your possession Martin van Maële, Ed Valigursky and Paul Lehr originals. I also distinctly recall a Frank Wilson drawing from *Supermanship* ("The Great Vice Versa"). Obfuscate again and the night physicals shall be accompanied with a very cold Roboleine spoon.

   – Tabs qua Tabs

To T.G.R., of TORONTO

Gatekeeper Of Tabbydom,

Happy tidings on the Marlana question. She has taken my disappearance rather poorly I am told; her crying fits have spilled out into public spaces now. Rumours abound that she cannot continue on without me, and has splendidly made one attempt already at taking her own life involving a piece of chicken wire (I shall spare you the details). The police have been notified concerning my disappearance, and I reckon they shall approach you about an interview for questioning. I feel my resolve failing, which is not to say that I do not believe in the "saturnalias of our conventicle" as you term it, but then again, a rubber truncheon in less capable hands makes for less desirable results.

I don't want to let you down again. I realize that breaking off communication was what doomed us the first time, so instead I want to make my fears perfectly understandable and ask for assurances (come what may). As comely as the attractions of Quail Pipe are, I am beginning to bristle at being under the floorboards for so long (there are only so many Hy Averback films you watch). Couldn't I step out to pick up a few things, Dovey? I might have to run an errand in Moss Park for a night or two...

I really think you are taking too much on your shoulders. Claude is a dear, but the polybabble that passes for conversation is so astonishingly poor that I really might quash his quongs one night with a coat hanger—I am sure that you would grant me that much. What a radgepot you have running this madhouse; châteaued out of his mind half the time from jimmyjohns he's hoisted out the cellar and rolled into his quarters.

In more cheerful news, I received word through protected channels from an old friend. Ingram Freleng, upon hearing of my disappearance after Goldie's death, began to fear for the worst. Far from presuming that I was absconding from the scene of a crime, his letter of concern went to great lengths to assure me that I had a friend who wanted to repay an old debt. He seems enthusiastic about paying homage to Goldie's legacy, and has expressed an interest in fencing the majority of the collection to international parties at white-market pricing. We will not be sending more than two pieces per party (and none to France naturally) to ensure they are not consolidated in one pool, and trackable by the authorities. But perhaps we should make some small allocation for Marlana—she will after all have limited means in Europe, and I do feel she will be hard done by, even *if* we make arrangements on her behalf.

Eagerly awaiting your return from the west. I have not moused off during your absence, as promised. I hope you will be feeling better in a few days. I agree with your sentiment that summer colds are the worst: predictably ill-timed, with a hint of insouciance for good measure. My anxiety unseats my mind. I fear it has made me disastrously unproficient in the goodly art of letter writing. Adieu for now, your
    – Serge

To SERGE MAYACOU, of TORONTO

Drippydick, Lovetick, Stypdick,

One must only have affairs when making love to run-on sentences.

You Cooper-Union dropouts are all the same. All duff and no grog, ineluctably doomed by a lack of imagination. I left Bella Coola earlier than communicated and should be arriving shortly after this letter reaches you. DO NOT SET FOOT OUTSIDE OF QUAIL PIPE YOU DERMOPHILIAC DUCK SHIT UNLESS YOU WANT ABROGATIONS OF YOUR PRIVILEGES TO RESULT. You will receive an Arthur Ranson if you comply.

Your recalcitrance will be our undoing. Claude has already apprised me of your undisciplined self-gratifications. Evirates are my speciality, remember?

Claude has rummaged through your rubbish and found enough evidence to damn an onery house. A night-diddle to buy his silence counts for hardly anything in today's delicate economy. I run a tight ship, jagabat. Never forget where you are—sowgelders aplenty.

Marlana is no longer a concern. I went to Bella Coola in part to negate her involvement in our future. Her kitling Prue Enz lives there, remember? We have always been on good terms. Goldie had long suspected that Prue was not produced of his bloodline.

I have to impart the paramount importance of my next question: you are *absolutely certain* Goldie included an infidelity or non-paternity event clause in his prenuptial agreement? I don't need to know particulars. I am with Prue as I write this, who assures me there is no love lost between her and her mother. Her recollection is that Goldie pledged to her that in the final event, she would be taken care of, but that should any proofs of Marlana's inconstancy turn up, Prue could expect courtly munificence on his part. Prue had always construed that to mean she would receive the Stanley Pitt painting. Whether or not this in actuality means, as I suspect, the whole kit and caboodle of the inheritance, you are my proof for this legal eventuality taking place and leaving Marlana to toy with only otiose recriminations in solitude and wonder.

I will give Marlana the option of giving chase to her *roi fainéant* and losing all stately entitlements to Prudence, or that of keeping the villa in Lourmarin, along with her share of the bequeathment (minus the unaccounted-for artworks), and the abandonment of her search of one "missing" business partner. Another nick in the notch wants looking after. What else is new? Is that a happy enough ending for you or do you want to go again?

More gambitfields to follow.
     – Tabs

Tita Esme's Room

RYAN AVANZADO

Shortly after my eighth birthday, Mom forced me to move out of my bedroom and into Jan's, because mine was the larger of the two and my aunt from Pampanga deserved to live comfortably. She wasn't related to us by blood—she was Dad's uncle's brother-in-law's niece—but I was to address her as either Tita Esme or Auntie Esme. Dad said it was only temporary, at most a month or two, but he had a way of pretending difficult things would be easy. I asked Mom how long I'd have to wait to get my room back, and after several exasperated huffs and a short lecture about how I should be more Christ-like, she explained that having this woman stay with us was necessary.

The afternoon I moved in, I scanned the pink and yellow wallpaper and thought to myself, *This just won't do.* Jan had about thirty stuffed bears and giraffes and an assembly of dolls that she lined up by height and colour on her dresser. I had with me my Stretch Armstrong action figure, my G.I. Joe and Transformers collections, and a full erector set, including a crane that picked up bolts and screws. Our beds were arranged on opposite ends, mine next to the closet and hers by the desk with an orange lava lamp that twinkled at night.

Dad picked up Tita Esme from the airport the following morning, after twenty-six hours of flights that began in Manila, stopped for layovers in Osaka and Vancouver, then finally landed in Toronto. She was waifish and ghostly, her skin almost pink, as if dashed with a spoonful of Pepto Bismol. Her cheekbones were high and round, and her hair was a raven so intense that I could hardly make out the individual strands.

39

Mom nudged me with her leg to greet her. "Mano po," I said, and reached forward, but she held my palm with her bony fingers and gave a limp handshake instead. The only grown-ups ever to shake my hand were strangers from Dad's office at the nuclear power plant. For everyone else, I was expected to bow slightly, take his or her hand, press it to my forehead and receive a blessing. I looked at Mom, who pretended not to notice, and at Dad, who shrugged. Then Jan swooped in and gleefully shook Tita Esme's hand as if ringing a large bell.

In the living room, Tita Esme sat in the corduroy recliner, my parents in the loveseat to her left, and Jan and I toppled over each other on the teal sofa. They made small talk about the arduous plane ride and frosty March weather while sipping glasses of orange juice. Every few minutes, I caught Tita Esme staring disapprovingly at me as I tried to kick Jan with my heels.

"Take a couple days to settle in," Mom said, "then we'll find you a husband."

Tita Esme leaned forward. "Is it that easy?"

"For you? Very easy. Ronald has friends he wants you to meet."

"They're good guys," Dad said.

That night, Jan and I stayed up past midnight making fun of Tita Esme's tight-fitting polka-dot sweater, how tall and scarecrow-like she was, how she didn't notice the grain of rice stuck to her upper lip. Shadows from the lava lamp danced across our faces.

"She wants a boyfriend so bad," I said.

"She'll let anyone be her boyfriend," Jan said.

"She'll kiss anyone."

Jan hopped onto the carpet and imitated Tita Esme's walk, sashaying her hips and waving to imaginary dates. She clomped her feet like a tiny pony and made smooching noises with her lips. I giggled and thought maybe sharing a room wouldn't be so bad. Soon, though, we heard Dad's heavy knock against the door, and we scrambled underneath the covers and pretended to be asleep.

I spent that first week confused why everyone was so hung up on Tita Esme. Mom introduced her around the neighbourhood as our *very single longtime family friend.* At church, one of the sacristans cornered Tita Esme near the St. Vincent de Paul collection box and begged her to attend his Thursday-night prayer group. At the Loblaws, an old woman stopped us near the produce aisle, took one look at Tita Esme, and warned Mom never to leave her alone with Dad. At Adams Park, a nanny asked Mom if it would be rude to approach her for an autograph—she mistook Tita Esme for the actress Gloria Diaz.

To me, she looked unhealthy. When I helped her with the dishes, I shuddered at the thick veins wrapped around her pallid forearms. She and Dad were supposedly the same age, forty-five, but his skin was plump and smooth, while hers looked ready to slide off the bones. Whenever I mentioned this, Mom disagreed and insisted Tita Esme was an ideal Filipina, slender and fair, straight from the pages of a catalogue. *Statuesque* was the word she used. Sometimes, if I squinted and crossed my eyes so that everything appeared a touch out of focus, Tita Esme did resemble one of those Greek figures at the museum.

Dad invited his friend Tito Allen over for dinner during the second week she was with us. He arrived with a box of chocolates and pants that rode too high on his waist. He was completely bald and had a trim physique, which he credited to pedalling his Schwinn along the winding paths near the Scarborough Bluffs.

"Do you like to go cycling?" he asked.

Tita Esme replied, "I don't know how to ride a bike."

"Really?" Jan said. "Even I can ride a bike."

Dad dropped his fork and sent us both upstairs for the rest of the night. I sat on my bed seething. I'd only taken a few bites of my pork chop and had missed out on the cassava for dessert.

"Why did you do that?" I said.

Jan tucked into a ball and draped herself with a blanket. I grabbed two of her Maxie dolls and twisted their heads, the sound like a squeaky door hinge, until they broke free. When she turned over and saw the headless dolls on the carpet, she screamed with such force I worried the windows would crack.

Footsteps raced up the stairs and Mom burst in, terror on her face. She looked at me, then at Jan, who pointed at the decapitated Maxies and began to sob and shake. Mom cradled her and stroked her hair, scolding me in a voice as shrill and terrible as crows.

The next morning, I gave Jan my Stretch Armstrong and told her she could do anything she wanted with it. At first she tried to tear off the head, but all that did was lengthen the torso. So she searched inside her desk for a packet of markers and coloured him purple.

Mom and Dad made phone calls and found Tita Esme work at a strip-mall bakery, between an eye doctor and flower shop. Suddenly the house smelled like croissants and ensaymada in the afternoons.

"I have this for you," Tita Esme said, presenting a wad of cash at the kitchen table on her first payday.

"You should keep it," Dad said.

"If she wants to give us some, let her," Mom said.

"Keep it, Esme. You already do a lot around here."

In fact, our house was humming. Tita Esme always rose before dawn to perform one of her self-imposed chores—dusting the Jesus and Mary figurines above the fireplace, scrubbing toilets, scouring the ring around the sink drain, removing water spots from the foyer's big mirror, ironing Dad's shirts and Mom's blouses, mopping the yellowing linoleum in the laundry room, hand-drying the dishes and silverware, watering Mom's potted aloe vera and Chinese evergreen plants, collecting the empty tumblers and coasters Dad left in his basement stereo room—then she'd take the bus from Dean Park to Kingston Road to Port Union, all before 8 a.m.

Dad liked whenever Jan or I helped her, but mostly we got in the way, and after we broke a few dishes and tipped over one of Mom's plants, Tita Esme stopped asking us. She was polite and pleasant, but distant. When she brought home free ube halaya or egg buns, they were considered treats *for the house*, or for Mom and Dad, never for Jan or me.

The evening Tita Esme first got paid, Jan and I pressed our ears to Mom and Dad's bedroom door and listened while they argued, first about the burden of extra groceries, then about the need to find Tita Esme a husband.

"She's so picky," Mom said.

"These things take time," Dad replied.

"You'd like it if she stayed here longer."

"That's absurd. Is that what goes on in your head?"

"I can see, you know."

Jan and I scurried to our beds when their voices grew louder. Dad's growl travelled through the pipes and echoed behind the walls. Mom's high-pitched wails came in through the air vents beneath the desk.

Mom made me her spy. Dad and Tita Esme were in the backyard chatting away their Sunday underneath the patio awning, teacups and butter cookies spread over the picnic table.

"Get out there and see what they're talking about," Mom said to me in the kitchen, scanning Dad's every move through the window.

"But they're boring," I said.

"I'll give you a dollar."

"That's it?"

"Take the soccer ball with you. Go before I get mad."

I stomped my feet and promised myself I would tell her nothing interesting. Not that I expected much. Dad and Tita Esme's conversations were usually about people and events they barely remembered. They'd grown up together in the countryside among a stretch of sugarcane plantations bordered by a shallow river. He claimed that they were once best friends before they lost touch, and she claimed that she was too cool to ever have him as a best friend.

I kicked my ball through the grass as they reminisced about the Easter week festivities in their town. Everything sounded torturous, more like a series of endurance tests than memorials to our salvation— the chanting recitations of the Lord's passion, the fasting of Good Friday and the dour silence of Holy Saturday, the three-hour Sunday vigil that began at the stroke of midnight.

"I'd visit every puni off the main road," she said.

"Wow, the devotion of the singers in those little chapels," Dad said.

"Oh, please. You'd listen for five minutes then head straight for the tables of pancit and adobo."

"I hate waiting, too," I blurted out.

"We all know how impatient you are," Dad said.

43

Tita Esme shifted in her chair. Even under the sunlight, her complexion was as pale as a toilet bowl.

"Not to worry. I don't have long," she said.

I rushed inside and asked Mom if Tita Esme was dying.

"If only," Mom said.

She wiped down a placemat and explained that Tita Esme's tourist visa lasted just six months and that the bakery paid her under the table. The whole thing sounded criminal.

"If she meets someone and they get married, then she'd be out sooner."

"I hope she meets someone now," I said.

"Me too," Mom said. "Is that all they talked about?"

"Easter and long masses."

"Easter is the holiest time of the year. Even holier than Christmas. Don't forget that."

I asked why Tita Esme had to stay with us in my room, why she couldn't stay with the neighbours. None of these were new questions. For a moment, her lips curled, the beginning of a laugh, though she quickly turned serious, the muscles of her neck tightening.

"You're a selfish boy," she said. "But you have a very unselfish father."

She seized my wrist and pulled me close. Her fingernails pinched my skin. I wasn't sure if she was mad at me or him or herself.

"If you only knew how much he was willing to spend," she said. "There was no arguing with him."

"Oh."

"We had to buy her. The family that kept her wouldn't let her go unless we paid them."

"You can do that? Does this mean *we own her*?"

"Of course we don't own her. What's wrong with you?"

Jan came downstairs a few minutes later and joined me at the table. We ate a bowl of grapes while Mom put dishes in the cupboard. Jan went on about how much she loved grapes, their sweetness, roundness, the feeling of tearing the skin apart with her teeth. Soon after, Dad returned from the backyard carrying the empty tea cups and cookie boxes. He mussed my hair and gave Jan a peck on her forehead.

"Who wants to come with me to get ice cream?" he said.

*

The first time Tita Esme babysat us was in June, three months into her visit. My parents drove downtown for dinner at a Greek restaurant, followed by a production of *Miss Saigon*. Tita Esme fed us roast beef microwavable meals and chocolate doughnuts, then plopped us in front of the television until bedtime. We tried to convince her to let us stay up for David Letterman, but she refused and turned out the lights by nine o'clock.

A half-hour later, I saw the glare of headlights on the bedroom window, heard car tires pulling in on our driveway, followed by footsteps on the porch. I thought Mom and Dad were home, but then came a knock at the front door and the open click of the deadbolt. Feet shuffled through the house the same way mine did when I was sneaking off for a midnight snack. Their voices settled, but I felt movement in the hallways, up the stairs, and into Tita Esme's room—*my* room. I woke Jan up, and we stood by the bedroom entrance staring at the sliver of light underneath my former doorway, soon blotted out by what I imagined were their shirts and socks.

A wave of rustling came, but little else.

"What are we waiting for?" Jan asked.

"Be quiet," I whispered.

I waited for the creak of mattress springs, the smacking of lips and skin. At one point I thought I heard panting, but it may have just been the air conditioner.

"Let's go watch TV," Jan said.

We tiptoed down the stairs. It was still too early for Letterman, and the stations were packed with legal and medical dramas. Jan flipped through channels on the remote. Under the flickering screen, the statues of Jesus (a child, in flowing robe) and Mary (hands clasped, in flowing robe) and Gabriel the Archangel (kneeling, with wings), our paintings of St. Francis of Assisi (face grave, holding a dove) and St. Christopher (waist-deep in water, child perched on his shoulder), all looked grotesque.

We didn't get to watch Letterman. We were curled up against the sofa armrests when Tita Esme woke us. Her bony hands led us back to our beds, and she tucked me in so tightly that my feet were pinned to their sides like a penguin.

We tattled to Mom and Dad the next morning while Tita Esme was off to her Saturday shift at the bakery.

"What do you mean she had a visitor?" Dad asked.

"He came after we were put to bed," I replied.

"Weren't you asleep?" Mom said.

"We woke up when the front door opened," Jan said.

"How do you know it was a man?" Dad said.

"'Cause they went into my room," I said.

"That doesn't mean it was a man," Jan said.

Tita Esme returned hours later with a white box of hopia, Jan's favourite dessert. I watched her eat four of the little cakes while Mom and Dad scolded Tita Esme in the basement. Part of me felt bad for getting her in trouble, but another part of me felt good. Having someone over unannounced, slithering and indulgent in my room of all rooms, was gross.

After that, Tita Esme stopped bringing home baked treats. She still attended to her litany of chores, but with eroding quality, just thorough enough that Mom and Dad couldn't criticize her without seeming petty. Bath towels weren't folded quite so neatly. The washroom sink had a rusty grime behind the faucet. By mid-July, she'd stopped having meals with us and took plates up to my room. She stayed out regularly past our bedtime.

"Is it safe for her to be travelling that late?" Mom said one afternoon. She grabbed a pack of hot dogs from the freezer and defrosted them in a bowl of warm water.

"We can't police her," Dad said.

"Fine. In that case, I really think she should be paying rent. We welcomed her like family, and instead she lives here like a tenant."

"We're not charging her."

"She has you wrapped around her finger." Mom sliced the package open with a steak knife and turned to us. "How many do you want?"

"Two," I said.

"One," Jan said.

"She needs that money for when she's on her own," Dad said.

"What's the use if she ends up going back?"

"Then it's even more important that she have the money."

Mom burnt the hot dogs on the skillet. I covered mine with relish and mustard and a handful of diced onions. Jan bathed hers in ketchup.

Jan guessed that Tita Esme must have saved at least $500. I guessed more like $1,000. Both amounts seemed more than any person could ever need. We entered my room, hoping to find her stash in one of the dresser drawers and confirm. Everything was different—my posters had been removed; the bedsheets were red instead of green; my desk was now facing the left wall instead of the right and was covered in piles of makeup and lotions; I saw none of my toys (I later found them under a blanket in the closet); a floral scent pervaded, overwhelming as you got closer to the window; and it felt several degrees warmer than the rest of the house.

We started with the bottom drawer. It was stuffed with scarves rolled up into cylinders, in leopard print, solid colors and stripes. We squeezed them in search of a papery texture but found nothing. The next drawer up overflowed with wool sweaters; the one above that, with printed T-shirts and jeans. We found her underwear and bras in the top drawer.

"Jan, you go through it," I said.

"Why should I do it?"

"You're a girl."

"So?" she said.

"It's not weird for a girl to go through another girl's underwear."

The drawer was too high for her to see into, and she was forced to reach in blindly while standing on her tippy-toes.

"Nothing so far," she said.

I stooped over the drawer and guided her one way, then the next. "What about now?"

"Nada."

She quickly removed her hand and tossed a pair of Tita Esme's underwear at me. I jumped and yelped. It skimmed my arm, which I pulled back and examined as if infected. Jan doubled over and snorted.

"It won't hurt you," she said. "Don't be a baby."

"Put it back in the drawer," I said.

"You put it back."

She walked to the desk and sifted through the makeup. I stood behind her as she swept her thumbs over the eye shadow and sniffed them, the money now fading from our thoughts. Powder flakes dusted her collar. She picked up tubes of lipstick, removed the caps, and arranged them from lightest pink to deepest red.

"This is way more than Mom has," she said.

"She needs them more than Mom does," I said.

"That's how she gets so many dates."

"Every day of the week."

"Except Sunday," Jan said.

"Even God rests on Sunday," I said. "Wish she'd marry someone already."

She reached for a jar of lotion and held it up. The lid read MIRACLE CREAM in cursive. "What do you think this does?"

"It's just lotion," I said. "For your hands and face."

"What if it makes miracles?"

"That's stupid."

"I'll put it on my face and walk on water." She dipped her fingers into the cream and smeared it like a mask. "Smells good. Try it."

"I don't wanna try it."

She streaked a dollop on my cheek. The scent of melons singed my nose.

"Do you feel any different?" she asked.

"Like I can make miracles? Nope."

She spread her arms wide. "Watch me fly," she said, straining.

She reasoned that we needed to fully commit for the cream to work. So we slathered ourselves in it, covering our faces and arms until we looked like mummies. We took turns jumping off the bed, higher with each attempt, landing heavier with each attempt. Drops of cream speckled the carpet. The entire time, I acted like I was humouring her, but at the apex of each leap, I wondered if there was a chance I could keep rising, break through the ceiling and glide into the clouds.

Mom caught us. We were startled to see her standing in the door-way, though it seems obvious looking back that the entire house must have been rattling under our weight.

She looked at our white faces and said, "You're not supposed to be in someone else's room."

"This is my room," I said.

"No, it's not. This is your Tita Esme's room now."

We stood with hands behind our backs.

"What's that all over you?" she said.

We pointed to the open container of Miracle Cream on the desk.

"We were trying to fly," Jan said.

Mom picked up the container, scanned the cursive, then the list of ingredients on the underside. "Sus! Get that off right now!"

We sat on the washroom counter as she removed our shirts, our little bellies spilling over the waistbands of our shorts. She dunked Jan's head underneath the faucet, then the arms, then covered her in hand soap before rinsing her off again. Mom did the same for me.

Drying us with a towel, she scrunched up her cheeks. "There's a rea-son you don't go through other people's things. Do you know what that was?"

"Miracle cream," Jan said.

"Skin-whitening cream," Mom said.

"What?" I said.

"It turns your skin white."

Jan and I stayed up late looking for signs that the cream had done its damage. We surveyed for spots on our elbows and foreheads. We compared the shade of our ankles with our wrists and thighs.

"Do my ears look lighter?" I said.

"I think I gulped a bit down," she said. "What about my tongue?"

"You think eyebrows can turn white?"

"I got it all over my fingernails."

"Fingernails are already white."

"What if they get whiter?"

We swore that if we noticed any changes, we would make Mom bring us to the hospital. Maybe the doctors would have a way to reverse our condition? Maybe the doctors could put us underneath lasers and burn the brown back into us?

But in a few days, Jan stopped looking for blotches. If I asked her whether I looked any different, she'd shrug and run into the yard. Sometimes I'd tremble at how pink her palms were, until I remembered that mine were pink too, and so were Tita Esme's, and so were Mom's and Dad's.

Tita Esme never mentioned the stray underwear or the opened lipstick tubes or the empty container of Miracle Cream. I'm certain Mom told her—or maybe Mom told Dad and he told Tita Esme— because she became even more withdrawn from us in the subsequent weeks. She hardly spoke to Jan and me at all, and only addressed Mom and Dad when they asked her a direct question. Often she'd slip out the back door in the early evening, only to return at dawn, and we guessed that she must have found a boyfriend or two.

The last time Tita Esme babysat us was in August. Mom and Dad left money for pizza and pop. I bet Jan that I could finish five slices, which I did, then spent the next several hours lying on the sofa, holding my stomach and groaning. Tita Esme gave me an extra glass of ginger ale, just as Mom would whenever I was nauseous. All it did was make me burp. I asked her if she had any other solutions, maybe a remedy from the Philippines, but she assured me I had just overeaten and digestion would run its course.

She reclined between Jan and me, an out-of-date copy of *Redbook* in her hands. The Blue Jays played on television. My breaths were loud and irritating, and sometimes I sighed for added effect.

During the bottom of the sixth, the tightness in my gut began to roil, and I felt a tide of saliva forming in my mouth. My throat rapidly clenched and released. I closed my eyes and counted backwards from one hundred, but at seventy-four, I sat up, leaned over Tita Esme, and vomited on her lap.

She squealed and tossed the magazine into the air. Jan took off running. Tita Esme held her T-shirt out from her stomach, trying to cradle the throw-up like a basket while jogging to the kitchen. She wrung the shirt over the sink and I vomited twice more on the couch cushions. By the time she brought me a trash bin, my stomach was tired and empty.

"You're the worst babysitter," I said, bile stinging bitter.

"That's not nice," she said.

She rinsed my mouth with warm water and dabbed the splatter from my sleeve. Once free, I climbed the stairs and found Jan, head buried under pillows.

"Are you sick?" she asked.

"I'm fine now," I said, changing into pajamas.

We walked back downstairs. Tita Esme was wiping the couch cushion with wadded up paper towels. Beside her were three rolls standing upright, the rubber trash bin, a box of baking soda, and a seltzer bottle. She moved through the clean-up with astonishing precision—soaking up the watery chunks of pizza, spraying seltzer on the leftover stain, blotting the moisture with paper towels, then sprinkling the area with baking soda and pressing it into the cushion with her hand.

"We don't like you," I said from the hallway.

"Yeah, we don't like you," Jan said.

Tita Esme poured another layer of baking soda.

"I don't like you either," she said.

"We hate you," I said.

"We hate you," Jan said.

Tita Esme stood up and passed us on her way upstairs.

"We hate you," I said.

She returned with two of Jan's stuffed bears, purple Stretch Armstrong and my Cobra Commander G.I. Joe. She waved them at us playfully, tossed them into the puke-filled trash, and shook the bin. Then she went back upstairs, returned with a polar bear, a giraffe, and my Bumblebee and Grimlock Transformers and tossed those into the bin. She removed the garbage bag and double-knotted it, slid that bag into another garbage bag, and double-knotted that. I was too dumbfounded to cry.

*

Even though throwing up is a natural, uncontrollable biological function, and even though Jan and I were the ones who'd lost possessions in the skirmish, Dad punished us both, equally. For all of August and into the new school year, we weren't allowed to play outside or see any friends, and television was off-limits, too. He told us to pass the time by drawing or doing puzzles, and made me help Jan with her addition and subtraction. Mom often read next to us in the kitchen, her literature of choice the Harlequin romances she picked up at the drugstore, shirtless Fabio types on the cover.

Tita Esme left the week after throwing away our toys. Jan and I didn't say goodbye to her. Instead, we hid in our room and listened to her luggage trundling in the foyer. She moved in with her boyfriend, a lanky insurance salesman with neatly parted hair and two daughters from his first marriage. Soon after, we heard they wed in a civil union at city hall. We saw them in the crowd most Sundays at church, and sometimes we ran into them at holiday parties. Her husband was a charming man who had a habit of complimenting others while downplaying compliments paid to him. The first time we met, he pulled a quarter from behind my ear.

At those parties, Jan and I mostly shied away from Tita Esme, preferring to run around with the kids our age. But once, when I was twelve, I found myself alone with her, waiting in line to use the washroom. She asked me what grade I was in, and said how tall I was becoming. She noticed that my voice was starting to change, which I was self-conscious about. I wondered if I was supposed to apologize for how I'd behaved years back, but it seemed like a strange thing to do in the moment. Instead, I replied with one-word answers and I asked her nothing about herself, and if she thought poorly of me for it, she gave no indication.

The night I returned home from my first semester of university, Mom and I sat on the living room couch, waiting for Jan to return from volleyball practice. I told her I found it odd that we'd never spoken about this woman who once lived with us. Whenever we crossed paths with Tita Esme, we exchanged cheek-to-cheek kisses, as if she were just another member of the community.

Mom told me that Tita Esme confessed what she had done to our toys. Tita Esme described the vomiting and the ensuing argument, and she apologized for acting in such a disrespectful manner. After all, Mom and Dad had spent thousands to bring her here, had rescued her from a life not worth living, had asked for nothing in return. She told them that before she came to Canada, she worked fifteen hours per day, devoted herself entirely to the family that kept her, raised the children as her own, all in exchange for a small room.

Mom and Dad already knew all of this.

She told them she didn't miss that family, but the children surely missed her. At night, sometimes she jolted awake, worried about some missed task. She speculated that was why she couldn't warm to Jan and me. She was afraid to become attached. But how she had acted was disgraceful, she said, and she proposed a solution she hoped they would accept.

She showed them the money from her work at the bakery. It was theirs, she offered. She would focus more closely on her chores, wake up an hour earlier to ensure their perfection. She would take care of us whenever Mom and Dad needed or wanted—on weekends, on evenings, on holidays. She was giving herself to us.

Hers would be an endless debt.

My parents looked at each other. Dad spoke first, then Mom. They couldn't accept this. Tita Esme protested. She talked about embarrassment and dignity and shame and sacrifice. Mom would not budge.

"I sent her away," Mom explained to me. "I didn't know if she would find a husband in time, even just out of convenience, or if she'd come up with another way to stay in Canada. Maybe she'd have hid in someone's basement for a few years before being sent back. That's really what she was offering to do—work for us for nothing until they took her."

I crossed my legs and exhaled.

"Actually, I was happy when she left," Mom said. "I had my house back, my husband back."

"You always had your husband," I said.

"Did I? Maybe. I never asked him what went on between them."

She rubbed the back of her hands against her thighs. She was about to say more, but she stopped herself and changed the topic to our biggest regrets. Mine was that I'd never had a real conversation with Tita Esme, that we'd preferred each other's silence. Mom thought for a second, then said she wasn't sure if she would have done it over again, let this woman stay with us for as long as she did, even if it meant Tita Esme would have spent the rest of her life in servitude.

"What kind of person does that make me?"

Baby Boomer

CARLEIGH BAKER

G reg hears dishes hit the wall upstairs. So often now, he can tell the difference between a shattering dinner plate and a saucer. He hears the word *bitch* screamed at his daughter—his only child—sweet Danica. So he takes action. Pulls himself up off the couch, where he and Manon have been watching *Judge Judy*. Makes for the front door.

Manon silences Judy with a press of a button. "Listen to them up there," she growls. "Do something!"

"I'm going for a walk," he tells his wife. Mama bear.

"You're going garbage collecting." Creases around her eyes. She's lost weight. Looks like a deflated foil balloon in her silver tracksuit.

There are latex gloves and garbage bags waiting at the door. "Recycling," Greg says.

"Greg," she says. "It's only a matter of time before he stops throwing dishes and starts throwing punches."

Greg tingles a little at the thought, but he meets Manon's gaze with a smile. He knows Travis won't get violent. He knows Travis's type, all bark and no bite. A goddamn coward.

Upstairs, a tin coffee cup ricochets—at least those are built to last. Greg needs some air. The suite is small and cramped with his books and the furniture Manon refused to part with when they moved downstairs. Credenzas full of bone china, saved for Dani. Dusty French colonial couches that smell like wax polish. Stifling in the humidity.

"Catch ya later." He gives her the finger guns, but she doesn't return them. Puts the latex gloves in his pocket.

Manon turns the sound on again. "Judy'd stick it to that little shit," she says.

It's been three years since Travis and Danica moved into the suite upstairs. A year before that, they were married. Danica was twenty-five, Travis twenty-seven. Not too young, Greg thought. Old enough for Dani to make her own decisions, whether he was onboard or not. Naturally, Manon disagreed.

"He's a bum, and Dani's blind!" she declared at the rehearsal dinner. "This relationship is doomed." Banged her fork on the table like a gavel.

Travis responded by throwing a pitcher of sangria at the wall. Greg remembers Dani, drips of wine trickling down her pretty freckled nose. Little pieces of nectarine stuck in the long brown hair she'd spent hours curling and twisting into an elaborate hairstyle. The smile never left her face as she rose from the table and retreated to the washroom.

Greg slipped the waiter a twenty to clean up the mess, then waited for Dani outside the washroom. "Honey, are you okay?"

"A little sticky," she said. "Good thing I chose the burgundy sundress!"

Greg brushed a piece of strawberry off his daughter's shoulder. "You're sure about this...about Travis?"

"He had it rough growing up." She kissed Greg on the cheek. "Not like me."

"Is that a reason to marry him?"

"Dad, I can help him."

Wisdom of the young, Greg thought. With a sigh.

When they got back to the table, an already skinny Travis had shrunk considerably. "Greg, man, this isn't me." He pulled Dani onto his lap. Buried his face in her neck, like a kid.

"Let's hope not," Greg said. Manon rolled her eyes.

So it happened: service at the Quay and photos at Queen's Park. The big magnolias in full bloom. Greg and Manon have one of the wedding photos on the mantel, next to Dani's high school diploma. Travis's family hadn't made it out from Toronto. Greg offered to pay the airfare, since it meant something to Dani, but Travis refused. He said they'd never make the trip for him.

Travis is stomping through the front yard toward Danica's car. Unwashed and unshaven, some kind of movie star look Greg doesn't understand. When he sees Greg, he's all smiles.

"Aw, hiya Greg! Sorry about the yelling. I guess I got a little carried away." He feigns a look of remorse. "Dani's bitchin' really gets under my skin sometimes, kinda like you and Manon, hey?"

"Not really," Greg says, noticing a large new tattoo of a shark on Travis's arm. "How's the job search going?"

Travis's grin evaporates. "Christ, you sound just like her." He gets into Danica's car and screeches the tires as he drives off. The smell of burned rubber hangs thick in the air.

Travis lost his job as a roofer six months after the wedding. He said he was injured, but Workers' Compensation wouldn't honour the claim. They said there wasn't enough proof. Greg certainly hadn't seen any. A few months later, Danica left the nursing program at the University of British Columbia to get a job as a waitress.

"Just until we get back on our feet, Dad," she told Greg.

Three years ago. Try as he might, there was nothing Greg could say to change Danica's mind.

When he really thought about it—how useless he was in the face of Travis's caveman rage—Greg wanted to throw something, too. But anger accomplishes nothing. So Greg started his recycling campaign. He would get Danica back into nursing school and get rid of Travis. But he needed more money. He'd made a reasonable living teaching at the community college, but money had been tight since his retirement.

The kitchen manager at the college was happy to let him pick up the empties after school functions. Sometimes several garbage bags full. He combed the alleys six days a week, through Queen's Park and deep into Sapperton on the other side of the highway. Manon would die if she found out how extensive the recycling operation actually was, but a few times a month he'd even take the car into Vancouver and fill it with empties from the trade conventions at BC Place. It was a full-time job, but his generation had never been afraid of hard work.

Not like Travis, and his whole damn generation. Millennials. What the heck happened?

Tonight, Greg takes a route all the way up Seventh. Crosses through alleys to catch the neighbourhood parks with bins that are emptied only once a week. Some of the big family picnics wrap up their empties and leave them next to the cans. This makes his job easier.

First stop is the back end of Queen's Park. Just past the picnic tables, there's a spot where a bunch of old cedars stand in a circle, and the air always feels a little cooler. Greg stops and inhales. He used to do this circuit in the morning, because it was peaceful and he could be back home before Manon even woke up. But lately he's been running into other recyclers. Chinese grandmothers who smile and nod at him, with no urgency in their movement. Sometimes one of those guys with the shopping carts. A switch to evening seems to have eliminated the awkwardness of competition. Greg pulls on the gloves and opens bin after bin, taking a few swoops through the top level of garbage, careful in case of anything sharp. Pulls out the empties with an efficiency that might make sorting through the trash seem natural to anyone passing by.

Next up is a little park where he and Manon took Dani when she was a kid. It used to have a zipline that ran from a tree fort all the way across to the other side of the park, until the city deemed it too dangerous for kids. Now it's just a couple of picnic tables and a "neighbourhood approved" safety swing set. No wonder kids got soft. Greg moves a couple of greasy buckets of discarded KFC and finds a two-litre Diet Coke bottle.

It's dark by the time Greg hits his last stop, a little park on Trafalgar with Japanese gardens and a duck pond. He walks over the stepping stones—almost indiscernible in the dark. Dani told him she's seen koi in the pond, but Greg's never seen anything but murk. Tonight he sees the glint of an empty Dr. Pepper can, but it's out of his reach.

By the time Greg gave his stockbroker a call two years ago, he had collected a thousand dollars in empties. He cashed in a GIC, and invested two thousand in Galena Ventures, a mining company that would pay off big if their new dig was successful. And it was. Six months later, Greg had five thousand, which he invested in a tech company in California. Fourteen months later, he sold high, put five thousand in a savings account with Danica's name on it, and reinvested the rest. He could have stopped collecting empties, but he didn't. Playing the market is risky, and things can go south in a hurry. But they didn't. Manon had no idea about the money. He anticipated the look on her face when he told her he had enough to solve all their problems. Maybe they could take a vacation. They used to go walking through the neighbourhood together, before the kids moved in, but she rarely leaves the house now.

Wednesday night family dinner. Manon is carving the chicken like it's an adversary. "He's still parading around the neighbourhood like some kind of vagrant!" Manon points the carving knife at Greg. She's got on the gold tracksuit tonight, which at least gives her a healthy glow.

"Yeah, Greg, have some self-respect, man!" Travis combs his hair with his fingers and reaches across the table. "I've been unemployed for months now."

"Thirty-six months." Greg passes him the potatoes.

"Whatever, you don't see me digging through the trash." Travis stuffs another mouthful of chicken into his maw and reclines in his chair. He's clearly relieved not to be at the receiving end of Manon's fury for once.

"I don't think there's anything wrong with it," Danica says and squeezes Greg's shoulder as she gets up to clear the table.

"No, leave that to me," Manon says, swatting at her daughter. "Just get *him* out of here before he settles on the couch."

"I heard that," Travis bangs open the door to the upstairs suite as he leaves. "Comin', Dani?"

"Coming." Danica watches Travis leave. She starts loading the dishwasher.

"Dani, I'll do that later. *CSI* is on." Manon lifts up the couch cushions, looking for the remote.

Danica glances upstairs. "You watch *CSI*? I thought you hated that cop stuff."

"It's interesting. All the different ways they can trace a crime back to someone."

"Your mother has become a regular sleuth," Greg says. "She must have half a dozen Agatha Christie movies out from the library. She'd be the one to talk to if anyone turned up stiff." He grabs two garbage bags. "How about we go for a little recycling walk, Dani?" he asks. "I got you a pair of gloves so you don't mess your nails."

She smiles. "I haven't had a manicure in—"

"Thirty-six months?" Greg says. When Danica smiles, he sees a grubby six-year-old digging up worms for their annual trip to Trout Creek. He sees a graceful twelve-year-old learning crosscuts at the rink and waving at him in the stands. And he also sees the future: Danica at her convocation, posing for a picture next to the rhododendrons with him and Manon. No Travis. He'll be long gone by then.

"We'll do the alleys, everyone will have their blue boxes out." Greg hands Danica a bag.

She smiles. "Okay, Dad."

There's a peekaboo view of the Fraser River from the front yard. It looks like mercury from the distance. The sky's full of pink sunset, but it's muggy again.

"Dad, can I ask you something?"

"Sure." Greg's cellphone buzzes—it's a text from his broker. Time to sell InfoTech.

"Was Mom always so…aggressive? Like, before you had me?"

"I think of it as passionate." Greg shoves the phone in his back pocket.

"Did you ever worry that it wouldn't work out between you?"

"I sure didn't," Greg says. "Worrying solves nothing. No problem is unsolvable, but you gotta take action, cupcake."

Danica leans over the neighbour's blue bin. "Smiths must have had a party."

"Everything okay, Dani?" Greg asks.

Her head drops a little for a second, and she pulls herself up to face him. "Dad, I think I've made a mistake."

"What do you mean?"

"A bad mistake. A big one." She puts a hand on her belly. "When I really think about it, he's the last guy I want to raise my kid."

"Oops." A bottle of white Zinfandel escapes Greg's grasp and rolls under the Smiths' car. "Oops, oops, oops. Have you told your mother?"

Greg tells himself that twelve thousand is enough. Twelve thousand is a lot. He calls his broker, starts the wheels in motion. He can keep two thousand for Danica and offer Travis the rest to get out. Forever. If Travis gets wise and asks for more, he can have it. Danica won't go back to school for a few years now anyway. The money won't be available right away, but Greg can arrange some kind of payment plan with Travis. He'll have to.

When Greg gets off the phone, he hears doors slamming upstairs. But this time, his daughter is doing the yelling. Maybe he should have told her about the plan, but if Danica can get rid of Travis of her own volition, everyone will benefit. That's not greed, it's logic. Twelve thousand is a lot of money. Greg and Manon could take that vacation.

"I'm going up there." Manon has been pacing like a puma since Danica told her the news.

"Don't you think it's best if—"

"—I think it's best if I protect my pregnant daughter from that piece of shit," Manon hisses. She flies through the door to the upstairs suite, and Greg keeps his mouth shut. His plan has been carried out seamlessly up to now, he can't let emotion get the better of him. But he can feel the beginnings: hot forehead, a knot in his stomach, shortness of breath. He shuffles some tax papers around on his desk. Checks his phone. Now all three of them are up there yelling. He knows Travis. Travis will blow off some steam, and run away somewhere for the night. Then Greg can explain to his family how he is going to make everything better.

"Greg!" Manon's voice booms from upstairs, but there's something funny.

And then Travis's voice. "Bitch. He hates you as much as I do!"

"Jesus." Greg takes his phone out and dials 911. The neighbours are going to talk.

"Greg!" The fear in Manon's voice is obvious now.

Greg stands and heads upstairs.

He hasn't been in the upstairs suite since he painted the bathtub for Dani last Christmas. There's a hole in the hallway wall. Burn marks in the carpet, a cigarette ground into one of them. An overturned Texas mickey of Bacardi rum is rapidly spilling its contents onto the floor. Manon calls for him again, as he picks up one of Dani's old track-and-field trophies from the mantelpiece. Marble, with a gold-painted pole vaulter on top.

Dani is sprawled on the floor under the kitchen table—the same ratty Arborite table she grew up eating breakfast at. Her nose is bloody, eyes are closed. So. Greg was wrong about Travis. Manon was right. And now she's backed up into a corner of their old kitchen, eyes wide, nostrils flared. Travis is pressed against her, holding a broken beer bottle, his back to Greg. Manon's eyes flick over to Greg's and back to Travis.

Greg's movement is efficient. The base of the trophy hits Travis on the side of the head and splits his skin near his temple. Bright blood spurts out. He goes down without a sound. There's always a lot of blood in head injuries, Danica had told Greg once, when she was in nursing school.

The gold-painted pole vaulter lands at Manon's feet. She picks it up and looks at Greg, saucer-eyed.

"Wow," she says. "Wow."

"I saved some money," Greg burps out, bile rising in his throat. "I saved us." They're so close now. Greg can smell her sweat. He feels the hair on his neck bristle, the muscles in his thigh twitch. Then Danica groans, sweet Dani, and they both remember.

Jamaica

TOM THOR BUCHANAN

This is what I know about my father:
He was born in 1931, in Okinawa, weighing four pounds and one eighth. It's my belief that never once in his life was my father the tallest man in the room. As an adult he barely surpassed five feet, and never weighed above a hundred and twenty pounds. The image of his ribs is as familiar to me as his face.

He met my mother somewhere in Michigan, where they both worked at a hotel, he as a janitor, she as a canoe guide. He was thirty and she was eighteen. My father was never clear on when he'd come to the US, or where he'd been during the war, and my mother said he was inconsistent on whether he had living parents, or siblings. She described him as a friendless, withdrawn man who had nonetheless pursued her shamelessly.

I was born on the day my mother turned nineteen, and my father was already a thirty-one-year-old man. That same year, we moved to Pittsburgh, PA, and in her first winter there my mother slipped on icy steps and had to spend the entire season lying on the living room couch, reading newspapers. Around the time of my birth, she had become engaged in a frenetic process of self-education, in the throes of which she taught herself Spanish, read early Marcuse and Isaiah Berlin, and wrote letters to city aldermen. I believe she was already incredibly unhappy. Periodically my father threw her down the stairs. Periodically he talked about leaving and moving to British Columbia. He was by turns raving, helpless, ghostly. This was in 1962, the year Marilyn Monroe died and Charles Mingus stood up at his Town Hall concert and offered people their money back. My father was working in a bakery then.

He would work from one in the morning until just before noon, twisting sour-smelling wads of dough into intricate shapes and shoving them into an enormous oven. Loaves he'd broken or burned he'd bring home. At street corners he would wait swaying with fatigue for the light to change, as the midday crowd streamed around him. Over his shoulder he would carry a milk crate he'd stand on to reach the counter at the bakery. One thing about my father, he was never embarrassed about his height.

My mother once told me my father was an intensely angry person. Angry at whom, I asked. She said that most people are angry because some presence they feel they deserve is absent from their life. Waiting around makes people very angry. She also said that my father had never been able to adapt himself to the particularities of poverty in America. In Japan there had always been a peasant class, who even when they were mistreated at least felt confirmed by the fact of their historical precedent. In America there was only the abiding faith in the ability of a person to change his station. And, of course, the pain of failing to do so. My father had expected his poverty to manifest an ethical dimension and instead it had manifested an economic one. Which produces a capitalist despair, she said. Which was my father's despair. These kinds of things, she said, are what constitute a culture.

I rarely saw my father. He was at work when I woke up, and slept through most of the afternoon and evening. But one day when I came back from school I found him sprawled out on the kitchen table. Instead of coming straight home from work he'd stopped at a liquor store and bought a quart of Old Grand-Dad to polish off on the walk home. He had taken his milk crate and thrown it onto some train tracks. When I came in he lifted his head from the table and looked at me. When he spoke it was in a mixture of English and Japanese, a language I rarely heard him speak. He told me about how sick this country was, how everyone got sick and stayed sick off of something. He told me that in Japan, in the south, people ate roots and that his grandmother's piss had been clear as water. He told me that my mother thought it was all a matter of where you were born and in what century, like two axes on a graph. All a matter of who was free and who had to get to work on time. He asked me if I believed that too. He said he'd slap me back to the Stone Age and we'd see if I believed that. This was our century, his and mine. His eyes rolled up, and he lay back down, and was quickly asleep. I stood there for a few minutes, watching his breath move inside his ribs.

My father did eventually leave. Up and disappeared like Charlie Parker. One weekend he went out for the night and on his way home veered left instead of right and that was it. When we saw his friends out in the world they acted sheepish. No one had any information. My mother was so angry she avoided bakeries altogether and for a time we had no bread in the house (this is a diet currently popular with the rich).

So for a while it was just the two of us, alone in a house at the edge of the City of Bridges. In some ways, our lot improved in my father's absence. My mother got a job as a secretary for a local radical lawyer, known for defending vandals and union agitators. She had a story about John Sinclair walking into the office without a word and sitting on her desk. For a time she wrote unanswered letters to Hannah Arendt. By the time I was a teenager she could afford to give me a little money, enough to buy cassette tapes and odd copies of *Bomp*. When I grew tired of the tapes I had I would record over them from the radio, or from the collection of dub records a pot dealer in the neighbourhood lent me. I made tapes that spliced together PiL singles with a day's worth of time-share ads from public radio, or that obscured King Tubby with a mix of static and distorted background noise. I became less interested in listening to music than making these tapes. I tried to make them impossible to sit through, learning as I went how to torture anything recognizable into something crazed and private. I did my best to avoid any patterns in the sound, and sense of structure, I wanted to make something beyond language. I saved enough money to buy a portable recorder and a microphone and used it to record traffic downtown, or people having screaming matches on Federal Street. I began describing my work as "stochastic," a word I learned from my mother.

In this way I occupied myself for four or five years until adulthood. I spent this time largely alone. I rarely spoke to anyone other than my mother. I cultivated no friendships. I can't recall if I graduated high school. My life was reduced to a selfish and ascetic set of principles, a state in which I would sometimes become suddenly aware of a lack of desire inside of me, a total absence of any kind of appetite, only a tired, animal-like distrust of anything that wasn't myself. Periodically I would feel a brief and lucid anxiety that I couldn't place, which quickly passed. I lived in a state of numbing personal poverty. I continued making tapes. I think I learned from that period that life in America passes quickly, and that there is nothing essential about it.

My father sent me a postcard when I turned eighteen. The return address was for Kingston, Jamaica. He said he was living there and making his living as a horse jockey. He said that he was now 52 and weighed one hundred and eighteen pounds. The reverse of the postcard showed two racehorses rounding a turn, their hooves speckled with mud. Two impossibly small men crouched like acrobats on top of their shoulders. At the very bottom of the card my father invited me to come visit him. Oh, I thought, in life, we do experience contingencies.

People are often surprised, or disbelieving, when I tell them I rarely thought of my father in the years we were apart, but it's the truth. I accepted his absence as a condition, similar to inclement weather or a tooth abscess. I remember once watching my mother getting ready for work, and pausing to lean against the kitchen counter to catch her breath, and becoming suddenly aware that she had become prematurely old, and that she was almost completely alone. This was as close as I ever came to thinking about my father.

Maybe I decided to go immediately. Maybe it took me a few hours or days to make up my mind. It's hard to remember how decisions are made. At some point I put the postcard on the kitchen table for my mother to see when she came home. She picked it up, read the back, and set it back down, said nothing except to comment on the handsomeness of the horses. A few days later at dinner she asked how I intended to pay for a ticket. She asked me if I knew how much a plane ticket to Jamaica cost. She asked me if I knew how to pack for a trip. She asked me if I even remembered what my father looked like. I looked at her and found her face unreadable. I suppose that she likely thought of my father more often than I did, but then again, what's a guess really worth, even among family. I told her I intended to sell some of my tapes, maybe outside of the Warhol Museum. She asked me if I planned to wear a silver wig and sunglasses. I shrugged and continued eating.

The price of a midwinter ticket to Kingston was more money than I'd even seen. It was apparent I could never pay for it with my tapes. I rarely had more than a few dollars; I would often get on the bus only to find that I had nothing in my pocket except for buttons or the plastic knobs from appliances. A job seemed out of the question. I was always tired and couldn't keep appointments, and people seemed unnerved by meeting me. The newspaper carried an ad for spray-washing graffiti for $3.50, week after week. Local drug dealers were knifing each other and being found in snow banks. Theft felt like an attractive option to me, having long been interested in the story of D.B. Cooper. Hubcaps gleamed on this year's Cadillacs along Elmsworth Avenue

At some point, I saw a flyer at a bus station for an organization (a "cultural association" being the term they used) that gave money to Americans with Japanese heritages. What makes a person part with their money once they have it is beyond me. I applied for a grant to visit my father. When they learned I didn't attend school I had to write an essay proving my literacy and betraying any anti-social world views. In early December I was invited to their Pittsburgh office, the basement of a Lutheran church near Chinatown, to discuss my eligibility. A committee from the foundation's headquarters in California attended. They arranged themselves in a semicircle while I sat on a plastic folding chair in front of them. They asked me how long it had been since I'd seen my father, whether he had any living family in America, and whether he'd spoken Japanese at home. They asked me to describe a time my father's status as a Japanese immigrant had been thrown into stark relief. I described a time when he'd nearly been arrested for wrestling a traffic cop who called him a chink. I also told him that I'd heard him speak Japanese once while drunk. His family was either dead, disowned, or otherwise indisposed. I gave them all the particulars they wanted, as clipped and honest as a traffic report. They asked me what my father's experience had been during the Vietnam War, and I told them for all

I knew he'd been 4F, being likely too small to hold a rifle, and anyway possessing the kind of disposition one imagines in those soldiers who become disgruntled and shoot their COs in the back. Before they had a chance to ask I told them I knew nothing of why my father was in Jamaica, or how long he'd been there. They asked if, to my knowledge, he could possibly be part of an existing Japanese-American community in Kingston. I shrugged my shoulders and was dismissed. I waited in the hall while they deliberated. A half hour later I was called back in and told that they were awarding me an amount sufficient to cover the price of an economy-class ticket to Norman Manley International Airport, in sunny Kingston. I booked one that same day and mailed my father back his postcard with the date of my arrival.

When I told my mother she didn't betray any surprise, nor did she ask where the money came from. Maybe she was worried I'd tell her I'd been letting men put cigarettes out on my chest. She told me she had always been very sensitive to the moment when things became inevitable, being something of a Hegelian. The day before I left she helped me pack a bag and pick what clothes to take. She gave me some caffeine pills and anti-nausea tablets. That night we dragged our mattresses into the living room, and stayed up talking obliquely about my father, my mother drinking gin from a coffee mug. She told me about the resort where they'd met, how my father slept in a cot under a stairwell in the back of the building. She described the ways in which his body had seemed impossible to her, the strange way he unsettled a room. She talked about how a person could become violent over the course of a lifetime and how you come to a point where talking in terms of happiness and unhappiness makes you want to laugh. She told me about a dream she'd had often after I was born, where my father held me, pink and new, on his baker's paddle, and how she could never tell if he was taking me out or putting me in. At some point I fell asleep, and when I woke up in the morning she'd already left for work. I grabbed my Samsonite and caught a bus to the airport.

Record of Working

PAIGE COOPER

His physicists leave their idiot mistakes smeared across their tables, and during the night Arthur marks his corrections. In the morning nonconformity meetings they raise their insulted eyebrows—he has not sourced incompetents, they believe they can police themselves—but there are mossier issues: embedment plaques poxing the housing assembly; blue-sky disruption mitigation schemes from Garching and Palo Alto; lists of additions to the already-biblical ark of conductor metals. His team of design integrators are only four now, and every day at eighteen hundred hours the updates are re-disseminated with deviations flagged in green. At the workstations, bleary engineers take these changes, sometimes, as incidental.

Arthur, the first and only Director General of the project, chides grown men like a grade school math teacher. He stalks around in deep-pocketed camouflage trousers and an old Cambridge rowing blazer. The project is six years old. It is three years and nine months behind schedule. Every day of work costs into the millions: the precise number fluctuates, given the exchange rates on the thirteen different currencies involved, many of which are inflating hideously. Every few months the accountants come from their Domestic Agencies and sit behind their stiff little flags at the horseshoe dais in the glass-walled amphitheatre on Level 6. Up there they can look out over the entire compound: the reactor's seismic isolation pit populated by four hundred and ninety-three concrete plinths, the trailers, the machines, the debris. At night the military bathes everything in starry silver spotlights. In the centre of the pit, one hundred and sixty degrees of the ring fortress is black, hollow as a promise.

What Arthur has told them: to reach breakeven, plasma must stream—or drift, or sawtooth, or tear—in a four hundred second pulse. And then again, and again. One day it will be self-sustaining. The scale is critical. The Venezuelan Domestic Agency complains of the concrete shortage, but it's food shortages causing the riots. Of course it's severe. The forest is virginal. The sea eats the cliffs under colonial ruins. Energy will be delivered in milk bottles every morning. This was Arthur's vision and everyone understands that his visions come true. For instance, the elemental woman waits sleeping in his bed. And the sun achieved ignition, did it not?

Redout coughs and delays, but Arthur, who has never been later than forty-five seconds for anything, is absent. Ten minutes pass. Redout reads emails. Sunlight at this hour tracks across the blue jungle, but doesn't angle inside the room. The noise of the construction in the pit is muted, but given enough time it accretes in the skull, sludges the blood vessels. Every so often a concussion shivers his collar, and reminds him of other, lesser reactors that have failed: cataclysms even when they were the size of kitchen tables.

Greenhalgh and Boucher drain their coffees and scowl at the green scrawls on their schematics. Van der Meer types on his phone. Six others are wilfully late. Seventeen have cancelled their attendance on a temporary or permanent basis. It's May. The men who remain are wretched for a break.

"Clear enough?" says Redout. The appeal of impersonating Arthur's daily philippic is minimal. Boucher stretches and scratches his belly.

"All right," says Greenhalgh. He picks up his papers.

Van der Meer rises and walks out without lifting his eyes from his phone.

"Let's do it like this every day," says Boucher.

Redout dials Magda. Three rings in, he remembers the elemental woman and hangs up. He considers paging Arthur, but his nose wrinkles at the crudeness. The construction crews will pour the second segment of the ring fortress today; that is, the remaining two hundred degrees of the circle in which they will settle the torus's vacuum chamber, when it's built. An empty crown. Whenever that is—the components must be built, shipped, assembled. Years from now. A decade. The Haemorrhoid Pillow of Eternity, Boucher calls it. There can be no hollering for the Director General like a lost child at a supermarket.

Magda calls back immediately. Redout stares at his phone while it flashes.

"What is it?" she says.

"Oh. Hello, Magda. I'm sorry I hung up. I was afraid I'd bother you."

"Kind of you."

"You weren't sleeping?"

"Sleep?"

He chuckles. He grasps for a different question to ask her. The air stretches in one long, lordly parabola between them. Redout tucks his fist under his armpit. His voice is light. "I was just calling. I was wondering if you'd seen Arthur this morning."

"You haven't," she says.

"He's missed the noncon meeting, is why I'm asking."

"And why would you call me?"

"I know," he says. "I realize."

Magda's silence is dead and wooden. Eventually: "Ask her, then."

Redout clears his throat. "Indeed. Certainly. I will."

The line dies.

Again, he considers paging Arthur. The man has never carried a phone, but since construction began here five years ago he has also never been anywhere but headquarters and the house the Japanese Domestic Agency built for him on the cliffs, atop the ruins. To Redout's knowledge, he's never even left the compound.

From the descending glass elevator, the half-complete ring fortress is a cavity decked in orange flagging and red scaffolding. Yellow machines scuttle like wasps masticating their paper palace. The noise is wholly dissected from its makers—spasmodic, demonic—trucks spin their liquid rock and engineers shout. A fleet of agitators roils the concrete into all available crevices. They sound like doom approaching. The pour will continue for another nine hours. The practice pour last week was identical in every way, and the result sits over by the treeline, looking like a newborn gulag dropped from the clouds. The elevator doors open onto the empty lobby, where an infuriatingly fine white dust laps at the cement floor and clouds the hems of the glass walls.

For no good reason, the parking lot's grade is as geometrically immaculate as the reactor's basemat will be. There's no telling the Jeeps apart. Black boxes that rained down from the German Domestic Agency back when construction began. The lot is mostly empty because the military insists the construction crews bus in from the closest village, twenty kilometres away. There was a brief time when car engines were machinated into bombs. To spare himself squinting at every licence plate, Greenhalgh has slapped a Manchester United sticker on the door of his Jeep. He used to cycle out to the village and back, until he was robbed the second time, less harmlessly than the first. Boucher's spray-painted a safety-orange peace sign on his rear window, and draped his side-mirrors with festive flagging like a child's tricycle. Boucher came from one of the failed tokamaks in Provence. Greenhalgh, meanwhile, came from fission, because fission is real and fusion only might be. In the beginning, it was easy to seduce the best minds to come devote themselves to this, the ultimate.

Right inside the military perimeter, where the local soldiers and their patriotic dogs make every morning a border crossing, Redout turns onto the dirt road that winds up the bluff. It's slippery. He used to feel some guilt over how the Jeep—which mutters of ecological and macroeconomic violence, war museums, bad television—is such a powerful comfort, as compared to the exhaustless aluminum capsule in which he putted around Palo Alto. But, as they've learned, outside the perimeter the Jeeps are more than just a comfort. Soon there'll be no more hawing and they'll have to tighten belts and enlarge the living quarters for staff inside the perimeter, to house the construction crews. They will fall another year, two, behind schedule.

Arthur's house on the cliff is, like every building in the compound, made of glass. It's grown from the old stones of a Spanish fortress, as unlikely as a bright future. Certain bits of wood adorn rather than structure it. Ledges jut out over the ocean. The cliffs are granite and don't seem to be falling into the waves at any human pace, but the house is so sleek it looks like it could launch itself into orbit and escape all this suffering. Currently, the sun has flared it into phosphorous, white and silver. Arthur moved out in February, down into the coach house at the foot of the drive. Itself a dowdy offspring of its dam, blocked from the same genes and rubble. Built for one. Or two who want to be constantly entangled in each other. The elemental woman has lived there since she arrived.

Redout couldn't say which door he'd prefer to knock on right now. Magda's doubtless sitting alone in the cavern of the great room, swallowing a hundred miles of horizon in her glare. She has the kind of beauty the mind craves, and, partially because of this, when he met her his notion of certain realities became rearranged. But her field of warp extends only so far, and these days when he sees her the sky remains blue. It was good, in the end, that he'd never said anything to Arthur.

Redout pulls in at the coach house, behind Arthur's decaying station wagon, and the elemental woman descends a step from her doorway. Her hair is a black plasma of whorls, her hands are striped in burns. She is wrapped in sheer textiles, throat to wrist to ankle. He has seen her naked many times, as many times as he has seen her. She is standardly naked, or undressing, or re-dressing various parts of her contorting wire frame. Arthur, drunk, had stood and recited lines. He'd mouthed her fingers. That was the last time Magda had invited the executives for cocktails on the balcony. There had been dozens of them then. Now there are fewer, and none except Redout will visit Arthur at home.

"He's gone, if you're wondering." The elemental woman's lips are wide and raw.

"Where?" Redout lifts his hand against the sun.

Arthur calls her elemental. Part of his Working. But she was born Karen Barwick in Weston, Connecticut. The man she came here with was Italian, an electromagnetic engineer, but a replacement for him was soon found and he left quietly.

"How would I know?" She lifts and settles a piece of cloth over her shoulder.

"Did he leave a note? Say something?"

"You must think I'm extremely stupid."

"Of course I don't. I only wondered—"

"Talk to your government friends," she says. "They'll be able to find him. They'll want to kill him when they find out."

Redout has already stepped backward twice.

"Wouldn't it be easier for you if they'd just kidnapped him? That's probably what you should tell everyone, if you want to get out yourself."

"I have no idea," mumbles Redout, "what you mean." He opens his wallet, lifts out his card. "Would you call me if he contacts you?"

"He won't." She withdraws from his extended hand, folding into herself. She is beginning to look like women do as they become useless. She is beginning to look terrifying. She steps back up into her house. Her voice is a lilt, a song: "I hope they catch him. I hope they burn him alive."

Magda watches Redout's truck slink back down the dirt track into the forest. From here, all she knows of the reactor is the occasional keen or drumbeat; it's invisible to her. Barwick's dollhouse is still. If Arthur is really gone then the woman is alone in there, turning from alien sink to alien bookshelf to alien bed. Potentially she is alive with agony. A current of emotion that can't be cut. Magda would tell her: one must wait until the generator runs down. One must have faith one will be left inert. There's no helping it. Whether a two-cylinder or a star. If it's a star, maybe, barbiturates. One must learn that being inert is the natural state. Magda has been titrating off the tranquilizers for three weeks now. She likes to lie on the balcony in last of the sun with her herbs.

Three possibilities: one, Arthur has left, maybe with a woman yet-unknown; two, Arthur has died; three, Arthur is still in there and has Barwick playing some new game.

Because of the third possibility, Magda will not walk down the steps to the dollhouse to offer succour. There is a constant temptation to expose herself to new pain. Like dwelling in the memory of the two weeks that Arthur and Barwick spent in the master bedroom of this house, while she lived here and Renata still lived here. She and Renata would drink tea in the autumnal January breeze and hear the animal sounds from the open windows. Ignore it like it was only the spider monkeys, the waves licking the ruins to dissolution.

Renata, eighteen by then, was grim. "Is this what I did to you?" she asked, once, as the fucking grew intolerable, the garden smell, the melodrama.

Magda palmed the girl's silky mermaid hair. "Of course not. You're my sister."

"Liar," said Renata. She had an instinct for self-preservation. She left within days. Wrote from Copenhagen that she'd paid her way in via shipping container. The girl spoke five languages. She'd found a job cleaning rooms. "You can come here!" she wrote. "No one's starving yet."

Another temptation toward pain: Magda still wears her wedding band. If she totals it up, week by week, she'd say she was happy for three months, all told. One month of those was ecstatic. It's been seven years since she met him, six and a half since she married him. She has seen the threshold of her tolerance. It is as wide and high as the horizon.

Immediately, Barwick finds that the house empty of him is so much more alive that breathing makes her giddy. She strips and burns linens and curtains. She opens windows and smashes the ones that won't. She avoids his rancid cave, cramped with the massive shrine of his work, except to throw every trace of him—books, clothing, papers— into it. Every day a ritual. He liked to tell her how he summoned her in there. A fortress of dirty objects. An insane person's altar to ego. He burned incense while chain-smoking and wore the same clothing every day without washing it or himself. He taped over the glass in every door and pinned the curtains to each other. He scribbled over the mirrors in black grease and stood naked staring into them, his fattening belly and soft penis. He starved himself and binged and shat. He read aloud to her from his daily writings and then locked his secrets away in a suitcase when he went to work on the reactor. His book, his Record of Working. Of course she read it, as the glamour of his genius dissipated in the stink.

You have had a result. The elemental. She is the perfect image in the heart of man, modelled by the awful lust in the space-time that forms all women, the insatiable and eternal. It vivifies the rose. Just as the little sister was used to effect transference of the weakness of the false woman's flesh to a critical period, just as your passion for the little sister also gave you the strength you needed at the time, confirmation of the Adultery and Incest in the Law, now The Elemental Woman has manifested in response to your call. The suspense and inquisition were your luck, you were enabled to prepare your thesis, formulate your will, take the Oath of the abyss and thus make it possible to manifest her in order to wean from wetnursing. She has demonstrated the nature of the woman in such unequivocal terms that you will have no further room for illusion on the subject.

He had her write, too, in a little notebook, her own record. Some days would rain dread as she tried to think of anything plausible enough to write down, knowing he would find it and read it. He'd scrawl in his corrections, steal whatever he liked as his own. He'd sneak out past the soldiers, who'd never been told how to recognize him. The phone would ring. "It's the President," he'd say. Arthur liked to orate to Barwick while he fucked her, an exposition of the women whose assholes and mouths he'd filled. He maintained an annotated list in his Record. Every time he fucked her, a new woman was described. The girl at the market who sold him incense; van der Meer's wife; any scientist or bureaucrat who had come to work under him and been possessed of an adequate form; Magda, that poor crumbling statue of herself. Who else—Barwick smirked—who else had demonstrated *the nature* unequivocally? The stories had begun to overlap and entwine, if he were drunk or had been drunk or just lying. He had certain words and actions he'd go back to, when failing. When he came, he came in her because it was part of the Working. Their child would be born as the reactor was born, a god of eternal power. He'd never mentioned contraception. It seemed to never have occurred to him that she had control of that, that she could leave, that she could, living in all these dirty proofs, perceive him perfectly.

Magda's hypothesis is that the military perimeter will soon flex and invert and everyone within will be punished. The power still runs silently in her kitchen, but the food delivery is two days late. This is fine. She has always hoarded what she can. When they first arrived it was possible to drive into the village and buy sundries from the people in the market, though neither the women at the stands nor the soldiers with their dogs would deign to recognize her. Living as a ghost with him had been much lonelier than this current solitude. When she lived in Manhattan, before Arthur ensorcelled her, there were many men who knew her name. Here, she no longer needs one. Last year a famous American actress was murdered in her private villa. A college girl in Caracas was raped by nine soldiers. Now people gather where food used to be and scream at the soldiers and die. The violence, says the President, is due to the influence of television. The climate's drunk, liable to mania and then sullenness and then lashing out. Most herbs die, left on their own. She has to pay attention, bring the plants inside from the balcony every afternoon. Hail.

Magda used to buy her herbs from a girl who sold them in paper cups from her skeletal motorbike. The girl's ears jutted out under her cap. Her face, if cradled, would have rested against Magda's breast. Her nails were carved into dark, dim points like a badger's. She always smiled for Magda. She let Magda speak a little in Spanish. She said, "Do you know which you like?" Having a scrawny female to protect must motivate half the world's efforts. When Magda imagines what men must feel it makes her own missile body ridiculous. Tiny asses make cocks look big enough. Barwick, for instance, is narrow and contorted as a child. Magda lives constantly shocked by her own ugliness and beauty. She wonders every hour what she looks like: sea cow? Valkyrie? Her data points—beautiful, hideous—would blotch the grid to blackness. The famous actress was on holiday with her ex-husband and five-year-old daughter. How much suffering people tolerate, lingering where love used to be. Screaming for it. If she had brought the herb girl here to the glass ruin, she would've sucked the dirt from under her fingernails and lived off the momentum of that small thing's trust.

Again, her phone rings. Surely Redout, who's never said anything but "Of course" to Arthur. Instead, the soldier at the perimeter gate says, "I have a woman for you. Will you accept?" They drive her up. It isn't the herb girl with her friendly ears. This woman wears a backpack and a camera, like a tourist or a journalist, and a long braid. She hops the steps up to the door like she's been here many, many times.

"I summoned you!" Arthur had crowed, in front of everyone, while Barwick began to laugh.

The boy with the assault rifle at the compound's perimeter asks Redout to spell Arthur's name, as if he's never heard it before. And a second time. Then he shrugs. There is no record of Arthur leaving. Not coming, either, in the last five years, though yes, there he is on the list of residents, his photo faded out past recognition. Redout is unsurprised.

"Could a man go through the woods?" he asks. Beyond the razor-wire gate, the jungle swarms in still life, breezeless, embalmed in flowering vines. On this side, the air carries biting insects and the sound of pouring rock.

The boy adjusts the rifle slung over his shoulder. "The dogs patrol all night."

It's eleven hundred hours. Redout must chair the weekly materials update. He goes back to the conference room on Level 4 as if he's spent the morning normally. Emails, coffee. Construction jitters the air. If they were on the schedule, they would be lowering the torus chamber, a flawless vessel fashioned from a single peel of material, into the housing by now. "The work is perfect!" Arthur always said. And yet, Redout never replied, the reality is not.

Greenhalgh and Boucher are the only men in the conference room. It is all men on the project. Redout used to hire women, in the beginning, because they are cheaper and easier in so many ways, but Arthur ran through them like a wasting disease. He'd leave them useless, ruined for work, and then Redout would have to find a reason to send them away. They all went: docile or hissing, but they went.

"Droste says he needs another ten," says Greenhalgh.

"If we give him fifteen you think he'll find a way to stop the tungsten erosion?" Boucher spins in a slowing circle on his chair: legs crossed, hands raised like little wings. "Or will he just show us more slides of that Klimt painting with the nipples?"

"Maybe the nipples can absorb the thermal loads," says Greenhalgh.

"Droste is testing all sorts of pulse frequencies on those nipples. Those nipples are the hottest materials he's ever seen."

"Found Arthur yet?" says Greenhalgh. "Speaking of."

Redout pulls his gaze from the pit, back into the room. "What do you mean?"

"You tell us," says Boucher.

Heat prickles Redout's neck inside his collar. He dials into the conference line with Droste in Garching, where the man's been bombarding monoblocks with neutron radiation for the last year and a half, and sending back drawings of the little fissures he makes. The reactor will produce no waste, except for the reactor itself. The walls transmuted, the equipment irradiated. The problem is that there is no material invented yet from which to build the torus chamber. Even though the plasma itself will spin like a yolk inside an electromagnetic sac, everything melts at two hundred million degrees. Out in the void, uncontained, the sun's core burns tepidly at fifteen.

The conference line plays U2 while they wait.

Redout's phone flashes on the table. He picks it up. "A woman came," says the boy with the gun at the gate.

"Who?" says Redout.

"Cortez," says the boy.

"Who is she?"

"We drove her to the house. But now there is another. Dubois, she says."

"Just a second," he says. "I have to take care of this. Reschedule with Droste."

Greenhalgh lifts a hand. Boucher is spinning again.

"Do you know what she wants?" Redout asks the boy.

"The woman in the house."

"I want to talk to her first. Bring her here to me at headquarters. I'll meet you in the lobby."

There is a pause. "She says no."

"Send her here," says Redout.

The boy sighs.

Once, the real military came. They'd taken charge of the perimeter while the President visited. No one had understood that the gate guards weren't real soldiers until that day. Arthur's friendship with the President was close and long-standing, enough that—despite the

Americans and Europeans—they had plotted together to build the reactor here, on this peninsula, where it would benefit them both first. Without Arthur there was no reactor. When the President had visited—toured the pit, sat behind his little flag on Level 6 during a woodenly optimistic diagnostics meeting—the gate boys had sulked around in their fatigues while the real soldiers manned every post.

Redout waits in the lobby, then the parking lot, but the boy doesn't bring any woman. They've ignored him. The elemental woman had said, "Talk to your government friends," but Redout is afraid. Droste's tungsten feathers like old bone. Arthur promised energy in milk bottles within ten years. Six hundred people once worked on this site daily, but that number has diminished as the coherence of the currencies drifts and families grow grey-faced behind barred doors at home. The thirteen Domestic Agencies supply fewer and fewer resources. There are wildfires in Austria and bread lines in Canada. It is difficult to ascertain at what point civilization has collapsed, because no one ever designated a quantitative measure, but Redout, if pressed, would say either they have thousands of years, or it's already over. Science will reveal all in the end. Superstition is the problem. Apocalyptic myths designed to scare people servile and meek. Women, whose bodies crack open like shellfish, who live for their naked infants, are so vulnerable to terror. Terror is what makes them humourless. They despair. They become murderous. Arthur, last month, drunk in his shrine at noon, held forth at volume: "God is the solar-phallic creative will, and the daughter is the virgin who unites with her father, stimulating him to reactivity and this begins the generative process all over again. This! This is what we're doing here. Four hundred seconds! It must be harsh! It's the scale of the thing!"

Redout finds his Jeep again and drives to the glass houses. In this last long, arid winter, amid all the other problems the project faced, Arthur began what he called his Working. Redout has seen the altar, yes. Redout was present as the seven verses were read aloud. Arthur naked and erect in a shroud of smoke. Redout had no choice but to record the proceedings, as requested.

Envision yourself a cloaked radiance desirable to her. As a man and as a god you have strewn about the heavens and earths many loves, these recall. Remember each woman you have ravished, think upon her, concentrate all into the elemental woman. Think upon your lewd Beast. Repent and recount your casual loves. Your lust belongs to her. Speak the Oath of the abyss. She is the Daughter of Fortitude, and ravished every hour from her youth. For behold, she is Rationality, and Science dwelleth in her; and the heavens oppress HER. *She shall absorb thee, and thou shalt become living flame before she incarnates.*

The door to the glass house is splayed. Bodies move against the aquarium sky, shadowed between windows. As he mounts the steps, another Jeep pulls up. Three women climb out. Their faces are familiar. A physicist, van der Meer's wife, a woman from the village market. They don't glance at him as they file past him, into the house.

Redout follows.

"I summoned you!" Arthur had crowed when they walked into his house one evening after work and found her standing there, smiling politely on the arm of the new poloidal-field magnet engineer. Everyone heard Arthur say it. Men's wives, Magda, three quarters of the executive, Magda's young sister. Arthur took the woman's hand, kissed it like a king's. His face shone terribly. Tears fell from his eyes. "Finally. You've come," he said.

Inside, the women are in the kitchen, on the balcony, clustered in groups, buzzing around. Low laughter. At least two dozen of them. On a couch, one weeps into another's shoulder while a third—he recognizes the girl Renata, sixteen when she first arrived here—strokes her hair. Each woman he recognizes as one of Arthur's. Each one has giggled secretly with Arthur in an exhilarated dark. Women Redout himself has castigated or bribed or soothed, as their temperaments required. A lineage, a genealogy of women. They inculcate one another like exiles, reunited.

The glass walls are open to the ocean. The vibrato scent of newly fused ozone smashes up from the waves below.

Across the room, Magda fixes her gaze on him. Beside her, Barwick looks like a savage myth. Their faces are still. They have already summoned their solution, and ignited it.

A hand is placed on the nape of Redout's neck. Of course the reactor will fail. It already has. If it wasn't a fantasy, it was a nightmare.

But he moved forward, didn't he? Is that not courage enough? In the face of it all, did he not do his work?

From above, the city lights are blocked black in irrational patches. The jet traces a descending compass curve. Skyscrapers are nothing but red pinpricks at their tips. Whole districts are deleted. Buckled in his seat, Arthur ignores the burnt-up map below, scraping in his journal with his green pen.

—because of this test Rationality is incarnate upon the earth today, awaiting the proper hour for manifestation which was never NOW. The elemental was as false as any creature, all the squealing and manipulating that came before, she was no Daughter no vivification no result no IGNITION. This is proved in her infertile hole, though all men laboured upon it. Yea, you must strive abominable and be clothed with barncloth until you come into power and purple though you be contemptuous and solitary. Await the TRUE WOMAN who will flame the TRUE WORKING. Prepare yourself for portents. Prepare for the slaver of the hordes. Prepare all your priesthood and power—

His pen doesn't leave the paper he's scoring, not as the landing gear descends, not as the plane bumps against the tarmac. Finally, as the herd around him scrambles, he stuffs his papers into his rucksack and pushes his way out of the machine. He took nothing but the funds he had apportioned for his own needs. He sacrificed everything. But not everything! He will contact Andrea, or Elisabet. To continue his work, his reputation will require a salve of loving dedication. One of them, or both, must publish a piece exposing the superstitions and corruptions that crippled him.

He passes through border control with his new passport and hurries through the endless bright corridor towards a taxi that can take him to an appropriate hotel. A woman is walking towards him. She is young and beautiful. The corridor is empty. She meets his eyes, and he slows as she nears. She is clothed in a ravage of angelic light. The flame of her. He cannot help himself; he stops.

"Arthur," she says.

He's speechless. Did he summon her? Is she false? She is empty-handed, as if standing before her creator.

"Don't you know me?" she says.

"You?" Hope lights in him. The true, the ur. He is a boy. "Is it you?"

Her smile suffuses him with radiance. In the distance, thousands of kilometres behind him, he hears a monstrous concussion. It is the sound of an annihilating force expanding, at impossible speed, towards him.

I'm Lonely Down Here

MARCUS CREAGHAN

I watched your broadcasts. Every single one. And I've come to some conclusions.

The two of you met at Skidmore. And the first footage shows you stealing. Standing in 7-Eleven, between two aisles, picking at a scab on your right index finger stuffed in the pouch of your coat pocket. Daniel's over by the cash, giving the sweet talk to a poor naïve girl behind the register.

"I'll distract her while you grab what you can."

You'd both phoned home with sob stories for your parents about indigent peers that needed help. Telling the folks that you'd emptied already pretty slim wallets, as in *No, no, no, I couldn't think of keeping a dime for myself while any of you are going without.* All lies. Worse still, you act like a babe in the woods ("What? I think I can manage—but if you insist") when pops offers to wire money to his sweet charitable daughter. Of course you two just blew it all on those gelatin capsules: MDMA cut with Ephedra and a squiggle of toothpaste to give 'em that touch of space-agey colour. After the come down you were left with the penniless post-fix hunger.

Daniel gives you a sharp look from the counter because you've raised your sightline in search of reassurance when he told you, he told you twice, to keep your head down and your hood up so the cameras won't see—so that I won't see.

Granted, your hands are shaking now. Even if you grabbed that dun-yellow bag of Fritos, your down-and-out moral delirium tremens are likely to rattle and hum until the vacuum seal comes loose, and you're sprinkling corn chip confetti across the room. But Daniel says he loves you, which you cannot afford to take as a lie. An hour before now you sat facing each other on his bed with the folds of black comforter. He thumbed your nose, held your face in his hands, and said: "Hey, listen, we can do no wrong because this is our time," which caused your brain to scream: Please leave me / Don't leave me / Please leave me / Don't leave me, etc.

This is all part of the story I tell about you.

Oh, and those films. Those films Daniel no doubt forced you to make. I promise, if I had been there, as your biggest fan I would have put a stop to it. I wouldn't have let him do that to you. Berating you for hours as the lens keeps itself keenly centred on your face. Those endless disturbing interviews where he would break you down slowly. Or maybe we should call them what they really were, because they weren't art, surely, and not really interviews either, if I'm being honest. They were interrogations, denouncements, tirades. Take your pick.

I learned so much about you from those films. Almost all of I what I know about this time in your life comes from them. But they are monstrous.

In the stilted, washed out colour palette of camcorder footage your face turned aggressively towards the viewer. Not with shame, but from a sense that you had been trespassed upon. A stilled moment freighted with antagonism. Even after he begins to ask you relentless questions, the context of the interaction is constantly shifting. Suspended in time, and left without resolution: endlessly on edge.

Questions like:

"When did you first feel as though your beauty was a source of power?"

and

"How have you abused that power?"

After graduation Daniel went off to France to make a different kind of movie. Made no promises. Said, It's selfish to hold on to someone while they're still young. Said, You'll thank me one day. Said, It'll be easier on us both if we cut it off clean.

Something inside of you went crooked. You caught yourself

breathing heavy in the middle of the night with a pain in your gut, as if you were drowning and all that sucking air was just putting stones in your belly. I feel the same when I've been betrayed.

Your organs curdled and you wanted nothing more than to return to the inner shine of something pure. If Daniel was a mistake why not return to the start, before he was inevitable? He hasn't eaten up your chance to go back. It's just a matter of finding when you well and truly wanted something only for yourself.

Returning, perhaps, to the idyllic time they show in documentaries about your life, when you and the other kids sprawled across grasslands, sampling a freedom forbidden in the school year.

On certain days, your heads would spring up, your eyes would cross the skyline. Attuned to the sense of a coming rain by hands run through the thickness of the air (or, more likely, by a shiver across the soft undershells of your ears). When all games surrendered to the coy ambling about, waiting for the water to fall. Because no play could ever quite compete with the joyful rampage when a hard sheet of it came down like a curtain on one side of the field, sweeping up each kid who ran into its enfolding.

You hit the porches and hung off the support beams of houses with hair dripping down your face as sun showers soothed the day into its passing. And when the mist dissolved into that evening sky, as if birthing the stars by its vapour, you'd hold as long as you could to save the pleasure before finally allowing yourself to look up.

In your innocence it didn't even seem that far. Because you don't know what belongs to you, only that if you claim everything you're sure not to lose it. The silence and the sky, pinholed with iridescent light—you spilled yourself into it all. And it welcomed you.

This is the origin story they tell about you. It's how they let us know that you were always meant for space.

When astronomers found out that Europa, that glistening Galilean moon over Jupiter, had an undersurface ocean sloshing around its core with more volume than every body of water on Earth run together, they went wild. A new potential for the galaxy to give back to ailing Earth. But NASA didn't have two nickels to rub together at this point, so it fell on the foam-ridden mouths of hungry private enterprise to fill the gap.

A conglomerate of global technocorps and entertainment gurus pooled venture capital to fund Cunningham-Uniplex: part colonial project, part reality television spectacle. The idea being to strap in some doomed volunteer to establish a base on the moon. A terminal specimen, laying the grounds for safer forays in the future.

But the legend of the American astronaut was absolutely dead in the water at this point, and this was a marketing problem. In the history of US space flight fifty-five astronauts were accepted into the corps during the "heroic" era of the Mercury, Gemini, and Apollo missions. That number ballooned to two hundred and sixty-six during the shuttle era of 1981–2011, and they became faceless in their multitude, losing the steely-eyed gaze and square jaw of their type. I remember the old heroes, equal parts fighter pilot and desperado pilgrim. Their private lives of alcoholism, beaten wives, and fractured families strategically hidden. They were myths engineered out of old storybooks. But their replacements were Ivy Leaguers, pointdexters with doctoral theses. The unwavering competency of the shuttle men and women resisted all personal identification. And so the legend died.

You on the other hand, you were someone to believe in.

You could read your own self-destructive urge, and so could the execs leering as you signed release papers. They had a stake in you burning out: it makes for good TV. And while initial suborbital test flights proved weak in terms of ratings, the unimpeachable charm of low survival rates promised blockbuster status after true lift-off. A group of grad students at MIT pegged your estimated post-launch lifespan at ≈ 2mth5d3hr1min5sec.

I want you to know that I was watching from the start.

"Will you get lonely up there?"

"I'm lonely down here."

Though delivered in a sullen tone, your answer is met with laughter from the gathered press corps. For them this is a puff piece.

You went through all the months of boot camp and of technical training somnolently. Glad to wake up with a set schedule and to fall asleep exhausted.

By the time you are aware that the moment has come for a decision, the moment has already passed. You chose to leave the planet because you were leaving the planet at the time when you finally asked yourself to choose. What seemed like free will was only the acknowledgement that things move beneath us, that the Earth shakes and we find footing where we can.

As g-forces pressed you back into the pilot seat you felt fixed, immovable in a way that was a passable substitute for belonging.

At first Daniel seemed to re-engage, no doubt buzzing off the association he could claim with an interplanetary celebrity. But he incrementally excised himself from your quiet victories, becoming bored.

"The soybeans are finally sprouting," your message reads.

"You must be so proud," he'd respond a couple days later, drawing a circle around your accomplishments to make them private: yours and definitely not his.

It was difficult to hide your disappointment from the cameras, which were ubiquitous and invisible.

Blinking lights in the cockpit, and along the body of the shuttle seemed to be user-friendly flags of important statistics—vitals, oxygen levels, communication arrays—and yet their carmine glow felt full of the potential for betrayal, doubling as they did for the bloody universal symbol of "recording," "watching," "waiting for you to act."

You asked for his future messages to be blocked and found a nook between the suspended sleeping unit and the air lock chamber that suited your need for a place where you could imagine yourself unseen. A place to hide yourself while you chewed the inside of your cheek and didn't cry.

You'd run for hours on the treadmill, I saw you, turning up the simulated gravity to test your strength. Only when completely spent could you really weigh that newfound hostility brewing up inside.

Sometimes you would slam a fist against the lockers just to hear the cold rattle of perforated metal that made you feel strong. And I bet you wondered what kind of person would watch you. Isolated in front of computer monitors, awake and raw after 4 a,m, in some antique chamber of the mind, looking to get invidious satisfaction from the caged life of an unhappy woman.

It was very unfair of you to think this way if that is, in fact, what you thought. Sure, sometimes my head felt like the inside of a coffee pot: drip, drip, echo. But only from being tired, only ever because of tiredness and nothing else. It disappoints me that you would think so little of your admirers. I lead a productive, fulfilling life. I work for the government. I get a modest but not insubstantial salary for what I do. What business is it of yours how I spend my leisure time? If I come home, sometimes very late because I am committed to leaving when tasks are done, not when five o'clock comes around and I am able, under normal social pretexts, to appear as though I am done for the day—if after that I want to sit down and spend some time with you, even if it amounts to several hours, what business is it of yours whether I should use my free time in that way?

It's in moments like these that I begin to have my doubts about you.

But after all you made it. The gargantuan planet had been visible through the keel porthole for weeks. Relays from home were full of felicitations and popped-cork noises as the scientists assured you that you'd "exceeded all expectations and were sure to continue to do so."

You found yourself staring at Jupiter for hours. Looking like smoothed round granite and marble, seamed through and belted with ochre clefts. Indented with a blurred red mark, because all beauty bleeds. You told the cameras that it drifted into your dreams, where you'd see yourself "soaring, naked, with arms outspread over the gaseous surface."

You wake up to a ringing alarm. Cascades of amber light shade the chambers of the ship. Mechanically, through muscle memory, you don your extravehicular suit, strap on an oxygen supply and corkscrew your fishbowl helmet into a locked position. Then you secure yourself on the palette of the safety rig with clasps gripping your torso to the frame of the ship. Eager for disaster, you tense up, feeling your breath coil along the glassy surface and smog back onto your sweating face.

By some counts Jupiter has sixty-seven moons, and one of them, about the size of a suburban home, pulled your ship into its orbit, ploughed one wing along its surface and then ricocheted the crumpled tin can back into the night.

The big suck of exhaust and a clicking like film being fed too quickly through a rickety projector, and then—silence. A massive swath cut across the starboard hull and you can feel the safety hoists struggle as you're pulled toward the new opening. Looking into the hole, then down at the clasps that keep you attached, you feel a coldness coming over you. Once more you must sense the body moving, as if without command. Releasing one carabiner, and then another, and then another. Unrigged from gravity's tender mercy and left to unspool yourself out into the chilly draw of the dark universe's dormant imagination.

At first you keep your eyes closed, to save the pleasure, and then, slowly, like the stem and the seed bud angling toward the sun, you open. Pellucid depths, rippling a gradient of pearl blue. Writing a ghostly line of coloured cursive. The planet's aurora borealis, cresting, limning the sphere and stretching out toward the moon of Io. It has a pulse and it glows, leaving a curved tail of emission, fading back through time as it degrades into darkness. Jupiter sweeps, and a million amps of current flow between it and all that cannot be left behind. Nobody has yet spoken for this. It's been waiting.

The cameras cut out, but a microphone, lodged in your helmet, records the final moments.

Even though you know you should keep calm the breath, save air, you repeat: "This is mine. This is mine. This is mine."

I know the feeling.

I start the video over again.

The Underside of a Wing

PAOLA FERRANTE

An albatross is a bird who doesn't go away, even though its body is capable of movement, long distances in fact, over nine thousand miles in fact. An albatross can circle the globe, stay in flight for over nine years without stopping. In Latin, an albatross means immutable, unchanging; eventually an albatross returns to the same island. There are at least nine species of albatross that are endangered; with a white underbelly camouflaged by black upper wings, an albatross is easy not to see. There are at least nine species of albatross that endanger; an albatross is a bird who will always bring you down.

1.

The albatross is riding the SkyTrain back from Commercial Drive. The albatross doesn't know why a girl even bothered getting on the SkyTrain, taking the bus all the way down the mountain in Burnaby, making her ears pop just so a girl could go to some graduate student meet-and-greet for the psychology department where the albatross avoided talking to anyone all night. She doesn't know why a girl bothered when the albatross ended up alone, in the bathroom, throwing up nine-dollar wine and playing PC classic solitaire on her phone. On the SkyTrain, a girl tries to make sure the albatross is not seen by the two other people who are sitting too close to the albatross, who are sitting just close enough to each other that the edges of their thighs are touching, just close enough to be a couple. The couple doesn't seem to notice the albatross; the couple is looking at clouds. That one's a seashell. That one's a heart. The albatross used to play this game with Rob, back when Rob was going through his Hitchcock phase in film studies, back when every third cloud was the blood in the shower scene from *Psycho*. The couple is able to name the shape of a cloud and agree; the albatross can tell by the reaction shot, the part where they kiss. Rob loved to talk about Hitchcock's use of the subjective camera, the reaction shot which follows the point-of-view shot where the image is the exact representation of the image as a particular character perceives it. At first, a girl thought that she and Rob were speaking the same language; she had done a minor in film too. But Rob never saw what the albatross saw, clouds that pour rain, clouds that eventually disappear, pushed higher and higher by global warming, causing the darkening of ocean water, the death of desert bacteria, the worsening of pollen allergies. "From Rob's point of view, Rob is better back in Toronto. It is better Rob doesn't see the albatross anymore. It is better if no one does." The albatross just can't see it. But that one's a plane, a bird, maybe.

2.

The albatross posts selfies, but they are taken in her bathroom mirror. A girl captions them with the goal of the day. Going to do the Grouse Grind. Going to run across the Capilano Suspension Bridge. In the background, no one can see the unmade bed where the albatross can't sleep, the stack of takeout sushi containers, the pile of Hitchcock DVDs she took from Rob's apartment. The murder in *Rear Window* reminds the albatross of the murder of Kitty Genovese, who was killed while thirty-eight people watched or listened without understanding it was an emergency. That murder was the reason Darley and Latane studied the bystander effect, which was the reason newer research found that the flight-or-fight response inhibits helping behaviour, which is the paper she should really be reading right now. But the albatross just switches *The Birds* for *Rear Window*, uses the DVD as a coaster the next time she cracks a beer. Going skiing at the top of Whistler Mountain in August before the real work starts. Going to sleep well tonight! From the point of view of Rob, against the right background, say the Lion's Gate Bridge, connecting Vancouver to the North Shore, the albatross will be hard to spot. From the point of view of Rob, it will look like she's having fun.

3.

The albatross is sitting across from a man who is sitting in the good leather chair in an office at the university. The albatross is sitting on a plastic chair, the one that has some padding but is not built for support like the leather chair. She is trying to make sure the albatross doesn't say too much, agrees mostly. From a man's point of view, the albatross is falling behind; the albatross is heading into academic jeopardy. A man does not understand the relevance of the albatross's references. An albatross's language is mostly sky-calls and bob-struts, the clattering of a girl's ring tapping against the chair, a constant hollow drumming like a heart inside her ears. Has she read the classic study on mistaken attraction due to activation of the flight-or-fight response on a suspension bridge? Of course, the albatross is making her leg jump up and down and up and down, making her look as though she is nodding; the albatross, with a wingspan of over nine feet, has to keep it together or a man is going to notice. A man is going to ask what's wrong. From the point of view of a man in a supportive leather chair, there's no room for the albatross in an office, at a university.

4.

A friend will want to meet the albatross for lunch; a friend will say she understands what's wrong. From the point of a friend, the albatross will just need to move on, get out, meet people. A friend will have answers, proper nouns. The albatross should try eHarmony. The albatross should try Moksha yoga. The albatross really shouldn't have another glass of Merlot. The albatross will appear to have so much going for her; a friend will say she just needs to stop worrying. A friend will describe how she learned to stop worrying when she went to Thailand, met her fiancé; a friend will show pictures of them on the beach with a perfect blue ocean and a perfect blue sky, skipping past the dark clouds from a waste-to-energy plant burning plastics beside a shrimp farm, past the animals kept by themselves in cages at the Pata Zoo. It's the albatross who will want to think the ocean is photoshopped; it's easy to photoshop tropical islands, Google images of beaches and hammocks. A tropical bird unable to fly in her cage is real. An ocean that blue is not. There are not even clouds in the sky.

The albatross will excuse herself to drink from a flask in her purse in the bathroom, cry while reading the graffiti on the stall that promises a good time if she calls someone named Dan. Last time, the albatross forgot to fix a girl's eyeliner and a friend said she wasn't looking that great; Is something wrong? The albatross texts to say it would have been great to see a friend, but she just can't make it. The albatross doesn't care how it looks.

5.

The albatross is not looking well, despite the concealer under her eyes; the albatross is not sleeping. The albatross is checking boxes on WebMD at 2:30 a.m. The albatross is supposed to answer always, often, sometimes, rarely, or never to get definite answers, but a girl is having trouble agreeing on the exact nature of the problem with the albatross. The albatross checks that she always has difficulties falling asleep, but she never has difficulties staying asleep: she can sleep in a lecture hall, or a cafeteria, or through the first-year introductory psych course she is supposed to TA at 3:30 p.m. She often experiences excessive worry; the albatross never experiences worry that is excessive. The albatross sometimes experiences worry in social situations; she always worries that others will notice the albatross. Tonight, so the albatross's roommate doesn't notice, she is watching *The Birds* with the sound turned off. Rob once told her that, in filming the attic scene, Hitchcock tied live birds to Tippi Hedren's costume. The fear on her face is real. Only a few of the birds she is afraid of are not real. Sometimes it's hard to tell. WebMD doesn't give definite answers; it says the albatross should consult a physician. But she often experiences a fear of the albatross speaking in public.

6.

At 4 p.m. in the university health clinic, the albatross is sitting behind the glass with her clinical supervisor. The albatross is supposed to be sitting in front of the glass while a woman named Mandy, who is doing her PhD, observes from behind the one-way mirror. Instead, a woman named Mandy is explaining to a man why no one can see if he has an albatross right now. Unfortunately, it's already four and they close in an hour. Unfortunately, they are short staffed because the albatross, who is still drinking vodka out of what is supposed to look like a vending machine Pepsi, is late for her practicum shift. (Unfortunately, there was traffic, there was a problem with her alarm, there was the fact that a girl needed the albatross to drink at least half of what used to be Pepsi before the albatross would stay quiet. Unfortunately, the albatross is going to have to wait to make a girl's excuses about why she's late *this* time until later; Can't she see Mandy is doing an assessment right now?) Unfortunately, there is a bit of a wait list, maybe a few weeks to a month, even if a man can't see himself waiting that long. They don't take walk-ins unless it's a real emergency. Unfortunately, the glass at the university health clinic is not real glass but tempered glass, supposedly the shatterproof kind wrapped in plastic coating, the same kind used in a marketing challenge that involved breaking a million dollars out of a West Van bus stop, known for visible distortions. For example, from the point of view behind the bus stop glass, five hundred dollars looked like a million dollars; Mandy says that from the point of view of her supervisor behind the university health clinic glass there is no way to see a man's albatross today. An albatross is not a real emergency. From the point of view behind the glass, a real emergency is a man banging his fists against the glass. A real emergency is a man threatening to break the glass; an albatross is not supposed to go behind the glass at a university health clinic. A real emergency means Mandy is going to have to call security; from the point of view behind the glass her supervisor doesn't see it as an albatross. A real emergency, according to page nine in the manual, is a sudden traumatic event, or a loss, or thoughts of suicide. Of course, the supervisor says later, a real emergency would have been if the man had told Mandy that he was planning to jump off the Lion's Gate Bridge, but he didn't tell her that. There was no way, from behind the glass, to have seen that coming.

7.

On a bench in Stanley Park, the albatross is drinking rum from a plastic iced tea bottle because she needs Rob to answer his phone; she needs to tell him she finally understands why it took Tippi Hedren almost losing an eye to tell anyone how she was afraid of Hitchcock. The problem is a girl needs the albatross to be quiet; she needs to read. She needs to read about how people who were afraid on high suspension bridges mistakenly felt attraction but the problem is that on her phone the albatross is reading that Hitchcock thought false fronts underneath a sheer nightgown would make Grace Kelly more attractive. Hitchcock was unable to detect when Kelly wouldn't wear the plastic insert breasts because she thought they would look fake. The problem, the albatross is now sure from her reading, is plastic is linked to cancer, anxiety in children at age seven, the death of albatross chicks whose bellies, cut open, are filled with brightly coloured garbage while no one notices. For example, even when it starts to spit rain in Stanley Park, the albatross doesn't seem to notice. She doesn't move from a bench in Stanley Park; she reads how no one noticed that Albert, an albatross off the coast of Northern Scotland, was alone for more than sixty years with gannets who didn't understand his language, the meaning of his cries. The problem is the albatross reads, but there is nothing in the literature to suggest that gannets could ever understand an albatross, that the albatross would ever be aware it wasn't a gannet. Most birds can't pass the mirror test, recognize an image as themselves. The problem is Rob doesn't pick up his phone and she needs to tell Rob how she can't tell anyone, but she is afraid of what a bird can do. She is afraid, especially when crossing from Prospect Point, to go back to her residence room. She is afraid, seven hundred metres above sea level on the Lion's Gate Bridge, that the albatross is unable to see her face in the water below.

8.

In a seminar room where people are sitting in bright-orange plastic chairs, a girl is supposed to be answering questions about the bystander effect. She is supposed to be explaining why, when Kitty Genovese walked home that night from a bar in Queens, thirty-eight people listened to her being murdered and didn't see it as an emergency. She is supposed to be explaining, but the albatross won't be quiet. The albatross isn't sure if the black T-shirt camouflage is working or if the people can see the white deodorant circles under her arms; the albatross hasn't been to the lecture for the course she is TAing in weeks. She is supposed to be explaining why, but the albatross doesn't know why people couldn't have understood it was a real emergency even though one of the people in the orange chairs is saying that actually, the first articles in the *Long Island Press* and the *New York Times* reported no witnesses; actually, a lawyer later on argued that very few residents of the nearby building could have seen the attack. Actually, new research suggests that people will help only provided it's a clear emergency. Actually, she is supposed to explain the difference between a real emergency and a clear emergency, but the albatross is talking in its own language, which is a drumming of her heartbeat getting faster and faster; the albatross, actually, is not talking in a way that makes sense at all. The albatross is saying how maybe Kitty was less scared of the man attacking her than of the people attacking her for being what she was, a woman who worked at a bar coming home late in Queens; maybe Kitty didn't want help, even though she was clearly screaming for it. Maybe the albatross is just breathing in and in and in and no words are coming out because an albatross can't explain how a real emergency is not a clear emergency; the albatross can't explain why she would go to the Lion's Gate Bridge because she needs to get off the island. It's a real emergency. It is the kind of emergency where she is seeing black, where everyone might see the white underneath part of her wings instead of the black, the kind where she might be having a heart attack. It is the kind where everyone is going to see the albatross as she passes out for a few seconds, then wakes up on the floor, where she can see only the feet of the bright orange plastic chairs.

9.

At Nanaimo Regional General Hospital, the albatross is waiting in the emergency room. The albatross doesn't like it here. Everything is made of plastic. The chairs in the waiting room she can see from the hall are made of the same orange plastic as the ones in the seminar room; she can't see her own reflection in the fluorescent light hitting the seat of the empty ones. The pen the woman in the booth behind the glass is using to write down what the albatross says is made of plastic; the glass itself is probably made of plastic because the woman says the albatross can wait, but it's highly unlikely the doctor will see her tonight. It's highly unlikely because they have a thing called triage. It's highly unlikely because the albatross is not bleeding or burning or having a heart attack. No, from what the albatross has told the woman, a girl did not experience the symptoms of a heart attack. No, she probably just had a panic attack and should go home and get some rest; a girl is fine. A girl is fine, but the albatross is not fine with the orange plastic chairs, or the plastic window; the albatross is telling the woman that plastic is killing the oceans. The albatross is telling the woman she wants to take one of those orange plastic chairs and hurl it through the glass. A girl is telling the woman that she can't go home to Toronto; the albatross is intent on leaving the island, will leave Vancouver for the North Shore via a bridge seven hundred metres above sea level. The albatross is telling the woman with the white undersides of her wings pressed hard against the plastic glass. Then the girl is feeling the body of an albatross thrown over and over against the glass; the girl is feeling how the wings of an albatross get pinched when held behind her by security. The girl is feeling the body of an albatross is her, face down on the ground where she can see the rubber, not plastic soles of a nurse's shoes.

10.

A nurse is saying an albatross is a bird who eventually goes away. Eventually, it learns to fly, long distances in fact, effortlessly in fact. The girl agrees somewhat that an albatross might be a danger to others. The girl might not agree, but a woman who is a nurse who came out from behind the glass believes an albatross needs to be seen. The girl might not agree, but Hedren never got Hitchcock to listen; Albert on his gannet-filled island spent years and years just trying to find someone to talk to so he didn't have to die alone. Kitty spent her last moments screaming at apartment buildings whose lights were on. The girl might not agree, but an albatross is a danger to herself. The girl might need to be seen as an albatross, at least for seventy-two hours. Eventually, the girl is told, an albatross can change; it can become extinct. Eventually, she is told, the girl can learn how to fly, without being in flight.

Madame Flora's

CAMILLA GRUDOVA

Victoria's menses stopped. Her nanny looked through her old diaper bustles, the ones that hadn't been thrown away yet. It had not arrived when it was supposed to. Her nanny checked the diary she kept of Victoria's menses. ("Light," "Regular," "Thick" "An Odd Smell.") Each sentence accompanied by a fingerprint of blood, from the moment little Victoria, age thirteen, held up a bloody hand saying "Nanny I am dying," to which nanny replied that the diaper bustle Victoria had always worn was in preparation for such bleeding and that the bleeding was best called blooming and the blood best called flowers by a young lady.

Ladies wore diaper bustles all the time so men wouldn't know exactly when they were menstruating. It was less obscene that way, the constant taffeta swish swish of the diapers that accompanied women's movements giving no indication of their cycle. They were large and scented, made out of cotton and plastic. Women past the age of menstruating still wore them, as did little girls, there was no sense of end or beginning. The bustles were reassuring: women would never leak. Women were like eggs made out of marble, not creatures made of meat.

Nanny told Victoria's mother, who told Victoria's father, that Victoria was dreadfully weakened. Victoria's father called the family doctor, who hurried over and, without shock on hearing Victoria's period had stopped, handed Victoria's father a bottle of Madame Flora's, saying he saw this affliction all the time in young ladies, it was nothing to worry about.

"It's such a horror, the idea of flowers from a woman's body. It seems a shame to bring it back when it has disappeared," Victoria's father said with the abstract disgust of a man who had never seen it before.

The doctor laughed. "It is indeed, but a necessity of life."

The bottle was made of milky green glass, opaque so the liquid inside wasn't visible.

They all knew of Madame Flora's. Her advertisements were everywhere, on billboards and magazines, illustrations of fainted ladies contrasted with ones of ladies dancing and carrying children. Ladies sitting on half moons, laughing, bouquets of blossoming flowers. In many shopping arcades there was a mechanical wax girl in a glass box, eternally consuming Madame Flora's. When the bottle reached her mouth, a blush spread through her wax cheeks. Madame Flora's was "The Number One Cure for Weakness, Nervous Complaints, Fainting and Dizziness."

Victoria's father opened the bottle and took a strong sniff, then another. He stuck his finger in and pulled it out: Madame Flora's was a dense dark-brown syrup. The bottle label suggested mixing it with tonic water or putting it in puddings or spreading it on toast with butter.

Victoria's Nanny tried a spoonful herself. The doctor and Victoria's father looked away with slight disgust.

She spat it into her hand then wiped her hand on her apron.

"Sir, it tastes of…blood!"

"Nonsense. It's a one hundred percent herbal mixture, I have read the label and prescribed it to many patients. I would not expect you to know what blood tastes like," said the doctor."

"I only know, sir, from the smell of it."

Victoria's father grabbed the bottle and looked for the ingredients, but they weren't listed.

In small letters on the bottom of the label it said, *For Extreme Cases, Please Consider a Vacation at Madame Flora's Hotel.*

The canopy curtains of Victoria's bed were closed. Nanny opened them. Victoria lay in bed, reading a book of nursery rhymes and smoking. Her long red hair was greasy looking. Nanny grabbed her cigarette and put it out under her boot.

"Nanny!" Victoria cried.

The doctor and Victoria's father chuckled.

Nanny prepared a glass of Madame Flora's in the bedroom kitchenette. Women weren't allowed in the main kitchens of houses, but kitchenettes were a place where they could prepare light meals —there was an electric tea kettle and a tiny plastic oven, which used a light blub and was decorated with flowers, that could warm toast and make little cakes but never burnt anything. There were boxes of powders that could be turned into various porridges, teas, malts, and seaweed jellies, and there was always a fresh bottle of milk.

Victoria tried to spit out the Madame Flora's but Nanny stopped her. She swallowed with a grimace. "Bring me a crumpet, Nanny, and some milk, to chase it down, please, Nanny."

"Be quiet, Victoria," said her father.

"Bring the child some milk," said the doctor. "The taste of Madame Flora's is not delicate."

Victoria was to be given Madame Flora's in the morning, at lunchtime, and before bed. She complained that Madame Flora's gave her fevers and constipation. She rinsed her mouth out after, and often went to the bathroom, sticking two of her fingers down her throat until she vomited it up. "I don't like iron," she said to herself. She did everything she could to get Madame Flora's out of her body. She didn't miss her menses, the gelatinous clots that reminded her of leeches, the fear of leaks even when she wore chaffing rubber underwear under her bustle. They tried the whole range of Madame Flora's products: in addition to the tonic, there were pastilles, pills, powder, bouillon squares for soup, and a line of chocolate-covered Madame Flora's jelly that looked like Turkish delight inside but tasted like rust, sulphur, and browned flowers.

Victoria poured Madame Flora's on the crotch of her diaper bustle hoping it would pass, but Nanny knew.

Victoria's father said he would send her to Madame Flora's hotel.

"Can't Nanny come with me to Madame Flora's?" Victoria asked.

"No, she must look after your mother," her father said, and Victoria was secretly pleased, for she wanted to be away from Nanny.

They took the carriage. Victoria wore a green taffeta dress. Besides her trunk, she had a small black velvet purse. Inside were love letters from her father's butler and one of her father's friends. One contained a dried daisy, stuck to the page with horse glue.

Victoria's mother brought a large tin of wine gums along for the ride, keeping it on her lap. It was all she would eat. The blackcurrant flavoured ones in particular. Her father brought cold roast beef, a spiral sausage that resembled a round rag rug, and paté along for himself. He didn't stop to eat it but let the smell fill up the whole carriage. "I feel so ill I want to die," Victoria said to herself. Women weren't allowed to eat meat. The smell of it was intolerably strong.

They had to stop twice, for forty minutes each time, for her father to go to the bathroom. There were men smoking and loitering about outside the men's public restrooms. On a bench by the bathroom door, there was a man with swollen red legs, his trousers rolled up to reveal them. He was eating potted meat with his fingers and grinning. There was a smell around the place, like burnt mutton, her mother held a handkerchief to her face as they waited. "Why do men take ever so long to toilet," asked Victoria, and her mother told her not to be vulgar, drooling as she spoke because of the wine gums.

Victoria knew the right amount she could piss in her bustle without it leaking or smelling. She did so. There weren't many public bathrooms for women.

Madame Flora's hotel overlooked the sea. It was a white building, like most in the town, a popular seaside resort. The words *Madame Flora's* were written in large gold letters and there was a billboard on the roof of the hotel with an image of Madame Flora's tonic surrounded by roses. The main doors were glass with golden bars. The veranda had no chairs, only large potted ferns.

The hotel foyer smelled of the bouquets of flowers placed everywhere, but it was overrun with suitcases, tennis rackets, and other sports equipment. In the centre of the foyer was an enormous, strong-looking young woman wearing a fur coat, her dark hair in braided loops pinned to her head. In one hand she held a lacrosse stick. There was a vase knocked over in front of her, the water turning the red carpet a darker shade.

"I want my own room," the girl said loudly.

"If ladies are in a room together, their flowers will blossom together," a woman in a purple dress with red frills and a matching hat said.

"I don't understand what you're saying," replied the girl. "Where am I to put all my things?"

"It is beneficial to becoming well again. It is our policy," the woman said, and she turned to Victoria and her family.

"A moment alone with the young lady please," she said, taking Victoria's arm and bringing her behind the hotel counter into a small room.

The woman had a fob watch hanging down her skirt. She was Madame Flora. Her bustle was huge, an exaggeration of one. She looked like a dining room chair from the side. She wore a small glass vial on a necklace. She said it was full of Madame Flora's, from one of the first bottles she had made. The liquid looked dried, dark, and old.

There wasn't a desk in the room, but there were a matching set of patterned couches, a drink service on wheels with crystal glasses and tonic, and a few little side tables with more flowers on them and porcelain figurines and fruit made out of plaster. Madame Flora shut the door and told Victoria to sit down. The walls were covered in photographs and drawings of babies. "From former guests at Madame Flora's, once their flowers returned," she said. "Madame Flora's is available for anyone to purchase, but our hotel is reserved for the most exclusive of clientele. I take a personal interest in all the guests here. Madame Flora's is made in a factory in the north, where the water is strong, but I prefer to be here, with the girls who need my help most, who need their flowers to return."

"I don't like it. It feels like a poison. I don't like it coming out of my body," said Victoria.

"And do you like taking your Madame Flora's?"

Victoria would've blushed, if she had the energy, but she knew her cheeks remained pale and slightly green.

"Well medicine is not supposed to be tasty, now is it?" Madame Flora said.

She poured a glass of her tonic and handed it to Victoria. Under her gaze, Victoria drank it.

"It is a policy here that girls share rooms, as you may have heard."

Victoria's mother handed her a wine gum wrapped in a tissue as they said goodbye.

The girl in the foyer was named Louise and she was the daughter of a Baron. She was assigned the same room as Victoria. They weren't allowed to take the stairs, only the lift. The stairs were gated off. Behind the gate the red-carpeted stairs were dusty. Victoria was afraid Louise would make the lift break with all her things. There were only three floors. The halls had dim lights and were stuffy.

Their room was on the top floor, filled with small beds, but pretty with rose-patterned bedsheets. There were lots of small mirrors, and nightstands with powders and Madame Flora's on them. There was a marble fireplace, lit, with a decorative brass fireguard in front of it, and potpourri in little china dishes. There was a small window looking out onto the sea, and a skylight. One wall had a mural of Mother Goose on it. A small pink door led to a bathroom. There was an indent with a curtain over it, which Louise pulled back, revealing another bed. There was a thin girl with pale blonde hair and a red scalp lying in it, holding a paper box to her chest. She wore a wrinkled cream-coloured nightgown.

"I was here first," the girl said quietly, not looking at her intruder.

When Madame Flora left, Louise pushed one of the beds under the skylight and, standing on it, tapped it with her lacrosse stick.

A few more girls came into the room through the door, carrying carpet bags, hats. One with black hair who took the bed beside Victoria's was named Eliza, and a girl with curls was named Matilda. None of them had shared a room with so many girls before.

They wandered around their small room, touching things. In the fireplace there was a bit of a stocking and a burnt crumpet. On the wall, behind Victoria's metal bedframe, someone had scrawled "Mutton".

There was a collage on the wall, of horses and dogs, badly cut out of newspapers. In the bathroom was a framed picture of a lady riding a rabbit.

Without looking at any of the girls in particular Louise talked, taking off her coat. Her dress had a sailor's bib and a strange cut, with low hips—it wasn't suited to her bustle. The sleeves were short. On one arm she had a Union Jack tattoo which the other girls thought shocking until Louise said her father had it done on her when she was eight, which meant her father loved her very much.

"After this I'm going to Fairy Palace, in Wales, to fix my teeth. My Hugh had his teeth fixed there. Then we are getting married."

She suddenly looked at Victoria.

"Are they going to send you somewhere to fix your nose next?"

Victoria covered her nose with one of her hands.

Louise continued talking "They've fixed my hymen twice now, both times it broke from riding horses. It has to be intact just before you're married so that a nurse hired by your fiancée can break it with a metal instrument. It's so he won't be put off by sight of blood after the wedding. Your fiancée gets a certificate from the nurse saying it was done." Victoria didn't understand what a hymen was, perhaps a little male china doll? Victoria's dolls had never bled, though she often checked and made them diapers out of tissue.

Louise pointed to the collage of dogs and horses. "Its shape is the Kingdom of Wales."

"No it isn't, I'm from Wales," said Eliza. Louise slapped her.

There was a diaper bustle dispensary, a tin box hung on the wall. Louise pulled out diaper bustles, throwing them into the room until they were called for dinner.

The dining room was full of small round tables; only two or three girls could fit at each. There were many older women there, who were married. The married women were in separate, individual rooms. It made Louise angry. "Bitches," she said. They spent most of their time playing cards in the parlour or writing long letters to their husbands and children.

There was a large bottle of Madame Flora's surrounded by tiny bottles and oranges as table centrepieces. Oranges were said to help with the constipation that too much Madame Flora's could cause. They were served bowls of mashed potatoes with sugar and milk, or bowls of white bread with sugar and milk, cups of tea with sugar and cream, and more oranges, there were bowls of peeled oranges and orange jelly, crumpets, tiny pots of jam, cabbage and boiled carrots, rice pudding. Victoria sat with a pudgy girl with dark circles under her eyes who said, quietly, "I've not stopped my flowers for the same reason as everyone else. Have you ever been in love?" Victoria thought of her father, her father's butler, and her father's friends, and said no. The girl ate too much cabbage and rice pudding and had gas. She told Victoria that she knew a girl whose flowers stopped after she saw a dead man in a ditch, but she was cured, at Madame Flora's, and that she herself would never be cured, which she said with a little giggle Victoria didn't like.

After dinner, the girls were told to go to bed. Rest was the most important thing. Louise stuck a photo of Hugh, a real lock of his blonde hair glued to it like a toupée, in the middle of the dog and horse collage. "He has more dogs and horses than all that," she said.

Louise's hands were surprisingly dainty and pudgy, with expensive feminine rings, including her engagement ring from Hugh Orville. Her nails were polished, red and sharp like vole's teeth.

Hugh Orville turned up the next day. Madame Flora wouldn't let him visit, but he left gifts for Louise with her—a stuffed swan toy, a box of chocolates. He drove around the hotel in his motor car playing a popular song Louise loved called "Tinky Tinky Too Too," a duet between a trumpet and a theremin. Louise moved from window to window, waving and dancing. Hugh was stunningly handsome. He wore a blue kerchief and a fur coat like Louise's, flashing his new teeth from Fairy Palace. Louise told everyone he was a duke.

Eliza had several black dresses, all velvet or silk. They all looked similar but she wore the same one every day until it smelled, and to bed, merely changing her stockings and bustle, discreetly, in the morning. Matilda's dresses were exceptionally ugly, Louise told her. They were calico, brown, mustard yellow, pink.

Each girl had her own way of taking Madame Flora's, of standing the nasty taste.

Eliza liked to mix Madame Flora's with black tea, Matilda with tonic water, so it was weakened. They put only a drop or two in. Victoria copied them.

The girl who slept behind the curtain and wouldn't say her name put it in milk so that it was a pink colour. Many in the dining room put it in their porridge.

Louise took a straight teaspoon in the morning, with lunch, and before bed, without complaining or grimacing.

She had an iron ball which she licked and threatened to throw at the other girls. Her nanny at home had given her the ball as an anemia cure, and she was addicted to it, but Madame Flora took it away saying it was bad for her, as were greens. "Spinach is poisonous. My tonic is the only safe source of iron for women."

Each evening, a maid came and took away their bustle diapers and dirty laundry in a cart, and examined the bedsheets and blankets for stains. It didn't feel as cruel as when Nanny did it, tuttering and sighing. There were so many girls at Madame Flora's. It wasn't personal.

Louise, who wore trouser pajamas to bed, talked into the night. There was nothing else to do, besides reading magazines.

"I saw a man eating a boiled egg. He grinned at me as he done so."

"I sniffed a rasher of bacon, once, in the kitchen at home."

"Hugh killed eight pheasants and a fox last spring."

There was a middle-aged woman who sat herself in the lift and wouldn't come out. Others squished buns through the brass grating, to make her eat, but she wouldn't let anyone pour any Madame Flora's in—she called it devil's juice. She wasn't married. Madame Flora put some of her concoction in a spray bottle and sprayed the woman with it but she turned around and crouched in a far corner of the lift. Madame told them to ignore her and look away when they passed. There were queues for the one elevator left. The woman screamed and shook the lift during the night and silently paced during the day. Louise spat orange pips at her whenever she passed by the lift.

One morning they came down and the lift was empty and clean again.

On his second visit, Hugh brought Louise a miniature golf set which she set up in the parlour.

"Exercise is the enemy of your flowers, Louise," said Madame Flora, taking Louise's golf club as she took a swing. Louise was so despondent that Madame Flora made an effort to provide entertainment. Victoria couldn't see how Louise could be bored. There were so many ladies' magazines to read at Madame Flora's—*The Modern Priscilla, Dainty Day, News for Ladies* in big stacks everywhere. Victoria's nanny had sent her some popular poems written out on card paper in brown ink. Victoria ripped them up. She was scared of Nanny visiting Madame Flora's like Hugh did, of Nanny circling the hotel crying "Victoria! Victoria!"

The town was full of hotels, shopping arcades, stalls selling postcards, seashell art ("Don't touch the seashells, girls!" said Madame Flora), and novelty tea sets with the royal family on them. There were rides and other amusements. Madame Flora hired a long covered rickshaw pulled by two cyclists to bring the girls around. The seats were very small, and metal. Louise struggled to fit in one, so she balanced herself on the back of the seat, her legs hanging down the arms. She harassed the cycle riders, telling them to go faster, or slow down when she saw something that looked amusing, especially the butcher's shops which had striped curtains covering the windows and signs that said Gentlemen Only. "What do they sell eh?" she muttered. "Sausage. Eggs. Snouts."

Victoria half covered her ears to make herself look good, but was intrigued by what Louise was saying. Louise could be distracted from the butcher's shops only by a carousel on one of the piers.

Madame Flora said yes to a ride on it and made one of the maids run back to the hotel and get some soft paddings to put on the fake animals before the girls sat on them. "Sideways, girls, sideways, like you do properly on a horse."

She nodded to the carousel owner once she checked that all the girls were rightly seated, but after it had gone round a few times, Louise changed positions on her zebra, so both legs hung down different sides. She had taken her bustle off and sent it flying. It resembled a swan as it fell into the seawater. Madame Flora shouted for the carousel to stop. By the time it did, Louise had wrapped her legs around the pole of the zebra, laughing wildly.

Madame Flora didn't let them go out anymore after that, saying it would use up the energy needed to restore their flowers.

Someone came and gave a lecture on ferns, bringing samples in misty glass jars.

"I don't want my flowers again, ever, I just want out of here. I never want babies," muttered Matilda, touching one of the glass jars.

Madame Flora could tell at a glance the difference between menstrual blood and blood from a wound. When Matilda told the maids she had her flowers again, and held up her sheets, Madame Flora came in and pulled up Matilda's nightgown, exposing her diaper bustle. Her legs and stomach were covered in small cuts.

"How could you do this to yourself, sweetest of hearts. We just want to help you get better—don't we treat you well?" asked Madame Flora. They examined her for cuts each week. They put bandages over the ones she had and checked to make sure she didn't rip them off and reopen the wounds.

As Louise continued to act restless, Madame Flora hired two performers, a couple with their small dog, who wore fancy hats and sang and danced and were popular in all the seaside towns. Madame Flora place a velvet railing to separate the girls from them. Louise made them sing "Tinky Tinky Too Too" twice, stomping her foot along so loudly the floor shook. Everyone was relieved to see Louise entertained, but the couple's dog went missing by the end of the show and they caused a fuss Madame Flora thought to be upsetting to her clients.

"Doggy, doggy!"they cried. "Where is our doggy!" The man begged Madame Flora to let him carry around a piece of cheese to lure it out from wherever it was hiding. Madame Flora told them they were disgusting and made them leave without payment.

"Must have gotten out," said Louise. "Must have drowned in the sea."

"Victoria thought that, once they were in their bedroom, Louise would pull the dog out from under her dress, but she didn't. "I'm not interested in mutts," she said. Hugh had bassett hounds, corgis, and Dutch partridge dogs he imported from the Netherlands despite the heavy taxation. They could hear the couple shouting outside the hotel. "Where is our doggy! Bitch, bitch!"

A few days later the dog was found dead in one of the halls. Madame Flora was livid at the thought there was now "meat" in her establishment. The hall was cordoned off, and the girls heard she burnt the dog in the kitchen oven. Victoria wondered if she was afraid to put it in the trash. The smell of burnt hair and flesh wafted up through all the rooms, and Madame Flora filled her establishment with electric fans and more bowls of potpourri.

*

None of the girls told Madame Flora about the time, in the chaos of getting up and getting dressed, a sausage rolled out onto the floor of their bedroom. A first they thought it was a dried turd.

Louise picked it up and ate it before Madame Flora and one of the maids entered the room having heard their screams.

No one knew who left the sausage, except it couldn't have been Louise because she would have eaten it beforehand. She ate things as soon as she received them because she knew she would always get more.

There was no change in Louise's pallor since eating the sausage, nor was she sick. All the girls who had been in the room watched her closely.

*

"What about girls who have too much?" Victoria asked in the dark, in bed one night.

"Too much what?"

"You know, too many flowers."

No one replied, except for Louise who said, "You need a licence stating you are male to buy meat, but I once heard about a woman who dressed up as a man and bought a rack of lamb and was arrested. Maybe the girls who had too many flowers were arrested too." Louise chuckled loudly, the sound filling the room like a horrid fart.

"Or died because they didn't have anything left in their bodies," said Matilda. "Maybe their hearts came out with their flowers."

After some silence, Eliza whispered:

"There was a boy, Thomas. He loved me. He cut himself, on his arm, and let me drink the blood. He did it a number of times, on his legs and his arms. He said it doesn't count as meat. I started to get better but he died of infection from one of the cuts."

*

A week later, Louise was shouting "In here!" standing on a chair below the skylight. "Open the latch," she growled.

It was one of the rickshaw cyclists. Louise had sent him a message through one of the maids, perhaps.

He had put on cologne and it filled the room. He had sweat stains under the armpits of his beige suit, a fresh and red young face, and a little moustache that had been waxed and curled with care.

He took off his trousers and underpants but left on his jacket, shirt, bowtie, shoes, and socks. He lay on his side on Eliza's bed, looking at them all and making kissing sounds. Eliza got up and sat beside Victoria, clutching her arm. "I want her to do it," he said pointing to Eliza.

"Sit up," she said to him, and he did, spreading his legs wide. She went in between.

He winced, but they couldn't see what was going on, her head was in the way. The man moaned.

"His thingy's in her ear," whispered Louise. Eliza turned around, blood on her lips. The man's thing was all sweaty and there was blood all over his thigh, where she had bitten. Louise went over but he said, "I'll come back tomorrow night," and pulled up his trousers, not thinking of the blood, as if he didn't know he was bitten.

There was a bandage over the bite when he returned.

"The other thigh," he said.

Louise didn't bite but tried to use her nail scissors. The man screamed and said no, use your lips and teeth. She did, but made a show of cleaning her face off with a hanky and perfume afterwards and all other the girls knew it was because he was working class.

The girl from behind the curtain came out and drank some too. Matilda and Victoria didn't.

"Bring a friend, tomorrow then," Louise said to the man as he left.

The young man didn't come back the next night, but another came and knew what would happen, taking off his trousers too. After Eliza and Louise drank, Matilda took off her bustle, climbed up on the man, sitting on him, and moved around in an odd manner that made the man giggle and yelp.

"What are you doing?" said Louise.

"I don't want any blood," said Matilda in a breathy voice. "I just want to keep doing what I'm doing."

Louise scowled and, grabbing one of the man's arms, made a cut in it and started drinking. He barely noticed. His other arm reached up and grabbed Matilda's breast, squeezing. It looked like it hurt to Victoria.

The next night, a different man came, and the same thing happened, Matilda sat on him while the other girls cut him and drank from him like a fountain in a garden. "But I don't want my flowers," said Victoria to herself, watching. The girl from behind the curtain copied Matilda and sat on the man too. Matilda said if you didn't have your flowers, you could do it all you want and you wouldn't have any children. All the other girls laughed, confused, except for Louise, who said, "Hugh wants twenty children," in a serious voice. Later in the night, Victoria woke to the sound of Louise trying to do with a pillow what Matilda did with the men.

They accumulated left-behind socks, bowties, shirts, jackets, trousers, shoes, suspenders. One man left his underpants, which Louise used as a nightcap. The girls tried them all on, taking turns, their bustles lying around the room like gigantic broken egg shells. How easy it was to become men.

"I could walk into a butcher's shop and buy myself a piece of ham," said Eliza.

One young man fainted after they drank his blood. Louise slapped him, and they poured Madame Flora's down his throat. He sputtered and sat up, then vomited up the Madame Flora's all down the front of his suit.

*

"I'm bleeding again," the girl from behind her curtain said weakly one morning.

"Wonderful, delightful," said Madame Flora when she entered, looking at the bleeding girl. Her smile disappeared on closer inspection. She called for one of the maids. Together, they carried the girl out of the room, blood dripping from her nightgown.

Hugh stopped by the hotel again to drop off a gigantic basket of fruit including a pineapple and three bananas. Louise ate too much and got diarrhea. She drank Madame Flora's straight from the bottle to stop it.

"I'll just have a small taste," said Victoria, next time a man came. Eliza was on one arm, Louise on the other, and Matilda was sitting on him. Victoria made a cut on his foot. Blood tasted like a fresh version of Madame Flora's, she thought.

At the end, they couldn't wake the man up from his faint. They poured Madame Flora's on his face but he didn't respond.

"He can sleep behind the curtain till he's better," said Victoria.

"He's dead," responded Louise. "He's meat now."

They put him in Louise's trunk.

All the blood from the man must have gone into Louise because her flowers started soon after. Wearing her stained pajamas she ran down into the foyer to use the telephone box. Everyone in the hotel could hear her shouting into it. "FLOWERS, HUGH, FLOWERS!" A few hours later a carriage from her parent's house arrived, followed by Hugh Orville in a motor car.

Louise took the trunk with the man inside with her. "I'll take care of it," she said to the other girls.

Her wedding was in all the papers a few weeks later. She had new teeth too, and they looked exactly the same as Hugh's. They both made sure to show the teeth off in the photos.

Eliza left soon after. She said she wished Thomas could see her flowers, which was a wicked thing to say even though he was dead. No one ever would, now, unless she had to come back to Madame Flora's. She didn't have a nanny at home.

"Give me a spot of yours," Matilda begged Eliza. She didn't just spread it in her bustle but inside herself and on her legs too. It tricked Madame Flora this time.

Victoria was left alone, except for the picture Hugh Louise had left behind.

I'll be in and out of here for the rest of my life, Victoria thought. I'll be stopping and starting my flowers, I'll be spitting up Madame Flora's, I can settle here forever with the parlour wives. There were leftover Madame Flora's bottles all over the room. She poured their contents into the toilet, without flushing, and giggled as she did so. She then sat on one of the beds and opened a magazine. On the cover was a woman using a telephone, her spare hand sitting atop a bouquet of roses.

Chemical Valley

DAVID HUEBERT

I kneel down and reach for the nearest bird, hydraulics buzzing in my teeth and knees. The pigeon doesn't flinch or blink. No blood. No burn smell. Sal's there in seconds, his face a blear of night-shift grog. He rubs his bigger eye, squats by the carcasses. Behind him the river wends and glimmers, slicks through the glare of sixty-two refineries.

Sal thumbs his coverall pockets. "Poison you figure?"

"Leak maybe."

Suzy appears next to Sal, seeping chew-spit into her Coke can. She leans over and takes a pigeon in her Kevlared paw. Brings it to her face. "Freaky," she says, bottom lip bulging. "Eyes still open." She wiggles her rat face into a grin, a frond of tobacco wagging in her upper left incisor.

I can't afford to say it. "Saving that for later?"

Suzy flares. "What?"

"The chew."

Suzy puts a hand over her mouth, speaks with taut lips. "Enough of your guff."

I snort. "Guff?"

She sets the bird down, hitches her coveralls. Lips closed, she tongues the tobacco loose and swallows. "Clean 'em up," she says, nodding at the pigeons. She spins and walks away, a slurry of chew-spit mapping her path across the unit.

What you might find, if you were handling a dead pigeon, is something unexpected in the glassy cosmos of its eye: a dark beauty, a molten alchemy. You might find a pigeon's iris looks how you imagine the earth's core—pebble-glass waves of crimson, a perfect still shudder of rose and lilac. What you might do, if you were placing a dead pigeon into the incinerator, is take off your Kevlar glove and touch your bare index finger to its cornea. What you might do before dropping the bird into a white-hot Mordor of carbon and coke is touch your fingertip to that unblinking membrane and hold it there, feeling a mangle of tenderness and violation, thinking this may be the loveliest secret you have ever touched.

I'm telling Eileen how I want to be buried, namely inside a tree. We're sitting in bed eating Thai from the mall and listening to the 6 p.m. construction outside our window—the city tearing up the whole street along with tree roots and a rusted tangle of lead pipes—and I'm telling Eileen it's called a biodegradable burial pod. Mouth full of cashew curry, I'm saying what they do is put your remains in this egg-looking thing like the xenomorph's cocoon from *Alien: Resurrection* but it's made of biodegradable plastic. I'm telling Eileen it's called "capsula mundi" and what they do is hitch the remains to a semi-mature tree and plant the whole package. Stuff you down in fetal position and let you gradually decay until you become nitrogen, seep into soil.

Chewing panang, Eileen asks where I got the idea about the burial pod and I tell her Facebook or maybe an email newsletter. "You click on that shit? Why are you even thinking about this now? You just turned thirty-four."

I don't tell her about the basement, about Mum. I don't tell her about the pigeons strewn out on the concrete and then going supernova in the incinerator and it gets you thinking about flesh, about bodies, about waste. I don't tell her about Blane, the twenty-nine-year-old long-distance runner who got a heart attack sitting at the panel in the Alkylation unit. Blane didn't die but he did have to get surgery and a pacemaker and that sort of thing gets you thinking. Which is how you end up lying in bed at night checking your pulse and feeling like your chest is shrinking and thinking about the margin of irregular and erratic.

Picking a bamboo shoot from her teeth: "Since when are you into trees?" She says it smug. She says it like Ms. University Sciences and nobody else is allowed to like trees. I don't tell her how we're all compost and yes I read that on a Facebook link. I also do not tell her about the article's tagline: "Your carbon footprint doesn't end in the grave." Reaching for the pad Thai, I tell her about the balance, how it's only natural. How the human body's rich in nitrogen, how when you use a coffin there's a lot of waste because the body just rots on its own when it could be giving nutrients to the system. Not to mention all the metals and treated woods in coffins. I tell her how the idea is to phase out traditional graveyards entirely, replace them with grave-forests.

"Hmm," Eileen says, gazing out the window—the sky a caramelized rose. "Is this a guilt thing, from working at the plants?"

I tell her no, maybe, I don't know. An excavator hisses its load into the earth.

"Is this why you were so weird about your mother's funeral?" I ask what she means and she says never mind, sorry.

"Do you ever imagine they're ducks?"

Eileen asks what and I tell her the loaders and the bulldozers and the cranes. Sometimes I imagine they're wildlife, ducks or geese. And maybe why they're crying like that is because they're in distress. Like maybe they've lost their eggs and all they want is to get them back and when you think about it like that it's still bad but at least it's not just machines screaming and blaring because they're tearing up old sidewalks to put new ones down.

"Ducks," Eileen says. "Probably still be one working for every three scratching their guts for overtime pay."

She stacks the containers and reaches for the vaporizer on the nightstand, asking if I love trees so much why didn't I become a landscaper or a botanist or an arborist. I shrug, not mentioning the debt or the mortgage or the pharmaceutical bills. Not mentioning that if I wanted to do something it would be the comics store but there's no market in Sarnia anyway.

I tell her it's probably too late for a career change.

"No," she coos, pinching my chin the way I secretly loathe. She smiles her sweet stoned smile, a wisp of non-smoke snaking through her molars. "You could do anything. You could be so much." Eileen lies down on her back on the bed, telling the ceiling I could be so much and the worst part is she means it. The worst and the best all mangled together as I reach out and thumb the curry sauce from her chin.

Eileen tells me she needs the bathroom so I help her out of bed and into her chair. I stand outside the bathroom door listening to the faucet's gentle gush and think about later, when Eileen falls asleep and I drift down to the basement, to Mum.

In 1971 the Trudeau government issued a ten-dollar bill picturing Sarnia's Chemical Valley as a paean to Canadian progress. Inked in regal purple, the buildings rise up space-aged and triumphant, a *Jetsons'* wet dream. Towers slink up to the sky and cloud-like drums pepper the ground, a suspended rail line curling through the scene. Smokestacks and ladders and tanks and tubs. Glimmering steel and perfect concrete, a shimmering fairy city and the strange thing is that what you don't see is oil, what you never see is oil. The other strange thing is that this is how Sarnia used to be seen, that not so long ago the plants were shiny and dazzling and now they're rusty with paint peeling off the drums and poor safety and regular leaks and weeds all over, stitching concrete seams.

*

On the drive to work a woman on the radio is talking about birth rates as the cornfields whish and whisper. Eileen doesn't know this or need to but I drive the long way to work because I like to drive through the cornfields. What I like about them is the sameness: corn and corn and corn and it makes you think that something is stable, stable and alive and endless or about as close as you can get. If Eileen was in the car she'd say, "as high as an elephant's eye in July." Then she'd probably say her thing about ethanol. How the nitrogen fertilizer comes from ammonia which comes from natural gas. How the petrochemical fertilizer is necessary to grow super huge varieties of hybrid corn products that mostly turn into livestock feed but also a significant portion turns into ethanol. Ethanol that is then used as a biofuel supplement to gasoline so what it is is this whole huge cycle of petroleum running subterranean through modern biological life.

On the radio they're saying how first it was the birds and then it was the reserve and now they're getting worried. Now they're seeing plant workers, especially the women, producing only female children. No official studies on the area because Health Canada won't fund them but the anecdotal evidence is mounting and mounting and the whole community knows it's in their bodies, in their intimate organs, zinging through their spit and blood and lymph nodes.

"Hey," Suzy says, slurring chew-spit into her Coke can. "What do you call a Mexican woman with seven kids?" I try to shrug away the punchline but Sal gives his big-lipped smirk and asks what. "Consuelo," Suzy says, her mouth a snarl of glee. She puts her hand down between her knees and mimes a pendulum.

I smile in a way that I guess is not convincing because Suzy says, "What's the matter Jerr-Bear?" I tell her it's not funny.

"Fuck you it isn't."

"Think I'll do my geographics."

"You do that," Suzy says, turning back to Sal. "Can't leave you here with Pockets all shift." Pockets being what Suzy calls me in her kinder moments, when she doesn't feel like calling me "Smartass" or "Thesaurus" or "Mama's boy." Something to do with I guess putting my hands in my coverall pockets too much.

I walk away while Sal starts saying something about Donaldson or Bautista and Suzy makes her usual joke about me and the Maglite.

Before she got sick, Eileen used to work in research, and on slow days (that is, most days) I used to think up towards her. I'd look up towards the shiny glass windows of the research building and think of Eileen working on the other side. Mostly what they do up there is ergonomic self-assessments and loss prevention self-assessments but sometimes they do cutting and cracking. A lot of what they do is sit up there staring at glove matrices and gauges and screens but I'd always picture Eileen with her hands in the biosafety cabinet. I'd picture her in goggles and full face mask and fire retardant suit, reaching through the little window to mix the catalyst in and then watching the crude react in the microscope. Because when Eileen was working she loved precision and she loved getting it right but most of all she loved watching the oil split and change and mutate. Say what you want about oil but the way Eileen described it she always made it seem beautiful: dense and thick, a million different shades of black. She used to say how the strange thing with the oil is that if you trace it back far enough you see that it's life, that all this hydrocarbon used to be vegetables and minerals and zooplankton. Organisms that got caught down there in some cavern where they've been stewing for five hundred million years. How strange it is to look out at this petroleum Xanadu and think that all the unseen sludge running through it was life, once—that it was all compost, all along.

In 2003 there was a blackout all across Ontario and the northeastern United States. A blackout caused by a software bug and what happened was people could see the stars again from cities. In dense urban areas the Milky Way was suddenly visible again, streaming through the unplugged vast. What also happened was babies, nine months later a horde of blackout babies, the hospitals overwhelmed with newborns because what else do you do when the power goes down. But if you lived in Sarnia what you would remember is the plants. It was nighttime when the power went out and what happened was emergency shutdown of all systems, meaning all the tail gas burning at once. So every flare from all sixty-two refineries began shooting off together, a tail-gas Disneyland shimmering through the river-limned night.

The day shift crawls along. QC QC QC. The highlight is a funny-sounding line we fix by increasing the backpressure. Delivery trucks roll in and out. The pigeons coo and shit and garble in their roosts in the stacks. Freighters park at the dock and pump the tanks full of bitumen—the oil moving, as always, in secret, shrouded behind cylindrical veils of carbon steel. Engineers cruise through tapping iPads, printing the readings from Suzy's board. Swarms of contractors pass by. I stick a cold water bottle in each pocket which is nice for ten minutes then means I'm carrying piss-warm water around the unit. I do my geographic checks, walk around the tower turning the odd valve when Suzy radios, watch the river rush and kick by the great hulls of the freighters. I think about leaping onto the back of one of those freighters, letting it drag me down the St. Clair and into Erie just to feel the lick of breeze on neck.

Time sags and sags and yawns. By 10 a.m. I can feel the sun howling off the concrete, rising up vengeful and gummy. Doesn't matter that there's a heat warning, you've still got to wear your coveralls and your steel toes and your hardhat, the sweat gumming up the insides of your arms, licking the backs of your knees. The heat warning means we take "precautions." It means coolers full of Nestlé water sweating beside the board. It means we walk slowly around the unit. As slow as we can possibly move but the slow walking becomes its own challenge because the work's still got to get done.

The river gets me through the shift: the curl and cool of it, its great improbable blue. The cosmic-bright blue that's supposedly caused by the zebra mussels the government put all over Ontario to make the water blue and pretty but if Eileen were here she'd say her thing about the algae. How she learned in first year bio that what the zebra mussels do is eat all the particles from the lake, allowing room for algae to grow beyond their boundaries and leading to massive poisonous algae blooms in Lake Huron and Lake Erie. So you think you're fixing something but really there's no fixing and how fitting that one way or another the river's livid blue is both beautiful and polluted, toxic and sublime.

"Heard about those bodies?" Sal asks, thumbing through his phone as I pass by the board. I ask what bodies and he says the ones in Toronto. "Like a half dozen of them, some kind of landscaper-murderer stashing bodies in planters all over the city."

I kill the shift as usual: walk around wiggling the flashlight thinking about the different spots in the river and diving into them with my mind. Thinking about what might be sleeping down there—maybe a pike or a smelt or a rainbow trout nestled among the algae and the old glass Coke bottles. Sometimes I think my way across the bridge, over to Port Huron. Wonder if there's an operator over there doing the same thing, thinking back across the river towards me.

I drive home the long way which means cornfields and wind turbines in the distance as the sky steeps orange pekoe. In the rearview a flare shoots up from the plants. Getting closer, I pass through a gauntlet of turbines, feeling them more than I see them. Carbon filament sentries. Once I passed an enormous truck carrying a wind turbine blade and at first I thought it was a whale. It reminded me of videos I'd seen of Korean authorities transporting a sperm whale bloated with methane, belching its guts across the tarmac. The truck had a convoy and a bunch of orange Wide Load signs and I passed it slowly, partly because of the danger and partly because there was a pulse to it, something drawing me in. The great sleek curve of the blade, its unreal whiteness.

Eileen's still up, vaping in her chair by the window. "Sorry," she says, spinning her chair to look at me. "Couldn't sleep." I tell her she can vape in the kitchen or wherever she likes but she looks at me with her stoned slanting smile and tells me it's not that. Says how she's been looking out into the yard a lot and when she does it she thinks about the teenagers. She looks at me like she wants me to ask for details. I don't, but she continues anyway. Rehearses how those kids in the seventies got trapped in the abandoned fallout shelter. "You know, the yards were so long because the properties used to be cottages and the old shelter was overgrown and the teens were skipping school and smoking up and the excavator came through and started to fill it in and no one realized the teens were missing until days later. The only explanation was that they were scared, so scared of getting caught that they stayed quiet, let it happen, hoped it would pass."

"You don't believe all that do you?"

Eileen shrugs, still staring out the window. "No. Maybe. I just like the story."

I ask how's the pain today and she says manageable. Turns her face towards me but doesn't meet my eyes. I ask her out of ten and she says you know I hate that. She asks is something wrong and I tell her no. "Something you're not telling me about?" I don't respond and she doesn't push it.

We watch the original *Total Recall* and when we get to the part with the three-breasted woman Eileen asks if I find that strange or sexy and I tell her neither, or both. Eventually Eileen drifts off but when I stand up she lurches awake. She asks where I'm going and I say just downstairs to read the new *Deadpool* unless she wants the bedside lamp on. She says no, asks when I'm coming to bed. I tell her soon and she says cuddle me when you get here. "Don't just lie there," she says. "Hold me." I tell her yes, of course, and head down to the sweet dank sogg of the basement.

Mum listens with tender quiet as I tell her about my day—about Suzy, about the pigeons, about the construction. Mum is gentle and sweet, her gold incisor catching light from the bare pull-string bulb. Eventually I check my phone and see that it's pushing eleven and I should probably head upstairs if I want my six to seven hours. I give Mum a goodnight kiss and tell her to get some rest and then I notice something strange in the floor, stoop down to inspect.

A hand-shaped imprint in the foundation floor.

Mum looks on, her face a void, as I toe that dark patch with my basement-blackened sock and find that it's wet, somewhat soggy. The hole's a bit sandy and when I get closer I smell it. Muskeg. Raw Lambton skunk.

I prod a little deeper and become a stranger, become someone who would stick a curious thumb into such a cavity. The oil comes out gooey and black and smelling sharp, a little sulphurous.

I dream of bodies, the ones buried in planters in Toronto. The ones I'd heard about on the radio—this killer targeting gay men in Toronto and the more planters they dug up the more bodies they found. In the dream the bodies aren't skeletons, not yet. They're in the active decay stage: their organs starting to liquify, the soft tissue browning and breaking down while the hair, teeth, and bone remain intact. I see them crawling up from planters all across the city. Not vengeful or anything. Just digging, rising, trying to get back.

"Would you have liked to become an engineer?" We're in the tent sipping iced tea and listening to a sweet chorus of loaders and bulldozers, the air heady with the lilt of tar.

"I am one. A chemical engineer." I can see Eileen wanting to laugh and fighting it. Not like I've got any delusions about my four-year

Lambton College diploma but technically it is a credential in chemical engineering.

"Maybe an urban planner," Eileen says. "Have you heard about all this stuff they're doing in cities now? Condos with elevators big enough for cars. Cute little electric cars that you'll bring right up to your apartment with you."

"Sounds more like an Eileen thing."

A bird lands in the armpit of the oak. A little black bird with a slash of red on its wing. The one I love but can never remember its name.

Eileen sips her tea and says yeah I'm probably right but it's just she can tell the hours are getting to me. The hours and the nights and the overtime. She reminds me how I told her, once, that it's like a sickness, the overtime. "You could do whatever you want," she says. "You could be so much."

The worst part is she always means it and the worst part is it's not true. Not true because Mum worked part time and Dad died so young that there was no money for me to do anything but CPET. I don't tell her because she already knows about the comic store, about how maybe I could write one on the side and I already have the character—BioMe, the scientist turned mutant tree-man after attempting to splice photosynthesis into the human genome.

"You're so creative, you could be so much. Like your comic store idea. And remember that musical you wrote in high school, *Hydrocarbonia*?" She chuckles. "There was that three-eyed coyote and the plant worker Village People chorus?"

"I think it was basically a *Simpsons* rip-off. Mr. Hunter went with *Guys and Dolls*."

"Still. You're a poet at heart."

"The bard of bitumen."

"What I mean is I love you but sometimes I feel like all you do is work and all I do is sleep and we never see each other and I just wish we had something else, something more."

A quick haze of stupidity in which I contemplate telling her about Mum. Then I see a seagull in the distance, watch as it catches a thermal and rides high and higher, an albatross floating through the glazed crantini sky.

"One more shift," I tell her. "Then four off."

She doesn't need to roll her eyes. "Look," she says, pointing up at the oak. "A red-winged blackbird."

On the drive to work they're saying about the fish. Saying about the drinking water downstream, in Windsor and Michigan. Saying about the tritium spilling into Lake Huron. You think Chernobyl and you think Blinky the three-eyed fish but what you don't think is an hour north or so, where Bruce Power leaks barrels of radioactive tritium into Lake Huron. They're saying how significant quantities of antidepressants have been found in fish brains in the Great Lakes.

I drive past the rusting drums and have to stop for a moment because there are some protesters forming a drum circle. They're holding signs that read "Stop Line 9" and chanting about stolen native land and of course they're right but I don't smile or stop or acknowledge them. Just park and walk through security, a new sting in the awful.

*

Ways people deal with constant low-level dread: the myth that the wind blows the fumes south, towards Aamjiwnaang, towards Corunna, towards Walpole. That the airborne toxicity lands ten kilometres to the south. That the people who live north of the plants won't get sick or at least not as sick. As if wind could really dilute the impact of living beside a cluster of sixty-two petrochemical refineries that never sleep, could change the fact that you live in a city where Pearl Harbour-style sirens sound their test alarm every Monday at 12:30 to remind you that leaks could happen at any moment. There's a joke around Streamline, a joke that is not a joke: the retirement package is great if you make it to fifty-five. Which is not inaccurate in my family seeing as Dad went at fifty-two and Mum followed at fifty-six and they said the lung cancer had nothing to do with the plants and the brain cancer had nothing to do with Mum's daily swims from the bridge to Canatara Beach. The strange pride among people who work the plants: a spending your oil salary on hummers and motorcycles and vacations to Cuban beaches with plastic cups kind of pride. A live rich live hard kind of pride. The yippie ki-yay of knowing that Sarnia is the leukemia capital of Canada and the brain cancer capital of Canada and the air pollution capital of Canada but also knowing that oil is what you know and what your parents knew and all your family's in Lambton County so what else are you going to do but stay.

We're putting on our face masks and backpacks while Don the safety protocol officer explains for the hundredth time about the new model of self-contained breathing apparatus and the new standard-issue Kevlar gloves. Telling us once again that personal safety is paramount even though all of us know that what operators are here for is to control situations.

I'm sitting there watching sailboats tack their way across the lake while Don goes on about the hydrogen sulfide incident that happened two years ago. Incident meaning leak. Telling us again how the thing about hydrogen sulfide is that you can't see it, so you can't actually see or smell when it's on fire. Two years ago when a vehicle melted in the loading dock. An invisible sulfide fire came through and before the operators could shut it down the truck in the loading bay just melted. The tires evaporated and the air hissed out of them and the whole truck sank to the floor, a puddle of melted paint on the concrete and nothing left of the truck but a gleaming skeleton of carbon steel.

*

We used to swim in the lake at night, just the two of us. Dad was usually home watching the Blue Jays, so me and Mum would drive up to a secret little beach in the north and we'd swim out into the middle of the river where the lights from Port Huron gleamed and wiggled in the darkness. Sometimes it would rain and the rain would make the water warmer than the air. I'd seen a water snake at the beach once and I always imagined them down there among our legs. Though Mum had assured me they were non-venomous I saw them sharp-toothed and cunning, biding their time. Sometimes Mum would dip down below the water, her head disappearing for what seemed an impossibly long time and I don't know how she found me but she'd wrangle her arms around both my legs and pin me for a moment while I kicked and bucked and then we'd both come up gasping and squealing and giggling in the black water, a gelatin dazzle of refinery lights.

"So what tree?" Eileen asks, watching the sun leak pink delirium over the abandoned Libcor refinery. Eileen in her chair and the van parked behind us. In front, the overgrown refinery that shut down thirty years ago after a mercaptan leak. When they left, the company kept the lot. Took down all the tall buildings and left a waste of concrete with a railway running through it, surrounded by a barbed wire fence.

I ask for clarification and Eileen asks what tree I'd want to be buried in and I pause to think about it, looking out over the crabgrass and goldenrod and firepits full of scorched goldenrod. "Think there are any animals in there?"

Eileen says yeah, probably, like Chernobyl. She knows about Chernobyl from a documentary. In the exclusion zone, there's a place called the Red Forest. It's a bit stunted and the trees have a strange ginger hue but the wildlife is thriving—boar, deer, wolves, eagles. Eileen says nuclear radiation might actually be better for animals than human habitation.

I stand quietly, holding Eileen's chair and watching the sun pulse and glow and vanish. She reaches back and takes my hand, rubs the valleys between my fingers. Eventually, without saying anything, we turn for the van.

"You ever think about concrete?" Eileen asks as I'm fastening her chair into the van. "How it seems so permanent. How it's all around us and we walk and drive on it believing it's hard and firm and solid as the liquid rock it is but really it's nothing like rock at all. Weeds and soil beneath it and all of it ready to rise up at the gentlest invitation. It's very fragile, very temporary."

On the way home we pass by the rubber plant and the abandoned Bluewater village and beyond it Aamjiwnaang and Eileen says "incredible shrinking territory." The reserve used to stretch from Detroit to the Bruce Peninsula before being slowly whittled down through centuries of sketchy land deals. Eileen's maternal grandmother was Ojibwe and she has three cousins on the reserve and we go over once in a while but mostly her tradition is just to say "incredible shrinking territory" when we drive by.

It comes to me when we drive by a bungalow, spot a clutch of them crawling up from the cleft of the foundation. "Sumac, I guess."

"What?"

I say sumac again and Eileen clues in and says aren't those basically weeds. I tell her no, they can get pretty big and I like the fruit, how they go red in autumn. I like how they're sort of bushy and don't have a prominent trunk. How they're spunky and fierce and unpredictable.

"Sumac." Eileen does her pondering frown. "Noted."

It's dark now and the lights are on in Port Huron, flickering out over the river. Looking out the window, Eileen asks me to tell her again how the county used to be. I hold on to the wheel and steer through the great chandelier and tell it how Mum used to. I say about the plank road and the Iroquois Hotel, how Petrolia was incorporated the very year Canada became a country, so we're basically built on oil. I tell about the gushers in every field, soaring up fifty feet and raining down on the fields, clogging up the river and the lakes until the fishermen in Lake Erie complained about the black grit on the hulls of their boats. I tell about the notorious stench of the Lambton skunk, and about the fires. No railway or fire trucks so when lightning hit and fire took to the fields they often burned for weeks at a time, a carnage of oil-fire raging through the night.

"Wild," she says. "Can you believe all that's gone now? That whole world." I don't say it's not gone, just invisible—racing through stacks and columns and broilers. I tell her what a perfect word, "wild."

Eileen goes to bed early so I head down to the sweet cool lull of the basement. The hole is the size of a Frisbee now, and it's starting to stink. Sit on the old plastic-plaid lawn chair and talk to Mum about work, about Suzy, about the fish and the pigeons and the ratio.

There's a long silence. I didn't know the whole thing was getting to me. Didn't know how it was building in me, fierce and rank. I tell Mum I'm worried. Worried I'm going to lose her. Worried about the smell, the rot, the secrets. Worried someone's going to figure it out, maybe talk to the taxidermist. And I can't tell Eileen and what are we going to do, what am I going to do?

Mum sits there and listens sweetly. Then she twinkles her golden incisor towards the muskeg hole and I see something strange, something wrong, something white. So I step closer, grab an old chair leg and stir the muskeg a little and yes it definitely is what I think it is: a small bone that could easily be a piece of a raccoon thigh but could also be a human finger.

I wake up at 5 p.m. and find Eileen making pesto which means it must be a good day. As I'm making a Keurig she tells me there's another one in the toilet. And once she says it I can hear the splashing. "Sorry," she winces, pouring olive oil on a mound of basil and parm. "I wanted to. Just didn't have the energy." She presses a button on the KitchenAid, makes whirling mayhem of leaf and oil.

I put on my spare Kevlars and head into the bathroom, pull the lid up to find the rat floundering, scrambling, its teeth bared and wet with fresh blood from where it must have bludgeoned itself against the porcelain. The water the colour of rust. The rat keeps trying to run up the side of the toilet, losing its purchase and sliding back down in a mayhem of thrashing legs and sploshing water.

Without quite knowing why, I reach in and pin the rat and squat down to look into its eyes. I guess I want to know what it's like to be a rat. Its head flicks back and forth in rage or terror, never meeting my eyes. Maybe it doesn't know how to.

If I let it go it'll just end up back here, in the toilet, in pain. So I hold its head under the water. Pin it as it thrashes and bucks and wheels its legs, switching its ghost-pink tail. Exhausted, the creature doesn't fight much. More or less lets it happen.

I walk it through a Stonehenge of pylons and descend into the guts of the exhumed city street. I lay the rat in a puddle at the mouth of a culvert and throw some sludge over it. Walk back between a mound of PVC piping and a wrecked Jenga of blasted asphalt.

Back inside, I tell Eileen I released it alive. "Good," she says. "I'm getting tired of this. Must have something to do with the plumbing, the construction."

"Should be over soon."

"What should?"

"Want to go down to the river?"

We park at Point Edward and I wheel Eileen down to the waterfront, where the river curls and snarls and chops its dazzling blue. Underfoot there's a belligerence of goose shit. We watch a pair and Eileen tells me they mate for life and get fierce about their young. They've been known to attack adult humans to protect them. I look at the geese and wonder how long their families have been nesting on this river.

"When did they stop migrating?" Eileen asks.

Which makes me think of a book I read once, where the main character keeps asking where the ducks go in winter. I can't remember what book or what the answer was if there was one. I tell her I don't know and she tells me how weird it is that there's this whole big thing about Canada geese flying south in winter but as far as she can tell they never leave.

"I think it's the northern ones, more so."

"And what, they migrate down here? Winter in scenic Sarnia?"

Beneath the bridge a teenager launches into a backflip. Executes perfectly to uproarious applause. His audience: a chubby red-headed boy and three thin girls in dripping bathing suits. Eileen stops for a moment and I can see her watching them and maybe she's thinking how comfortable they are. How cozy. How nice it must be to just have a body and not think about it.

Above them, transport trucks arc through a highway in the sky.

The four off blur by in a haze of Dominoes and Netflix and assuring Eileen there's no smell from the basement, that it's probably just the construction. Eileen and I watch all of *Jessica Jones* then all of *The Punisher*, listen to the bleats and chirps of loaders and excavators. On Saturday I find a bone like a human elbow joint in the muskeg, another like an eye socket. Rodent hip, I convince myself. Raccoon brow. Squirrel bits. More rats.

Then it's Sunday, meaning back to night shift for eight more on. I whiz past cornfields on the way to work when I notice something strange, something I've never spotted. Which makes sense because it's in the very back of the field and it sort of blends in with a little patch of windbreak trees behind it but there it is: a rusted old derrick in the middle of the cornfield. A wrought-iron steeple rising up through the swishing haze like a puncture in time, a throwback to the days of gushers and teamsters, when the fields were choked with oil and fires burned for weeks.

Eileen texts me to say there's still that weird smell in the house and she's pretty sure it's oil or gas. Maybe it's the stove, should she be worried. She's thinking of texting her brother to come check it out. I tell her no, don't text your brother, I'll open the windows when I get home. Which is when I hear the enunciator.

The blare of the Class A and then the radio crunches and Suzy comes on saying there are a few malfunction lights on Zone 1 and a flare shooting off.

"Main concern is FAL-250A. Flow transfer failure could be a big one let's get on it."

When a Class A sounds, everyone goes. So it's not just us CDU operators scurrying around it's also Naphtha and Alkylation and Plastics and the unit is full of bodies. Todd puts on a SCBA though nobody's sure why. Derek and Paul smash into each other at full speed on the Tower 1 scaffold causing Suzy to yell, "No fucking running rule still fucking holds." Stan, one of the night engineers, says maybe it could have something to do with the sludge blanket level in the wastewater valve.

Suzy wheels on him. "How the fuck is that?" When Stan starts to explain she tells him to go back to his craft beer and his Magic card tournaments. Jack tries again: "Backpressure?"

Suzy glares at him, leaking chew-spit onto the floor. Stan walks off muttering something about valve monkeys. Suzy stares at her board and calls orders out while the rest of us scramble around checking valves and lines and readings.

Sal finds the problem: a release valve is down and there's buildup in the main flare. A buildup of hydrocarbon waste in the thirty-six-inch flare where the tail gas should be burning off, which means a lot of flammable gunk and Suzy's board is telling her the flare's going but the flare is not going.

"Looks like a problem with the pilot flame," Sal shouts from halfway up the tower.

"Getting enough oxygen?" Stan shouts back up.

"Should probably call research," Sal says. Suzy says fuck those fucking lab monkeys then moves towards the tower with a gunslinger strut. Grabbing a rag from a maintenance cart, she starts tying it around a plunger. She sets a boot down on the rubber cup and yanks the wooden handle free. Then she climbs up the tower to the first platform. As she's heading up Sal races down and I'm backing off too as Suzy leans back, shouts, "Heads up," and sends the plunger handle arcing towards the mouth of the flare.

The workers scatter—scurrying into the warehouse and the delivery building, hunching behind trucks and the board. I find a dumpster and cling to the back of it. Sal hits the concrete and joins me just in time to watch the plunger arc and arc and land in the maw of the stack.

The air shimmies and buckles.

The flare lights.

Lights and blasts seventy feet into the moon-limned sky. Air swirls and booms and I clutch my chest because I can't breathe.

The dumpster jumps.

The dumpster becomes a toad and leaps ten feet across the floor. The flare lights, a hissing rage of tail gas, a seventy-foot Roman candle stabbing up at the sickle moon.

No one gets hurt. No one gets in trouble. Stan walks away shaking his head along with the ten or twelve operators gathered on the floor. The enunciator goes quiet and Suzy walks down from the stack brushing off her knees.

Sal looks over at me, muttering something about being too old for these shenanigans. He walks away huffing, pauses to curse towards the dumpster's skid mark, which is longer than a car. Suzy calls me over and tells me I didn't see shit, then tells me to look after the flare for the rest of my shift.

"What do you mean look after it?"

"Stand there and watch it Stephen fucking Hawking." So I stand there and watch it.

The moon grins down and the flame shoots up beside it for ten min-utes, then twenty, with no sign of abating. I pace around Tower 1, checking pressures and temps and turning valves as needed but always keeping that flare in eyeshot.

One hour. Two.

Down by the river I see the lakeshore going liquid and sort of throbbing. At first I think it must be gas. Then I think I must be hallucinating because the shoreline itself has turned semi-solid as it refracts the flare's corona. It looks like there's flesh down there, a great beast sidling up to the fence.

I walk down and shine my flashlight on them and see that it is flesh. Not one creature but thousands. Smelt. Thousands and thou-sands of smelt cozying up to the shore, coming as close as they can to the flame.

I don't notice Suzy until she's gusting sour breath over my shoulder. "The fuck is that?"

"Smelt."

She stands there looking at the fish awhile, spitting into her Coke can. Then she turns back to her flare, gives it the up-down. For a moment I think she might genuflect.

"Fucking smelt," she scoffs, walking away.

I spend the rest of the shift watching the smelt shudder in the balm of the flare. Thousands of fish inching towards the tail gas column as it roars and rages through the punctured dark. Light licking them silver and bronze, the smelt push and push against the shore—close and closer but never close enough.

I drive home past the wind turbines thinking as I often do about a hundred thousand years from now when maybe someone would come across this place. I talked about this once, with Mum. We walked into a cornfield just to look at the turbines and when we got there I asked what would happen if there were no corn or soy or farmers left, just the turbines marking the graves of fields. How maybe a thousand years from now there would be a new kind of people like in *Mad Max* and they wouldn't remember farms or electricity or the nuclear power plant in Kincardine. How these future humans might find this place where turbines sprouted up taller than any trees, their arms like great white whales. The surrounding farms all gone to wild again. And what else would these new people think but that these massive three-armed hangmen were slow-spinning gods? "That's very well put," Mum said then, as if she were the teacher she'd always wanted to be instead of a woman who answered the phones at NRCore three days a week. She stood beneath that turbine, staring up at its bland white belly for a long time before she finally said, "It does sort of look like a god. A faceless god."

Eileen's still sleeping when I get home so I pour some merlot and head straight down through the oil-reek into the basement. Eileen was right. The smell is getting bad. Detectable from the kitchen and almost unbearable in the basement itself and what this means is a matter of days at most. Below, the morning sun winks and flickers through the cracked foundation. The hole is the size of a truck tire, now, and there are more bones floating at the surface. I grab an old broken chair leg and stir the muck around, transfixed by the bones. One that looks like a splintered T-bone, one that may be a gnawed nose, another that I'm pretty sure has part of a fingernail attached. A row of molars like a hardened stitch of corn.

The teenagers. In the yard. The story I've never believed.

"It's all right," Mum would say if she could speak. "It's all right, sweet Sonny Boy. You're all right, you're here, everything's going to be fine."

And Mum would be right. For the moment everything is nice and cool and dark and we sit there in the gentle silence until Mum wants me to tell her some of the old stories so I do. I tell them the way she used to tell me. I tell about her grandfather, the Lambton oil man who sniffed for gushers and got ripped off on the patent for the Canada rig. I tell about the last gusher and the time lightning struck the still and all the dirty land sales the companies made to get things started in Sarnia. Water, I remember her saying once. It was all about water. They chose Sarnia because they needed to be by the river. I tell her the same now and she sits there smiling faintly, a twinkle in her gold incisor, and for the moment the two of us are calm and happy and together.

*

When I creep into bed Eileen wakes up. She reaches for her bedside table, produces a rectangular LED blear. "It's almost noon," she says. "What were you doing?" I tell her I was in the basement. She asks if I was playing *WoW* again and I say no just reading some old volumes of *Turok*. She murmurs the usual: just don't take up Magic like her brother. I laugh and tell her no, of course not.

Then she rises. Sits up in bed and I can see even with the blackout blinds that she's gone serious. She asks if there's something going on with me lately. I tell her no, of course not, just a hard day at work. And how could you expect what comes next:

"You know I'm never going to get better?"

Times like this, I'm not good at saying the right thing because there is no right thing.

"It's just," she continues, "sometimes I forget, myself, that it's not ever going to end, that it's just going to keep going like this for who knows how long. And I just want to be sure that you know the full extent of that."

I tell her yeah, of course.

She squints through the dark. "It's just, I know it's hard for you, and if you ever wanted—"

I tell her no, absolutely not, whatever it is. Whisper that I don't want anything different, don't need anything more than what we have. I go big spoon and nestle into her until I'm hot, until I'm roasting under the blankets and wanting to roll away but also wanting just to melt, to seep, to burn hot as compost in nitrogen night.

The day Dad died, Mum and I sat in the bug tent in the backyard watching a horde of blue jays eat the heads off Mum's sunflowers. Any other day she would have gotten up and screamed carnage at those birds but she just sat there watching. He'd weighed about forty-five pounds at the end and it was not a nice thing for a wife or a fifteen-year-old son to watch. It ended graciously, in sleep. The ambulance came and Mum went with because there were checks to be done, forms to be signed. After she came home we sat in the backyard watching those ravenous blue jays pick through a row of twenty or thirty six-foot sunflowers. I said how I didn't know blue jays could be so vicious and Mum said oh yeah, everything beautiful has a dark side, just like everything wretched has a loveliness. When there were only three heads remaining and the blue jays were pecking tiredly, half of them gone, Mum told me those sunflowers had been growing in the spot where she'd buried her placenta after I was born. She said she'd always figured that's why they grew so well there. Said how the placenta had enriched the soil so in a way I was feeding those blue jays, we both were. And so the two of us sat there watching the birds gobble up the vegetation we'd nourished together and I saw each one grow a face. The last three sunflowers became me and Dad and Mum and I watched the blue jays shred those yellow faces into mangled tufts.

I take the long way to work and when I see the wind turbines I find myself driving towards them. Driving down a farm road and then onto a corn farm with a turbine on a strip of grass and weed and I'm leaping out of the car and sprinting up to it, kneeling while this terrible white demiurge churns its arms in slow rotation. I kneel there thinking up towards that turbine and feeling overpowered by something blunt and terrible and awesome. The sound of the thing is huge and steady and sonorous, an Olympian didgeridoo, and I remember about the bats. How this strange hum draws them in and then the arms send them plummeting into the fields where the farmers have to burn them so they don't attract pests. The arms spin slow but in their slowness there's something massive, something enormous and indifferent and nearly perfect. I imagine myself chopped into atoms, into confetti. I see tiny particles of my hair and skin feathering over the field, blending with the earth and the soil, becoming vegetable, becoming corn. The wholeness of that resignation, a longing to be unmade, to wilt beyond worry and debt, pension and disease.

The farmer whizzes over on an ATV. Behind the quad there's a trailer carrying a blue chemical drum, the skull and crossbones symbol on the side. The farmer asks if I'm all right and I tell him sure, fine, never better.

"Well then," he says.

I walk away wondering how much ethanol's in the soil.

*

The night shift sags and sputters. Clouds brood and curdle over the river. I get a text from Eileen saying she's smelling that oil smell again and is she going insane. I text back not to worry, it's just the construction, I'll phone the city tomorrow. I tell myself don't check the phone don't check the phone and then I check and it says that Eileen's brother's on the way.

What I do is panic. What I do is leave, which is a fireable offence. What I do is vacate my coveralls there in the middle of the unit with Suzy walking through shouting don't even think about it but I need to get home and so I just say, "Be right back," and hustle to my car without even showering.

What I do is drive tilting and teetering and when I get home there's a cruiser in the driveway among the shadowy hulks of graders and loaders lurking against the orange plastic mesh. Eileen's in her chair at the top of the stairs saying sorry, she had to, her brother saw what was downstairs. She looks at me, a little broken.

"I'm sorry."

"It's okay. It's weird, super weird. But I love you. We can talk about it."

I head down into the basement where a red-headed cop and Eileen's brother stand kneeling over the muskeg pit, their backs to Mum. They've moved her slightly, pulled her beneath the stark light of the pull-string bulb. Up close, she looks bad. Wrinkly and purplish, with a sickly glaze.

I reach out to embrace her and the cop says no, don't, you can't do that. I ask him am I under arrest and he says you watch too much TV but this is basically unprecedented and we're going to have to ask you a few questions downtown.

I nod to Mum. "What'll happen to her?"

The cop winces. "Probably have to confiscate the body. Evidence."

So I don't let go. I don't consult the cop. I step closer and hug Mum tight, press my face against hers and kiss both cheeks. Pull away and look deep into her face, which has been in the shadows but is visible now, a mangle of resin and vein.

My pocket beeps. A text from Suzy: "The fuck are you? Get back here emergency all hands."

The enunciator's going Class A and everyone's running around frantic as I scramble into my coveralls and grab a SCBA and head out to Tower 1. Sal's walking away from the scene heading for the parking lot. "Fuck this," he grumbles into his SCBA helmet. "Not worth it."

I ignore him, keep going, suddenly beyond worry, over fear. When I look up I can see a red alert light blinking by the broiler on Tower 1, so I head over and climb the stairs.

Suzy's down below and shouting, "Back inside back inside," but she can't be talking to me because I'm floating. Floating very slowly, the world turned heavy and blurry. There's a strange heat and a blur in the air and Suzy's shouting, "inside inside," but now I'm starting to think she might be shouting, "Sulfide," is clearly shouting, "Sulfide." Which seems funny. Which seems hilarious. Which seems perfect.

The enunciator ratchets up a notch, becomes a didgeridoo.

Below, the hydrants swivel their R2-D2 heads and let loose. Twenty hydrants sending millions of gallons of water arcing through the air to knock the gas off and that, too, is hilarious.

In the distance, turbines churn and churn and churn like children's pinwheels, blowing all the bad air far far away.

I keep climbing. The hydrants arc and spit and soak me. I slip on the latticed steel stairs and recover and get to the valve near the alert light, start to turn it but it's heavy, wildly heavy. Comically heavy as I lean in and stagger a little and then get it turning, get it shut.

On the way back to the stairs my legs are bendy like bubble gum. I take a step and then wilt into a kind of human puddle. Writhing onto my stomach, I see through the platform's steel grid two ambulances and a fire truck raging into the parking lot. My SCBA's bleating like a duck or a bulldozer and in the distance there are sirens, beautiful sirens. The hydrants spit their applause, twenty tearful arcs of triumph.

Eileen appears beside me, flapping turbine arms. I move to speak her name but she shushes me, fern teeth wavering in the bog of her mouth. Her tongue is a hundred sea snakes and she's saying shush, never mind, she's come to take me away. As I'm clutching the nubs on her scaly green withers, I ask what happened to Mum, to the basement muskeg. She tells me diverted pipeline and the company will pay us off and Mum's all right now, it's time to let her go. And of course she's right, Eileen. Of course she's always been perfect and right and brave, so brave.

She starts to flap her turbine wings and soon we're chugging up and soaring, cruising, swooping high over the river, the hydrants swirling through the sky below. Eileen curls into a loop-de-loop and when we come back up I can see that the hydrants have become gushers. Twenty black fountains arcing and curling through the flood-lit night. Down below, a million neon-blue smelt dance calypso at the surface of the river. Mum stands beneath the bridge, looking up and waving, her face no longer discoloured, her gold incisor winking.

I glance over at Eileen, green eyes glowing elfin and wild. I tell her I have something to confess and she says she knows, she always knew. She says it's a little weird, the thing with me and Mum, but what isn't a little weird?

We catch hold of a thermal that takes us up fast, too fast, high above the black arcs of the fountains. The air strobes and changes colour and Eileen twirls a wing and says, "Look." What I see is a sky full of plants. Coral and krill and strange ancient grasses and we're riding it, soaring on the spirits of five hundred million years and for once it is not bad, is not sickening. All around us the gleaming ghosts of sedge and bulrushes, zooplankton and anemones and all of it pulsing green again. Below the river full of dancing neon smelt as Eileen spreads her wings and jags her beak and tells me it was true, was always true: we were all compost, all along. I tell her thank you and I love you, cling to her wings as we rise up burning through the broken brilliant sky.

Good Bones

JESSICA JOHNS

When my sister finds her eulogy, she's really not impressed. And she should have been quite happy, I think, considering I managed to come up with so many nice things to say about her. She squints into the paper like she's having trouble seeing it. "Why are you writing my eulogy? I'm not dead. I'm not even dying."

"Why are you going through my stuff?" I am quite upset with her. It is a nice eulogy, probably one of my best.

"It was on your table."

This is my fault. It should have been filed away with the others in the closet cabinet. The blue folder, for family. Yellow Post-it Note denoting the latest revision.

She had been hovering in the kitchen where I left it out. She wouldn't sit on my bed even though it's the only seat in my apartment other than the kitchen chair currently covered in bone-thick yarn for a blanket I'm knitting for Marv. It's mustard-coloured, like his hair. She has this thing about boundaries. What I'd said in the eulogy was that she was a protective sister. Growing up, she had always made sure to turn off the lights of our bedroom when she'd sneak her boyfriend in for sex. She'd also given me pink and blue earplugs. See, boundaries.

She's already putting on her boots and I wonder if I should try to explain or if she's already filed this away as just another weird thing. I offer her a banana before she leaves, even though I'm still mad, and she takes it.

Yeah, okay, so I go to the bar afterwards. Not The Archer, the one I work at, but the one farther down Jasper Avenue with the *Jurassic Park* pinball machine and *Tapper*. I'm only there for a few hours—until I run out of loonies and beat my own *Tapper* high score, twice.

I walk home like I'm being carried by a swarm of bees. The woman walking in front of me has one of those plastic umbrellas you can see through, so her hair looks wet even though it isn't. On her black tote, a Rod of Asclepius pin. *Public servant*. I think. *Poisoned by improperly prepared pufferfish. Only ate the yellow jellybeans because she believed the rest gave you cancer.* Even after I offer her a spot in the bee swarm, she gets mad when I reach out to touch her wet-dry hair. That's okay. I want to stop at the 7-Eleven anyway.

When I get back to my apartment building, Marv's on the front steps. I'm munching on a chicken wing and catching my heels in the dirt. I tell him about my sister and then about the eulogy cabinet, for context. He asks for a piece of chicken and I give him a drumstick because I hate the drumsticks. Marv is houseless and likes to walk this street. I feel comforted to see him; he fills space like a balloon.

"Write one for me." Chicken skin hangs from his mouth. I feel honoured that he would even ask and rush upstairs to do just that, deciding to use the black fountain pen and put him in the green folder, marked friends. *Loved animals. Held fear gingerly between two fingers. His mouth wet like a teardrop.*

Okay, the drunken eulogy wasn't my best, but I haven't really thought about Marv's death yet. I have imagined the deaths of almost everyone I know. My dad dies in weird ways. He's murdered with a samurai sword on a busy street, or his parachute malfunctions while skydiving. My sister gets swallowed up in things. An open manhole, quicksand, the ocean. I have imagined the deaths of people who only imagine their own, and I wonder if they'd match up—our versions of the most horrible thing that could happen.

I can't imagine Marv dying; that's the problem. I can't imagine him not on the stoop, or feeding rabbits in the side alleyway, or at the back of The Archer by the grease trap.

I file the drunken version away to think about later and then run down to give him the rest of my 7-Eleven Pepsi. He's gone, so I leave it for him in the shade of the step. I hope it doesn't get too warm. If it were winter, this wouldn't be a problem. The pop would stay ice cold, freeze maybe, make a slush. Edmonton summers are just as depressing as the winters, but nobody says so. They're almost worse because everyone truly wants them to be good. But just because something is no longer terrible doesn't automatically make it good. People don't like to admit things like that, though. It just depresses them more.

*

Mom calls the next morning. I knew my sister would tell, little snitch. My phone has a crusted circle of 7-Eleven nacho cheese on the screen and I try to wipe it off as we talk.

"Is this because of your co-worker dying?" she asks.

Safe assumption, I suppose. Though I started the eulogies long before Duncan died, and I'm glad I did, too, because now I have his eulogy all ready. Red folder, marked miscellaneous, because I don't yet know where he belongs. Or rather, I *still* don't know where he belongs.

Before Duncan died, he'd disappear into himself every now and then—go on benders or road trips to somewhere with sand. I used to picture him dead in side-road ditches marked only by numbers, on white-tiled bathroom floors, cold on a friend's sofa cushion. I never imagined his deaths as violent. They were lonely ones though, and I think that's worse.

When he came back from wherever he'd been, he was good as ever, holding on tight to some hanging thread. He'd wear his banana shirt, freshly washed, and kiss people he just met on the mouth. Loud laugh at any small joke. Slowly peel the lint off his bones.

"Does it make you think about Rhi?" Mom asks, even though I haven't answered the first question.

Rhi and I used to live together. Before going to work one night, she had a brain aneurysm in her car. Slumped over the wheel, seatbelt fastened, keys in the ignition but not turned on. I told her dad later that she looked peaceful because I thought it would make him feel better. At Rhi's celebration of life, her fiancé, or ex I guess, read out a very touching eulogy, which during some later research, I found on wikiHow. I wondered how many people could fit into the same template.

Rhi was the first real death. Duncan was the second, and he did die lonely, after all. I asked him after our bar shift if he was staying over. He'd had one shot for every one he gave to a customer and on those kinds of nights he was too bright and warm to take himself home. His long black hair had come loose from its bun, but he didn't seem to notice. It was 3 a.m., meaning miles of time left for drinking, but he said he'd come over after; we couldn't be seen leaving at the same time anyway.

When Duncan's roommate found him in their garage the next morning, the car parked at an impossible angle and the hose in the window, he told everyone he looked peaceful, too. It didn't make me feel any better, but I guess it was because I knew he was lying.

"Maybe you should go back to see Dr. Boxma," Mom suggests. Dr. Boxma was a wonderful woman who really tried her best, but you just can't admit weird things to a person with a perfectly symmetrical face.

"No, I'm fine," I tell her and then rush off the phone on the pretense of cleaning out my fridge. Mom's died a hundred times since Tuesday. It's always her mind that goes first.

Okay, I do clean out my fridge, but I only just did it a couple days ago so it takes no time at all. I shove my latest draft of Duncan's eulogy in my back pocket before I leave, grab a pomegranate for the road.

I check downstairs for Marv first, but he's not around. I hope I see him later, at least after Duncan's celebration of life, a term that has now, at my annoyance, become a trend. I can't stand around and wait for him though, because the cracks in the road are extra wide and I might sink into them if I don't keep moving. Plus it's being held at The Archer in an hour, so I should probably go early and have a drink. Hope to get swarm-carried again.

Fine, so on my walk over I stop at the liquor store. The Archer is only three blocks from my apartment but three blocks is a long ways if you want to loop through the alleyways and take a break at the park.

The mickey of Jack Daniels Fire is cheaper than usual, so that's nice. The store clerk's nametag says Allen, and he takes his time ringing me through. *Trampled by wild horses. Diverted awkward conversations in large crowds. Kissed his reflection in every mirror he passed.* As I wave away the paper bag and shove the bottle in my purse next to the pomegranate, he smiles.

The park is the most beautiful thing about my area and it's still ugly as all hell. Two basketball hoops face each other across a patch of grass, rims bent at upward angles. A square of gravel looks like it tried to be a playground but gave up. Two swings, a giant abacus, one metal slide.

They are going to play Duncan's recording of a Lumineers song over the loudspeaker, the one he always sang at karaoke nights. Everyone will listen and quiet cry into their beers. He hated that song, only ever sang it to pull girls, at least before he started dating Jane. When he came over one night, slipping in quietly at 4 a.m., he played his recording of "Famous Blue Raincoat," the song he learned for her, because of her name. It was beautiful, better than the real version. He learned the guitar parts for it and everything. I guess I should have been jealous, but I wasn't. Mostly, I was envious that anyone could love like that at all.

When the song had finished, he turned his phone off like he always did. His breath smelled like whiskey and something earthy, like dirt. "Marv is downstairs again. I gave him my toque, he looked cold."

"Good."

"You owe me five dollars for that Cavaliers win," he said, pulling the blankets tighter around us, cocooning in the cold from outside.

I slipped my feet under his. "I wrote a poem for you today."

I read it to him off my phone. It ended something like "the sound of soldiering air / through a window crack."

"You're the most goddamn sentimental person I know," he said. "Always busy looking at what the light shines on instead of where it's coming from."

I liked the way he spoke. The way his mind worked around things. He hooked his hand in my underwear and pulled me towards him. "Send it to me with the five dollars."

They should play one of his Leonard Cohen recordings today. That's what he would have loved for real. I take a sip of Jack Fire, but that's all I want. It doesn't taste right for today, and the pockmarks in the metal slide are warping my reflection, so I can't stay for too long. I don't want to slip into them, either.

I loiter in The Archer's back parking lot between a Civic and a rusted Jeep the colour of sawdust. Counting the people going inside, I guess it's pretty near full and only 2 p.m. The bar is going to make a killing today. Nothing makes people want to drink more than celebrating a marriage or mourning a death. Trying to act happier than you are is hard work.

Ben, my manager, walks through the side doors behind a girl I've never seen before, his hand on the small of her back. A couple months ago, I asked Ben how often we cleaned our beer lines. He was eating a piece of jerky. "I don't think ever."

"Isn't there some sort of Foodsafe guideline?"

He kept chewing, tried to work his cigarettes out of his back pocket with his jerky-free hand. "There's actually no legal requirement to do it. Most bars don't. It takes a lot of time. Couple hours probably."

He tapped a cigarette out of the pack and offered me one, knowing I don't smoke. This made me sad, imagining the clogged arteries of our underground machine. Poor girl. She'll probably die soon too. *Heart attack. Never let her guests go thirsty. Made sure everyone always thought the best of themselves, even if it was a lie.*

That shift, it had been my side duty to clean all twenty-four beer taps. My fingers were rubbed raw and the handles didn't look any different. That was the thing about The Archer; everything could be spit-shined, waxed, sanitized, and still always look just a little foggy, like it was smudged. Duncan used to say that it was part of her charm, our bar. She was a never-ending fixer-upper, but she had good bones.

Today, Ben will probably make a speech because Jane will be too choked up. He'll crack jokes and not mention suicide and probably pour everyone a round of Guinness, Duncan's favourite beer. He won't actually buy it though; he's too cheap for that. He'll void it off the computer and mark it as spill, accepting thanks from everyone meekly like he's swallowing small pills. This will go in Ben's eulogy. Along with what is already there: *Died in a bushfire of his own making while camping. Pushed his dick against women as he close-talked.* Filed away in the orange folder, marked shitheads.

Danielle pulls up in her pink scooter and I can't really avoid her so we go in through the back. She only just started working at The Archer and I don't know a lot about her yet.

She pushes me into the staff washroom right away so we avoid the mix-ups that happen when you talk to people and refer to a dead person in the present tense and then have to correct yourself. After Rhi settled comfortably into the realm of *was* and *used-to-be*, a group of us tried to celebrate her birthday, but not many people showed and I wondered what the polite amount of time would be before I could leave. I wanted to eat chips and watch TV in bed. That's just what happens though, the sting of things eventually covers up the sting of other things and we keep having parties for dead friends.

Danielle and I do our second line of coke off the back of the toilet tank before the thought comes to me. "I bet these washrooms never get cleaned. Who knows what we're snorting. Crusty old drugs probably. Little poo particles."

Danielle licks the white powder off the edge of her student card. "Really? You wanna talk about poo right now"

I'm confused by her confusion, but I guess she just thinks I'm being crude. She changes the subject, anyway. Talks about *The Bachelorette* instead. A bunch of men lying their way through a long line of other men to get to a woman. I don't see the appeal.

She moves to the mirror and reapplies her lipstick. "It's kind of awkward for us, hey? Not knowing him that well."

I rub the back of my jeans, Duncan's eulogy crinkling under the weight of my hand. I pick through my own purse trying to find a lipstick, but I haven't put any on today. Besides the pomegranate and bottle of Jack, I find an old Tootsie Roll and a green crayon. The bottom of Danielle's lipstick says Ruby Woo, but it looks more like Russian Red, and the bathroom is too small for two people.

I go out the back again, not bothering to look into the bar because there's no point in that. I sit next to the grease trap on a cracked concrete parking block to wait for Marv. Maybe he'll want the bottle of Jack. I don't think this is what people have in mind with a celebration of life, but maybe that's okay. Duncan didn't fit so easily into things anyway, and I've thought of a great death for Marv.

On a space expedition heading for the moon, he ejected himself from the spaceship because he didn't want to be just another guy who went to the moon. By some magical space miracle, he and his teardrop mouth floated all the way to Jupiter where he got side-swiped by Io, one of Jupiter's big ugly moons, and started careening toward its surface. He was terrified the whole time. He held the fear gingerly between two fingers and shit in his astronaut pants. Vomited too. But he never felt empty about being emptied; he wanted everyone to know that. A moon volcano melted his head, but the rest of his body remains protected by the cracked compression of the moon's silicate crust. The moon has been renamed Marv after our dear friend, because he deserves it and no one liked Io anyway. Loved animals to the end, he will be missed by many street rabbits, and of course, by me. I miss him too.

Minor Aberrations in Geologic Time

CODY KLIPPENSTEIN

1.

Breathing is harder now than it was when I set out: every time I stop to cough I bring up a tacky bit of blood. I guess you could say it's my own fault. Early this morning while the lab was still dark, I surprised some white coat whose nametag I didn't have the chance to read—another Canadian, by the look of him—before he swung an elbow against my sternum, nearly crushing my goddamn heart. I'm trying, at the very least, to leave a confusing trail for the bastard, and for every bastard he must've gone and woken up. One dark smudge on the tree not ten yards from the Mazda pickup that I left tire-deep in the spongy grass at the edge of the wood, another in the low-hanging leaves to the northwest and southeast, double back for a few more, leave the rest up ahead...

The air is wet and smells like rot. Even my ponytail is dripping with sweat. Apatosaurus (Female) is quiet and compliant despite having never been outside the testing room before. I'm quite proud of her. At a little under four weeks old, she is approximately as tall and as heavy as a full-grown German shepherd. It is a dog harness, in fact, that I've lifted from the shed behind the institution gate to make sure I don't lose her. What do you think, Matheson, will they use the dogs to track me? Will they threaten me with lead bullets or stun? I've got just one LCP .380 hidden under my windbreaker, safety on, which I took from the guard post after one too many drinks at the staff party last night. It's not my aim I'm worried about if that's what you're thinking—everything I learned from you I learned well—it's that I've never fired at another person before. In the back of my brain I've got this spectre of you stretching your legs, tapping on my optic nerves in time to my frantic breathing. *Oh, kid, you're in over your head.* I know it, Matheson, I know.

2.

It's not an easy trek, especially in this condition. Roots draped in moss rise from the mulch. Cloaked arms of Death, all of them—stumble once and I might not feel like getting back up again. Step high. Apatosaurus (Female) takes passing interest in every leaf and branch in our path. I glance down at the roaming eyes on the sides of her head and rip a handkerchief-sized swatch of moss from a nearby limb to tickle her big square mouth with, holding it in front of her nose like she's some snotty kid in need of a clean-up. With excruciating sloth, she opens her maw and accepts it. Chews.

I tug, stop, turn, tug. She appears pensive.

What exactly do sauropods think about?

I'd been working out of the nowhereness of the Ginoza lab for less than two weeks when I first saw Apatosaurus (Female) twitch in her sleep. Some old stone broke in my chest then, and forgetting the wife you returned to, forgetting the words you'd said to me, I got into that piece-of-junk truck the institute lent me and rushed back to my micro-unit to call you, damning the time difference of all things. *She dreams, Matheson! Imagine that.* I went so far as to pick up the phone and hold it against my face before remembering it had been three full seasons since my voice was not an intrusion. In this life, an era.

Grey light through trees means close to dawn. Christmas Eve, I realize. It has been a full year now since my transfer to Japan. On another island in the Pacific, half a world away, it is cold enough to be snowing.

Infant apatosauri can run in short little bursts on two feet—you knew this already, of course, because it was you who first told me, holding my wrists, guiding my fingers over the casts of bones you'd excavated: *tarsals, metatarsals, phalanges, ungual*—but I couldn't quite believe it before seeing it for myself. When it suits her, she pulls me in her wake and I'm flying: legs clumsy over uneven terrain, free hand pressed against the space between my ribs, willing myself not to trip or cough again. Mostly, though, as now, I'm the one straining ahead and it is her that's slowing us down. We are so close to water I can smell it over the forest's decay. *This way*, I keep telling her, though she makes attempts to wander in every direction but toward me. *This way*, you murmur with me. *This way*.

3.

We made some pretty grand hypotheses, Matheson. You have to admit. You intended to make promises when you were able, assuming you were able to bring yourself to leave her. I said I'd follow you wherever the old bones of this earth called you. When we fucked, it was an ancient tooth you spoke of giving me—I don't wear jewellery—from somewhere far away. Ulaanbaatar, maybe. I don't remember. You'd bring it back and I'd know I was wearing something that endured. I promised flesh and blood in exchange.

So here I am making good on it, though not in the way I expected.

Pebble beach at last: large sky-coloured stones receding into stone-blue water. Inflatable lifeboat beached on the shore like a soft-shelled reptile, equipped with two oars and a non-working motor. Farther out, an old tugboat shrugs in the waves and waits. I look from the lifeboat to the tugboat to Apatosaurus (Female) slack at the end of her leash, lifting one front leg and setting it down again gingerly on the pebbled terrain.

S'matter, kid? you say in my ear. *Can't stop now. It's too late.* And here I feel you run a finger—ring finger, gold-ringed finger—from the sweaty gulf between my clavicles down to my coccyx, like you're cutting me open.

That's the problem with us a species, isn't it, Matheson? We can't stop digging up what should stay dead.

I inhale, grip Apatosaurus (Female) under her belly, and lift, and together we waddle to the lifeboat. She lifts her head and peers over the rubber sides that cradle her. Bracing my back against the craft, I push my weight against it and it hurtles into the water. Goodbye, solid ground. Apatosaurus (Female) bellows. Despite the bovine face, the knollish body, that long, trusting neck, she has the cast and pitch of a woman on her knees in the bathroom, shoulders squared off to the toilet, cordless phone in hand, *God-willing-any-minute-now-he'll-call-to-take-it-back*, phlegmy and incapacitated by grief. In the water I shiver and sweat, cold up to the knees and feverish above them. Blood comes up when I cough again. Step high. Not long, now. Matheson, I'm coming for you. I'm coming home. It will be New Year's when I next land on your doorstep. I know: when I knock and you open up, when I smile, when I take a nice, even breath, when I step aside, when I show you what I have to give you, you will—

The Stunt

MICHAEL LAPOINTE

I'm the only man in the village who subscribes to *The Hollywood Reporter*. The latest clipping, which I paste in my scrapbook, is just a column inch, an ad for waterbeds on the reverse.

> *Black Water* director Edgar Van Buren is once again facing criticism, this time for his decision to host a lavish party for the jurors who acquitted him of manslaughter. Held at the director's midcentury home above Coldwater Canyon, the party marked the one-year anniversary of the verdict, on May 15, 1988. All twelve jurors attended. The father and former manager of Doretta Howell, who intends to sue for wrongful death, has called the party "proof you can't find one good man in Hollywood."

I recognize the byline. The writer had tried contacting me countless times throughout the trial, but I could not be reached for comment. Because I was non-creative personnel—below-the-line, as they say— and had no height from which to fall, I could avoid the most public disgrace. But behind tinted glass, the studios don't forget. Without the help of the courts, they took everything from me, my whole life in America. And I can't imagine where I'd be if they knew my version of what happened.

*

After a morning of being thrown through a window, Dot Howell collapsed in the honeywagon, unable to proceed with her French. I remember handing her a Yoohoo and picking sugared glass from her hair. Edgar Van Buren insisted his actors perform the stunts themselves—no body doubles—and as I testified, she obeyed his every direction.

Dot and I wouldn't get our three hours that day. On the set of *The Chasm*, our lessons were just ten-minute fragments before she was hauled off again. The few times I cornered a producer—and once, disastrously, Van Buren—he wouldn't take me seriously. I said Dot needed those hours, there on the shag rug of the honeywagon, chewing Skittles and microwaving in the desert heat. I said she needed to be a girl for three hours a day.

I asked her, "Do you think he got the shot?"

She shook her head, a shimmer of glass.

All she could focus on was the model. A medieval French castle surrounded by the sodden country of my native Normandy—it was our class project; we had a different one on every shoot. Now Dot cracked the lid on another tub of clay and slapped some on the hillside. I didn't protest, but lately the clay had been piling higher and higher while the castle went unfinished. It wasn't encouraging that she pictured Normandy as a muddy wasteland.

"Soon we'll need to add the servants' homes," I said, in French.

Dot massaged a lump into the landscape.

Finally, she said, "I need to tell you something."

I kept picking at her hair.

"Stop it," she said, freezing my hand.

Dot had never addressed me so formally. I sat very upright behind my desk and put my fingers together in a steeple, as if to show her that when you speak like an adult, everyone around you grows cold and severe.

"Dad and I made an agreement," she said. "When he gets here, he's going to be my manager."

Betraying nothing, I said, "He was supposed to be here yesterday."

"I know that."

Dot's first assistant pounded on the honeywagon door. It was time to go back through the window.

"Do you think he'll come today?" I asked.

"Probably, yeah."

"That's not very professional."

Dot looked at her dirty hands and suddenly lurched at me like a beautiful, filthy little vampire.

I neither flinched nor smiled.

*

God hated *The Chasm*. If I believed in predestination, I'd observe how He arranged the production's calamities to torment Edgar Van Buren. The director's perfectionism was the stuff of renown—dozens, sometimes hundreds of imperceptibly different takes to achieve the one. That's why, despite everything—despite the drinking, the verbal abuse, the reckless endangerment—everyone wanted to work with him. It was a chance to be a part of something everlasting.

Yet on that project, everything conspired against him. Twice the set was ripped away by sandstorms that gathered on the radar, blood-red and too late to evade. That's when Dot and I laid the foundation of the castle, the honeywagon rocking in gale-force winds. And we had further opportunities to work when the elder star, Xavier Braun, stepped on a rattler and was bitten three times, fast as automatic weaponry, and had to be air-lifted back to Los Angeles.

The Chasm was Van Buren's first horror film. Having asserted himself in almost every other genre—comedy, history, war—it was an aesthetic challenge he'd set himself. But what was it about? The script was impressionistic, constantly reappearing on different-coloured paper as it underwent another visionary mutation. I don't think he really understood what horror meant—not yet.

In the latest version—mustard yellow—a narrative spine had formed at last. A runaway orphan (Dot) hitchhikes into the desert and comes upon a seemingly abandoned chapel, only to discover a man (Braun) living inside. The orphan mistakes him for a priest, but as it turns out, he's an escaped convict, a child murderer. The title, as I gleaned from the mustard-yellow version, referred to the psychic underworld into which the killer initiates the orphan. But everything else remained indistinct. The budget was ballooning. The studio was terrified.

Van Buren's indulgent, improvisational method was a Hollywood anachronism. He'd inked a famous contract in the late 1960s, wedding him to the studio in perpetuity but guaranteeing certain artistic protections. At the time, it had seemed like a colossal mistake. But by the '80s, he was the last of his generation's directors still to be provided unlimited budgets and vast creative leniency. As his fellow auteurs found themselves directing second units on third sequels, Van Buren remained untouchable. He took as long as he liked; the budget was just an abstract figure to him. At night, he'd start a bonfire and drink to semi-prophetic excess, sweat shining in the flames, and everyone waited to hear what he'd discovered and transform it into cinema.

I didn't care about Edgar Van Buren or his *Chasm*. I was there for Dot, Dot alone. I dreaded only the one calamity: that Ryder, her father, was coming to take over her career. And what would that mean for us?

*

It was dusk when Dot's bike finally skidded to a stop outside the honeywagon. After a Yoohoo, to my amazement, she took up her math textbook and moved through the algebra with vigour, as if her mind were ravenous. In our classroom, all was orderly and French and still as a mirror. In fact, it was I who spoiled the environment.

"Is there anything I can say to persuade you?"

Not looking up, she said, "No, Pascal."

"He's a day late. He doesn't call. Is this the behaviour of a manager?"

She placed the pencil by the page.

"You don't know him."

Something in her voice frightened me, a kind of echo from a place I didn't understand. I corrected her pronunciation and poured some Skittles on her desk. She exaggerated the sticky gnashing of her teeth—that was better.

And then I heard the crunch of tires, and we were outside, headlights sweeping over us. As the truck rolled to a stop, it nearly mangled Dot's bike.

Ryder slammed the door of the Ford F-Series, which she'd bought for him. He was bald but wore a red beard, dense as a forest observed from a jet, and his barbell biceps were unevenly patchy, the hairs like scratches. Already he looked northern and overheated.

"Doretta!"

He could barely support her when she leapt into his arms.

"This is Pascal."

We shook hands.

"You're the teacher."

Dot cleaved to me and said, "Mon astre."

"What's that?"

I felt a warmth in my cheeks.

"There's no good translation," I said.

"I've told you about him."

"Sure," he said, "I remember."

"And she's told me about you," I said.

"All right."

Ryder told her to look at the sky. Wasn't it indigo? Wasn't it beautiful?

"It's like that every night," said Dot.

"Is that your bike?"

"Yeah."

"Good for you. Remember where I taught you to ride?"

"Lake Erie."

Ryder glanced at me.

"I found a little spot with a view of the valley," he said. "Get in the truck. We'll catch the last of the light."

The sky was fading fast, but Dot humoured him. He heaved the bike into the cargo bed, and in another moment, the truck veered away.

I replaced the textbook on the shelf and dropped her pencil in the oblong ceramic cup we'd fired together. Then I corrected her algebra—so many mistakes—and my day's purpose was fulfilled.

*

Awake on the honeywagon's narrow bed, I listened for that shy knock on the door. Then she'd come inside, as she'd done so many times, and wordlessly curl up on the carpet. I'd imagine her sucking her thumb as we fell into our dreams.

No one ever appreciated what those children went through, not until something happened—and then everyone had an opinion. But they were a lot like a movie set, like the chapel they'd built for *The Chasm*: pristine from certain angles, behind which the trash collected and a producer was smoking.

Eight years old, Dot had been given to me on a set at Nickelodeon. I mean that in earnest: her mother, Roxane, just a bruised little child herself, entrusted Dot to me. After a brief, impulsive marriage to Ryder, Roxane had fled to Los Angeles with some inarticulate ambition, but before she even had headshots, she was drinking for breakfast and coughing.

The limelight isn't morbid; it skipped over Roxane and fixed on her daughter—Doretta "Dot" Howell of the rosebud hair, the endless eyes. Doctors said they were actually growing too big for her head. With that monumental face, Dot appeared like an adult you'd once known or had, at least, once seen on screen.

Those are my fondest memories, still glowing. I recall Dot as an energetic blur. At Nickelodeon, we'd play hide-and-go-seek, and she'd give herself away with laughter. She'd do anything for Skittles; she'd imitate the sound of French. When the *Enquirer* started following Roxane around, just to catch her drunk in public, Dot began staying overnight.

After Roxane's death, I gave up my other children and wholly devoted myself to Dot. I banished the charlatans and moneylenders. I gave her an idea of God, telling her there was always a beautiful man watching her. And so, I was the one she asked about the bleeding; I was the one who told her what it meant.

As for Ryder, on certain melancholy nights I'd hear about him. She had so few memories, she always returned to the one good summer on Lake Erie, stretching it out until it seemed like a marvellous history. When he took her on his back, she said, she didn't fear the water. The way she spoke of Lake Erie, I sometimes felt she was still waiting for him to take her back and finish those lessons.

Meanwhile Nickelodeon became Disney, and Disney became Fox. And then the *Chasm* script arrived, on fresh white paper. It was the first script she wouldn't let me read until she'd finished. From the very beginning, she was doing this for an idea of herself. Now fifteen years old, she had to choose: orient yourself toward Oscars, or be an unserious girl forever.

The *Chasm* set was unlike any I'd ever been on. They weren't creating this movie to be happy or to make others happy. Lying awake that night in the honeywagon, I heard the crew's drunken laughter, the hiss of someone pissing on the sand. And Dot didn't come. I said a prayer for her, alone in the night. She was still so unknown to herself.

*

Van Buren suddenly took Xavier Braun and a small unit up into the mountain caves. They were gone for days, but Dot and I still didn't get much done. Ryder would scoop her up after breakfast and shoot through the desert toward the cliffs or the Indian reserve. They'd fire off guns together, blowing up the Joshua trees, or skid around on ATVs with a recklessness I'd begun to see as common to them. By the time she got back, she was more depleted, more useless to me, than after the most violent Van Buren workdays.

Yet nothing was so contemptible as what Ryder asked me as I filled my flask at the water station.

"Pascal," he said, "what exactly do you teach my daughter?"

He'd accosted me outside the shade, the white sun hovering, a pitiless disc, above his head.

I said, "A standard Californian curriculum."

"And more besides."

"Well, of course. The state mandates that studio teachers be certified welfare workers. I manage Dot's well-being, whether it be getting her inoculated, or discussing the morals of the script, or just keeping her company—being there for her, you understand."

"I don't want to offend you," he said, "but Doretta seems, sometimes, a little stunted."

"Stunted."

"Basic things—things she should know—she doesn't."

"And you're to judge what she should know."

"The names of presidents, yes. The cause of the Civil War. All fifty states."

"American things."

"It isn't only American," Ryder said. "She's slow with simple math. She knows nothing about tectonic plates or how tornadoes form."

"I assure you, Mr. Howell, Dot's developing perfectly well."

"Then why can't she take the proficiency exam?"

I'd been in Hollywood long enough to get guarded when a parent mentioned the exam. The fact that he even knew about it already betrayed him. If an underage actor could test out of high school, she became eligible to work longer hours, overtime, even through the night. A sick green glow always emanated from the heart of a Hollywood parent.

"You'd better leave that up to me," I said and began to walk away.

He put a hand to my chest.

"All the same," he said, "I'd like to sit in tomorrow afternoon."

"I don't think that's a good idea."

"I'm her manager," he said. "I have the right."

He'd kept me there just long enough for my nose and cheeks to burn.

*

Dot was dabbing pink paint on the little princess when he entered. She dropped her brush and Ryder sat, ridiculously huge, in one of her chairs.

In French, I said, "Your father is going to spend the remaining time with us."

And Dot answered, in American English, "I know."

I clucked and reminded her to sustain the French, as we'd agreed.

"But it isn't fair. He won't understand what we're saying."

"As you wish." And I looked to Ryder. "But you see, there was something being taught here, and now, no longer."

"Noted."

I didn't dare give her Skittles. I handed her the math textbook and told her to work on the algebra. At first she was confused, thinking she'd seen the problems before, but then she settled in.

As I stared at Ryder, I gradually perceived that he was struggling with the conditions in the honeywagon. Everyone thinks they understand what it means to work on a movie. It was pushing a hundred; the walls were sweating. The toilet was close, unclean. Soon he was fidgeting. I'd applied cold cream to my face and could sit there for hours, deriving austere pleasures from how Dot gripped the pencil, how she turned it idly in her fingers and nibbled the edge.

I broke my pose only upon hearing the commotion outside. For days, the set had been held in a kind of scorched suspense, but now there were shouts and laughter, cars swooping through camp, refreshingly. Van Buren had returned from the mountains.

Ryder seized upon my distraction to shoot a spitball at his child. "Hey!"

I turned to see Dot clutching her ear, Ryder laughing like an ape.

She balled up a page from her notebook and rang it off his dome. Now he was looking at her with appetite, and in one brute motion, he cleared the desk away and grabbed her at the waist. She let him pull her to the carpet, laughter breaking into hiccups. I moved the castle to safety and watched them roll around.

Ryder caught my eye, and he must've read my satisfaction there. He disentangled from her and righted the chairs.

He said, "I don't know what came over me."

Dot was still heaving on the floor, hair strewn over her face. She blew it off her lips and said, "It's fun here, isn't it?"

I said, "Isn't it?"

"Get back to work," he ordered. "Start working, Doretta."

*

Ryder befriended Van Buren. At night, I'd see them, crackling bronze figures by the bonfire. They'd pass the Jim Beam and, when it was empty, set the bottle out in the clear moonlight and blow it to smithereens.

Van Buren had come back changed by the caves. He said *The Chasm* cohered for him there; he was throwing out most of what he had. In the day, producers waited anxiously outside the tent while Van Buren rewrote the script, ash dropping into his chest hair. They called the studio; they tried to explain what he was doing. At day's end, he'd have the latest scene copied and issue it like law.

Drunk in that infernal light, he and Ryder unfolded Dot Howell's future. If she got *The Chasm* right, there would be more projects, all the awards, unimaginable money. I could hear them howl together—"Yes, yes," went her father, her manager—and more gunshots.

*

I found the pink pages on my desk. She'd left them for me. I took them out to the plastic chair beneath the parasol with a view of the hills. They were just piles of Martian-red rocks, as if a giant had ground up mountains in his fist. As the sun set behind a dusty film, the sky purpled and dimmed.

At once, I saw why she'd left the new script, why she didn't want to face me as I read it. *The Chasm* was darkening; it was becoming real horror. Before, the relation between Dot and Xavier was all innuendo, arresting suggestions between cuts, but Van Buren had made it explicit. So this was what you learned in caves; so this was genius—the molestation of a child on film.

When the night had gathered around the camp, I went looking for him. There was no one by the bonfire, but I heard the pop, the breaking glass, and followed them out to where Van Buren and Ryder were shooting. The light of the moon was so pure, the men seemed to stand on stage, the sand flat and crossed by the shadows of the Joshua trees. Off to the side, three women sat on lawn chairs, smoking in fur coats, their legs bare and blue. They noticed me first, and their silence alerted the men.

I stood with the pages, observed by Van Buren. Behind him, Ryder reloaded.

I said, "You have a wicked heart."

Ryder hooted, plunking in the bullets.

"What did you say?" The director stepped forward, close enough that I could toss the script against his chest. He caught the wad, glanced over it, and threw it aside.

"I said there's a worm in your soul."

All the while he was coming toward me.

"What do you know?" he said. "What could you possibly know?"

"Ease up," called Ryder. "It's only the teacher."

"I know she won't do the scene," I said.

"But she will."

"I won't let her."

Van Buren shoved me with both hands, and stumbling back, I tripped on bramble and landed hard. He sent me back down as I tried to scramble up. I felt his drunk, elemental strength.

I managed to say, "I'm not afraid of you."

"You're a fool, Pascal."

Now he crouched down and slapped me, once. I briefly saw the women, and then my cheek was to the sand. I thought of snakes and scorpions.

"You're a fool."

The shots rang out in rapid succession—a woman yelped—and Van Buren stepped back.

"Enough," said Ryder.

Dot's father hoisted me to my feet and brushed me off, motioning for Van Buren to stay where he was.

"Why don't you go to sleep, Pascal?"

I was staring at Van Buren, his eyes full of moonlight.

"She won't do it," I said, to myself.

*

I couldn't find Dot in the morning, and everyone had a different answer. They sent me to makeup; they might've seen her with the first assistant; she'd just biked by—see the tracks? Finally, I approached the chapel, where they were setting up the scene, and over a producer's shoulder, I saw her.

"Dot!"

He cut my angle off.

"You can't keep me out. I'll have this whole thing shut down. Dot!"

I snagged her eye, and she said to let me through. The chapel smelled of fresh sawdust but was staged to signal years of decay: a collapsed wall, the Virgin caked with grime, doves in the rafters prodded by the handler on a ladder. And Dot—her dress was bloodied and torn, blotched with black fingerprints and sticking with sweat.

"You don't have to do this scene."

"Pascal—"

"I know we haven't talked about it."

"We don't have to."

"Can't you see what they're doing?"

Van Buren was riding the camera like a dark horse, and Ryder stood nearby, reading the pink version. How could he let the scene play out in his mind?

"Don't let them do this, Dot."

She seemed confused by how I took her hand.

Van Buren tapped her on the shoulder and, without even looking at me, said, "Let me explain this to you."

Actor and director angled away.

I got as close as I could to the scene. It was just a squalid mattress by the altar. Dot sprawled as if drugged, eyelids thick and heavy as a toad's. Her legs were bare, bruised. I'd never seen her thighs, and I remember wondering, absurdly, where she learned to have thighs like those.

Van Buren called for action, and Xavier squatted down. He was strangely clean, grey hair wet, pulled back. The beads dangled from his neck like grapes. It wasn't artifice—it was lust. It was real in his eyes, and on his fingers, and blazing through his lips. Van Buren thrust the camera forward. I heard them murmuring. Xavier pinned her by the wrists, and she writhed—not against his strength but within it. He cupped her chin—her soft cheeks bunching, lips squeezed into a square—and leaned into a suctioning kiss. Her eyes closed voluptuously, horrifically. Then she put his hand to her breast and pulled him back onto the bed.

Suddenly Dot sat up straight and shook her head.

My heart thrilled. Van Buren yelled cut.

The director wiped his mouth. Someone brought Xavier a cigarette, and the actors lounged there on their elbows. Van Buren crouched down to Dot and called for Ryder. The four of them had a quick conversation.

Ryder came back to me through the crew.

He said, "She can't do the scene."

"I can see that."

"She's asking you to leave."

Doves shuddered on the roofbeams.

"What?"

"She can't do the scene in front of you. Will you go back to the classroom and wait for her there?"

I looked to Dot. She put her eyes everywhere else. From a distance, Van Buren was watching me.

"Let me talk to her."

"You're wasting everyone's time, Pascal. Now she's asked you nicely—go."

*

I'll never know if she came back to the honeywagon afterward. I'd taken the bottle to the hills. My sister sometimes sent me Calvados from home, though I almost never found occasion to drink. I'd been working through this bottle for a year, but that evening, I sucked it worshipfully, as if it were the very pith of Normandy.

The desert stars came out, and my mind turned to Roxane. I wanted to pray to her, but the stars were cold, withdrawn. I knew I'd disappointed her. She'd urged me to take her daughter; shaking, she'd pressed the beads into my hand. It was a promise, soul to soul.

And the old picture came, man and wife on a little plot of Normandy. He's reading in the shade, apples dropping from the tree, the castle in the distance, tall. The children sprint past and she calls to them, still a child in her heart.

But I found no direction there. The picture hovered in two dimensions. The Calvados tasted thin, even putrid at the edges.

Instead a story Roxane once told, chasing Stoli with milk, invaded me. Ryder would have her smear lipstick on his erection, she said, as if his penis were a cheap whore, and then she'd suck it like a woman's lips. And I thought of the women, naked under fur coats, and I thought of all the money Ryder had now, Dot's money.

I broke the bottle on the stone, and the liquor burst over my hand. I knew where he slept. The jagged edge of glass caught moonlight, and I felt like Roxane, way out on some private rampage, pursued by journalists. But I didn't realize how drunk I was until I stood and moved unsteadily, rock by rock, down the hill, and then all I wanted was to be buried underground, asleep.

*

I grew formal over the coming days. I'd taught adults before. No Yoohoos, no Skittles—and where had the castle gone?

Doretta knew I was angry—there were times I thought she sensed the rest—but didn't attempt a reconciliation. It would've been the death of the woman she wanted to be, the icon looming over her, beckoning her out into the world. So it was already written.

She failed at the new lessons I gave her. She had to stay late, do them over. She put on a show of not minding. She tried harder but still wasn't ready.

Meanwhile *The Chasm* was collapsing—that's something that never made the papers. The producers tried keeping rumour in check, but the studio's anger was known; it had seeped into the cast and crew like guilt, everyone but Van Buren. He only responded with further provocations.

But in private, as we'd learn during the trial, he was tormented, blocked. *The Chasm* had no climax. It needed something spectacular—a permanent image—and it was then that water, black and deep and strong as steel cables, began to rush across the desert sands of his imagination.

*

On the morning of the stunt, he had us up before dawn and announced that we were going to the sea. It was all arranged; he'd sent the crew ahead. Now Doretta, Ryder, Van Buren and I piled into a truck and headed west, dust blazing up behind the wheels.

I remember Doretta was excited. This was why you worked with Edgar Van Buren—so you could reminisce, later, to *The Hollywood Reporter*, all about the time he had you up at dawn and took you to the sea because he'd seen the movie ending in a dream.

In the truck he passed around the mint-green pages. Escaping the murderer, the orphan would plunge into the cove. Later, they'd shoot her underwater on a stage at the studio, feeling her way into a cave. But, for the drop, the location was perfect, said Van Buren: a little cove of ink-black water.

He said, "A shot of you falling—it could be immortal."

With the stunt, *The Chasm* would be whole, at last.

"We shoot at sundown."

But his star was staring out the window, the stooped desert trees rushing past. In sunglasses and with a kerchief tied around her head, she looked like a woman twenty years older, twenty years ago.

"What's the matter?" he said. "Don't you like it?"

Doretta's head turned toward me, but she said, "I love it."

"The audience will know you've given them everything," said the director. "The Academy despises doubles. They want to see you act every frame."

Only I knew what she was thinking, but I also knew she didn't want me to speak for her, not anymore. In her shades, I could see myself, just a small man in the corner of the truck, indistinct, like the memory of someone you knew as a child.

*

After weeks in the desert, I relished the breeze that pulled off the sea. All day was spent setting up the stunt, the crew bobbing in lifejackets down in the cove. The water swirled around them, black and deep, like a pit. Doretta would drop from the cove's rocky wall.

No one ever asked if she could swim.

I wandered away from the set, over to where the sheer cliffs plunged, and stared out to the hovering line of the horizon. Already the sun was lowering and flashing off the water. It wouldn't be long before the stunt.

I heard: "Pascal."

It was Ryder. He came to my side and peered into the wind.

"Everything takes forever," he said. "But I guess you're used to it."

"Yes."

He laughed, "Don't be so high-strung, Pascal. I come in peace. I know we got off to a bad start, but I've been thinking—I was wrong. I mistook her excitement for immaturity."

"Excitement."

"For me to be here. She was just being my girl, like before."

I wanted to say there never was before.

"Shake hands?" he asked.

I'll never know for certain, but in that moment, I sensed he'd had me fired, that in the morning, I'd be recalled to Los Angeles. Over blinding water, Doretta Howell's future stretched out to the vanishing point.

We shook. Ryder stepped to the very edge and looked straight down. The rocks pointed up like bayonets; the current ripped into the open sea. I remember my hands felt light, inspired, primed to push.

But the spirit deflated. He'd prevail, anyway. The bulb inside her had finally split; a powerful stalk had broken through. I saw the mud she'd slung beside our castle. It piled up before my eyes, incompatible with life.

There was a call: "Pascal!"

I turned to see Doretta's first assistant, and Ryder and I came running to the makeup truck.

We found Van Buren leaning over the chair where she shivered and gasped for breath.

"What is it?" Ryder asked.

"It just came over her."

"Give her space," I said and knelt. "Breathe easy. You're safe."

She'd gone bright red, and hot tears issued from the corners of her eyes, though she wasn't really crying. I took her hands; the wrists rapidly pulsed.

"You're safe."

"We were reviewing the stunt," said Van Buren. "She's never been this way before."

"What is it, Doretta?" asked Ryder.

She was regaining composure, I thought, or a sense of audience. She said, "It's nothing."

"Maybe the water," the assistant offered.

There was a brief silence while the men decided whether to take her seriously.

"But she can swim," said Van Buren.

"Of course," said Ryder. "I taught her myself—you remember, Doretta, on the lake."

She nodded.

"I remember."

Later, no one would recall how they all looked to me, even her. But if I forget every other instant of my life, I'll still remember how I said, "She can swim."

"Maybe it's the drop," said Van Buren. "But the water's deepest right where you're landing, and anyway it's not as high as the window. All right?"

She touched the tears from her eyes and pushed out a smile.

"All right."

Van Buren clapped. Ryder helped her up.

"I'm sorry to be so childish."

The first assistant cooed, "Not at all, darling, not at all."

Van Buren was out the door. "She's fine," he reported to the producer outside.

"I'll put you on my back," her father joked.

"Just get me to the set," Doretta said. "Then I'll do it on my own."

*

I remember the light was perfect. From where Ryder and I stood, we could just see her pressed against the wall below, her famous rosebud hair precisely tangled. The cove whirled beneath her, swallowing. The camera lowered to the surface. I heard Van Buren's call for silence, for action. "Go!" he shouted. "Go!" There was still something I could've done. Then Ryder started running, but it was a six-minute climb down to the water. The camera never stopped rolling. The footage was never made public.

My sister has set out coffee and *Le Monde* beneath the apple tree. The fruit is full of worms; a drought has killed her garden. This isn't what I'd pictured, what I'd tried to make out of the girl once given to me. But I can see the castle, and the indifference of the stone—watching everything, anything—is like the love of God.

In *Le Monde*, I find another clipping. I will paste it in the scrapbook. There are fewer all the time; soon they'll vanish altogether. Translated into American English, it reads:

A film by Edgar Van Buren, *Black Water*, premieres in Paris this week. Critics say the film subtly reworks the tragedy of child actor Doretta Howell, which derailed Van Buren's last production and nearly cost him his freedom. *Black Water* has been nominated for Best Picture and Best Director at the Academy Awards, and has grossed over $40 million in the United States.

Today Is Cool

JULIE MANNELL

I think each time I try to kill myself I don't actually want to. I emailed Jude through his girlfriend, Audrey, because Jude had sworn off the internet for a year or so, since he left Montreal for New York. That was a while ago, that was before he left New York to go live with Audrey and her family in Toronto. Jude and I had conducted a weird sexual experiment two years ago where I told him how to convince girls in the University Students' Association to fuck him. It never failed. My success rate at getting Jude laid imparted me a tremendous confidence that was quickly followed by a complicated jealousy and then I fucked him too. I fucked him. I fucked him on his bed. I fucked him on his chair. He picked me up, digging his fingers into my ass cheeks, and I let him fuck me on top of his dresser, knocking his pant drawers shut with my ankles. It didn't turn into a romance. He had Audrey. He still has Audrey. I emailed Audrey and I told her to tell Jude I was wanting to kill myself again. She said she would and asked for my phone number and asked if I wanted to talk to her about it, which was considerably kind considering I was weirdly reaching through her to her boyfriend whom I had weirdly fucked two years ago.

The act of killing yourself is pretty desperate in itself. Just saying you want to kill yourself, the utterance, the threat in the utterance, makes you an abuse, not the words you say, you yourself are an abuse. When I closed my computer I wondered if I'd abused Audrey.

I never asked to be born anyhow. The situation was these two people, let's call them my parents, decided they wanted to give birth to someone and I ended up being directly implicated. Sometimes I think about how my grandfather died. Frequently I involuntarily flash back to the time my father died. I often recollect this thing my aunt, the nurse, told me. She said that usually when someone is sick to the point of insufferable discomfort and permanent unhappiness the hospital will just pump them full of painkillers and it is the overdose that gets them in the end. How can you be sure something is permanent when forever hasn't happened yet?

Montreal is so vapid these days with people flaking constantly, never accountable for the consequences that come with being inconsiderate towards others. I'm not sure if it is a geographical or generational issue. Also, I can be biased. I grew up with farmers and factory workers in a small town in Niagara. I can be judgmental; the friends I made at McGill are different than those I grew up with.

I am a lot of things.

I'm the best girlfriend. I'm the worst girlfriend. I try to be a good girlfriend, but my boyfriend's never happy. At most he'll allot me an automatic confirmation of "I love you," or "You are beautiful," but they sound like the prerecordings on answering machines.

The movie crushed me and I asked. "What are you thinking?"

"Nothing," he answered.

He sat up in bed, sweating, perhaps a dream, "What are you thinking?"

"Nothing."

I slip into a nightgown with a lace hem complementing my thigh. "What are you thinking?"

"Nothing."

"But this." I pull it up towards my navel and point my left toe.

"You are beautiful," he laughs. "I love you."

He isn't bad. His name is Lachlan and he has cool hair and interesting things to say about music and history. He's the kind of boy other girls get jealous of. He's the kind of boy who is nice and who looks good in photos and comes from money and doesn't have working class problems. He's the kind of boy you can appreciate when you have working class problems, and you've had the bad boyfriends who are born of the problems of your class, and you aren't the prettiest, but he is so awkward with women that you know it's a kind of miracle he stumbled across you and didn't have the experience to know that he could do better. Sometimes I feel like such an asshole for complaining. He's the kind of boy whose family has more homes than he can count, including a summer mansion on an island in the Laurentians.

I met his parents there. They were the kind of people who fussed over their sons and fussed over the state of their houses—what to buy and what not to. His mother was almost overly eager to be my friend. She asked if I shared her opinion that they ought to invest in a third boat considering the age of the other two. I told her I thought it was smart to buy a new boat, just in case. I said it like it was something I'd considered and I knew what I was talking about. Lachlan's family was so rich and handsome. His mother gave me a fur coat to wear when the night got cold. She introduced me to her collection of eccentric hats. His father cooked me a steak and complimented me on my rural Canadian accent like it was something he was a part of now that I was a member of their family. They fussed over the wellbeing of their unemployed but artistically gifted sons. "Aimless," said the mother, beneath a feathered boudoir cap and amaranth wig. "I worry they are aimless but now is the age for discovering yourself."

They bought another boat. Then they took off on the boat and left us alone on the island together.

When they were gone, we began drinking, and Lachlan's brother Lennox kept poking fun at my thick rural Canadian accent and how it became thicker as I got drunker. At first it seemed so innocent; we played Scrabble. Lennox won and Lachlan lost and I ended up in the middle. The evening fell behind the hills across the lake until sky and water were one.

Earlier that day, before his parents left, battery acid had spilled on Lachlan's favorite shoes. I watched him sit alone on the dock, barefoot, pouting. His mother swore that she would buy him a new pair. "They are only shoes," I suggested. It seemed unreasonable to get worked up over anything when you get to live in a mansion on an island, let alone shoes that had no sentimental value other than looking kind of cool. His mother retorted, "No, I understand, he's just like me. We both care about our things. For us things have emotions."

These people thinking I had no feeling for objects confused me; I've always thought of myself as quite sentimental. My relationships with objects were the only aspect of the visit that left a bad cloud over me as Lachlan's girlfriend. I wondered about the childhoods of the families that cried over physical things and justified temper tantrums over stuff breaking.

We still played Scrabble, and Lachlan lost after having an already terrible day with the shoe travesty. He drank until his eyes went blank and sociopathic. It was a look that started fights, fights that might as well have taken place between me and a pile of bricks. He looked about as smart as a pile of bricks. I asked him to slow down. He said he'd stop. He disappeared. I caught him sneaking whiskey through a reflection in the window between the kitchen and the outdoor dining room. It didn't really shock me. He looked like Daniel, Ryan, Brad . . . all of my old boyfriends from my old life, the small town life where drink was sport. I poured his glass down the drain and he expressed regret—for the booze being wasted, not for him lying to me.

I was pretty fed up by that point. I stole the bottle of Wild Turkey—I remember buying Wild Turkey because we'd read that was all Sinatra would drink at Capote's black and white ball. I hid the bottle in the pocket of a bathrobe in one of the forgotten upstairs bathrooms. I locked myself in the darkness of one of the west wing bedrooms. I realized I had no real friends whom I could call. Montreal had become so insipid. My sadness would bore them. The threat of sadness would be redundant. My sadness is not special.

Lachlan came up to my room to offer me salt and vinegar chips as his penance. I tried to reason with him. I tried to explain to him my life story and why I was upset and why it was scary to be on an island, in a mansion, with no friends, no cell service, and a drunken blank face that resembles every terrible ex-boyfriend I've had to change my locks over. Never try to reason with the drunken blank face. At one point, I became so frustrated I began to hit myself in the head. "Why do I always love the fucked-up addicts?" I said out loud to no one, to myself and stupid brick-head slumped in on himself in the corner. Lachlan was from a good, well-to-do family and had an education and still he was like this. Every time I am in a relationship with someone like this it always somehow feels like my fault. So I began to punish myself: smashed my head with my fists repeatedly. Awoken from his stupor, as if the thuds on my skull were a primordial alarm, he grabbed my wrists and pulled me onto the bed. I backed away from him and cried in a corner on the floor. He said to himself, he said to himself about me, while looking out the window as the sun rose, "Why do I keep doing this?" Then he calmed and nursed me back to bed.

He woke up confused but somewhat sober, the innards of his eye resting on a peripheral lash.

I can be very mean and unforgiving when I'm scared and alone in a mansion on an island. I was very mean and unforgiving of his drinking and his stupid attempts at hiding the drinking and his grabbing me. I reminded him of the night's dramatics while we were under the blanket, both of us curled inwards like snails hiding in shells. I didn't leave out a detail; every fingerprint and stray hair was accounted for. He cried when he heard about himself the way I told it to him.

This wasn't the first time this sort of thing happened. Earlier that week he'd gotten drunk, accused me of costing him a fortune, and broken up with me. In the morning he'd forgotten he'd broken up with me and I just sort of decided not to remind him.

After the island was my birthday: a celebration of the most radical thing I ever did by accident. My birthday cast a thick emotional weight over what would have otherwise been a normal day. I spent the whole afternoon watching *Orange Is the New Black*, waiting for Lachlan. Checking the clock. Wondering what was up. When he finally appeared at my doorstep I found out he'd been in the park hanging out with Mara and her dad. Part of the problem was Mara—he follows and fumbles after her. I can tell he's in love with her, at least more than he's in love with me. He can't even muster the words to say why I am more worthy of his love other than to kind of mumble, "She's flaky."

The other problem was his great love for her dad. I have spent years trying to recreate my own father through various mythological representations. At twenty-five, I have no idea where my father is or what he thinks of me. Science tells me he's decomposing and thoughtless. Lachlan's being with Mara's father on my birthday reminded me of a void I often imagine lives inside me and makes all my experiences somewhat incomplete.

He acted like I was being a melodramatic baby and maybe I was, but this was Mara, and this was Mara's father.

"Look, he's funny and he likes me, and he was in town, and he wanted to see me. My thinking was I'd stop in the park and have a few beers and you would have time to get dressed."

I wish I had a father Lachlan could meet and get excited about. I wish I could be flaky like Mara and sort of cruise through life with a trail of boys and friends and family members all excited for what was to come next.

"Mara is excited for your party," said Lachlan, like he was awarding me a badge.

After I expressly begged him to not get drunk at my birthday party, he did. He screamed at me until I wanted to crawl inside my own stomach. Then he broke up with me again, and again by the following morning he'd forgotten he'd dumped me. We went for brunch.

We tried to have a calm and measured phone conversation. It began with him dumping me because "we both just make each other miserable." I feel like he does terrible things and then blames me for holding him accountable and then blames me for the guilt he feels for being so terrible to me. I explained that there is a difference between us. I am always held accountable for everything in life: payments on bills, rent, fixing broken objects. His family's money relinquishes him from any and all accountability because all of his needs are taken care of. He is able to obsess about wants or objects. Wants are different from needs.

Earlier in the year, after I'd been fired from a retail job for speaking French with an English accent, I put forth the suggestion that we move to Toronto, where we might have an easier time finding work, even as a barista or whatever.

Lachlan responded, "If I left Montreal for anywhere it would be New York."

"I don't have my citizenship. I'd have the same problems there as I do in Montreal."

"I think we have different interests."

I suggested we probably have a different definition of "interest." Moving so that I can have a job and shelter and food is, for me, not an interest but a necessity. For him it meant that I wasn't a true bohemian.

I also brought up maybe moving in together so that I could pay less rent while I search for a job. He replied, "I think we want different things." Again, he misused "want."

I began to wonder when I had ever truly been allowed to want. It was like a skill I'd never been taught. When I was very little I had wanted to stay a virgin until marriage because that is what the church had told me I should want. I had wanted to have a big Victorian house with a bunch of daughters because I'd watched *Little Women* on repeat. I aged out of religion and into an economic crisis. Life taught me to skeptically want and slowly urge towards the likeness of whatever small desire I had, while keeping that desire a private secret. If the desire was private and it failed, then I wouldn't be publicly disappointed, make a spectacle of my disappointment, and be embarrassed all the more for ever having wanted anything in the first place.

In the world of Lachlan, if somebody wants a boat—just for the simple fact of wanting a boat—the thing materializes on the shores of a private island. Their dreams are possibilities. The wants are magnetically attracted to their money.

As the measured conversation continued, he said that I needed to take a more active role with his friends because I keep him from them with my crazy jealousy.

Mara was the big one. She'd never been anything but nice to me, but I had an idea that she'd stolen my life from me. I'd seen the way Lachlan hawed over her, disappearing into back rooms to share secrets with her. I used to do that with Jude before he followed Audrey. Then there's Liv. Liv was my best friend until she abandoned me for Mara. It was slow. They worked together and then started hanging out after work. Eventually we didn't see each other as much. Liv stopped calling me to tell me about her romantic prospects or mental health. Where we were once confidants, now Mara was the keeper of her secrets. I did not want to be friends with Mara.

In the winter, Liv had made plans to move in with me. She said, "I'm very serious about this if you are." I said I was also, but expressed concerns about the last time we lived together, when her bulimia had revealed itself as particular and controlling: where I left my books, how I organized the cupboard, what I ate, and who came over—she said these were all very triggering for her disorder. In retrospect, she did other things that bothered me. For example, she would throw parties and then leave the parties to have sex with her boyfriend and

I would be stuck playing hostess to strangers. There were a few times I had to ask professors for deadline extensions because I was "sick" when really I was busy listening to her cry about frivolous things like what name for her new cat would most impress her then-boyfriend. I did care and I didn't. I thought I loved her and that was what you do when you love someone. I'd assumed the feeling was mutual

Why had I stayed friends with Liv for this long? She uses phrases like "Maid of honour at each other's weddings" and "You are like a sister to me" and I've always longed for that kind of best friend. I've never had a "best friend" relationship with my mother. She lives far away and was why I had moved so far away. My mother used "daughter" as in "You are not like other people's daughters" as if by some deficiency I was not and never could be her daughter. I didn't exactly disagree with her. I felt annoyed because she was the one who chose for me to be born in the first place. If she wanted a different daughter then she should've had a different husband or an abortion. Familial words have always had a strange power over me. Liv had used them. A person should never tell an orphan they think of them as family unless they really mean it. It's sick. It's a basic social law. It's like how you don't visit the SPCA unless you are really looking for an animal of your own. Don't call a girl your sister. Never call a girl your sister, never.

I hadn't heard from Liv for a month, so I called to confirm the living arrangements. "I didn't think you were serious," she said. "I've made plans to live with Mara and Siobhan and those girls." Liv disappeared with Mara into their secret world and then, months later, magically reappeared at my birthday party as my "best friend of seven years."

All of our friends, Lachlan's and mine, had come to my party. Some even brought me presents. We all sat around a wooden table on the bar terrace. Everyone talked about how great I am. Everyone put on a great big parade of what big liars they are and I smiled because I am a liar too. I love Lachlan. I love Liv; she is like my sister. It's nice your dad is in town, Mara, and so on.

Cathleen is Lachlan's friend who says she has schizophrenia. She speaks in a high voice and is fond of giving advice to others. She gets all preachy at me about emotional and physical turmoil, as though she's lived through things she assumes I haven't. Once, while drunk, she wrapped her legs around Lachlan's waist very sexually, very much in front of me, on my bed, in fact. I'm not sure if she was trying to make me jealous or, more likely, probe how inhuman, unfeeling, and irrelevant Lachlan is as a silly plaything/chew-toy for girls to paw at innocently. The innocence comes from it being Lachlan and not the act itself.

Cathleen used to be best friends with Mara. At my birthday party, she also drank too much and kept trying to be my instant best bud, kept trying to share her secret hatred of the other guests to see if maybe her feelings would match mine and we could be friends. Friends through hatred, or something. She thought we could be close like sisters and Cathleen told me she'd always wanted a sister. She'd been ripped off by Mara's friendship with Liv and, like me, had no place to live. I didn't want to live with Cathleen. I didn't want to hear her talk about mental illness, like hers is the same as mine. I wasn't yet ready to covertly embarrass myself with another girl. I also didn't fully trust her with Lachlan. "Lachlan is like my brother," she'd said and I knew, because I used to say the same thing about Jude, when a girl says a boy is like a brother it means, in its own twisted way, that she would fuck him. I didn't want to be friends with Cathleen. I didn't want to be friends with Mara. I didn't want to be friends with Liv anymore. I kind of loved Lachlan.

Moses is Lachlan's socially awkward friend who knows a lot about stuff. He disappears for months, upsetting Lachlan—who has no other real male friends—and then reappears as if nothing has happened, as if he'd been there the whole time. I suffer the consequences for Lachlan's misery because of the reckless nature of Moses's disappearances. When Moses is gone, Lachlan sticks to Mara and then drinks and then fights. When Moses comes back, him and Lachlan sit in a room and talk about outer space, or British New Wave, or war. Things between us are more peaceful.

Moses could not make it to my birthday party. Things were becoming insufferable. I knew I needed to suck up my anxieties and reach out to my boyfriend's friends because I loved Lachlan and I wanted him to love me. My want was a need this time.

I thought a surprise party might remedy everything.

Lachlan's birthday is only a month after mine and Moses swore up and down that he was coming back to Montreal for good this time. He would be here for July. He would come to his surprise party.

I ordered Lachlan's present a month in advance with my own birthday money because I was nervous I would have nothing left come July 1st. The beginning of the month is always the worst time. I had a dream of his present and then had to Google search to make sure the dream present was a real thing that I could buy. I ordered a custom pair of pajamas that looked like Scotty's uniform on *Star Trek*. I have hated *Star Trek* ever since I was little, when I decided rice was made by putting a cheese grater to Captain Picard's bald scalp—a gross but captivating idea that's stayed with me. I thought the gift would matter more if I got Lachlan something he loved but I hated.

Next, I organized an event on Facebook that was secret and invited all of his friends. His friends got very into the plan. I knew I had to involve them because they are so flaky. I had to make them feel like they had some small ownership in making the event happen, otherwise nobody would show up and Lachlan would be more depressed and that would be my fault too.

"We shouldn't say anything about his birthday all day!" said Moses.

"That's so mean! Let me at least send him a text," interjected Cathleen.

"Can't wait!" Liv remarked, speaking to me for the first time since my own party.

The day before the party, Mara said she couldn't make it. She was taking a bunch of our friends on a trip to Boston. They had just decided that day. Mara is awful. I was grateful that at least three were still supposed to be coming, and I hoped they would actually make it because somehow, in the big mess of all of these people and their weird hang-ups, Lachlan's loving me, and my worthiness of a boy like Lachlan, rested on people materializing at this party. I had to manufacture Lachlan's childhood, like his wants could still magically unfold before him, as if the party could prove I was an adequate girlfriend, and lover, and person, somehow.

That day, I baked his favourite vanilla confetti cake and made the frosting bright blue: his favourite colour. I covered it in dinosaur sprinkles and wrote "Frak" because he loves *Battlestar Galactica*. I purchased a special tiara for him to wear and those birthday kazoos that unravel when you blow in them. Cathleen picked them up beforehand. She promised that at the very least her and Liv would be there. Nobody had spoken to Moses, but Cathleen said she would find him and drag him to the party if she had to. Cathleen really, really wants to be my friend.

Finally, I curled my hair with curlers and put on the pink and white "present dress" that is his favourite because it makes me look like '50s kitsch, and it also makes me look like a present, which I guess is what privileged boys find sexy. Maybe it has nothing to do with privilege. Maybe it's just nice to have your girlfriend wrapped up for your birthday.

When I arrived at his apartment, he was slumped over a coffee table littered with empty Pabst cans. "Nobody remembered my birthday," he said, staring darkly into the carpet. For a moment, I marvelled at the innocence of his heartbreak. There was a genuine sweetness in the fact that he felt comfortable enough to share with me his shame, however misinformed. Was I to him what Liv was to me? He was revealing a deep unfulfilled want and I felt incredibly terrible that I couldn't tell him the surprise I'd planned with his friends behind his back.

I held his hand and told him that we were going on a silly adventure. We walked down St. Laurent Street, past little shops, and then through Chinatown. He kept guessing at where we were going. First it was the seedy bars, then it was ritzy bars, then it was any of the ridiculous flashy restaurants with mechanical cats waving at us through blinking windows. I walked with him, hand in hand, all the way to Old Port, where we stopped in front of a fancy steakhouse and I said, "I know steak is your favourite."

The meal cost me my rent money. The *Star Trek* uniform had cost me my birthday money, a lump sum of $50 mailed from the grandmothers. I had hoped I'd gotten it right. "I'm sorry," he said. "This is perfect, and I love you, and you're beautiful. I'm just really upset and miss my friends."

I told him I was taking him to another bar, a bar that was our bar. We didn't talk the whole bus ride. I looked at him looking out the window. I reached to hold his hand, and he responded by gripping mine but kept his face towards bus stairs and then the sidewalk, a cement necropolis for stamped out cigarette butts.

When he walked in, the cake illuminated Cathleen, Liv, and, miraculously, Moses blowing kazoos. "Happy birthday!" they shouted, and then they told him all the details of the scheming we'd been up to.

Mara texted him a photo of herself in Boston holding a sign that said "Happy Birthday Lachlan." Liv just kept talking about how great her new apartment is and how we should come over and use their grill. Moses got drunk and said I was the best girlfriend ever, though he said it while Lachlan was outside having a smoke and couldn't hear. I studied Lachlan through the window. I thought that he was beautiful. I hoped that he was happy and I hoped that he loved me. I wondered if spoiling children was a form of abuse because their parents just gift them incessant joy before they, these little people, have really had a chance to earn or appreciate it. If excruciating happiness is the default of a child's world then there is nothing left but a devastating fall. Reality alone was his rock bottom. I wondered if the adult life of the spoiled was really just a second life where nothing is a surprise, not even a party, so you just kind of wander through moments jaded because everything that is good has already been given to you. Lachlan was spoiled but he wasn't bad, and he looked so precious through the window, and I was the best girlfriend ever, and I hoped he knew it, and I hoped that he loved me because I loved Lachlan.

After the party, Lachlan and Moses set off firecrackers in the park, and we ran away from the police. Then Moses used Lachlan's bathroom, had a beer, and eventually left us alone.

Lachlan was drunk but not as drunk as he'd been on my birthday or at the island mansion. He put his head on my lap and began to bawl like a newborn. He threw a temper tantrum and said that I had done a horrible thing, letting him believe his friends were too busy for his birthday.

"You make me feel bad. I feel worse than I've ever probably felt in my life."

"I'm sorry." I pet his head like he was a cat.

"How could you make me believe that none of my friends cared about me? I was sick all day. This is the meanest thing you've ever done. This is the worst birthday of my life."

He was sober enough to not dump me, but I felt dumped on and sat, dumbfounded, for nearly an hour, as he told me that I am an awful person who does awful things to people, and he was talking about himself when he said "people."

I barely slept that night. I can be very mean and unforgiving when I'm scared and lonely in a relationship after throwing an epic surprise party. His apartment was different from mine: he had good knives, organized in a straight line in his kitchen drawer; his windows had blinds that were purchased, measured, and installed by someone other than him; his couch was new and his table was new—both designed to appear old but function like new, as they were.

In the morning I was furious. I kicked a scuff mark into his wall and threw the cake tray across the kitchen floor. I called him spoiled, entitled, a brat. I told him Mara would never fuck him or blow him or love him the way he wants her to. He said nothing.

Saying nothing is Lachlan's most annoying tactic. He lets me talk and not answer. Instead he makes me watch him be blank, indifferent, unmoved. Sometimes he makes me watch him not speak for twenty to forty minutes. When I yell at him to say something, anything, he simply rebuts, "I don't know what to say," or excuses himself to get a glass of water or visit the washroom. Then, when he returns, the conversation is over. I am the bad guy for yelling and name-calling. The loudness of my frustration always makes me the bad one.

But then there are other ways he makes up for it, to be fair. He brings over his vacuum when my apartment is infested (it is always infested). He helps me clean when the mess becomes too much. He pays my rent sometimes if I'm in a bind. He brings over groceries and always foots the bill at the end of the night. Am I being inconsiderate?

When we have sex it is always the same. I make the first move, never him. This makes me feel undesirable and unwanted and ugly. He barely goes down on me and it makes me believe my genitalia is disgusting and revolting. He goes slow on top of me until I make myself experience something like an orgasm. Then he pumps at me, frequently pulling out too far and then painfully jabbing me with force in a place somewhere outside of my vaginal opening, but still in a sensitive part around it. I feel more like a prop, a fleshlight, than a person. He can do this for hours without cumming. He can do it until I am raw. His failure to cum feels like a failure on my part. I go to pee and by the time I am back he is smoking a cigarette, talking about other things, as if the sex never happened.

We didn't have sex after his party, obviously. We hadn't had sex in a while. Neither of us had really felt it towards each other. I kind of excused a lot of the sex by remembering his lack of experience. Talking about it always seemed to elucidate his sensitivity to everything, anyhow. I couldn't even bring it up or make it better by pointing to parts of my body or making delicate suggestions. I felt neglected. My body felt neglected. I began to be embarrassed by my body. My body itself was a confession.

"I love you," I'd say.

His robotic response, "I love you too."

"Why do you love me?" I'd ask.

He would look like he's thinking, then say, "I just do. Just the little things that you do that I can't define."

"What do you love about me?"

"Everything."

"Like, what thing? Name a thing. Name everything that you love."

"Everything. I dunno, your face, your body, you're smart and funny and the funny smart things that you say."

He didn't know me and therefore also didn't know what to love about me. I was his girlfriend. I was just there.

Days after Lachlan's spoiled post-birthday meltdown, and the consequential near-demise of our relationship, I bought him breakfast at Beauty's and then we stopped at a bar without a name. He had a beer and I had a caesar, extra spicy. We were waiting for the exterminator to finish killing the spiders in my closet and the cockroaches in my kitchen.

Lachlan went to the Rialto with Cathleen to watch a World Cup soccer game. I went home to vacuum dead bugs then fix my cover letter and resumé for a prospective paid internship with a company through Youth Employment Services Montreal.

A job counsellor suggested I find a passion for "data entry" and, consequently, I found within me the exact opposite. She asked why

I couldn't move into my boyfriend's apartment since he had money and we'd been together a while.

After leaving the office I made an appointment at TD Bank to consolidate my student debt. Any talk with banks stresses me out. I hoped it would be fruitful, the consequences outweighing the concerns. Maybe I could be optimistic. Perhaps there was some way to wraggle free of this rut.

Mara texted me. She invited me to a "grill night" at her and Liv's new apartment where Lachlan and I could eat her grilled meat. It would be a good idea, I thought, the invitation was one of good faith, for her to have Lachlan and me at the apartment she shared with Liv and other girls. Still I couldn't help conceiving it as anything other than an elite treehouse I'd been exiled from because there had been room for other girls, and none of those other girls was me.

So I met up with Lachlan at the new place, where Mara pattered about, offering us little cheese biscuits and wine with ice in mason jar glasses, and she took us into her living room, explaining that it had come with the grand piano. I made an effort. I played "Ode to Joy."

Cathleen was bizarrely giddy; like me, she'd been shafted from the girls' treehouse, and she was giddy to shit-talk everyone. From her bedroom she sent me text after text asking about how pretentious the table setting was and what pathetically desperate outfit Liv was sporting and whether their couch was vintage or Ikea. She caused my phone to beep so much that I turned it silent. I didn't really want to commiserate, but I told her they were being okay and their couch used to belong to Mara's grandparents.

I'd wanted to get to Mara's place on time. Just, even, to make amends for Lachlan, just for Lachlan because I love Lachlan.

I did arrive on time. As soon as I entered I knew it was a bad idea.

The mess of cardboard boxes and girls' pretty duvets and girls' little makeup bags and girls' tiny couch pillows made me hyper-aware of the meaning of my exclusion. The meaning folded in on itself in multiple layers condensing loose annoyances and reasonable grievances into sedimentary loathing. My exclusion meant having to stay in my current apartment that I couldn't afford, not just because of the steak dinner I'd bough Lachlan, but because I couldn't get a job. I couldn't get a job because of Quebec and language laws and life as an Anglo in this city. Also Lachlan doesn't want to leave Montreal and I love Lachlan. Having to live alone and every day face my loneliness in a much shittier apartment than theirs, a shittier but more expensive apartment that I couldn't afford—them not inviting me to live with them—was an affirmation of my loserdom and arriving at this apartment for a visit was, in its own way, a humble acceptance of that loserdom, admitting that I was inferior. Visiting was a way of saying that I need them because I am lost without them. Visiting was a way of saying that everything was cool between us, and that would be a lie, that especially would be a lie.

"They are trying so hard to be grownups. They are thinking about putting blinds on their windows. Fuck," I texted Cathleen.

"OMFG ROFL," she responded.

I ran to the bathroom after quick hellos. I needed to pee and collect my thoughts. When I calmed down and entered the living room, everyone was gone. I awkwardly wandered around the apartment, the different half-assembled bedrooms, the kitchen with its somewhat ordered knives that unevenly jabbed into a wooden vessel. I spotted Liv's cat and tried to pet her, but she turned on her belly and aggressively scratched my wrist. She didn't like me anymore, not like how she did when Liv and I lived together. I could hear Lachlan laughing. I followed the laugh to a hidden back porch where he had disappeared with Mara.

I felt abandoned. I marched out onto the patio and sat between them. I gave Lachlan the stink-eye, which infuriated him. I intentionally tried to belittle him.

He said, "I like to explore abandoned urban decay."

I responded, loudly, "Yeah, now that you have an audience."

I made everyone uncomfortable.

Liv acted like the pretentious nitwit she is. That narcissistic, self-involved débutant excused herself to "work on things." "Work on things" meant drafting a business plan for some juvenile idea for a vegan bakery that she'd been plotting to co-found. The plan evidently had to be drafted on the rare occasion of my visit. My darkest self wished she'd realize she wasn't interesting or smart or strangely beautiful enough to be the soulless social climber she so desperately aspired to be. I wished she would understand that her desperation was evident to everyone around her. I wanted to be the one to tell her. I wanted to watch her cry about it.

So this was the apartment: walls, windows, and two porches, but at what cost? I mean rent was cheap, but at what cost? What did the cost of the apartment say about my value? Why was there so much at stake in these wood floors and popcorn ceilings?

When my snide comments had angered Lachlan enough that he, in typical fashion, excused himself to the bathroom, then it was only Mara and me. Mara, I guess, had never done anything directly wrong.

Sometimes I think that I am in the business of creating dangerous messes.

Mara and I discussed the many reasons we were sick of Montreal and the conversation itself revealed the differences in our childhoods. Her light concerns were about dreams unrealized, my heavy concerns were merely preoccupied with survival; wants vs. needs.

Then I said something, and it came out like a rambling confession. She turned to me to watch me say it because it was important and it was weirdly eloquent and it grew out of some deep gut place where I'd had it written all along, written inside of me on the internal surface of my skin. I said, "The problem with people here is they make choices based on appetite and not hunger. Every choice is grounded in personal preference and self-indulgence. People here, our friends at least, make powerful transformative decisions with possibly gargantuan ramifications for others, and they make those decisions as if choosing ice cream flavours. They can just hide behind their parents' wealth and, because of that wealth, no one is ever accountable for their actions. If there is no accountability, it makes the pain they cause somewhat unreal and so we are all just holograms of feelings that aren't really feelings, the feelings are just space, all of the people are just space. Anglophones who can somehow stay in Montreal after their degree is over anyhow."

I didn't say it in an accusatory tone, but it was meant as an accusation. It felt like the first time, in a long time, that I had really spoken. I'd maybe never spoken a real word in my life until that moment.

"You're really smart," said Mara. "I've always admired your ability to see through things. I'm so happy we've become friends."

We were quiet. Then we weren't. We talked about how much we both hate Liv's stupid cat, my monologue drifting beneath the conversation.

Mara served me grilled avocados and sausage. Lachlan returned and he hates avocados but he picked at my sausage and touched my leg like nothing had happened.

Liv eventually came back but didn't converse. There was maybe, I guess, something to be called conversation, but it was like non-conversation about stupid superficial things she's too stupid to actually really consider.

She's never seen a beautiful thing in her life, I realized, and now she has this tacky girly apartment to show for it.

I watched the rehearsed elements of her pointedly relaxed stance.

Then I watched Lachlan watching Mara who looked towards the skyline that set behind many roofs pointed like chins on heads tilted upwards.

Cathleen's rampant texts felt violent, but she meant them as comforting with "It's always like that," or "Mara and I have been having difficulties in our own friendship," or "If you need to talk I'm here," and more intensely, "Talk to me if you need someone." Cathleen so gravely needed someone to say that she wasn't being crazy—that Mara's a snaky bitch. Cathleen needed someone to need her need.

I took Mara's plate.

"Thank you," she said.

"Thank you for dinner," I responded as I brought the dishes inside.

I introduced myself to a faceless roommate whose name I didn't hear. I put my dishes into the sink and then, with quiet purpose, walked out the front door, down the steps, and onto the street. I didn't say goodbye to anyone. I just walked away and kept going.

I started to run at the corner. I ran down Avenue du Parc. I thought about how I originally saw us, Lachlan and I, the weeks after the first time we kissed: two tiny, long-haired fairies picking flowers for each other inside of a bubble.

There was no soot on my hands, but I could feel the weight of the labour of the men back home. I could feel every fruit my grandfather ever grew, and watered, and canned for other people to eat. I could see Mara and her very lively father eating the pears in the park on my birthday while I waited. Also, Lachlan's family sitting and eating my dead grandfather's pears. I could see the very educated parents of Lachlan, and others I know, drinking ice wine and discussing the ice wine and the ice wine having come from the soil where my father is dead and buried.

I got it in my head—not that I had to die, but that I had to legitimize my sadness in some kind of concrete way. It was a sadness that could not be translated into the language of Lachlan or Liv or Mara or any of those people. The sadness was not a word. The sadness was an action. I needed to hurl myself into the void or else I'd just be another allegedly sad person standing on the outside looking in.

I wrote a long sprawling letter absolving everyone of any responsibility, explained that it was my life, a life that only I could live and therefore would always fail to accurately communicate to anyone other than myself. Sick to the point of insufferable discomfort, I thought. Permanent unhappiness, I thought as I laid the pages of the letter in a straightish line on the floor. I don't want to be canned and distributed, a product that can be bought. I want to be frozen and sweet, like a fallen pear when late autumn frosts the orchards in the place where I was born.

I drank and drank alone in my bed. Permanent unhappiness. Nobody seemed to have noticed I was gone. Insufferable discomfort. I swallowed fistfuls of Clonazepam, Benadryl, Gravol, and after that it was just simple wishful thinking.

Not really. I cried. I cried and I hoped to God that what I was doing was going on some great infinite adventure. I understood it was selfish, but my sadness was illegitimate without the act to affirm it. The feelings weren't real unless I died.

Lachlan called about an hour and a half in and said, "I'm sorry, baby. I'm sorry."

"It was too much. It was all too much."

"I know, baby, and I'm coming. I'm coming home."

By "too much" I meant my grandfather's gargle right before he died with his mouth open like a toothless cave, my father in the ICU with his spine as some sort of Jenga game for people with PhDs, the way I was a daughter to my mother and the way I wasn't a daughter to my mother, my landlord telling me that I had to pay my rent (rent I'd spent on steaks for Lachlan's birthday) or I'd lose my apartment, the early morning threat I'd received that Bell was going to shut off my internet, Lachlan's continuous and relentless rambling drunken threats to leave me, how easy it was for people to just leave me, the student loans—a consequence of my ever dreaming of acquiring an education for myself, Mara's indifference, Liv's betrayal, my father again and my father again and my father—everything he is to me in his forever absence, the many nameable exes: Daniel and the aborted pregnancy, Ryan taking off in a car, Brad saying I wasn't special, what I'd done to women with Jude, Jude wanting Audrey, Jude not wanting me—all of it was too much on top of that pathetic girlish Montreal treehouse membership and its prosthetic affirmation of eliteness.

I fell asleep under a quilt stitched by my grandmother and awarded to me when I was born. I was awoken by Lachlan stumbling over my pages of embarrassing wants and wishes, my suicide notes.

"I love you," he said and then burped and then hiccupped in my ear. "I'm sorry," he said. He couldn't stop burping in my face. I turned downwards; he'd left footprints on my suicide notes.

As I stayed silent on the bed with my head still on the pillow, I could hear him snoring on the couch, the formidable and final stroke of indifference to my existence. Maybe he would recycle my suicide note. Probably, he would just toss them in the garbage.

Cathleen, who is easily unnerved and perhaps appropriately so, had a feeling. I don't remember sending the words that gave her the feeling. She had asked in one of her million texts how I was doing. In my drugged up stupor I accidentally betrayed myself. I texted back, "I'm going to kill myself." If you text someone that you are going to kill yourself then people get a feeling that you are maybe trying to kill yourself. Cathleen got the feeling so she called 911 while running to my place. I awoke to a paramedic shouting in my face, "YOU WILL DIE!"

In the ambulance, they—Lachlan, Cathleen, the paramedics— just wanted to keep me awake.

I tumbled between conscious and unconscious until I came to, discovering that I was in the hospital. Horrified, I screamed for Lachlan, and a severe Nurse Ratched–type threatened to tie me up. The only thing worse than failing at suicide is having your limbs trussed to a gurney while you're forced to confront your failure by being alarmingly and annoyingly alive.

They released me the next day. They'd given Lachlan my phone, wallet, and keys. All I had was a dress and flip-flops and, because of all the fuss I'd caused with my shouting and yanking out my IV over and over again, they refused to let me use their phone. Payphones don't work the way they used to, or maybe I was too high to make a collect call, or maybe the operator had it out for me.

I didn't know where the fuck I was. I wandered until I recognized the corner of Berri and St. Denis. I still had bandages from places they'd stolen my blood right out of my veins and they hadn't removed the stickums the doctors used to spy on my heartbeat. This was maybe the hottest mess I'd ever been. I was so high that I kept wandering off the street and into oncoming traffic. I felt like shit. I had failed at dying. I tried to reimagine it as a postmodern resurrection. It was an arrogant thought, but I needed something, and I was just trying to get by, just trying to get home.

I don't know how—I seriously have very little memory—but I got all the way up to Parc and Fairmount, where a couple saw me waddling in the street with the white square Band-Aid inside my elbow and hospital bracelet. They asked if I was okay and vowed to get me home. They are the kind of nice people Oprah should give cars to.

Lachlan was at my house. At first he was relieved to see me. Then he almost dumped me for trying to kill myself, but then he didn't because I politely asked him not to. He fed me a sandwich and pizza as I drifted in and out of consciousness. Most of the rest is a blur. I kept trying to load a TV show on my computer and then passing out before I could press play.

The next day Lachlan and I went to Youth Employment Services Montreal where I applied for a job and Lachlan looked at jobs too. While we browsed prospective opportunities, Lachlan's mother texted him that he should apply only for jobs that speak to his passions. Lachlan and I both share a lack of enthusiasm for data entry.

On the way home I could barely stand but still pretended to be happy. Lachlan left me in bed, where I took the last remaining Clonazepam, two Benadryl, and two Gravol.

I woke up today with texts from Lachlan that said: "Hey bb, how are you doing? I love you and if you are asleep I hope you have only good dreams and that the TD Bank meeting goes well."

Today the money from a job I worked in March came through and I was able to fill a small envelope with my rent money. I met with a man at the bank to consolidate my debt. He told me I have to cancel my internet and Netflix and everything so that I will be viable for debt reduction. I have to prove that I am really really poor.

I purposely didn't tell the banker, an observant but monotone, serious man with a suit and an earring, about the trip to the island. How much does it cost to buy an island? Montreal is an island.

My phone dings with a text from Cathleen, in good faith, to hang out, but I am embarrassed and don't want to bond over our mental illness. It isn't something I'm proud of or want to make friends through.

I haven't responded to Lachlan's kind texts. I have a missed call from Jude. I have an unread email from Audrey. I think Liv is with Mara. I don't care. I care a lot.

The scary part is that I think I would do it again. All of it. The scary part is that I think I would do it again, and again, and again, forever, whenever I get the chance. People will leave me. I can sense them gathering themselves to do so already. I am an abuse. They will confide to one another, they loved me then left because I am an abuse.

Today is cool, sunny, alive with pedestrians, and I've been alone and, somehow, still alive, with Band-Aid scabs here and there. Sitting on a bench, I watch couples holding hands, birds singing in the trees, children playing in the fountain. Summer is disgusting. Today is cool though. Keep thinking it to myself, today is cool.

Roxane and Julieta

SOFIA MOSTAGHIMI

"Juls, you want to know something?" Roxane swivelled on her stool in the Dufferin Mall food court. She was loud and her eyebrow was pierced and she didn't care who heard her when she talked.

"What?"

Julieta was the heftier one with round, wet eyes and soft, pulpy features that even when she worried seemed puffed up with extra skin.

"I had an abortion once—before I knew I was a lesbo, obviously." Behind Roxane, a row of old men drank coffees, greedy in their stares; she grabbed a French fry from its carton, and the spring of the chair swivelled her back around towards her girlfriend.

"When?"

"Like, six months ago, maybe?"

"Whose baby was it?"

"It was a fetus."

Roxane's long white arm moved to fetch more fries. The tattoos on it of sea creatures and waves seemed alive.

Julieta's jaw clenched. She swallowed.

"Okay, well whose *fetus* was it?"

"Juls, I just felt like telling you that and now that's all."

"So like, what? Was he married or something?"

"Juls, stop."

Roxane sucked the salt off of each of her fingers. She felt concern vibrating off of her girlfriend as if it were an invasion. Even the pulsing eyes of the old men nearby seemed less threatening.

"Oh my God," Julieta said. "Or did he like...assault you?"

"Juls..."

Fingertips still moist from licking them, Roxane pushed a strand of Julieta's black hair back behind her unpierced ear. Julieta gave a little kick with her voice—this was how she always whimpered when she felt powerless—and Roxane kissed her. She wasn't supposed to kiss Julieta in here. Any one of her mother's friends who worked in the Walmart down at the other end might spot them. Julieta pulled back then, receded alongside the eyes of the men, and put her mouth on the straw of her drink.

"Those creepy old men behind us think we're so totally hot, eh, Juls?" Roxane shot her eyes at them.

Six months ago, when Roxane was already a high school dropout, Julieta was finishing up her senior year. In every classroom she'd sat in the front row. Her evenings she'd spent studying. Her Sundays she'd spent in church with her mother. She'd never even kissed a girl before.

"Well, don't worry," Julieta said.

In Roxane's broken, blinking eyes, Julieta saw something like sadness slinking.

"About what?"

"I don't think you're going to hell or anything."

Before they'd met, Julieta used to stare at Roxane on her walk into work in the afternoons. Dressed in her blue Walmart uniform, Roxane would be standing in front of the dumpsters in the Dufferin Mall parking lot, feet in dirty white Converse, neck tilted to one side, smoking joints and daring mall patrons with her eyes to say something, anything.

Roxane noticed Julieta a few weeks after that, in the bathroom of the food court when it was still the spring, the chubby girl with the puffed-up face and big wet brown eyes.

"Are you okay? You look like you've been crying," she'd said to her, leaned over the faucet under the bad yellow lights of the bathroom.

"Fine," Julieta had said, but she slept easier that night. If a stranger could notice your sadness then this world, it wasn't hopeless.

When Roxane finally called out to Julieta, it was only a week later but it was the summer now. It was hot. Across the pavement, on the horizon, air quivered. Julieta crossed the parking lot in her black

Starbucks uniform. Roxanne had already finished her shift and changed into short shorts and a tank top. And it was curious and sort of hot how Julieta gawked at her body without saying a word. The feeling of anticipation had been almost unbearable, and for Julieta too, who knew she stared but couldn't help it. And when Roxane called out to her, it was like a fresh breeze coming up off an ocean and delivering them from the beating of the sun.

"Yes, you!" Roxane shouted. "Want a puff? I'll share if you give me a free coffee next time I come in. Deal?"

"I can't smoke before work. It'll make me anxious," Julieta said.

"Well what time does your shift end?"

"In six hours."

"Okay," Roxane told her. "I'll be here."

Julieta walked away smiling so wide that she could barely see out of her eyes with those cheeks of hers pressed up against them.

"Tell me about that guy, the one who got you pregnant," Julieta asked Roxane as they lounged naked on her living room sofa. Her mother would be home soon from work but until then Roxane was curled quietly into the small spoon of Julieta's big one, staring at the wall opposite the sofa. Both the TV and Julieta's mother's Catholic altar had been set up there, on the same translucent white table cloth, on the same cheap long fold-out table.

"Did you like doing it with him?"

Roxane blinked and stretched her arms over her head.

"Yeah. Sometimes," she said.

"So you're bisexual? Do you think?"

Roxane laughed hard and purposefully, and the sound was like a gurgle.

"I think everybody's bisexual. Now, let me go. I need a cigarette."

"Wait."

Both of Roxane's skinny tattooed legs flopped from the couch to the rug.

"What's wrong?"

Roxane could feel out of the corner of her eyes her girlfriend's breasts slumping towards each armpit, and for a moment, she wondered if she actually did feel anything for this person.

"Nothing's wrong. I just need a cigarette."

Julieta tried smiling. Her voice was quiet but her eyes were bright. "Come back."

"Your mom's gonna be home soon. If I don't smoke now, I'll have to wait for her to go to sleep, or until I leave."

"You should quit."

Roxane bent over and found her pack of smokes in her purse on the floor.

"Ha. Quit," she echoed. She pulled her T-shirt over her head then took off to the fire escape.

The fire escape where Roxane smoked flanked the north side of the detached red-brick house from which Julieta and her mother rented the second-floor apartment. Above them, on the third floor, lived Joey, the landlady's son. He had recently moved in after separating from his bitch wife because, as he told it, she'd had the nerve to tell him that she didn't love him anymore.

"Can you fucking believe that?" he had said, a few hot nights back, from the landing above theirs.

Roxane was standing on the fire escape lighting the tail end of a joint. Pressed against the back door as she was, she had a clear view of Joey at the top of the stairs. He was a huge burly man with heavy feet and thick porous skin; his hair grew in curly, black tufts that hovered over him like a dark halo. "I can," she said.

"After everything I did for her. The wedding. Everything. I can't fucking believe that."

Slowly, she'd walked a few steps up towards Joey then leaned against the railing, dangling another question.

"So you're divorcing her?"

Joey, in the middle of an inhale, had stopped and turned his head to watch this bold skinny girl materialize below him.

"Jesus Christ," he said. "How many tattoos you got there?"

Roxane laughed.

"I told my boyfriend, ex-boyfriend, he could use me for practice. He was a tattoo artist. I think I have thirteen, or fourteen...We used to live together. We both loved the ocean so they all have to do with that, like with the ocean. See?"

With his mouth pressed around his cigarette, Joey ran his eyes over the mermaid's tail drawn around Roxane's bare thigh.

"You like the pain, or what?"

Roxane cocked her head up and made a small nod.

"And you know," he said, "I could arrest you for smoking that. You know I'm a fucking cop, right? You know that?"

He had almost reached down to pet her hair in approval, and in her memory, he had.

So then that afternoon when Roxane walked out onto the fire escape for a cigarette in an oversized black T-shirt and a lacy purple thong, she was waiting for Joey to come out.

But Joey didn't come out. Instead, Roxane finished her cigarette and the girls waited until Julieta's mother came home to have leftover spaghetti with too-garlicky tomato sauce. Since her first invitation into Julieta's home, Roxane had preferred this one to her own. She loved Julieta's mother, a small brown woman with a rounded stomach and black eyes who loved to dramatize the loud, hard footsteps of Joey above them.

"He walk like he possessed," she repeated tonight during dinner. "He walk like he, I don't know. Like he crazy."

"We should move then," Julieta said.

"Where? You want to go back to Mexico? You never been!" A low, fast grumble filled the room as Julieta's mother laughed.

Julieta rolled her eyes.

After dinner, while her mother watched her telenovela, Julieta begged Roxane to sleep over. She loved to set her cold feet against Roxane's skin while they slept and imagine that with every sleepover, she saved her just a little bit more from a life of bad, mean boyfriends and sad abortions.

In the middle of the night, Roxane was awoken by a low thud followed by a shaky and muffled woman's laugh. Roxane looked at Julieta, who still snored, snuggly in a small cocoon at the edge of the bed, and strained to listen. She heard a door closing upstairs. More laughter. Then silence. She sat up with fear or excitement, or some combination of both that was neither of those things, and felt the wall at her back start to rattle like a tok, tok, tok. She thought she heard the rush of a moan, too, pale and wanting. Julieta still snored. Then again there was that moan, raw and surging.

Roxane thought of her ex-boyfriend, of his bare back as he lit a cigarette and the smoke rolled out backwards, to collide with her naked body on his bed. She didn't know why this was the image that had come to her, except that this was how babies were made, via these sounds and grunts and this sweat that truly requires no intimacy, not really, and of how after the abortion she'd told her boyfriend, ex-boyfriend, about how the first step to the procedure is the insertion of seaweed to dilate the cervix. "No way," he'd said, between two pulls of a joint. Before they'd broken up, she'd insisted that he give her one last tattoo, underneath her bellybutton, of strands of seaweed. She searched for it now in the dark, green and undulating.

In the morning, Roxane rolled onto Julieta's belly and tried to tell her about the man who had gotten her pregnant and whom she'd dropped out of high school and run away from home to live with, and about how he had reimagined her body with images from a book about the ocean they both loved to look at in the mornings, after long nights of drinking.

"If you ask me something, anything, I'll answer it," Roxane said. She was wide-eyed and expectant.

"All right." Julieta rubbed her eyes. Her face was swollen from last night's sleep, and she smelled strong, like wet earth. "All right, do you love me?"

"Of course I do," Roxane said, too quickly for thought. She rolled off the thick warm body of her girlfriend and stared up at the ceiling.

"You do?" Julieta's body rolled onto Roxane's now, and she stared at her with a soft, smudged-out expression of relief. "I love you too."

They heard the front door closing. Julieta's mother was gone to church, and a weight wasn't quite lifted, just suspended, temporarily above their heads. In the shaky quiet, both girls drifted off to sleep again and Roxane had wild, bad dreams, and sometime before noon both were awoken by the same banging, the same moans as last night's.

"Oh my God, are they doing it up there?" Julieta's face lit up. Her amazement seemed simple and childish but inside it was like a door was opening, and she fluttered to get out.

"Sounds like it."

"Does that mean? Do you think Joey hears us?"

"We're not loud enough."

Roxane got dressed. Julieta got dressed too, in a too-small tank top, then followed Roxane out onto to the fire escape. Outside was bright blue, without clouds. The girls sat on the landing, feet dangling between the iron bars, saying nothing, they were completely quiet. Just as Roxane finished her cigarette, the door above them swung open, and Julieta gasped, and a woman coughed, and Roxane lit another cigarette.

"Roxane, I think it's a one-night stand. Like he just picked her up last night or something."

Roxane looked at the backyard where she registered nothing but a rusty old oblong bathtub in the farthest corner. Above them, Joey and the woman talked about the weather.

"Hello? Roxane. What do you think?"

"Juls. I don't know. Who cares? Why don't you ask him if you're so curious?"

Joey talked loudly about his ex now. She'd turned out to be an unappreciative little cunt; that's how most women are and it's to be expected, when they get everything handed to them the way they do. "Imagine growing up knowing a man's always going to fucking financially take care of you?" he said to the girl who laughed hysterically at rhythmic intervals.

"Can I try some?" Julieta took the cigarette from Roxane's fingers and put it against her lips.

"Juls, are you sure?"

She pressed it to her lips cautiously, as if she weren't sure of her own depth perception, and as Roxane watched her inhale, she felt protective and guilty and a little bit in awe of Julieta's innocence. Julieta coughed, but only mildly, and once she had, the world felt bright and dizzy. The door above them slammed shut.

"Oh my God," Julieta said. "Imagine having sex with someone like Joey? He's like one of those Neanderthals. Like a brute."

Roxane felt very tired and very heavy.

"Let's go inside, Juls."

"I don't want to. I want another drag."

"I'm going inside."

Julieta pressed the all-white cigarette back into her mouth, inhaled, then tossed the thing into the landlady's grapevines.

Before she met Roxane, Julieta used to kneel at the foot of her mother's altar, next to the TV, and pray to the Virgin Mary that she not go to university a virgin. Having remained a virgin her entire life, Mary was the one person Julieta thought would understand her delicate and somewhat sinful plight the best. Her favourite figurine of Mary on her mother's altar was small and plastic, and she'd hold it and shut her eyes and hand so tight that Mary's silhouette would leave a mark on the inside of her palm that lasted for hours sometimes.

Even then it was clear to Julieta that she was gay. Boys didn't fascinate her, they didn't scare her, they didn't make her nervous. They were boring and predictable. Girls confused her. They made her blush. She liked the way they walked with asses and breasts that hung off of them like thick chains of silver. Still, when a woman caught her staring she'd bow her head down in shame and wish that she'd been born different.

When Roxane appeared, Julieta knew her prayers had been answered, and if her prayers had been answered then it wasn't wrong, who she was, how she felt. Roxane taught her these things with the sudden force of lightning.

"Who the fuck cares what anyone else does in their own bedroom?" Roxane had said to her. "We can do whatever we want. And it doesn't even have to stay in the bedroom, actually." Roxane had kissed Julieta straight on the lips. "Now kiss me back," she'd said. "Who cares? What are they going to say? If they say anything, just watch what I'll do. You can't always just be like, reading books. You got other parts to your body than just your brain, you know that, right? I'm serious. Kiss me. I know you want to."

Julieta had swallowed hard then pressed her lips then tongue into Roxane and they'd both fallen backwards, into the grass. On a warm, sunny day in the Dufferin Grove Park, surrounded by fifty people or more, they'd kissed and touched each other over their clothes for close to an hour.

So then it was true. Julieta knew.

Most weekends now, Joey came home late with a different girl who made varying levels of noises and degrees of moans that Julieta, in her small teal-blue bedroom, studied with curiosity. Her mother, if she heard the women, pretended not to, and if Roxane spent the night and was awoken by them, she would only shrug and roll back asleep.

The effect was Julieta herself became louder when Roxane pleasured her, and she insisted on being pleasured more often now. At work, during their breaks, the girls would meet in the food court, and the same old group of retired men would watch them as Roxane kissed Julieta's neck, her lips. Julieta also developed a system that she used to report on the different kinds of women Joey brought up to his apartment. Levels one through three were quiet, and level tens were so loud, they shook the wall against her head at night. Then within that, Julieta explained, were gradients and subtleties. Some drew sound out of Joey, while others didn't. Some were screamers, others moaners.

"It's like this whole other world," she said.

Then one night when Julieta's mother worked a night shift, the girls got drunk, and Roxane told Julieta that the major difference between them was that she was brave and Julieta wasn't. She wasn't passive, and Julieta was. It was an off-topic, mean thing to say, without context.

Instead of rage, Julieta felt crushing tiredness like a wave.

"What makes you say that?" she asked.

"Well, I do what I want. That's why you're still so innocent. You do what people want you to do."

"That's not true."

Roxane grabbed her pack of cigarettes from her purse and left for the fire escape. Joey wasn't home. All of his lights were turned off, and it was Friday. Roxane thought how fucking wonderful it must be, to be a guy, to have no conscience. She sat, and she felt that she was floating, waiting for something, not someone, or maybe it was someone.

The back door opened and Julieta stumbled outside with the bottle of rum, begging for a whole cigarette this time.

"See. I do what I want," she said.

"Be careful."

She sat next to Roxane, and their feet dangled over the black-blue darkness of the backyard. The city was loud, yet it all felt very far.

"In grade ten, I called our gym teacher a *fucking homophobic misogynistic sexist asshole* because he told this guy to stop 'whining like a girl.' I got in so much trouble, my mother beat me with her shoe, but I didn't care because it was true. And another time, I helped this girl, that I didn't even know, I just saw her on the street and this guy was hassling her, so I told him to leave us alone because she was with me, and I'm kind of big so I think he got scared and he did, he left. So see."

Julieta inhaled hard on her newly lit smoke then tried suppressing a cough. Roxane reached for Julieta's hand. She wished she could sink into her, love her.

"I'm sorry, Juls," she said.

"But I know you're more brave than me. It's just the truth. You just say the truth that's all, right?" Julieta held the bottle of rum with both hands and drank.

"Right."

"Like I never had a tattoo or an abortion or had sex with lots of people or flirted with everybody that I meet, all the time, because I'm so insecure and need their attention, or I've never not said what I'm thinking, all of the time, because I need secrets to make me special, or I've never been too wrapped up in myself to notice how anyone else around me is feeling or been so scared to let go that I won't even let myself have an orgasm."

Roxane laughed like how she did when the words would not come.

Julieta held the cigarette in one hand and the rum bottle in the other and she seemed a hundred years older than she had on that first afternoon in the parking lot when she and Roxane had met.

"You don't understand me at all," Roxane said.

Julieta set the bottle of rum down beside her and latched onto the railing to lift herself upright. Through the bars of the landing was this city that felt like nothing but a trap to Julieta, who had wanted to leave for school, or see the world, but staying here was all that she could afford, and with this girl, this girl she thought she loved or she did love, it had sometimes felt, on some days, that that was an all right thing, an adventure in its own way.

"Good. I'm glad," Julieta said. She turned around and went back inside.

Roxane stayed up late watching TV in the living room while Julieta slept. Then at 4 a.m., she heard Joey's loud, hard footsteps banging in the stairway outside. She wore only a T-shirt and a lacy thong when she stepped out with her pack of smokes and lighter, and when he saw her on the landing, he wore a pair of dark jeans and an unbuttoned shirt. He was alone.

"What are you doing up so late?" he asked. He was drunk, like she still was, and his eyes were red. His voice was raspy.

"What are *you* doing up so late?"

"Shit night at the bar," he said. "Got any weed? I need to take this edge off."

Roxane slipped one of her pre-rolled joints from her pack and, barefoot, walked up the steps onto Joey's landing. It was only one storey, but she felt infinitely higher, and the backyard felt infinitely smaller. On the horizon, the darkness was turning to blue, and she felt rushed and anxious to talk. She lit the joint, and when she passed it to Joey, his hand was fat and hairy and throbbing, bent over her skin, buzzing. Little goosebumps blew the little hairs on her skin straight up.

"Goddamn, fucking heat. Won't let up, eh?"

"I know," she said, loosely. "My mom's place doesn't have any AC, that's why I'm always here."

"Yeah? Was starting to think you two were lesbians or something," Joey said. He was much taller than she was, and when she talked to him she had to look up, and she liked that feeling of being immersed in a man's presence.

"You know we can hear you," she said, finally.

He passed the joint back to her.

"Hear what?"

They both looked at each other, and the air between them was thick.

"Your footsteps. When you walk. You walk really loud."

"I do, eh? Good thing my mom lives on the first floor."

Roxane nodded, and as she did, Joey touched her hair, pushed it back behind her ear.

"I don't usually think girls with tattoos are hot, but you are," he said. He folded the cartilage of her ear forward. "Got any back here?"

"I don't like it when they're too hidden. I like it when they show."

"What else do you like to show?" Joey stepped forward, and she felt his hot sour breath on her neck and shoulders, so unlike Julieta's, which was soft and tasteless.

"What are you doing?"

"What does it look like I'm doing?"

He buried his mouth into her neck, he licked, he pressed. Roxane shut her eyes, and she could see the letters that made up Julieta's name inside of her head, flashing like a neon sign, but her legs wouldn't budge.

He kissed her. The kiss was wide-open, full of spit. His tongue felt thick in her mouth. She couldn't tell if she kissed back, but she must have. She thought she must have been. There was comfort to something so gruesome as this. Her thoughts organized themselves effortlessly before her despite every one of his forceful gestures. He tugged on the string of her thong and grabbed for her pussy. His thumb rubbed it hard. She was wet. He groaned in smug satisfaction.

"You like that?" he asked.

He walked forward so that she had to walk backward, into the wall behind her, which was the door to his apartment. She felt his arms on either side of her, her boniness against him, his hand, which felt cold, against the heat of her.

"Wait," she said.

The door downstairs swung open and light rushed out onto the empty landing.

Roxane felt the breathing cut underneath her like with a sword. Joey breathed heavily against her. She waited for Julieta's eyes to wander up to her where she was now, this brute Neanderthal pressed up against her. He would stop if she saw them. He would have to stop, and she would have to explain herself.

Julieta grabbed the railing and looked below at the backyard then on the other side, towards the street. When she was finished, she turned around and went back inside.

Joey had gone back to licking her neck, her mouth.

"Wait."

"Why?" He pouted, as if a child.

"Fine."

She couldn't help it, in a way. Her pussy throbbed and he was strong and he smelled like sex. "Finish me off but then I have to go inside."

Joey's eyes were glassy. His breath was like whiskey.

"You're all the same," he said.

He rubbed her like she was made not of skin but something tougher, like rubber. It felt good in the way that pain can and then it only felt good, being rubbed like that. And as Roxane came, Joey covered her mouth with his hand and she felt that she was receding into some kind of vivid blackness, small and memory-like. Then the world moved into focus again and what hadn't seemed like her fault a moment ago now crushed her with the weight of her choice.

"I knew the moment I saw you you were a nasty girl," he said.

Roxane nodded meekly and said goodnight.

In bed, she folded herself over Julieta's body, which was warm and rigid and still for the remainder of the night.

If Julieta knew, she never said a word about it. The next time they had sex, Julieta was loud, the loudest she'd ever been, and afterward, Roxane asked if she loved her, and very soberly, Julieta said that she did.

"You say I don't understand you but you're just scared for me to. You're wary of intimacy," she said.

And the summer moved the way summers do: slowly at first, then the days tumbled together, gaining momentum. Julieta followed

Roxane to parties in her neighbourhood. They got drunk and smoked cigarettes on the balconies of strangers' apartments, talking about which classes Julieta should take in the fall, and what was Roxane going to do, and what did she want to become when she grew up anyway?

One night, after cabbing home from a party, the girls waited to hear Julieta's mother's snores through the wall before remembering that she'd picked up a night shift. Julieta took off her pants and top then fetched two glasses of water and set them on the coffee table.

"You know like 60 percent of the human body is made up of water?" she said, then she plopped her body on top of Roxanne's slim, bony one.

"Get off of me. It's hot."

"The AC is on."

They heard footsteps. Roxane felt this thud of a panic that what if Julieta's mother hadn't gone to work and found them here, half-naked? She floundered against Julieta.

"Oh my God, relax," Julieta said and slipped her hand up Roxane's jean skirt.

"Your mom. I can hear her. Julieta. Get off of me. Julieta."

Julieta was delicate in her own way, careful not to hurt Roxane as she struggled against her, and the footsteps carried up slowly.

"Julieta."

"Stop it. Let me."

"Why? Get off of me. What is wrong with you?"

"Roxane."

The footsteps moved up, past their feet, up their heads, to the top floor.

"Come on." Julieta still pressed. "Why do you never let me?" She had stuck her fingers up her girlfriend and into her, she kissed her neck—

Roxane thought that maybe she imagined these sensations flitting across the darkness of her body, black-orange and unwinding into near explosion. She wanted to scream, to cry. Instead she squirmed. She knew then that if she was powerless to this then she was powerless to everything. She moved like a boat without a motor, moaning then feeling the terror of this closeness, she screamed. Julieta fell backward.

A *tok* sound rang across the room as Julieta's head hit the coffee table, then she was sliding between it and the couch, her hunched back exposing thick rolls of fat on her belly.

Julieta looked up at Roxane with those innocent wide eyes, rubbing the back of her head with her still-wet fingers.

"Oh my God," Roxane said. She thought of Joey on the fire escape. She thought of her ex, and of all the ones before him, like a string of lights that burnt out as you went along, made a popping sound as they did.

The air conditioner switching back on made a made a long, low grumble.

"Juls?"

Julieta started to cry.

"Juls. I'm sorry."

Julieta's sobbing was hushed and jumbled. At times, no sound came out, only her shoulders bobbled then she would come up for air, a giant gasp, as if she'd been underwater and were only now just reemerging.

"I'm sorry, Juls. But you can't—I can't—we—"

Roxane wanted to shake her, tell her to stop.

"Never mind. We're just drunk." Julieta got up off the floor, grabbed her clothes and glass of water, and went to bed.

In the morning, the two girls sat on the landing and smoked cigarettes. Julieta rested her head on Roxane's warm bony shoulder. Upstairs they heard the door to Joey's back door opening, and with him was a girl who sounded not much older than they were. He was making fun of her.

"Sometimes I think if I never met you, I'd still be so dumb," Julieta said. She lifted her head and looked at Roxane, who stared back at her.

"I'm sorry," Roxane said.

In September, Julieta started school. A Pink Floyd poster of light refracting through a prism went up on her back door. She started to keep something she called an "ideas journal." Stacks of books filled the floor next to her bed and she switched to wearing glasses, started to decline drags of cigarettes. From a cool, restless distance, Roxane observed these changes with the sad, clairvoyant smile of a mother. By October, they were broken up.

Property of Neil

TÉA MUTONJI

1.

Spring 2012. My first week living alone has Neil written all over it. He was the first boy I had ever had in my bed. My bed which I mentally owned, which I came home to, night after night as an adult child, which had pillows and a comforter and a matching bedside table that I had paid for. The room and the bed went for $550 a month. It was a room in a house that was falling apart, but I didn't care because it was mine to fall apart in. The cockroaches were mine, the spider webs were mine, the sinkhole driveway was mine—even the sun that hit the window at exactly at 5 p.m. was mine. I always thought I would look back and remember everything as being mine. I left my mother's house believing that nothing in the world could ever hurt me again. Today, I try to hold on to this still. I say it a few times. I shut my eyes, I think of all the things that supposedly belonged to me, all the things that could never cut me, even if they tried—my kitchen, my frying pan, my toothbrush, my breast, my left ass cheek—and all I see is "property of Neil," written in big bold letters. I think of my life before Neil: I am twelve, I am fourteen, I am seventeen, neurotic because the world is round regardless of where you're standing. Now: I am nineteen, I am twenty-four, I will one day be one hundred. The world is squared. We lay down our elbows crushing the pavement, trying to get back up. All this because Neil was round, all this because Neil was squared, all this because Neil was everything I had ever wanted.

Scarborough was small. Everybody who lived here came from somewhere else. We all migrated to the same parks and the same bars and the same waterfront. This is what made it so special: nobody wanted to be alone, or everybody wanted to be alone but only metaphorically speaking. The bar down my street was the bar down everybody's street. And every night, some runaway woman-child found herself doing blow in the bathroom stall, giving an old man direction towards Kennedy Station, crying over a mountain of roadkill. Sometimes, that girl was me. I saw Neil my first night out. Thick brown hair, skin like a caramel cone, shoulders like a treehouse. I was in love with him like a matter of fact.

"If I didn't know any better, I'd think you were stalking me."

"What if I was?" I said, also as a matter of fact.

"What are you drinking? Gin? Vodka? You look like a whiskey girl. Firebomb whiskey. You've got that whole wild hair, hysteric mannerism thing going on."

"I like beer."

"All right, all right. I like a good curveball, let me look at you." Neil cupped my face, signalled the bartender for a pitcher, something light and slightly crisp. He led me through a crowd of old men and young men. Only a few women; many little girls. Everything felt sticky and delicate. The combination of sweat and alcohol and youth. We found his friends in a booth in the back room. They cheered when he walked in. He was a kind of a prophet. Everyone gathered to hear what he had to say. I didn't like beer. But he had a lumped belly, so I assumed he liked beer. I squeezed into the booth, glued to him by the hip, drinking the beer quickly, forcing it down my throat.

"Slow down, champ," he said, bringing me into a chokehold and keeping me there. "I haven't stopped thinking of you. I go to sleep and there you are. You have taken possession of my mind, woman. How are you settling? Where have you settled? Have you met Clay? That's my buddy, Clay."

I told him I hadn't to please him. He liked to be heard. He liked to bring people together, always for a celebration, always for the sake of being together. He was notorious for this. Clay I recognized from the week before when I was visiting the city and getting familiar with its people. Clay was somehow connected to everybody; he worked with at-risk kids, he volunteered at the youth homeless shelter, he sold blow for less than regular street price. In comparison, Neil was eerily beautiful. In that his beauty could terrify a woman, steal her from herself. He gave Clay a kiss on the cheek, then he leaned forward and gave me a kiss on the mouth. I decided that he was in love with me too.

"I was thinking about what you told me last time."

"About what?"

"That guy—what happened to you in high school."

"Oh."

"I just wanted to say that I feel for you." Neil pressed both thumbs on either side of my forehead, "You're strong and unstoppable—nothing and nobody can touch you. You're a wolf."

"Thanks."

"Say it."

"What?"

"You're a wolf. Say it. I'm a wolf."

"I'm a wolf?"

That night, we stretched on his bed. His bedroom was smaller than mine, furnished with a desk, a bed, and a miniature window. The floors were possibly carpeted and possibly hardwood. It was impossible to tell over all those books, and the clothes, and the towels he kept so perfectly spread. There was a wall covered with notes and letters he said he wrote. They were each folded in half and pinned shut. He had a map of Canada that hung over his bed. Little red dots to signal places he'd been, or places he thought of being, or just places. Neil told me he'd been in love once and that it was like being locked in a burning vehicle. He had a wonderful smile while he was remembering. He got naked in front of me as if putting on a show. As if undressing to show me what being in love had done to him. Underneath his left breast he had two large cuts. They might have been from skating, from getting bruised in the rink, but he ignored them and began jerking off. I kneeled in front of him and held him in my mouth. He drew a line on my head and took it from my scalp.

"Want some?"

"I'm all right."

"Are you sure? It's the good kind."

"Clay?"

"How did you know?"

"It's a small town."

"It will make you feel better."

I'm not entirely sure what vibes I must have given to suggest that I had not been better. If this was another story, I would tell you how we met: hotel party, downtown Toronto, lots of cocaine, cocaine on my forehead and cocaine on his midriff. Then, we kept bumping into each other like a thing of serendipity.

The next morning, I examined the tissue underneath his breast. Of course, we were up all night, avoiding the obvious questions, Where do you work? What did you study? Where do you see yourself in five years? But I learned that Neil was interested in writing, that he had learned to write by composing letters to his previous lover, the burning car lover, and had been interested in philosophy. "I think love is something you can physically feel, not necessarily from touching. We have these microreceptors that allow you to feel the love around. Right now, I can feel you hugging, I can feel you all over. Anyway, writing is like jerking off." I was standing in the room moisturizing my skin. "You can feel me from all the way there?" Neil dug his index finger into a baggy and stuck it up his nose. He walked over, dug in the bag, then, with that same finger, he dug into me.

He grabbed a contraception box from his dresser and threw it at me as I dressed. "Safety precaution."

"We used a condom."

"Plastic?"

"I'm on the pill."

"Yeah, but you're going to miss it today. When do you usually take it? In the morning? It's already evening." Neil walked over to me, put me in a second chokehold. "Come on, baby."

We lived down a long road from each other, Neil and I, and went walking to my place that evening after we had finished drinking. We saw a man stroking a tree with his arms. It was an odd sight, something like a vivid photograph that had been photoshopped, except it was actually happening. Then, a homeless man came out and showed us his fingers. I could tell he was homeless because he smelled like grass covered in piss. Neil reached out to him, said, "Ted, fucking eh, my man." Reached in his pockets and took out three cigarettes. We had spent the night fucking, then dancing, then snorting. Now we were smoking with a homeless man. He was sticking his tongue out at us.

"People get hungry and eat their own fingers," he said. "Look at this, look at this—see that? All fingers. I got all my fingers. Neil brings around sweet things and doesn't starve. Who's this? Lady with fingers."

Neil wrapped his free hand around my neck. If I had choked and died at that very moment, I would have died happy. "My girl," he said, giving Ted the rest of his cigarettes. A $5 bill.

"Where's all your fucking money, man? Buy yourself something nice, eh."

I think I was once a weightless body surrounded by weightless bodies, a little push and I'd float. My mother said I am unusual, not what she had hoped for. Not a person that could belong to somebody else. Not hers, certainly not hers.

I saw Neil every night that first week. He sat on the edge of my bed. Asked to hear a poem. Nibbled on my ear. Told me that the world was open and that the world was like an apple pie. "Have you ever stuck your dick in an apple pie. I mean, if you had a dick, I mean." Around his friends, he would look at me from across the room and wink. Pet me on the forehead whenever I said something to impress them. He felt good. Everything about him felt good. He was kind of like a blank canvas. Every day with him was like starting over. I liked it because I needed a lot of starting over. I needed a new chance for all the ones I had blown up. My mother couldn't look at me anymore. I had done something. It didn't matter now—nothing mattered anymore. I was sticking my dick inside of an apple pie.

A month went by and I saw him less. Then, two months went by, and I saw him when he felt like seeing me. Then, three months. Every night was the same. He sat on the mattress, his belly squeamish on the bedspread. His shorts always hanging around his waist. He smelled like ice, though his skin was perpetually soft and pink from the booze or from the heat. He spoke hysterically about the puck and the skates, how his face smashed the glass seven times during the game, leaving a smooth finish on his left cheek. I had never been to any of his games, but he recounted them vividly. I'd sit in the corner of the room, or on the porch where we often sat after a long week, and imagine him, lost and slow. I heard he was great, unstoppable on the rink, but something about the way his fingers jazzed made me believe he was probably just messy. He said the impact always got him going and he needed me to relieve some stress. He stressed easily, since his convocation, since the divorce at home, since his dad began sleeping on the sofa. He'd beat himself off to regulate his serotonin levels. He'd tell me shit like this when we were sexting. Always I answered, "Neil, Neil, Neil," and he'd say, "Yeah, yeah, yeah." I'd nod and adjust myself to fit where he wanted me, between his leg in a doggy position, knees and arms bent, arched back, ass sticking out. I'd check his rolls to see if he had been hurt. A couple scratches underneath his nipple. A bruise on his neck. I'd press two fingers and he'd grab them, pop them in his mouth, and begin to chew. We were sweating. The air conditioning had been broken all spring, now the end of July, his chest hair glued to my breast.

On my birthday, he came and sang to me. He had a terrible singing voice. But he loved to sing. He poured liquor down my throat, stretched in his underwear, sang a dramatic lullaby. He sat up and cried about dying, said, "When I die, all the shit I have inside of me will boil and I'll explode. It will be a natural death." He talked and talked and talked. When he was done talking, he vomited. I heard him, I always heard him: I'd press my ear on the bathroom door, listening to his groaning. Getting a rush from it. I would help him brush his teeth and he would fall asleep on top of me. I was so happy I wanted to die. The thought wasn't an active or physical one. It was more of a pornographic thought. It stemmed from a place of internal stimulation. The more I thought about it, the more aroused I became. I went about my day and waited for Neil to show. When he did, I was certain I was coming closer to death, so I fucked him certain I would die. I would snort another lizard. I would be resurrected.

"Okay, baby, it's time."

Neil gave me the contraception pill and fell asleep. I flushed it down the toilet, took a sleeping pill instead. My bedroom walls had princess characters printed on them. The princesses looked like dinosaurs or pornstars or firemen. I took a third sleeping pill. Neil tossed awake, sticky from a dream. "Hemingway blew his head with a shotgun."

"Plath burnt her head in an oven."

"Fucked on blow."

"Neil, Neil, Neil."

"Do you miss your mom?"

"No."

In the morning, I woke up, and he was gone. I never saw him again. He might have gone back to his room on the second floor of his parents' house. That's where I believed he took me and kept me, ate pieces of me so as not to eat his own finger. I felt like something was missing. In search of me, I began walking around my house. Everything in it felt distant from what it was supposed to be. The fridge became a walk-in shower. I'd open it night after night to clean myself, stand in front of it and freeze because I was perpetually hot. I missed him. I stayed awake from missing him—drank a lot from missing him. I even saw Clay, sometimes for the street discount, most times in hopes he would transform into Neil and I could live another day. They both had split-open faces. In that, you could see inside of them by staring directly at their foreheads. I even considered fucking Clay to feel Neil inside of me—he was growing inside of me. I could feel him, doing somersaults in my belly. I looked everywhere, behind the park, at the bluffs, on Highland Creek—Scarborough had become larger overnight. When I looked up, I noticed the sky had disappeared too.

2.

Summer 2013. Maggie and I moved to a sizable apartment on Morningside and Military Trail. There was a large hole in the oven door, so we often ate cereal. We told stories of what might have happened for the oven glass to crack so largely. My favourite scenario: it gave birth to an explosive banana bread that broke through from the inside out. I like to think I was a banana bread who broke out of her mother's house. The faucet in the washroom didn't work, so we brushed our teeth in the kitchen sink. Maggie majored in psychology and neuroscience and said that I had matured emotionally since last spring. When we talked about moving in together, she offered to make our home alcohol-free, but I had gotten better at drinking and drinking had never been my problem.

Her boyfriend was this tall African god who spoke multiple languages. He fixed everything around the apartment except the open oven. It became symbolic of our friendship. When she couldn't sleep, she'd get in bed with me and I would hold her, I would rock her between my breasts and kiss her behind the ear. I had gotten better at sleeping, but sometimes I hurt myself in my sleep. We needed each other. Not in a way that was desperate or out of bounds or even sexual. It was realizing that loneliness was overwhelming, overtly fetishized, that people who craved it were most susceptible to internal organ failure. It was better to open yourself up to the world.

I worked a serving job that kept me in check. The job was demanding. The people were needy. I got exactly two minutes of solitude per day. It excited me, and it made me crumble. I kept busy by writing. I kept writing to not think. I wrote these long poems, wrote about a boy who moves his furniture every Sunday in accordance with the sunset. I once said to him, "Feng shui?" and he replied, "Sanity." I often thought of that boy's mother, but I didn't know why.

I took on a few passing lovers, but the walls of my inside had lost all sensation. Fucking felt like breathing. Breathing felt like nothing. You know you are breathing only because you're not dead. I once brought a lighter to my vagina to see if I'd feel anything. The doctor said it might be PTSD.

Maggie said it might be lack of arousal. "Maybe you're having a hard time relaxing. David does this thing before we have sex, he gives me a full back massage, we'll like, be together for an hour before we dive into foreplay. It's like pre-foreplay."

"That sounds like a lot of work. Should sex even be worth that much work? I mean, my introduction to it all was fucked up. I was doomed from the start. I don't remember ever even enjoying it. I remember wanting to, roleplaying myself too. The entire thing is literally overrated."

"You just haven't found the right guy for you—wait, are you doing girls now? You just haven't found the right human for you."

"Do you not watch porn?"

"What?"

"Porn is not what ruined sex. Romantic comedy ruined sex. Nicholas Sparks ruined it. I can absolutely promise you at no point do birds begin to chirp in the middle of sex. Fucking *Titanic*. Sex is literally disgusting and bloody and mostly painful. You don't get an accurate, authentic, organic representation of sex anywhere but in porn. Maybe also on HBO, but less so."

"The sex you're having is hardly considered sex. Do you even want to have sex with any of these people? I worry about you sometimes. That sounds really numbing."

"Was there porn in Shakespearean time? Romance, courtship, that entire thing was also fucked up back then. Porn's recent. Porn's like reality TV but scripted."

Maggie continued tossing the salad in our kitchenette. She cut slices of cucumbers with a lot of malice. I wondered if she had been suffering in silence. "I think David and I will get married. I think he'll propose after graduation."

"You should probably start watching porn to regulate your expectation of all of that."

"You need to go see a doctor." Maggie grabbed my hand, pressed it against hers. "I need my maid of honour to have a working vagina in case I need to pawn you off to one of David's brothers, who are all rich and handsome and probably African royalty."

"I did see a doctor. My vagina's perfect. All psychological."

Everybody outside of our apartment seemed broken. If not broken, poor. You could tell from the ashy elbows or cigarette teeth. Now, loneliness felt foreign. Like something I had to actively reach out for. That's the problem with solitude, I thought, as I was giving myself a time-out, walking around the mall, having just finished drinking a bottle for the sake of drinking. You go out looking for a place to be alone and you find crowded malls and crowded parking lots and movie theatres and resto-bars. You stay home to be alone but you find furniture, casseroles with people's name written on them, televisions, books, magazines. You get so beaten up and that's when it happens. Solitude is that emotional response to the lack thereof. Not a physical space or an abstract thought. You gotta stop looking for it to fall into it. Romance, sex, destruction. I liked drinking by myself. I liked being in a public space having just drunk my water weight. I was fine like this—I was in my head like this. I looked up and Neil was standing in front of me, his thick brown hair, thick as ever—his mouth madly trembling.

"My, my, my," he says, "my, my, my."

Now I'm thinking I'm drunk and hallucinating, that the world is spinning, that my head has just been cracked open, "Neil?"

"My girl," he says.

"You're drunk."

"My girl," he says.

Neil had friends. He had people who loved him. They grouped around us, cheering him on, or I was in such a state, I felt like an animal getting eaten alive by a pack of stupid wolves. Then, I had been airlifted by a pack of wolves and went bar to bar until none of us had anything to show for it. Until Neil, who had a weak stomach and a large throat, began to vomit on the sidewalk, and then vomit in the parking garage. I had forgotten how bad he was at drinking, how much blow he needed to stay wired, how much discipline he lacked.

Now we were in the backseat of somebody's car, Neil and I, and he pulled a bottle of wine from somewhere, which terrified me, so I reached for the bottle and I drank most of it because I instantly remembered who he was. Then, all I felt was fear. I couldn't remember where the fear came from, but I flinched when he offered himself to me. I tried to remember being terrified of him, but all that I remember was saying his name repeatedly to anchor myself back to reality, Neil, Neil, Neil.

The car stopped, and he pulled me out on the street. We were alone underneath the moon, and I felt actual solitude for the first time. It was equivalent to getting your blood sucked out of your veins, like a fatigue that was nauseating, like feeling the wind blow through your body, feeling it fuck you from your belly and coming out of your back dimples, feeling the air pass through, knowing that there is a hole in the centre of you, a sick solitude, like you could die from being alone.

I could tell we were on his street. I recognized the elementary school and the cracked trees. The way he held on to me terrified me.

But it wasn't the holding that held me in place. It was the fear that if he let go, I would be overcome by vertigo, and I wouldn't wake up from it. He began to kiss me, and I pulled him towards his house. He lifted me slightly, then, my back was pressed on a wall. He was going for my neck. He was going for my breast.

"Why can't we just go back to your place?"

He pressed his mouth to my nose and began to suck on it.

"Do you fantasize about fucking on a school ground?"

I couldn't get a word out of him, so I let him fuck me. It was conveniently warm that night, sticky. While he was inside of me, I began to miss him. He had been tender. He had been electric. I was in so much pain I began to hurl. Then, I became afraid hurling would hurt his feelings, so I began to moan. When I was moaning, I could tell he liked it, so I began to laugh. I laughed until it was over.

Back at his place, we stretched out on his bed and I sang him to sleep. "Happy birthday to you, happy birthday to you, happy birthday dear Neil, happy birthday to you."

The next morning, I asked him if he missed me, and he told me that he hadn't stopped thinking about me all year. I asked him if he ever loved me, and he said love was such a strange concept. I toured his bedroom to refamiliarize myself. The bed was now pushed on the side of the door. The desk now faced the window. The walls were still covered and pinned by the same letters.

"Is it over with Elizabeth now? I heard you guys got back together end of last summer."

"Love is such a strange concept," he said again. "I can drive you home. We just need to stop at Shoppers and get you Plan B. I didn't use a condom."

"If I take it—will you stay?"

"Yes."

Back at my place, I took the pill and he got in bed with me. That evening when I woke up, he was gone. Maggie and I cuddled on our living room floor, staring at the popcorn ceiling, saying nothing at all. There was a dark spot on the ceiling, like a dried puddle—with enough pressure, the ceiling could fall and drown us both.

"I think David's breaking up with me," Maggie said, fighting back a crack cry, gasping for breath. "He said he's feeling depressed, and he needs to work on himself."

The phone rang and it was Neil. It was early in the morning, late at night. A friend of his was on his way to pick me up. He needed to see me and it was urgent. I rolled over and kissed Maggie on the mouth. "Neil needs me," I said.

When we arrived, the house was empty. We went through the backyard, guided by the fire pit, smelling the wet grass. Neil's parents had installed a beautiful campfire last summer. We often sat around and drank, heard stories of growing up in a multicultural city, of Ted pissing on the tulips in the front porch. This August had been balmy and damp, full of pollen and moisture. I found Neil on the kitchen floor— his vomit spilled on the tiles. I wondered for a minute what it would feel like to lose him permanently. I felt a sense of relief, like coming out of a burning vehicle and only later realizing it was a burning vehicle.

"Neil? Neil? Neil?" I said, again and again, but all I got back was the echo of my own voice. I looked behind me and his friend was gone. It was just the two of us again. I reached for him, I pulled on his hair, I lifted his arm.

Neil tossed and rolled over, "What are you doing here?" he said, swinging his arms so hard—he got me on the nose. "Fuck you," he said. He rolled on top of me, bit on my ear. "Sorry," he said. We laid like this for a moment. After some time, ten minutes or so, he rolled on his side and kicked me in the stomach.

I thought about crying, but I had forgotten how. I imagined myself suffocating underneath a mountain of plywood. I imagined myself like a baby bird being driven over, like the roadkill on the streets, like those epic romance blue blues from the movies. But I laid there, next to him, thinking that if I died tonight, it would be an incredibly lonely way to go.

The friend came back and picked me up from the floor. He offered to drive me home, but I insisted on walking. I let myself out the back door. I walked up to the driveway and sat on the curb. When I moved out of my parent's house, all those months ago, I sat on the grass and hoped my mother would come after me. I waited for an hour—I waited until I knew for certain that nobody would come.

WunderHorse II

FAWN PARKER

My office was moved from the second floor to a split room by the front entrance of the factory. They said it was so I could be more readily available to offer my wealth of knowledge. You might not believe it but I was one of the best and most precise at WunderHorse II, despite my being moved and consoled. I had the steadiest hand in the factory and sometimes I even painted other employees' copyrights and years on their horses' bellies for them.

You also might not believe it because I didn't look the part. I didn't have anything eclectic going on with my clothing. But that's how us true professionals are; we don't always look the part. We don't hone the aesthetic component because we're busy honing our craft.

I painted the small plastic horses in such a way that I could have gained international recognition, if not for the WunderHorse II company name overshadowing the identities of its individual employees. When Gary Malkez from my same floor came to me and confessed he was having trouble with the gradient pattern on the dapple gray, I got him doing it in an afternoon.

That was the first day Gary Malkez kissed me, in my old office on the second floor with the paintbrush still in his hand. He held it behind his back like he was embarrassed and when he left the room it was still behind his back, all the way back to his office like a pair of crossed fingers.

Gary Malkez was something of a hero in my opinion. He had it rough growing up, as he was born in the middle of a lake. He floated up one day, a full-grown man, and now a buoy marks that place, marked

"Gary Malkez." He took the hardship of being born out in the middle of a lake and turned it into a talent. Now Gary Malkez was one of the best swimmers you'd ever meet.

Me and Gary Malkez did some fine work at the WunderHorse II factory. You would have been impressed had you snooped on us painting the small plastic horses. Though you would have found it nearly impossible to snoop due to the abnormally high level of security at the factory.

When the others' office doors were shut, me and Gary Malkez would paint our horses together and come up with made-up names for new horse breeds. Gary Malkez would joke that he would start painting them on the horses' bellies and wait for them to become integrated into normal horse-lovers' vocabulary. When I thought of a really funny one he would laugh for a long time and then kiss me.

I loved Gary Malkez. The women on the second floor of the factory didn't like me for loving him, but I didn't care. The women at the WunderHorse II factory didn't like the men at all. You should've seen their quips in the newsletter and their faces and their middle fingers in the photographs.

Sometimes I would ask Gary Malkez to tell me the story of his birth, at least what he remembered from it. He did such a good job telling it that most times I would start to cry, and then maybe once in a while Gary Malkez would start to cry, too. His tears came out not salty at all but like lake water. I would kiss his eyes, left and then right.

*

My new office was beside the office of the receptionist, Sarah. I should mention my name is also Sarah, but I am a painter of the small plastic horses. Sarah the receptionist was in charge of answering the telephone to let companies know when the small plastic horses were being shipped out and what colours were available and how many was the minimum amount and was there a discount if one were to buy a sufficient amount of the small plastic horses so long as they were all one colour? I liked Sarah the receptionist because she got to go through the returned shipments of small plastic horses and pick out all the defects, and if I asked her she would give them to me.

Me and Gary Malkez set up a shallow shelf in his office on the second floor and lined up my defect plastic horses all in a row, and labelled them with the funny new horse breeds. He gave me a spare key to his office so I could go in and see the defect horses whenever I wanted to.

One evening I stayed late and repainted a defective plastic horse sky blue and painted "Gary Malkez" on its belly. Gary Malkez had already gone home so I used my key to go into his office and put the sky blue horse on his shelf.

All of the defective plastic horses looked very beautiful up on the shallow shelf all in a row. One of them near the end was a palomino missing one of its front legs, which I had not seen before. I took Gary Malkez's mystery palomino and put it in my purse.

The next day I saw that Sarah the receptionist was in her office with the door open so I went in with the defect palomino and said, Please, please other Sara, tell me about this palomino horse. She refused to look at the horse but she told me Gary Malkez had kissed her.

I went back into my office and dropped the defect palomino out of the first-floor window. On my smoke break, instead of having a smoke, I went to the staff bathroom and made myself orgasm thinking about Gary Malkez kissing the Sarah who answers the phone.

I wrote Sarah a note that said thank you for all of the defective plastic horses, and slipped it under her office door.

I kept my mouth shut around Gary Malkez. I brought him more horses but I stopped painting them beautiful colours like the colour of the sky. When he saw the sky-blue defective plastic horse, he kissed me for a very long time.

Me and Sarah became good friends and it was easy because I'm nice and she's nice and we're both very pretty. She invited me over to hang out and we sat on her living room couch and put our hands in each others' pussies. She had a way of smoking a cigarette that didn't crinkle up her mouth, and when I pointed it out she said that it was on purpose.

When I got home I cut up my driver's licence and my library card and all of my pieces of paper and plastic that said Sarah, Sarah, Sarah.

Gary Malkez sent me an email while he was in his second-floor office and I was in my new office on the first floor. He attached a spreadsheet with all of our made-up new horse breeds and numbers from one to ten rating how good he thought they were.

I went up to visit Gary Malkez in his office and we laughed about the spreadsheet and then we kissed.

In the factory an alarm began to go off and the lights were flashing. The receptionist Sarah called up to Gary Malkez's office and told him that a pipe had burst and employees were evacuating the building. Gary Malkez felt upset thinking about all of that water and how it related to his miraculous birth in the middle of a lake.

I waited in Gary Malkez's office while everyone evacuated the building. I got up close and looked at the photographs on his walls, of different angles of Gary Malkez sitting at the desk in that very office. I opened the drawers in his filing cabinet and pulled out all the pages with handwriting. In his desk drawers he had notepads and journals and a photo album. I looked through all of Gary Malkez's documents one by one.

A woman came onto the second floor with a stack of plastic buckets and brought one to Gary Malkez's office. She said, Use these to catch the water. I followed her up and down the halls placing buckets down by leaks in the ceiling and then I went back to the first one that had half way filled up, and I brought it back to Gary Malkez's office.

I poured the water over Gary Malkez's documents and I felt like I'd eaten him and swallowed him up whole. I paged Sarah who wasn't in her office because she'd evacuated but I'd already swallowed her whole too, anyway. I'd made both Sarah and Gary Malkez cum and I'd read both of their diaries. I sat down like a three-headed monster at Gary Malkez's desk and gathered the sopping wet documents into a clump. Then I went to the shallow shelf with all of the defect plastic horses and I paired them up in twos so that they looked like they were kissing.

Portland, Oregon

CASEY PLETT

Life being what it is, one dreams not of
revenge. One just dreams. –Miriam Toews

A drienne smelled cat urine when she woke up, but because her building was freezing the smell was faint and diluted by icy air. *They didn't call,* she thought as soon as she woke. She'd been desperate for one of the girls to call. She wrapped herself in blankets and got up, shivered over to the window and drew back the cloth she used for a curtain. Pale sunlight lit the room. She stood on her tiptoes to get a better view. She lived in a basement apartment and the windows were small and near the ceiling. *Snow's gonna set in any day now,* she thought. *Then God, who knows how long it'll be till I see out of here again.* She heard a car chug-start outside, then the *shkkkt shkkkt* of an ice scraper on the windshield.

She drew the curtain and checked the answering machine on her nightstand to make sure she hadn't missed anything. Then she padded to the bathroom. There was a puddle of cat pee in the corner. She wiped it up and scrubbed the floor, then slipped on her flip-flops (the apartment had been her boyfriend's at first, and after multiple cleanings the bathtub was still gross) and ran water. When it was hot enough she threw her blankets in the corner.

When she got out and went back to the bedroom she checked her machine again. No messages, though she was also like, *What, dummy, like they'll need you to drive at seven in the morning?* She put on clothes and a scarf and combed her breaking hair. *Maybe I'll just do nothing today,* she thought. Yeah. It was her day off from her regular job anyway.

She washed the bathroom floor with Mr. Clean and then went to the kitchen and decided she'd have breakfast. She split an English muffin. The cat nudged her leg. She sighed. "La *la* la *la* la *la*," she said irritably in descending tones. "It would kill you for me to eat first, wouldn't it?" She reached under the sink and dumped a yogurt cup of food in his dish. He gave her a scornful look. "Yeah whatever," she mumbled. She was almost out of cat food. Fuck. Maybe tonight they'd call.

She took a two-pound jar of strawberry jelly from the fridge and leaned against the counter while the muffin toasted. The cat stopped crunching for a second, stared up at her, then went back to eating. He was a big cat. His fur was grey with rounded black stripes, and he had yellow eyes and an awkwardly large chin.

An ant crawled up the wall opposite her. She made a face and smudged it with a paper towel. They should be gone when it's this cold.

She rinsed a plate and pushed up on the toaster lever, then scooped on jelly and climbed into the green armchair in the living room. She was small and the chair was big and she could fit in it easily, curled under a throw rug. Her head made a divot in the chair's back. She really hoped one of the girls would call tonight. She adjusted the rug so it went up behind her and made a cushion.

She slipped back into the apartment around eight—when the woman had said they might call her again—and leaned her frame against the wall. When she stood upright, off-yellow paint flakes were on her coat. She took it off and shook them out and went into the kitchen to heat up soup. Soon she was back in her armchair.

The cat wandered over and lolled on her feet. He was deceptively large; he looked average-sized enough as he walked but when he sat on his haunches his weight spilled from his sides like pudding. He leapt on the armchair and squished in beside her and the armrest. He filled in the space like caulk. She stroked his head. "So I was a bitch this morning," she murmured.

"Slightly," he yawned. "I suppose I deserved it. I did pee on the floor."

"Yeah," she said flatly. "That was kind of gross. Were you drunk?"

He cleaned the back of his paw. He enunciated carefully, like a mid-century businessman. "Maybe. You *did* leave the lid down."

"Glenn, *please* go in the bathtub. I'll like that a lot more than you going on the floor."

"Fine. I won't do it again."

"Okay."

"Okay."

She blew on her bowl. "It's frosty in here. Hey! Will you be okay with the winter? Because I could get you a heater." She nodded to him and slurped. "I can do that."

"Not at all, Adrienne. You see, I'm a Norwegian Forest—"

"I *know* you're a Norwegian Forest, dude."

"Well. I just need you to understand. I don't wither easily."

She scratched under his chin. "Tough kitty. You're sure? You tell me. I want you to be comfortable here."

Glenn closed his eyes and sighed with a high pitch that sounded like a wheeze. "I will let you know if I am cold. I wouldn't suggest worrying about it, however."

She nodded quickly. Then she ate her soup rapidly and he fell asleep.

She tried to crane her neck to look at the phone in her room. She really wished they would call.

She gave Glenn a little kiss on the side. The black stripes on his fur grew when his body rose with his breathing.

She tried to get up without disturbing him but he woke up.

"Goddammit," he said.

She laughed. This always happened. "Whatever, man! Like you need more sleep." She put the kettle on. "Do you want some tea?"

"I've never had tea."

"It warms you up better than rye. You prefer rye, right? Isn't that what you like to drink? I keep forgetting, I'm sorry… I always think you like gin for some reason."

He came into the kitchen, leapt on the counter and then the fridge. "Piddle. And yes, that is what I prefer. And, actually, sure, I'll have tea. I've never had it."

"How'd you grow up without having tea? Weren't your owners all snobby?"

"My former humans drank Scotch and hot chocolate. Well, and rye. But not, in fact, tea."

"Mmm, my kind of family."

"No, absolutely not."

When the kettle went she put a teabag into a bowl and poured the water in. She was almost out of tea too. Goddammit. She went to check her machine just in case. Nothing. Fuck.

She sat on a chair in her room. Then she picked a pillow off the floor and hunched up with it on her knees. They'd told her what they'd pay per call and she'd counted on making that much soon, but if they didn't call her in the next couple days—

"Adrienne?" yelled Glenn. "This is far too hot. I can't drink it."

She came back to the kitchen and blew on his bowl a bit. "Here," she said, "cool-a-rific."

"Thank you." He tentatively lapped it up. "Heyyy, wowee." He lapped more and looked up. "This is remarkably tasty. Is all tea like this?"

She grinned and bobbed the bag in her mug. "Nope. There's thousands of different kinds, actually. This one would be called English Breakfast."

"English Breakfast?" Glenn kept his nose in the bowl. "Yes."

"Do the English really drink this for their breakfast?" He continued lapping, and she drifted to the window where snow had just begun to fall.

"I don't know, Glenn," she said absentmindedly, staring up through the glass where she could almost make out the flakes hitting the ground. "I really don't know."

The apartment door shutting woke Glenn up the next morning. That was disappointing. He liked seeing her off to work. Must've slept through her alarm. Oh well. He would be seeing more of her anyway, with winter coming.

He stretched up from her blanket and hopped to the ground. He sniffed a pair of underwear on the floor. Humans smelled interesting enough anyway, but there was always this faint tangy smell in her underwear he could never place. It made him think of honey and human underarms, but it wasn't quite those things either.

He went into the kitchen. She rarely forgot to feed him, and he appreciated that. His former humans forgot a lot.

His mother had only given him and his siblings one piece of advice, as she was cleaning them one morning. *Your humans have one job*, she said. *To give you food, every day. If they cannot do that right, leave. I am not sure you need to know much else.*

Those old humans had been shits. Still, it had taken him a while to get out of there.

He ate then looked for leftovers from her, but like usual she hadn't eaten breakfast. He couldn't understand that. She had food. He had no problem with humans as a rule—he enjoyed their company more than most cats, really—but it aggravated him how little they used their things.

In the bathroom he found the toilet lid down. He thought of peeing in the sink to make a point but went in the bathtub, which thankfully was dry.

Back in the bedroom, he saw that Adrienne had left her closet door open, and he padded over to look. He always wanted to see more of her clothes, but they were jammed in tight on the rack and they were sorted by colour so they all blended together. And daily she usually only wore a T-shirt and jeans and the same sweater when it was cool.

He stretched and returned to the bed. He padded over the flowered blanket and plopped himself against her pillow. The phone rang and no one left a message. Adrienne's sheets were a violent purple hue and the colour filled his vision when he closed his eyes.

When Adrienne got home that night she yelled, "It's freezing out!" and took her gloves off with her teeth and went to put the kettle on. "Glennnn!" she yelled. "Do you want hot chocolate?"

No answer. He was sleeping, she supposed. She got her tape deck and the tape with soothing pianos from the living room. When she played it, Glenn wandered in from her room and she brightened. "*Monsieur!*" she said. "*Cette soir, je faiserais un petit de lait du chocolat. Voulez-vous?*"

He stretched and scratched his neck with a hind leg. "I heard you when you said hot chocolate. As did the entire building. Far too sweet. Tea instead please."

She washed a bowl and laid it on the other side of the stove.

"That is strange music," he said. He jumped on the counter and sniffed the tape deck.

"It's Chopin."

He cocked his head at her.

"It's from a piece I played in high school."

"This is you!" he said in awe.

"No!" she laughed. "I just played it once. And then my boyfriend got me the tape. Of someone playing it better." She paused and thought to herself. "Huh. I'm glad I didn't take that the wrong way."

"Hmm." He went on top of the fridge and settled. "Why isn't he your boyfriend anymore?"

The kettle whistled. "*Him?* Oh I—it just didn't work. Sometimes these things don't work."

"No? How so."

"It just didn't."

"Did he not want to see you anymore? You do not talk about him much."

"I don't really like him, so no, I don't."

"And why's that?"

"I don't know, lots of reasons! This was like a year ago, man, give it a rest!"

His ears flattened. "Oh I'm sorry! I am very sorry."

She sighed and poured his tea. "Oh fuck. Don't, it's okay."

"I am really very sorry," he said earnestly.

"It's okay."

"I am so sorry."

She made her hot chocolate then bent in front of her fridge. He lapped at his tea.

"But what was he like?" he said.

She emerged with a Tupperware of beans. "Hmmm?"

"What was he like. That boy. Or what are boys like. I don't know."

She opened the beans and sniffed them. Then she took out cheese slices and peas and put water on for rice. "Well for one, he was young," she said. "Young as me. But he had very old skin, for some reason. His face was so rough. Sometimes I thought I was going to bleed when I kissed him."

"Huh." He lapped at his tea exactly once then said, "And was he fun?"

She set down the bowl she was about to wash. "You're trying to ask if the sex was good."

"Well, not necessarily. Though I am interested in that, yes."

"The sex was good. And he could be kind of a bastard. But yes, he was usually fun."

"So he was fun!"

"Yes, Glenn, he was fun."

"Okay!" He was excited. He liked discovering more about her life. "So. What I want to know then is: What does fun mean between you and a boy?"

She stared blankly at the fridge, rubbing her fingers on a bag. Then she smirked and added rice to the water. She washed the bowl and lined up two hot sauces. She finished her hot chocolate and put the kettle on again.

"God, would you just talk," he said disgustedly.

Her eyes flicked at him then back to the stove. Then she settled against the counter. "I used to tell a friend of mine: Girls always say boys are oblivious. You know. And they have the right idea. But they're wrong about the words. What boys are? Boys are innocent. Even if they've been through a lot, even if they're monsters." She opened another thing of hot chocolate. "Boys are more like—" She mumbled and trailed off. "They suspend things. Like in that moment there's only their dumb jokes. They're so fucking stupid. Nothing else matters except whatever, like... stupid thing they're interested in. My boyfriend from high school? One of my favourite things used to be going to watch his a cappella group practise. Like they were five guys in this kid's living room or whatever. I went to every single one, and they were so *bad*. I never told anyone I thought this, but they sounded so awful." She laughed and suddenly choked back a sob. "I can't believe I'm going to cry about this. They really couldn't sing for shit. And they would *argue*. About the stupidest things. But I loved watching them. I had so much fucking fun at their stupid fucking rehearsals. It's so dumb. I loved them." She rubbed her face and smiled at him. "It really was the dumbest thing. You know?"

"Hmm." Glenn studied her unblinkingly. "And yet you loved going there. That is certainly quite interesting indeed. Hmm."

She looked up and saw his lack of expression. An image of a particularly emotionless professor from her one semester suddenly drifted into her head.

She narrowed her eyes. "I suppose it is," she said. "Interesting."

She made her hot chocolate and stirred her rice.

"What was this particular boy's name?" Glenn asked.

"Rob," she said, not looking back at him.

"Well I suppose I don't get it. But tell me—" he started, but she just laughed and went to check her messages. She took her bra off and changed into pajama pants while listening to her sister vent about money. No calls. She sat down on the bed then got up almost immediately and went to the living room to put a movie in the VCR, and sullenly Glenn followed and waited for her to sit down.

The movie ended and she clicked the set off. "Glenn." He woke up. "Yes? What?"

"I'm sorry I'm waking you—"

"No problem," he yawned and stretched. "What is it?"

"Do you like your food?"

"It is not bad. I have, of course, eaten far worse."

"Okay," she murmured, "I'll buy you different stuff. Just if you want, I'll do that. Just if you ever decide."

"All right."

He licked himself for a few minutes then hopped down and licked her empty bowl. "Adrienne?" he said. No reply. "Adrienne?" Eventually he heard her snoring, softly, in short, irregular bursts. A streetlamp from outside was reflecting soft yellow light through the packed snow, onto Adrienne's head and her chair. She looked shiny and small, like a—fairy, that was the word for those things? Maybe it was something else. He hopped back up and burrowed his head in her side. "Okay then," he said sleepily. "I'll tell you tomorrow."

The phone rang hours later, around one, and Adrienne jerked and unballed herself—Glenn woke and yowled and ran into the kitchen before her feet hit the floor—and she said, "Yes oh God please," and bolted to the bedroom. "Hi?...Yes...Yes I can definitely drive...Six four seven. South Greenwood. Okay got it. I'll be there in twenty. Goodbye. Thank you!"

"You're driving somewhere?" Glenn yelled from on top of the fridge.

"Yeah!" she said. "Thank God!" She put on a bra and pants and a coat and boots and was out of the door. Glenn blinked and licked at his empty bowl.

When she got home as the sun was rising she rushed in without speaking, slept for two hours, then got up and went to work without feeding him.

He reminded her when she got home, and she apologized a ton and loaded up his bowl. Soon she got a call to go out and drive again. She didn't stay out as late and when she came back she made both of them some tea but didn't eat. She chatted with him for only a bit before going to bed.

"What is all this about?" he said crossly. "Where are you driving?"

"It's for an escort agency."

"What?" he said, lapping. "I don't know what that is."

"Prostitutes, Glenn," Adrienne sighed. He kept licking.

"You're not serious."

"Absolutely I am," she said, taking off her bra and throwing it in the direction of her room. "Oh hey, in cooler news, I was able to get you some rye."

A couple nights later she didn't go out at all but slept for ten hours. Then left again without feeding him.

"Adrienne," he said when she got in that night, "my food please."

"Oh, right. Fuck," she said in an exasperated voice. She dumped a cupful in his bowl. "I'm sorry. I know that's like—really not cool."

"No it's not," he said and began eating. "You won't let it happen again, I trust?"

"No. No. Promise."

"Thank you."

But the next night she left around three and didn't come back at all until the next evening. When Adrienne stumbled in he simply yowled, "*Adrienne! ADRIENNE!*"

"Fuck I'm sorry, I'm sorry!" she said. She rushed into the kitchen and poured the bag into his bowl until it overflowed then leaned against the fridge and blew on her hands. She pulled off her hat and gloves and dropped them on the floor. "I'm sorry. I'm sorry. There were all these calls and I had a morning shift and—" She moved to the bedroom. "I'm sorry, I'm a piece of shit, I'm sorry." Then she kicked off her boots in the hallway. She doubled back into the kitchen and took out three cheese slices, which she unwrapped and ate in succession.

She watched Glenn sink his head farther and farther into the bowl of food. She reached out and scratched his back. He kept eating.

She straightened up and finished eating and had a thought. "Hey!" she said. "Maybe I'll leave the bag out for you. Hey? Can I do that? Let's do that. That way you could even just eat whenever you wanted."

He stopped mid-crunch and blinked at her and said, "I'm sorry, *what?*"

"Yeah, you know," she said. "That way you don't have to wait for me to get up in the mornings either."

His insides bunched. "I never mind doing that," he said quietly.

"But see that way if I forget you're not going hungry." She took out some rye and swigged a bit, then poured out a saucer for him. "Like, doesn't that make sense? You shouldn't have to go hungry because I suck. Doesn't that just make sense?"

He swished his tail, which had become the size of a feather duster. "Why would you keep forgetting though?"

"Oh, I—" She bunched up the slice wrappers on the counter and made a gesture of helplessness with her hands. She was so tired. She put the wrappers in the garbage. She was so incredibly tired. She was already moving to the bedroom. "I don't mean to forget. But also like today, I couldn't come home…I'm just like, I just think it makes sense." Suddenly she was irritable. "What works. That's responsibility, right? What is going to work, what the results are!"

He didn't understand but also didn't really care. He leapt on top of the counter then the fridge and looked at her, coiled. "I'll overeat if you leave the bag out," he said desperately.

"Really?" She was taking her coat off now and tossing it with her hat and gloves on the floor. She reached for a little more of the rye. "You never ask me for more."

"I will," he said. "I will eat and eat and I won't have any control. I don't even like it." It was half a lie, and a rotten one, a shitty one, because though he did overeat sometimes, he wasn't actually worried about it being self-destructive or anything like that. His body was still quivering and his tail was still huge. "Please do not do this," he said. "Please. Just put food in my dish in the morning. It's not hard. Please. Please. Please. Don't do this."

Adrienne stopped and looked into his eyes. He blinked slowly.

She shuffled to him at the fridge, reached up and put a hand on his back, then on his ears, and scratched him lightly, then scratched under his chin. "I'm sorry," she said. "Know it's not an excuse but I'm sorry. I'll feed you like normal. Tomorrow. Promise." He purred and rubbed against her hand and she went into her bedroom, dropped her jeans, took off her bra, and got into bed. He lapped up the rye then joined her.

The phone rang almost right away. "No. No!" she said as she woke up. "*Nooo!*" And it came out like she was sobbing but she wasn't, really. "I'm so tired," she whispered to herself and threw back the blankets. "I'm so tired. I'm so tired." She picked up the phone. "Hey…Yes… Yes…I can drive again…The outskirts?" Glenn didn't hear her come home and he fell asleep at four.

*

This went on for a while. Adrienne would forget about him every few days and Glenn would be seething and on edge every morning when he checked his bowl. She apologized more and more each time and swore it wouldn't happen again, but it didn't really change. He tried to be patient. He knew she had started a second job, that humans weren't perfect, it didn't mean it would be this way forever. She tried to bring up leaving the bag out again, but he just hissed and that was enough.

And it wasn't all bad. Adrienne seemed less stressed, for one. Calmer. Even if there were nights they didn't really get to talk. And they did still have fun. When her calls were slow they got drunk late and watched *Keeping Up Appearances* and made dumb imitations.

"OHHH LORDIE," said Adrienne, "MY TEEVEE'S GOT ALL THE EXPLETIVES IN IT!"

"JOLLY BAD!" Glenn cackled, lapping at his saucer of rye and missing, "JOLLY BAD BAD BAD BAD!" lurching around and managing the pretty impressive feat of falling to the floor on his face.

*

"What are those?" Glenn asked one night. Adrienne was cleaning out her bag in the living room and had set a Ziploc baggie of pills on the coffee table.

"T3s."

"Hm?"

"I'm going to go to bed soon," she said. "If they call again, they can find someone else. I have to go to sleep." It was around four and she'd just gotten home after leaving at eleven. On the table she'd also put books, condoms, stray cigarettes, some twenties, Chapsticks, lighters, pennies, nail polish remover, pens, napkins, a small hand mirror, a notepad. She returned to her bag only the notepad, two pens, the condoms, the mirror, and the lighter. Glenn noticed that she was moving strangely, slowly.

She still hadn't fed him that day.

He sigh-wheezed.

"Could I have some food?" Glenn asked.

"Oh shit," Adrienne said. "Yeah. Yeah. Sorry." She moved up jerkily. She was so tired. She was so incredibly tired. She felt every part of her body clunking and straining. She moved to the kitchen in slow steps, bent in front of the cabinet to take out his food, dug in a yogurt cup, and instead of pouring it, placed it in the bowl. When he went over to look at it, only a third of the cup was filled. He turned around; she was closing her bag, leaving the extra things on the coffee table and heading into her room.

"Glenn," she said, "come with me."

"Hmmm?"

"Come with me."

He followed her to the bedroom and she undressed, pulling her bra out from under her shirt, unbuttoning and dropping her jeans in one motion, putting one knee on her bed then letting her weight fall on the whole thing. She put the blankets over herself and Glenn jumped on them.

She picked him up and placed him on her chest, then leaned forward and scratched him under the chin. She said, "Glenn. You're really..." She closed her eyes, like she was saying something difficult. "I am grateful. You are in my life." Her head nodded down. She was so tired. It felt like a slow but firm hand was pushing her whole body deeper into her bed. She focused on getting words out and making them sound like words. "But I. Am? Hurting you."

Glenn blinked at her and said, "Oh. Well. I. Perhaps sometimes. Hm?"

She leaned her head back onto her pillow, gently and gradually, then sent her hand to rub her forehead. Her skin was so dry the sound it made was rough and quiet, like a book moved along on a carpet. "I'll be better," she said. She laid her hands above her blanket on the side of her body, breathed in and out deeply, her head farther and farther in her pillow. He could see her gently sliding away, and she was feeling herself leaving, like the warmest, softest plastic wrap was going around her brain. She lifted her hands once more to stroke Glenn—this seemed to take forever—then she said, "Could you tell me something nice? Just tell me. Something nice. That's happened to you." She felt each of her fingers sink into the blanket then disengage from response. "That's something you could do. That I'd really like..."

Glenn blinked at her. He didn't know how to reply so he said, "Hmmm," to stall and blinked and waited for her to say more. He was only thinking *I asked you. And you didn't even give me a full cup.* She didn't say more and he turned around and went to eat.

*

One night, after another two days went by without her feeding him— she was hardly home during this time at all, actually—Glenn gave up and started pawing at the cabinet where his food was but he couldn't figure out how to open it. He butted it and clawed at every edge from top and below but he couldn't do it. He tried for a while.

In the sink there were some peas in the bottom of a soup bowl. He ate those and felt a little better, but then he hacked it all up on the carpet an hour later.

Glenn was right, though, that Adrienne was less stressed. In some ways. Money wasn't as much of a worry, for one, and thanks to a few of the girls she could always get someone to pick up for her. Adrienne was grateful for these things (and those T3s were nice). But she was disconnecting, feeling more and more removed from the world, never unsleepy, awakened multiple times a night. She knew she was neglecting Glenn, that not only was he angry about the food but he missed her being around—though, she thought, he always had booze now and *nice* food and it was always actually *in* the house—and at her day job too she felt the faces receding, speaking to her like water. She wasn't exactly un-okay with this—the work itself was boring and peaceful most of the time (most of the time). Though she did hate the sleep thing. More, she felt like she was watching herself drift farther and farther from the known world. She never turned down calls, except for that one night, which the woman who ran the agency hadn't been happy about. (She liked the girls better than the woman.) Adrienne knew they liked that she was so reliable. And not only was the money good but like—she felt some pride in that. So she was out almost every night, and she would drive home in wee hours from bungalow suburbs and mid-grade hotels back into her part of the city. Sometimes it wasn't quite morning yet, so the streets would be quiet, but sometimes she'd be out late enough to see people on the dawn shift straggling out of their buildings, with parkas and coffees, zipping up their kids' snowsuits and waiting at bus stops. And when she watched them it was like nothing had ever felt less real. She didn't feel sad per se when she saw them, just impossibly heavy, unmoored. Like they were lives she was watching from far away and had been familiar with long ago.

When she came in that night, around four-thirty, having taken the last of her T3s an hour before, she swayed and zagged to her bedroom, losing her hat and gloves and coat to the floor on the way and not really hearing Glenn's mewing or yelling or noticing the vomit, shovelling food in his bowl zombie-like and only stooping to scratch him once before putting a knee on her bed and muttering, "I fell asleep in my fucking car."

*

The next day around eight he woke up as she was showering, but he pretended to sleep. He listened for the sound of the yogurt cup. When it didn't come and the front door slammed, he went to the kitchen and found her dishes unwashed and—

Okay. There was more food. He just didn't hear her.

Phew. She had cleaned up his vomit too.

After eating he went to the bathroom and found the lid down. He hissed at the bowl, which he knew was silly, but it made him feel better. He sighed. The bathtub would still be wet from her shower. He went back to the kitchen and leapt on top of the fridge. He gave a single lap at the tea bowl from a few nights ago. He wondered if she would remember him tomorrow. It really made him bonkers sometimes, not knowing. Perhaps he should have saved the food—

No.

What he should do, he thought, was go. He should just leave. He could bolt through the front door before she knew what was happening. He could do the same in the lobby. Winter'd be over soon. He could just go.

He swatted the bowl and knocked it onto the floor. A piece broke off.

The phone rang. He paused, considered, then wheeze-sighed and leapt down and went to the bedroom. The phone was on her dresser. It kept ringing. He jumped on the dresser and tried to gently turn the receiver over. God, he hated this noise. He pushed it once and it didn't budge. It kept ringing. He pushed it harder but his paw just slipped over the top.

He tried to lift it up from the bottom but it was too heavy with just one paw. Then he put lifting pressure from the bottom and butted it with his head, and the receiver turned over onto the body of the phone then slid off and over the side of the dresser, where it bounced suspended about a foot off the floor.

"Hello?" came a woman's voice. "Hello?"

Glenn leapt to the floor and got close to the receiver. "Hello?" he said. "This would be Glenn?"

"What?" said the woman. "I can't hear you."

"*HELLO?*" he said again.

"*WHAT?* I don't understand."

"*HELLO?*"

"I can't hear you—where's Adrienne? Can she drive?"

"No!" he tried.

"I can't understand you. You don't even sound like a hum—okay never mind." She hung up.

He blinked at the receiver until the dial tone turned into the alarm-drone sound of a phone off the hook. Then he jumped onto the floor and peed on a pile of clothes.

*

It was later that night, around three, that Adrienne came in and bolted a glass of orange juice and looked around the apartment. Glenn didn't seem to be around. Strangely she wasn't tired. She wasn't hungry either; she'd just eaten. She wished she had something to drink, but they'd run out last night and she'd forgotten to get someone to pick up for her. Or get some pot. Shrooms? Maybe. Glenn had drunk the last of the booze too. She put the juice glass in the sink then saw she'd left the front door open a crack. Oh Jesus. She shut the door and locked it.

She went to her bedroom and put most of her money away. She called the one dealer she had a number for. No answer. She smelled the pee on the clothes pile and thought, *Goddammit, Glenn*, and sprayed them with Febreze and threw the pile in the laundry. She tried the dealer again, no answer.

"You know what I don't get," Glenn's voice came from behind her, "is how you can hardly afford rent but you have no problem paying what must be an enormous phone bill."

She wheeled around in surprise. "Glenn!" She picked him up and rocked him in her arms. "Crazy kitty, were you there the whole time?"

He wriggled out of her hands and landed soundlessly on the floor. "You still haven't answered my question. How can you pay for the phone?"

"That's getting better now!" She bent down and scratched under his chin. "You never answered my question," she accused lovingly.

"I was sleeping and then you woke me up, so now I am here. I am also extremely hungry, if you don't mind feeding me again tonight."

"Yeah sure, no problem, of course," she rushed to the kitchen, and then she remembered: They'd run out of cat food this morning. "Shit. I didn't get you..." She trailed off and put her hands on the edge of the counter. She pressed onto it as hard as she could. She pressed hard enough that purple ridges appeared in her palms when she stopped. Okay. Whatever. She'd go to the store now. She'd go to the store and buy a huge bag. She would do it right now. She threw on her coat and said, "I'm going to Safeway! Coming back with food for days!" She yelled it as if Glenn were in another room. She pulled her boots on, and then she had an idea. "Ooh, I'll get some cough syrup too. Yeah. That's what I'll do." Glenn's eyes bugged slightly.

"Cough syrup?" he said. "What are you going to do with cough syrup?"

"You'll see! I'll be back in a bit!" Glenn turned and slunk into the kitchen and she left. She went up the steps to the lobby and was slammed with cold air and snow as she went outside. She retied her scarf and walked faster to her car.

∗

"Are you sure you are okay?" he said. His glowing eyes zoomed down on her from far away.

"Yeah man..." she said from the floor. "I'll be fine. I'm safe. It just feels so nice down here."

She had been lying there for a long time. He hated taking care of her. It didn't feel natural. He went over to his food bowl and said nothing.

"Fuck off, man!" she said. "I don't get mad at you, Glenn. Do I?"

His tail swished. She sat up to face him, which spurred a churn of nausea. She lay back down and said, "Noooooooo!" to the ceiling.

Then she said, "Okay so I want to talk. We should always be talking? Right? Like I'm thinking about you drinking and your family. Why did you leave that family? I feed you shit and this apartment is small, ha, I'm small. I'm cold. I'm in debt. I am an ower. Hahaha that means I don't own."

She stuttered for a bit and then said, "You do not make sense!"

"Oh I don't make sense."

"I'm sorry," she said.

"I'm sorry."

"It's okay. Goddammit!"

"What! What!"

"I wish I could know," she said, pointing at the moulding on the wall. "I never know when they'll call. I never sleep. I don't know what will happen. And sometimes the guys, they—there's this one girl I worry about so much, she—nope nope we are not going to, never mind. I never sleep. I always worry. I just never know. My goddamn car. I don't even need it to go to work." She slapped the floorboards hard. "Day work," she corrected.

"Here is a thought," he said. "You could sell it!"

"I couldn't visit my family then," she said plainly. "They don't even run Grey Gooses out there anymore. Fuck Grey Gooses."

"See, I find that curious," he said immediately. "Because I must say, you don't speak about your family very positively."

"My parents are bastards. I love my brother and sister. Fuck, I have to call her back."

"Hm." Oh! Glenn had a thought. "You wouldn't drive now, would you?"

"No. They probably wouldn't call me? Now? Though? It's very late."

"That job really does sound so interesting."

"It's really not and I want to talk about it except no." She dragged her fingertips up along the floorboards then put them on her face.

"I just get curious. I'm not trying to judge. I'm just curious."

"No," she said beneath her hands.

"It is nothing salacious or anything!" he said. "I promise."

"Mmmm."

He hesitated then said, "I'm just so curious as to what the escorts are like. What kind of people are they? Where do they come from? What would make them do this?"

Her face went dark. She sat up and panned her head side to side, like she needed to see him from every angle. "Glenn," she said. "Maybe you don't need to hear every detail about all the sensational things you've found."

"I'm just curious. Like I said, I'm not going to judge. I just want to know."

She looked at him darkly again, and she said, "Oh yeah?" Then she hit her hand on the floor once, twice, three, four times. "Oh *sooooo interesting!*" she said. "You're just cuuuuurious! You like stories, huhhh?"

"Don't you?" he said. "I remember you mentioned wanting to be a writer at some point, yes? Maybe this will inspire you?" He was trying to be helpful.

"Inspire me!" she said. She had that way of laughing and yelling at the same time. She lifted her head up and pointed a finger at him. She tried to talk but kept stopping. She made little starts of sentences that sounded like quasi-burps. "I'm sorry, I don't like that," she finally said.

His ears had flattened. "Well!" he said. "You talked about wanting to be a writer once! That would be all I meant."

"Heeeeeeere," she said. "You can have allllll of my stories." She bunched her hair up by her head and drew a circle on the side of her scalp. "Here you go. Everything that's happened to me *and* everything I've ever heard. But hahaha it's you, like, *you* ever open up about *shit!* I—" She hiccupped and looked at Glenn in the face, goggle-mouthed, like something new about him was dawning on her. "*Wow, fuck you!*" she said breathlessly.

She crawled to her bedroom then up into her bed, and pulled over the covers.

"Why am I here?" she said. "I'm so cold. I'm always so cold. I just want to be warm. I would give—" She snorted and chunks of mucus came out and glistened on her skin. "Guhh I'm sorry!" she called out. Glenn padded in and said, "Oh you're *sorry,* are you?"

Adrienne rolled over and fell on the floor. "Fuck," she said, "this is stupid," and Glenn coldly said, "Think, perhaps, about what is stupid," then immediately nuzzled her foot. Adrienne said, "Glenn, this is stupid." And Glenn said, "Adrienne, come on." He tried to nuzzle her neck and accidentally inhaled the awful syrup smell still on her lips. "Adrienne," he said. "Come on. Get into bed. You'll feel better in the morning." She laughed and hit the floor again. His tail bushed and his hair stood up and he said, "Adrienne I will leave you alone if you get into bed! Get into bed!!" She said, "You really mean that?"

She got up and into bed and he lay down on her stomach. When the phone rang she said, "NO!" without really meaning to and it sounded like a sob again, like no, please, please don't make me do this. But she picked up anyway and the woman answered and Adrienne said: "Hi. Oh…no.…oh no I'm so sorry I can't drive, I drank this…I…okay I'm sorry, no I know you can't keep having—" Then there was a dial tone and she looked at the receiver until the alarm-drone sounded. She spasmed and screamed and the phone squibbed out of her hand. She stared at the ceiling and couldn't cry. She made dry choking guttural sounds from her throat. Glenn ignored them and fell asleep. She watched the faint outline of his body go up and down. Then back to the ceiling. The room was rotating slowly, subtly around her bed like it was trying not to be noticed, and Glenn looked so small. It was like he was shrinking, like she could reach out and clutch his whole body with her hands.

*

Glenn woke up before she did for once, around ten, when the sun had been fully up for an hour and the light was fully poking through the snow to the room. He went to pee then checked around the apartment. Nothing was out of place except that her hoodie and coat were bunched up against the front door; other than that, normal. That was good. Once, she'd taken mushrooms and emptied all of the drawers onto the floor. Organizing, she'd said.

He went on top of the fridge and lapped at a few drops of cold tea that were still in the bowl. He looked out the window and the new inches of snow on the ground.

He felt bad about badgering her last night. He felt bad about a lot of things he'd asked about her life since he'd known her, about her past with boys, her job as a driver, dropping out of school, her parents' marriage. He just never paid attention to how she was reacting to him until it was too late. He got caught up. He really was just ferociously curious. And he did want to know everything about her. He loved her, she was his best friend, and she took care of him—she would get better about feeding him, of course she would, she was a good human, good humans fed their cats—and she was almost never mad at him, not even when it came to stuff like the piss and the vomit and the broken bowl. And she had had such a turvy, fascinating life over her twenty years. (Was she twenty? Around there anyway.) He was five, and he'd never see what she had, even if he made it to the age she was now.

Sometimes that bothered him. He realized, looking out the window at the wooden fire escape on the building across the way, that he had to explicitly admit that to himself. And that it was his deal to work on, not hers. Something about her life made him feel bad and insecure about himself. His world was mostly this apartment, and, well, as long as Adrienne was here, that was how it would probably stay. After he'd left his old humans last summer, he'd lived on the street for only two weeks before Adrienne had taken him in, and while nothing too terrible had happened besides awful food and a couple small fights, he'd been terrified enough during that time that he knew he wouldn't be much with the venturing again. It just wasn't for him, not with the safety and love he had here. Irresponsible, erratic, off-the-deep-end as Adrienne could be. He did love her, and he knew she loved him. He wanted to stay. He did. And he wanted to know all about her and her life, her world. He didn't want to be her, no, but he did want to be strong like her, funny like her, alive like her. Know what she knew, see what she'd seen. And he hadn't understood how those desires were not only impossible but also, well, kind of bad. But he knew now, he knew he needed to leave some things alone. He knew he wasn't always the greatest friend. He knew it didn't come naturally to think about what she was feeling. He didn't understand how she worked, how girls worked, humans worked.

He was trying to figure this out. He wanted to be better. He wanted to stop making her feel bad without realizing it. He wanted to stop thinking her world was tragically glamorous when in reality she was just usually in pain. He wanted to not break shit and pee on stuff when he was angry. He wanted to be less insecure around her, and he wanted to deal with that on his own without mucking her up in his bullshit in the process. He wanted to be good to her, on her terms. He wanted her to feel better. He wanted to be a good friend. He wanted to try.

*

She woke up sweaty. She had slept clothed under the blankets and now the sunlight from the window was baking her. She remembered the phone call. Fuck.

It was one o'clock. She had an evening shift in a couple hours. Well that wasn't so bad. She'd call the agency tonight too and apologize, say she'd had a bad night but was ready to work again.

She rubbed her eyes and breathed. Went to take a long shower. Put on some mascara when she came out. She dried and straightened her hair. She had so much breakage it was light-socket-frizzy. *Conditioner*, she thought. *I need to buy conditioner today.* She put on her jeans, a shirt, and a sweater. Brushed her teeth, went to the kitchen to feed Glenn and toast an English muffin. She made some coffee too.

"Hey there," she mumbled when he walked in.

"Oh hello," he said. He looked up once at her and swished his tail. Then he dove at his food.

"Sorry about last night," she said.

"No no, it is okay," he said. "It really is okay."

She drank a glass of water then went into her armchair. Glenn leapt up and squished beside her. She should really have more people over in here, she thought as she ate. Maybe her friend Tina from work. "How'd you feel about me having a girlfriend over here tomorrow?" she said. "Be nice if we had some company, huh? What do you think?"

"Oh, well yes, that would be nice!" he said. "And of course, if you would like some privacy or such I can gladly scamper away, that's just no problem."

"Oh no!" she said. "No, no, I'd want you here! Thank you, though. Thanks for offering that. I might take you up on that. Some point."

She scratched under his chin and he purred. "Of course," he said. She finished her food and he climbed onto her lap. He closed his eyes and let out a sigh-wheeze.

"Adrienne?" Glenn said.

"That's me."

"We can try leaving the bag out. We could perhaps give it a try and we could see how it goes."

She looked at him. He had opened his eyes. He was staring straight ahead at the wall, and his usually Zen face was heavy and sad. She leaned over and put her forehead on his. Her hair made a curtain around his head. She was silent for a while, and then she said, "I'm sorry."

He turned his face up and licked her cheek. "It's okay." He thought: *Sometimes mothers are wrong.*

The coffee burbled and she made to get up. He leapt down to the floor. At the sight of her back leg straightening and going upright, he suddenly had a memory.

"Oh say," he said, following her. "I am sorry if this is not an okay question, please tell me if it isn't. But whatever happened to that one friend of yours? The one with the, er, tattoos. I think she worked in an old folks' home?"

"Tracy," she said. She looked up at the window and saw the building across the way. "Hey, they cleared the snow on this side." Then she smiled and took out some cream. "That's an okay question."

"Oh good," he said. "Yes. Tracy. I liked her."

"Me too," she said dreamily, stirring her coffee. "You know what we used to do? This is before you came along. We used to put soap in the fountains at night. We weren't even drunk, it was just like, something to do. Hey? One night we walked like thirty blocks from downtown to her place. In the summer. It was beautiful. She was such a good musician, too. She had one of those velvety voices, y'know? Did you ever hear her sing?"

"Yes," he said. He closed his eyes and yawned. "I definitely thought it was nice as well. It sounds like you miss her? If I'm correct in that?"

"Yeah. God, she could charm the horns off a bull with that voice," she said. He was still on the floor, and she sat down opposite him, her ass on the linoleum, under the window. "And ambition," she said, sipping from her mug. "For all her wildness, like, that girl had gleams, like, *conquest* in her eye. I always thought she'd be on TV by now. Or at least in a music video or something."

He had questions, but he decided to listen.

There was a little silence before she spoke again. "What happened to her," Adrienne said. "She moved to Portland, Oregon. Isn't that funny? Of all the places."

"Oh hm," he said. He padded over to her and curled in her lap. "Is that strange then? Well, I am sorry she's gone." "Yeah," she said. "She was a ball. I get a letter from her every few months. She's always complaining I haven't gotten on email yet. But I guess she's doing well for herself out there."

She drank her coffee, and she petted her cat.

She set the half-full mug down on the linoleum.

She had to go to work soon.

The wind got strong outside. It was snowing again. She noticed for the first time that the wind had two sounds to it, a whistle and a blow. The whistling rapped and seeped through the window and sounded closer; the blowing stronger but farther away. "I really do hope I see her all famous someday," she said. "I should write her again soon."

Adrienne sighed and leaned her head on the wall. Her eyes fell on cracks in the ceiling that intertwined and looked like diamonds. She drank her coffee. Glenn was starting to fall asleep.

She massaged his fur. She felt unforgiven, needy. Not weak or bad but—unspecial. She saw herself here, in her apartment, the two of them growing, in summers and winters, looking up together to the ground.

She bent down and kissed her cat. She had to go to work soon. She had to get tea and conditioner on the way home.

Girls Who Come in Threes

RUDRAPRIYA RATHORE

Kitty had learned how to step out of her skin. That was how she understood it, anyway, when she lay flat on the faded green sofa in the afternoons, legs and arms spread out so they wouldn't touch and stick. The hot blood in her head felt like it was expanding into the dead air of the living room. With every inhale, she filled the space around her, until she felt the paisley-papered walls pressing in, and then she let herself drift into the other rooms like a fog, staying up near the ceiling so she could examine the cobwebs. The drone of the refrigerator or the neighbour's lawnmower throbbed through her as if they were the motor keeping her aloft.

Looking down at the hallway carpet was nothing special, but when she got to her mother's room, all kinds of things became visible. A condom, wrinkled up like a dried tadpole at the bottom of a paper cup and stuffed behind the dresser. Little butterfly hairclips on the bedside table, next to the pincushion stuck through with earrings. The clay figurine that looked halfway between a fox and a cat, hand-painted by Kitty in the fifth grade, tipped onto its side on the windowsill. She bobbed around, making note of where everything was and what it looked like. When she descended, she did so slowly. The threads of the netted canopy tickled her as she passed through on her way down to the bed, and by the time she touched the white expanse of sheets, she felt herself all crumbled into particles. She'd nap there, and if there was time afterward, run her hands back and forth through the clothes hanging in the closet, which smelled of perfume and the star anise pods that her mother used instead of mothballs.

"Does it work every single time?" Miranda, her only real friend in the world, displayed the clinical skepticism she felt about everything she hadn't accomplished herself. The day blazed around the two girls as they jaywalked across the empty street into High Park.

"Whenever my mom's not home," Kitty replied. "When she's there I can't focus hard enough."

"Can you, you know, make stuff happen with it?" Miranda kicked a pebble into swaths of burnt yellow park grass. A scene from Roald Dahl's *Matilda* played out in front of Kitty's eyes, the little girl concentrating on moving various objects with her eyes as her pretty teacher watched in awe.

"It's not about making stuff happen. It's spiritual."

"Okay, but if you could make stuff happen, what would you do?" Miranda pressed her.

"I don't know." Kitty batted at a cloud of mosquitoes. "I've always wanted to be able to turn into something else. A shapeshifter, sort of." At this, Miranda rolled her eyes. "Or maybe I'd make things disappear," Kitty said hurriedly. "And reappear. People who annoyed me. Like my mom."

Kitty's mother often moved like she was skating, letting the bottoms of her socks slide against the kitchen laminate. Or she travelled from room to room with a sheet wrapped around her shoulders and trailing behind. She holed up in the corner of her bedroom, or wore purple lipstick on the balcony and smoked a cigar she'd stolen from her boyfriend, Ashok, or spoke only in a Southern drawl all day. It depended on what she'd been watching on the television and on what mood she was in. She was what Nani, Kitty's grandmother, called "impressionable," and what other relatives, most of whom Kitty met only once or twice a year, called "loose."

When she came over, Miranda moved from armchair to armchair as the vacuum chased her, pushed by Kitty's mom in hair rollers and a silk robe. "*Attention,*" Kitty's mother squealed in French, and Miranda threw her head back and laughed and said she looked like Brigitte Bardot.

During those moments, Kitty sighed into one of the *Cosmopolitan* magazines her mother kept on the coffee table and said nothing. Miranda had never seen Kitty's mother's other moods, the quiet and scary ones that were reserved only for Kitty and her grandmother. If she'd had the confidence, she would have said, "Miranda, stop acting like she's a normal mom when you know she is the bane of my existence." It was a real desire of hers to say that, to say "the bane of my existence."

Now, Miranda said, "She seems fun to me."

"She's just unpredictable. That's not the same thing."

They sprawled across a shaded bench in an attempt to cool down. Both were starting ninth grade at the high school on the next block in two weeks. In anticipation, Kitty had emailed the two quiet acquaintances she'd sometimes eaten lunch with in middle school when Miranda ran off with other friends. *Are you in homeroom 9C with me? xoxo Kitty Minhaj.* Maybe because Sarah and Emily sat with her only out of obligation, or because their lack of personality prevented them from being actively mean to Kitty, neither girl had replied.

"And she's pretty. Moms are almost never that pretty."

Kitty pinched her thighs below the hem of her denim shorts. It was true that her mother was beautiful, her pointed chin and big eyes a match for the women her grandmother watched on Hindi channels at night.

"Some of the Bollywood moms are really pretty. When they're still young. My mom's much darker than those women, though." Kitty repeated this fondly, having heard Nani say something similar while warning against too much sun. "Anyway, there's nothing special about having a proportionate face." Miranda furrowed her eyebrows at this, as if to gesture to Kitty's own round cheeks. "Not to say I'm any better, obviously. I'm just lighter, 'cause of my dad."

"I mean, you're cute."

Kitty heard a familiar tone of obligation, but she appreciated it anyway. Miranda was far closer to a thing boys and teachers might call "cute," her pouty lips and reddish hair easily offsetting a pimply too-wide forehead. And though they were about the same height, Miranda was round in the right places, small-waisted and busty instead of childishly pot-bellied. Placed side by side, Kitty was not the prettier girl—not quite ugly, but certainly not pretty. In some ways, this set the balance of their friendship, because Kitty knew she was smarter.

She knew it when she was flipping through her journal, touching all the full pages, or composing her "Notes to Future Self" blog. She knew it when she finished reading a novel and all its possible meanings flashed spontaneously into place. She especially knew it when she felt her thoughts circling and wondered whether *they* created *her* instead of the other way around.

While imagining the new high school's crowded cafeteria at lunch-time, though, she had the sinking feeling that the number of books she read over the summer wasn't going to matter. The line between mild and certain ugliness was far more likely to determine whether one could make new friends.

"You should teach me," Miranda said, lying on her stomach with her breasts pushed down into the bench so that they bulged from the armpits of her tank-top. "How to float, I mean."

"Maybe," Kitty said. She swiped at her upper lip, which had produced a film of sweat.

*

The weekend before school started, Kitty's mother left the house. She got up and wandered for an hour in a man's shirt she told everyone was Ashok's, but was actually, Kitty suspected, just her own, bought from Walmart for $7.99, because it made her feel sexy. She let it fall away from her chest as she leaned over the counter, telling Kitty to empty the dishwasher while Nani cooked breakfast.

The dish was made with *poha*—a grain like flattened rice—and peas and chunks of hard-boiled egg. Every time she made it Nani explained that, traditionally, they put scraps of whatever they could find in it, the last bits of onions and potatoes. It tasted better when you knew nothing was going to waste, she said.

Kitty's mom disappeared upstairs and reappeared in a halter-neck sundress, applying mascara with the help of her compact. Ashok was going to pick her up for a day at the beach, and Miranda was coming over to spend the day with Kitty in the air conditioning.

"Summer's practically over, you know. You've wasted it staying inside so much. You should go out and do something fun before school starts." Kitty's mother spoke with her eyes half-closed, waiting for her lashes to dry.

The three of them knew that she herself had loitered in her bedroom eating ice-cream sandwiches for most of the summer—Kitty had seen the wrappers stuffed down in the bottom of her trash—and moreover, that there was no one Kitty could go with to the beach except Miranda, whom Kitty was too scared to ask. Every time they made plans, Kitty's pulse quickened with anxiety. She dared not do anything to upset the fragile social balance that made it permissible for Miranda to see Kitty occasionally, even while belonging to the clique of Roncesvalles girls who had pool parties in their backyards all summer. Kitty pushed the eggs across her plate, eating around them. The yolk, soft and meaty, was lined by a bit of grey where it met the whites. If she stared only at that in-between grey for long enough, the rest of the egg and the plate and the room grew blurry and faded, like they weren't there.

"*Ciao,*" she heard her mother say before going out to wait on the porch. Still she stared, and the filmy, eggy grey dominated her vision. She heard Nani get up to put the dishes away, heard the taps run, heard the scraping of the pan. Your eyes might never see anything else again, she thought. When she heard Ashok's car door slam and the wheels pull out of the driveway, Kitty let herself blink.

Later on, in her bedroom, which felt more like a cubicle because of its size and the fact that it had a bead curtain for a door (her sixth-grade decision, now deeply regretted), she wrote down "Vision is crucial" in block letters. Trying to pass the time until Miranda arrived, she opened up the section she always saved for last when she swiped copies of *Cosmopolitan* from downstairs, the one where readers sent in their most embarrassing stories. Usually, even when they had to do with periods leaking and denim zippers breaking, Kitty didn't find them embarrassing. Picturing a lean thigh or a belly button or even someone's ass suddenly revealed, she wished for something shittier, uglier. It seemed impossible that the smooth white girls who wrote in could feel anything like shame. Were *Jessica, 19* or *Maddie, 22* really almost-naked in their college classes if they looked like women were expected to look? Could you ever be naked if you didn't possess the specific roll of baby fat that Kitty carried on her stomach?

When she got hungry, she went out to the edge of the stairs and looked over the railing. Nani was lounging on the couch below with one of her dozens of transparent scarves draped across her shoulders. There were potato chips in the kitchen cupboard, but Kitty didn't want to risk arousing suspicion by grabbing a crinkling bag, and she especially didn't want to risk being told to eat her leftovers from breakfast. She looked over to the hallway linen closet instead. One of the five shelves had been turned into Nani's prayer corner, which held small statues of Ganesh and Shiva and Krishna. Among the incense and the cotton balls and the ghee, there was sometimes a little packet of sugar, the kind you could get only in Indian stores. It came in hard rocks, like candy. When she found it, Kitty poured it onto her tongue. It tasted the way Nani's clothes smelled, sweet and old. The rocks scratched the roof of her mouth before they began to dissolve. Too soon, she realized she'd eaten so many that it would be noticeable if she put the packet back, so she finished them.

She waited for Miranda, first through midday, then through the afternoon. The minutes crawled by as she tried to remember how to float, how to describe floating so that her friend would understand it. "You just focus on the air above your face," she said to herself. "Focus on the space between your skin cells." It was important that Miranda believe her. Kitty needed that—the sense that she could show Miranda something no one else could. Like the time she'd worn a pair of Nani's heaviest earrings to school without permission, the gold-set rubies and diamonds pulling her earlobes taut. *These are part of the jewellery chest my grandma got at her wedding,* she'd told Miranda. *They're the oldest and most expensive things in my entire family.* Miranda laughed at first, but Kitty caught her looking at the earrings later, and it was worth the stinging she felt in her earlobes for a full day afterward. She walked home with them in her pocket, twin tokens with a power she'd never possess herself. After the house was asleep, she put them back in the velvet-lined box Nani hid in the laundry room, under a stack of clean towels.

In her mother's closet, Kitty dug out a slippery black dress that felt like it was made of plastic. SMALL, the label declared. She pulled out other small things, tank tops with sparkly thread woven through them and skirts that buttoned, she knew, tightly below her mother's belly button. She pulled on a denim tube top that zipped in the front and a checkered pair of pants and, before even turning to the mirror, pulled them off again. After fiddling with its zipper for a few minutes, Kitty fit into a flowing red dress that fell to her knees. If she unfocused her eyes and pretended she was a foot taller, the shape in the mirror became familiar. Nothing had ever made her look like her mother before. Kitty examined the fabric's slight distance from the skin of her waist, the way it moved without clinging to her flesh. "Let your brain get fuzzy," she instructed. "Imagine that you're made of static noise." She paced the hallway in the dress. She wore it past five o'clock, when Miranda had swimming lessons every Saturday. Cold in the understanding that her friend would not show, Kitty sat at her desk. She fingered the too-soft fabric that belonged on her mother's body and watched dog walkers make their way to the park from the window.

*

"I don't know why all this Kitty business started in the first place. Your name is Kirti." Nani sat with her bag of yarn and a glass of club soda in front of the television, watching a Hindi soap opera. It featured a bearded man and a greying father and two sisters, and it was clear one of the sisters had framed the other for stealing the family jewels. Outside, it was getting dark. The dog walkers and joggers had gone home, and Kitty's mother had gone out to dinner with Ashok.

"Everyone just said it like that."

"So? You could correct them, couldn't you?" Nani wound yarn round and round one of her palms until the wad consumed her whole hand.

"Mom started calling me Kitty too."

Nani sighed. "Your mother doesn't understand, you know. She never understood the value of speaking Hindi around you. Ever since you were young."

"I know," Kitty said. "She didn't even eat her poha today." Nani shook her head in agreement. "Do you think she's right? About how I wasted the summer?"

"What does she know? You'll have another summer next year.

Just because she goes around in dresses with men, she likes to say that kind of thing."

Kitty felt hot and prickly all over her arms and chest. "Why does she do that?"

The commercials came on. A small brown boy placed a slice of Amul cheese on his bread and grinned, and then his mother, who was pale and long-lashed and devoted, chucked him under the chin and took a tiny bite from his hands. Kitty felt embarrassed watching commercials on the Hindi channels, like she knew something the actors didn't.

"She had you too young. With that Brian." The blue TV light gave Nani bags under her eyes, making her look sadder than usual. She tipped the remnants of her soda down her throat. On the television, a lady waggled her hips in a crowd of dancers. "I was young too, when I had her, but it was different. I was married."

"That's no excuse to be a pain," Kitty said. "That's no excuse to be mean."

Nani smiled in a way that Kitty hated, with pity and love mixed up in a soupy mess.

"You're right. I used to say the same thing about my sister when she stole my clothes. She was my mother's favourite, and she got away with everything. I'd tell her I wished she was dead, that I had a brother instead."

"None of us have brothers," Kitty said, feeling herself sink into a satisfying misery.

Nani nodded. "That is true, us three girls. There was a rumour, years ago, back home." She hiccupped, and Kitty understood it hadn't been only club soda in her glass. "My grandmother's cousin was so angry when she had her third daughter, after years of praying for a son. She got sick of listening to everyone who told her what to eat, how many rupees to donate, which temples to worship at, as though that would make her babies male. Finally, she went to a shaman in the village and got him to put a curse on her cousins and their next few generations. So they wouldn't have sons, either."

Wanting to cry, but finding herself unable to mask her excitement, Kitty hiccupped in solidarity. "And it worked?"

"Well, my mother had an older brother. But he died young."

"Oh," Kitty said.

Kitty's mother didn't get home until after they'd gone to bed. Kitty had lain down and immediately started to feel herself grow bigger, even without any effort. Her skin pulsed as though it was struggling to contain her. She thought about her father, the Brian that appeared in a handful of photographs from the year when her mom and Nani had first moved to Canada. He wore wire-framed glasses. There was a scruffy beard and a funny, lopsided grin and a strip of white flesh in a shot where his swim trunks had ridden up, with the lake in the background. And there was the fact that he'd left her this way, crossbred and alien. She knew there was a man walking around in loafers and buying pizzas on Fridays somewhere who could have chosen to claim her, to raise her, and he had chosen not to. Maybe the curse had something to do with that, too.

Quietly, without any real effort, Kitty felt herself move up and up, towards the ceiling, and then drift through the dangling streams of her bead-curtained doorway. She knew without looking that her body was still on top of her striped covers. She knew that she was most authentically herself now, when she was apart from its bulk. She knew that beyond the dark hallway was the door to her mother's bedroom, and she saw as she approached that it was slightly ajar. Inside, the lights were off but the glow from the streetlamps revealed the shapes of things: the translucent canopy hanging over the bed, the two pillows stacked atop each other, the dressing table a mess of bottles and tubes. Kitty hovered. Her mother had touched everything within these walls, and her influence made each piece of fabric and plastic and paper look like it was vibrating. She couldn't be sure, because as soon as she focused on one thing, it stopped, but when she looked away it began again. It was as though each object had taken on a life in the darkness. Each thing was ready to tell her some crucial bit of information, but didn't know how to begin, and shivered nervously instead.

Downstairs, the front door opened. They were home. Kitty heard Ashok's rumbling laugh as the lock turned. They would go into the kitchen and find the bottle of gin Nani might have left on the dining table, and pour themselves a drink. They would rummage through the fridge for a piece of cheese or bread, avoiding the plastic-wrapped bowl of poha, and they would talk for a bit before coming up.

Feeling that her time would soon run out, Kitty observed her hands opening one of the bedside table's drawers. Inside were a jumble of papers, an empty bottle of contact lens solution, and a plastic container of pills from the pharmacy. They were familiar, Kitty felt. They were blue and calm and important. She wondered if she could have them without anyone noticing, as she'd had the sugar. Probably, she felt— though she couldn't be sure—probably, they were sweet. She could take one and then another, swallowing before they dissolved. The label on the container gave her all the information she needed. There was her mother's name written out in capitals. After popping a few into her mouth, she might feel tired of kneeling on the floor, and she might let herself into her mother's bed. Kitty had never been so comfortable before. I'll wake up before I hear them come up the stairs, she thought, and even if I don't, they won't see me here. Her mother's room sighed with relief. In between the sheets, Kitty felt that everything within its walls loved her unconditionally.

The Aquanauts*

ELIZA ROBERTSON

the sea is another story
the sea is not a question of power
I have to learn alone
to turn my body without force
in the deep element.

  −"Diving into the Wreck," Adrienne Rich

1.

Fifty feet up, beachcombers pad their handbags with sand dollars, sea glass, sun-bleached urchins; honeymooners share a bowl of stewed conch across a gingham tablecloth; a mother washes her infant in the tide while Dad crams five quarts of discount rum in their safety deposit box; a dentist's wife sleeps under a sea grape tree; Dicky Jr. slingshots butterflies; a perfume of parrots shakes from the banyan; the beach is a shock of white sand; three NASA officials and two behavioural psychologists crowd a bank of video monitors inside a mobile trailer. On the screens, four women in bikinis eat enchiladas around a hide-a-table. Harry Nilsson plays in the background. The women discuss their day. Everything in the kitchen is submarine blue except the aquanauts' bikinis and the General Electric fridge, which is yellow-brown like envelope paste. A fifth woman floats outside the porthole window.

2.

2:15 p.m.
No. 5 unpacks her duffel in crew quarters. No. 3 confirms checklist with the *Pinafore*, the surface support barge. No. 2 organizes the dry lab. No. 1 and No. 4 dismantle the air scrubber system, which filters carbon dioxide from the air supply—
2:16
Topside pings. No answer.
2:16
Topside pings. No answer.
2:17
Topside pings. No answer.
2:17
No. 5 unpacks bag of masa flour and a tortilla press.
2:18
No. 1 and No. 4 remove cache of sherry from air filtration system, which they reassemble before anyone asphyxiates.

3.

In my observation journal I am supposed to record emotions like what is my daily mood in relation to the colour of the habitat's interior and perceived level of privacy. So far I've recorded two notes. First: No. 3's eyes are brown on land but underwater they blur into a sort of marshy green. Second: you never really sit into chairs; you fall.

4.

Our project is named after the glassy rocks found at the bottom of the sea the shape of spheres, teardrops, dumbbells, or as we scientists describe them: molten terrestrial glass ejecta of meteorite impacts, a.k.a. tektites.
 Speaking of bells you would be incorrect to imagine our habitat as a diving bell. Our habitat is two eighteen-foot silos connected by

a flexible tube. Each silo houses two rooms. The main entrance a.k.a. wet room is on the right. Above that, the engine room. On the left: the bridge a.k.a. dry lab and library. Below: bunk beds, refrigerator, stove, sink, storage cupboards, hide-a-table.

5.

Truthfully I have two observation journals. The feeling journal, described above, and the science journal, where I monitor how blind cavefish (*Astyanax mexicanus*) respond to shadows. The feeling journal is red. The science journal is green.

6.

Truthfully I often misplace one or other of the journals, or else one is in the bunk downstairs when a thought presents itself, and so there is some cross-contamination between feelings and science.

7.

7:15 p.m.
No. 4 and No. 2 lie on their bunks in crew quarters. No. 5 sits at the table with a book on Caribbean reef fish. Ravi Shankar plays on cassette. No. 1 speaks to the Pinafore. No. 3 showers.

7:18
No. 2 wants No. 1 to join them for freeze-dried spaghetti. No. 1 still talks to Topside. No. 3 towels off in the wet room.

7:20
No. 2 announces she will eat No. 1's share. No. 1 says something to Topside about eating for two.

7:24

No. 3 joins the others in crew quarters. No. 1 has hung up. She crouches on the floor of the bridge and watches the others through the hatchway.

7:32

No. 2 prepares the freeze-dried spaghetti.

7:33

No. 3, No. 4, and No. 5 discuss the acronym SNAFU.

8.

Pinafore is perhaps the most graceful word for "bib."

Blind cavefish lost their eyesight over a million years' evolution, but somehow the larvae detect my shadow and swim toward it.

I keep mispronouncing the scientific name as "asyntax mexicanus." I've never been to Mexico, but that's probably accurate as far as my Spanish goes.

This morning I found a poem in the library. It's by a woman called Adrienne Rich. I copied it into my green journal with the following amendment:

"A woman in the shape of a monster
a monster in the shape of a woman
the seas are full of them"

9.

Rehydrated tiramisu for dessert. We go around the table saying how many kids we want.

"I'd have one more," says No. 4.

"Jeff got a vasectomy after Melinda," says No. 2.

"Two," says No. 3. "A boy and a girl."

"I hope I have twins," says No. 5.

They all look at me.

"I have a PhD and three kids," says No. 2. "You don't have to choose anymore."

Can I choose if I want though? I ask in my head.

10.

"Topside gets happy hour why don't we?" says No. 4. "I hate sherry," says No. 3.

No. 3 is the whiner.

The bar at base camp is called the Hurricane Hole. They fashion cocktails like the Re-breather a.k.a. rum + Coke and the Baralyme a.k.a. Chardonnay + 7 Up + whatever else is going. The US Virgin Islands are one of three places in the world where the duty-free alcohol limit is five litres. The other places are Guam and I forget the third place.

In the wet room, we tape a playboy pinup to the shower curtain to give the boys upstairs something to look at.

11.

I haven't told the others I ran into trouble last year. Only my sister knows. She got a phone number from a toilet stall in the student union building. The number led to the answering machine of a woman called Jane. Even our parents didn't own an answering machine.

We met Jane at her house for coffee. She showed us a diagram of the cervix, which I knew about, but Jane, whose real name was Libby, looked fifteen, so I was relieved she knew about it too. She showed us a plastic model of the speculum and said, "We'll use this to open the walls of your vagina. We have a mirror too if you want to see."

"Don't take this the wrong way," I said. "But are you the receptionist?"

12.

How do blind cavefish detect my shadow without eyes or photo-sensitive pigments? The response is strongest among young. Maybe a protective instinct—to seek shelter from sighted predators. Maybe they like to feel hemmed in. Cupped by amniotic darkness on all sides.

The working title of my thesis is *Dark Seekers*.

13.

My virgin dive, eight years ago, coincided with my first period. I think because of the homonym, I expected it to arrive as a red dot. Just a grammar correction in my underwear. I was not prepared for the gore of it. The wetsuit kept the blood in, but still. Would the sharks know?

The other thing is boob implants. I don't have them myself, but friends ask. What you have to worry about here is gas bubbles, which lead to a small increase in volume. They don't pop though.

14.

At the place, they gave me a doughnut and orange juice. My sister came too and ate all the Triscuits.

It happened in Libby's bedroom under a poster of Janis Joplin. She gave me a shot in the bum, then inserted the speculum. She was not offended when I said: "Oh it's you. The 'we' before was strictly royal, wasn't it?"

You're not supposed to name it, but I keep meeting women called Shelley. Shell. Shell-belle.

15.

I have taken it upon myself to open all of the mostly closed pistachios. No. 4 offered her oyster shucker, but the blade was too thick, so I wedge my fingernails into the slit, and it feels like I'm popping off falsies, which I'm not wearing, that would be impractical, so it feels like I'm popping off real nails, which must be a dream trope, you know how teeth always fall out. My teeth don't fall out in dreams, they sort of soften into my gums like masticated food.

16.

Mood Adjective Checklist:

Concentration	50 g concentration / 100 g H2O x 100 = 50%
Activation	If you don't mind
Social affection	Así, así
Pleasantness	Highly
Nonchalance	✓
Deactivation	?
Aggression	2/10
Egotism	so-so
Skepticism	Healthy
Depression	4/5
Anxiety	Who's asking?

17.

5:05 p.m.
No. 2 and No. 5 lie in their bunks in crew quarters listening to *Beggars Banquet* on cassette. No. 1 works in the wet room. No. 3 and No. 4 are out on a dive.

5:11
No. 2 leaves her bunk and flips the tape. No. 1 gets a ring on the phone from the Pinafore. She talks to Topside.

5:14
No. 2 sits at the desk in the bridge and works.

5:16
No. 1 goes into the water with sample containers.

5:20
No. 1 returns inside after sending the samples to the Pinafore. She removes her wetsuit and has a shower. A picture from a men's entertainment magazine is taped to the shower curtain. A woman lies naked on a red carpet, a mollusk's CaCO3 deposits winding between her breasts, which she covers, mostly, with her hands.

7:15
No. 3 and No. 4 return from their dive. They still wear bikinis. Everyone sits at the table in crew quarters while No. 5 mixes masa flour and water. No. 1 takes the camera off its holder and aims it at the others. No. 3 shields her face with her hands. No. 1 takes a close-up of No. 3's navel. No. 2 ignores No. 1 but says, "Topside can't believe we're not drunk." No. 4 says, "Hey there's an idea. Who wants sherry?" No. 1 rocks the camera from hand to hand and makes wind and wave noises. No. 4 asks Topside if they've got big swells. Someone flips the Rolling Stones tape. The overhead lights switch on and off.

18.

On the surface we're all smeared with suntans but at depth the melatonin drains into a lunar pallor. The moon brightens the night sky, but it's not a source of light. The moon reflects the sun, fattening and withering every 29.5306 days. Nothing reflects off our faces down here.

19.

Q: Can man, who evolved from the sea to dominate the land, reverse the process by returning to the oceans and asserting control over the depths? —*New York Times*, 1970
　　A: Don't count on it.

20.

Some fish dig holes in the sea floor by blowing water out of their mouths. Others drill into the bottom with their bodies constantly churning. A four-foot barracuda lives under the habitat. I call him Mick. No. 3 says: "You know you shouldn't name them."

21.

After my shower this afternoon, I saw my foot from the corner of my eye. You know how toes curl in, un-prehensile. This deep, the water holds us up and down. If we stayed here, would our feet learn to clasp the coral? Would we grow seahorse tails? All that time suspended in fluid. The shrimp are a bit like fetuses.

22.

7:30 a.m.
No. 2 and No. 1 lie in their bunks. No. 1 writes in her journal. No. 3 and No. 4 sit at the table, discussing their dive plan. No. 5 makes coffee.

7:32
No. 2 says, "I wish we could stay another week." No. 5 says, "What about your fiancé?"
　　　No. 2: "He has a microwave."

8:30
No. 3 and No. 4 go to the wet room to suit up. They check their plan with Topside. No. 5 puts the table back.

8:37
No. 2 throws her Mood Adjective Checklist off her bunk. "Why are all the mood adjectives nouns?" No. 5 doesn't reply. She puts the coffee away and wipes the counters. No. 2 says, "And I dispute whether 'activation' is a mood."

23.

The pineal gland is the blind cavefish's third eye. It contains the light-sensitive pigment rhodopsin. When I remove the blind cavefish's third and only eye, the larvae stop swimming toward my shadow.

An old grief returns, at first only dampening the edges.

24.

In the wet room, No. 3 says, "I saw some mating today." I unzip her wetsuit and turn so she can do mine.

"Oh yeah how would you rate it?"

"High levels of activation and pleasantness."

"Was it the moray eel? I get the sense he's really riled up."

"Two tiger groupers."

"You know what I'm waiting for?"

"A red hind."

"No."

"Slippery dick."

"No."

"Go on then."

"The French grunt."

She laughs. "You think Topside are blushing?"

"Wait wait. French grunt and sergent major."

25.

6:27 p.m.
No. 4 relaxes in the bridge. She turns the volume down of a cassette by The Kinks. No. 3 notifies No. 1 her delivery from topside is in the trunk. No. 1 retrieves it. No. 3 still works in the wet lab. No. 5 changes the baralyme. No. 1 talks on the phone to the Pinafore.

6:36
No. 4 asks what the people topside are reading. She noticed they were reading. They're reading Tom Wolfe.

7:01

No. 1 digs through a box of tapes in the bridge. She finds the Spoken Arts cassette library. "This is wild," she says to No. 4, who plays The Kinks on her ukulele. No. 1 puts on a tape of Shakespeare sonnets.

7:11

No. 1 turns off the Shakespeare after listening to four sonnets. She puts on a tape about Olympian mythology. A man with an English accent describes the birth of Aphrodite.

26.

Aphros means "foam." Aphrodite was born from the severed genitals of Ouranos after his son, Time, threw them into the sea.

I never asked Libby where they put them. The remains. Surely they didn't have access to a crematorium or medical waste bins. But then, where did medical waste wind up?

My sister and I used to own a three-inch angelfish named Gertrude. When she died, I scooped her from the water. Her silver body filled my palm like a compass. Her wings, I mean fins, pointed northeast and southeast, to where the sun rises.

Where's my angelfish, I wonder. The one I haven't named out loud. Is it possible we're floating in the same molecules of salt and other people's excrement? The thought disturbs and comforts me in equal measures. We flushed Gertrude down the toilet too.

27.

7:44

Everyone sits at the table and eats their TV dinners. No. 1 says, "how much of us is out there already, do you think?"

No one answers.

7:45

No. 1 continues: "In the sea, I mean. How many dumps have we taken before now? And are we floating in all of that?"

Still no one answers.

"You know what I mean?" says No. 1. "The sea is One, unified. Water mingles everywhere. The boundaries are in name only, for the convenience of land dwellers and maps." No. 2 nods. She says she knows what she means. No. 5 mentions NASA—how the men on NASA missions go nuts. No. 4 suggests calling the base camp physician at 3 a.m. for No. 1's abdominal pain. They could stage a mock birth. No. 1 pushes the rehydrated beef stroganoff around her plate.

28.

When an earthquake shook the Virgin Islands last week, five women were sleeping in a steel capsule at the bottom of the ocean. The tremor disturbed their sleep, but the aquanauts checked their habitat and confirmed no damage had been done. "If you want to weather an earthquake," the team leader told control center, "the best place to do it is the habitat. I had a feeling of remoteness, like nothing could hurt me." At depths of fifty feet, the human body withstands 2.5 times our regular surface pressure. The time to re-acclimatize to surface pressures is 24 hours. Too rapid a return would cause the excess nitrogen in the blood to bubble up like fizz in a shaken bottle of Coca-Cola.
—New York Times, July 1970

29.

It is 11:23 p.m. We all lie in our bunks. Someone snores. Another rolls over clunkily.

I'm thinking about how I feel more at home underwater. The ocean a reservoir of our collective grieving. There are no walls down here. So many of us in the West have forgotten how to mourn.

My angelfish might be out here too. Maybe we'll find each other through eyeless, pineal knowing.

I'm thinking about how, by 2020, women could return to the sea. I imagine the movie voiceover: "Fifty years ago, nuclear war broke out between America and the USSR. Only the female aquanauts remained safe, tucked in their habitat at the bottom of the ocean. It was a giant leap for mankind."

How would we procreate? How would our new environment alter the psychology of living? How would it change our moods, with no shift in the season and no sunsets?

29.5306
Our hearts beat differently down here. Light shines from the moon's other creatures. Feelings of serenity and utter detachment. It's easy to forget what I came here for.

*In 1970, the US Department of the Interior and NASA co-conducted a psychological study of scientific work teams living in isolated environments. In each mission, four scientists and one engineer would inhabit a station on the ocean floor for ten to twenty days while psychologists observed them from the surface via CCTV. The underwater scientists were known as "aquanauts."

Eight Saints and a Demon

NABEN RUTHNUM

Thaïs
8 October 2009

Colin kept pronouncing it as though he were talking about people from Thailand. He wasn't following the patient, enunciated lead Ms. Rawley gave him in her intro: the way she stretched the *i* before sucking in air at the end of the *s*, making the trema talk. She interrupted Colin after the first paragraph or so of his presentation to explain the ¨, applying it to the whiteboard with two darts of her marker, then writing *diaeresis / umlaut / trema.*

"And since I would never even try to say 'diaeresis' repeatedly in this classroom, and umlaut is a bit of an ugly word, we'll call it a trema. Go on, Colin."

Colin always worked shabby jokes into his assignments and would inevitably focus on the Thai prostitute angle for his *Penguin Dictionary of the Saints* presentation on a reformed fourth-century "notorious harlot" from Egypt, who'd achieved beatification by burning all her clothes and jewellery, then latched onto a team of nuns to clean her soul for death.

Instead of listening, Julian practised getting the *i* to work for him the way it did for Karen Rawley. He sat at his desk making the small fishlike moue that the word demanded, while the room of fifteen-year-old boys waiting for their turn laughed intermittently at Colin, and Ms. Rawley stared at her desk. The assignment had been inspired by the discovery of a sealed box of the paperback dictionaries lying in the supply room, untouched since 1965. The books were beautiful, the liquid black of the borders and the sharp colours in the cover painting of Saint Jerome vivid and new, as though they had been mailed from the past.

"Since it pretty much says in the book that Thaïs probably didn't exist and that she is basically a Catholic bedtime story, the project, overall, was getting me to research a lie told to scare people into not having fun."

"What a penetrating argument, Colin, thank you." Karen looked up from her desk, watching Julian try his ï. He looked thoughtful and breathless, a drowned saint in living glass of blue and pink.

Pazuzu
31 October 2013

During Karen Rawley's hearing, Colin became Julian's best friend. This was in their senior year, when both boys switched out of Hemdale Catholic in favour of the enormous, identity-blanching public school between their two suburbs. Colin kept best friend status through their freshman year of college and two months of the next. In that last month, they watched *The Exorcist* on Halloween, trying to, as Colin put it, "get the fear back."

It worked. Just not in the fear-of-God way that Colin intended. They sat on separate couches in Julian's living room, which was weakly heated by baseboard units and chilled by powerful movements of air through and around the papery, century-old panes in the large window behind them. Colin and Julian were each caped in wool blankets and eventually drew their feet off the floor, pressing legs close to bodies.

The bit in the movie about Father Karras abandoning his mother was what got to Colin, who hissed a little bit at the scene of the depleted, betrayed old woman in her bed at a chaotic mental hospital. Colin's transfer from Hemdale had been followed a few months later by a local news profile of him and his boyfriend, a fairly stupid boy named Luke Strachan who was mainly appealing because he had his own place and made decent money selling stolen phones online.

They'd done the interview in Luke's bachelor apartment, the door open so the camera setup could get a decent angle on Colin and Luke sitting on the futon couch that unfolded into the bed they shared. Colin's mother was not the kind of Irish Catholic to embrace this aspect of her son, especially when she first encountered it through her husband screaming at her from the living room to come to the TV.

"All her fault, definitely, but it still felt like mine too," he said to Julian, when they paused the movie to get a wax-coated whiskey bottle open.

Nothing in the movie got to Julian quite as much as the death of Max von Sydow, which happened offscreen and was an accidental triumph of the devil, who'd been helped by the old priest's weak heart and broken assistant.

Colin kept talking after they'd gotten the whiskey open, talked through the whole rest of the movie, but Julian had maintained his ability to ignore him even after they became friends. He concentrated on little Regan, a couple of traced scars on her face as she hugged the priest in the last scene, until she got into the car and was driven away from the house where she'd been invaded by the demon Pazuzu. With the film over, his ears began to accept Colin's frequencies again, noting only that he was still talking guilt, before the names surfaced.

"And Latham didn't even see you with Ms. Rawley. I just told him about you being in her car after lunch. He pretended he saw, like he was the scandalized star, and added all that stuff on top of the kissing. Stuck to it the whole time, once his parents told the cops about the texts they saw. And he only pretended because he was a glory hog, not because he didn't want to rat on me, for sure."

The Exorcist credits were interrupted by Netflix pointing out similar films to stream next. Julian usually liked to watch credits through to the end, but he hadn't made a move for the controller, or any move at all.

"I always felt weird about telling you. Don't get mad, okay?"

Julian didn't grab for the controller, stepping onto and over the coffee table instead with his hands in loose fists. He tripped and smashed his face into Colin's teeth, setting his forehead and his friend's mouth bleeding before the first punch.

Vulnus
Julian Proctor
10 October 2009
English 10
Ms. Rawley
St. Vulnus

Vulnus began his life in ninth-century Baghdad. He was born from the union of a travelling merchant from Spain and a courtesan, who knew that she was to be decapitated for granting favour to someone other than the caliph. Vulnus's mother composed a song for her son, understanding that she would be executed when his skin and eyes were seen at his birth (the caliph at the time being decidedly dark, and the traveller from England rivalling the palest of his countrymen, his skin constantly blistered by the lacerating heat and rays of the desert sun).

Indeed, her head was ordered struck off before Vulnus's feet had left her womb, the court vizier having seen the boy's blue eyes, and a scimitar-bearing guard attending the birth. (Another version of the Vulnus story holds that the vizier, whose own eyes were blue, was the father.) Many accounts say that the boy Vulnus was delivered of a dead woman, as Jesus was delivered of a virgin.

The song composed by his courtesan mother, plucked from an oud every morning by the slave woman who'd offered to nurse him (the boy's survival being another indication that the vizier, and not a wandering merchant, had been the father), was an eleven-note strain full of the east with a recurring lyrical thrill that was not to be heard in Western music until the baroque period. The surviving notated scrap of "Vulnus's Dawn," taken down by a Renaissance musician from Sicily who had heard it at a Persian wedding, is considered by musicologists to be a key bridging element between classical music forms in several different cultures. Earlier renderings of the song, if ever they were notated, were lost in Hulagu Khan's devastating assaults on Baghdad.

Vulnus was raised to be a musician, castrated at an early age to preserve the sweetness of his voice and to further reinforce the caliph's claim on the courtesans that the young man spent his days with.

He fled the castle and Islamic rites on his twenty-second birthday, but not before releasing a dozen captured Christians who had been working as slaves in the kitchens—he clothed them in garments that would be invisible in the city and provided them with funds for their escape, refusing to flee alongside them as he knew the caliph's men would concentrate on capturing and killing him.

After two days, when none of the escaped slaves had been recovered and all were judged to be a safe distance from the city, Vulnus reappeared at the castle gates and surrendered himself to the caliph's men, declaring his hope that his deed had cleansed both him and his mother, while acknowledging the betrayal of his duty toward the caliph, who had fed and clothed him since birth.

Vulnus was beheaded in the same chamber where he was birthed, and his head rolled upward along the slanting stone floor to come to rest where his mother's had. On his face was an expression of total peace, which, when his executioner saw it, caused him to retire his role and take up work in the kitchens, where he became the court's greatest baker. But that is another tale.

Julian, I can't decide if this is a little bit racist (not intentionally, of course), and that 'Arabian Nights' turn at the end is wrong, tonally (despite making me desperate to hear the story of the Executioner-Baker), but your Vulnus entry is excellent, and you've done a great job of emulating Attwater's prose from the real Dictionary of Saints. A definite A / A+. Overall, I would be proud to have written this myself.

—KR

Eugenia
25 December 2014

Eugenia was Karen Rawley's favourite female saint story, both for the audacity of the holy bullshit and the Shakespearean hook of the cross-dressing woman-as-monk. The beheading ending was a downer, but Karen had corrected it in her latest piece—four pages of crowded handwriting on yellow paper that she folded together at the upper-left corner and slid into a folder with the rest—before knocking on the inside of her own door and waiting for it to be opened from the outside.

Threats that she'd made up and bruises that she didn't have to invent had gotten her what she'd wanted: twenty-three hours a day in solitary confinement, the kind that was usually earned by committing a few in-prison murders or by entering far more notoriously than Karen had. Whenever she asked a few hours in advance, the guards shuffled her up to the chaplain's office. Today they took her up immediately. The Father had special Christmas hours just after the morning mass, which Karen never attended.

"Nothing better to do today, Father?"

"I never have anything better to do than discharge the duties of my office, Karen," said Father Mackle. He was bald, cauliflower-eared from boxing young and cauliflower-nosed from daily drinking after hanging up the gloves. The guard who'd made the walk with Karen, a silent obese woman with a large facial mole, left when Mackle waved her off. What would have been an exposed brick wall behind him was painted a pale, fishy yellow, to match the rest of the surfaces on this floor of the prison. The desk wasn't institutional, though: a hunk of cherrywood that looked like a real piece of the outside.

"Did you bring that from home? I always mean to ask."

"The blotter? The desk. It was a gift from my first congregation. I've been hauling it with me ever since. What can I do for you, Karen?"

"I want to run my penitence past you, Father," she said, presenting the file she had brought up from her cell, pushing it across the red wood toward the priest.

"What's this?"

"I've been writing a series of dialogues between me and saints of my choosing and enacting them in my cell. I perform them out loud, I mean. I wanted to tell you so you can let the guards and the Warden's tentacles know that I'm not going insane. I'm talking through my sins."

"Yes. Well, that isn't harmful, necessarily. But I have to tell you that it is weird, Karen. Not a replacement for confession." Mackle paused, likely realizing that any alternative he could present would involve him doing much more work than he wanted to do, and devoting more time to Karen Rawley than she had fair claim to, in a facility of this size.

"Can you read one out with me? Whichever you choose. Just so you can see that it's harmless, even if it is weird. The guards. Soller, you know her? With the long arms and the bad front teeth?"

Mackle smiled at the description, able to place the woman instantly, though he'd never known her name. "Yes, I think so."

"She keeps on rapping on my cell door and asking what I'm up to when I do the readings. Clearly thinks I'm going insane. Just pick one out and you'll see. It's narcissistic, at worst, but I want you to see that it's a genuine expression of a kind of faith, Father."

"You choose one," Mackle said, pushing the file back at her. "I'll get it photocopied so we can do it properly."

Ursula
21 October 2009

Julian knew Ms. Rawley parked her car in a small strip-mall parking lot a block from the school. Her dad owned Ham and Tony's, the sandwich shop in the mall, and Karen had told the class a few stories about working there when she was a student at Hemdale. No kids from school went, choosing the McDonald's around the corner instead. Mr. Rawley had regularly kicked out teenagers who lingered too long at his stools and tables during the lunch rush, and this had been enough to kill the place for Hemdale kids and make it a teen-free oasis for downtown office lunchers.

Julian waited in front of Ms. Rawley's car, the cold of the pavement pushing through his cotton uniform pants and boxers. By the time he realized that he really wanted to get up he'd seen Ms. Rawley approaching and didn't want to look fidgety.

"Hi, Julian," Ms. Rawley said. "Following me?"

"No. I just saw once that you park here instead of the teacher's lot."

"Yes. When I finish work I don't want to talk to anyone, really, and the other teachers tend to chat in the parking lot. I get all chatted out." Ms. Rawley kept her car keys in her pocket, not her purse, and already had them in hand. She put them back in her pocket and leaned against the door of her aging Honda. Julian stood.

"I was wondering if I could get my Dictionary of Saints thing back. Even if it didn't count."

"You have it in your computer."

"I want to know what you said about it," said Julian, staring at Ms. Rawley's stuffed shoulder bag, which bristled with white papers and pulled her body slightly to the right when she walked. With its weight braced against her car, she was straight again, except for her small, usual slouch. He knew his entry was in that bag.

"Whoever told the school admin about the project, not that they were wrong to do so, I'm not running a secret classroom, ended anything to do with our new dictionary. I tried to explain that it was an exercise in style. Inventing new entries for saints who didn't exist is not the same thing as inventing new saints. If anything, it wasn't a creative exercise but an exercise in restraint."

"I know," said Julian, not really knowing. "I figured you got the idea from Colin's stupid comment about how Thaïs didn't exist."

"Ten points for pronunciation. And yes, something like that, although I'd never call Colin's point stupid. If anything, I was stupid for suggesting the assignment at this school."

"Did you read mine?"

"Yes."

"Did you like it?" Julian asked. Ms. Rawley shrugged out of the shoulder strap and rested the bag on the hood of her car while she got her keys out again, opening the driver's side and doing the double-click turn that unlocked all four doors. She tossed her bag in the backseat, which was teeming with volleyballs.

"We can talk about this a little farther away from the school, Julian, if you have time right now. Some restaurant near your house?"

On the drive Julian asked Ms. Rawley about her favourite entry in the real dictionary, clarifying that he meant which entry, not which saint. She told him about her second favourite, instead. It was Ursula, who hadn't wanted to get married and had corralled either eleven or eleven thousand maiden virgins to ditch Britain with her. All of them went on a pilgrimage to Rome and were massacred for their faith by Huns on the way back home.

"None of it could have happened, none of it's proved, but still. Eleven thousand and one virgins on a road trip, and all those blades at the end of it."

Anastasia
25 December 2014

Anastasia: You've called for me.
Karen: Yes. You're supposed to be an exorcist.
Anastasia: A rumour from long after my martyrdom. I've had very few conversations with the adversary.
Karen: You died in Serbia. I'm half Serbian, maybe that's why I chose you.
Anastasia: You've summoned me to confess.
Karen: No, for an explanation and a few questions.
Anastasia: I'll do my best with the time we have.
Karen: Martyrs want out. You have to acknowledge that, on some level, they all just want out, even if they have to go through torture first.
Anastasia: Christ?
Karen: Between what was going on down here and being King of Heaven forever? I never understood the sacrifice. I've read the reasoning but I've never felt it, myself. What was there to lose?
Physical pain, ostracism. Surrounded by lesser beings he was compelled to love.
Anastasia: A basic theological question that has been thoroughly answered.
Karen: I'm trying to understand the damage I caused. I confessed to everything I did and much more I didn't do, to spare Julian from the courtroom, from my "infamy." I described filth that had nothing to do with us. I picked up on every suggestion the judging machine made and I agreed, enhanced, amplified. I buried myself here.
Anastasia: But you did do wrong.

Karen: Yes, but how much?

Anastasia: Several kinds of sin. Worse, you corrupted acts of virtue. You degraded generosity and charity. You weren't helping and guiding Julian. You were trying to fuck yourself in all meanings of the word.

Karen: That sounds unsaintly.

Anastasia: I'm one of the made-up ones.

Cyprian and Justina
26 September 2011

She liked it when Julian walked around naked after they fucked, only letting him put clothes on when it was time for him to put in his writing hour.

"You still do this on our days off, I hope."

"Yes."

"An hour a day? On loose-leaf, not typed? Because this doesn't look like an hour of work." Karen flipped through the four pages he'd brought in, culled from the printer in his dad's study and containing about half the story of a saint named Akhen, in unacceptable handwriting.

"Sometimes an hour, sometimes longer. Is that okay?" Julian didn't like hearing the sulk in his voice but didn't know how to shed it.

Karen made him use her old university laptop, a clunker that no longer connected to the internet, closing him in the tiny breakfast nook in the kitchen and watching him through the windowed door as he wrote.

Each semester that they'd been doing this, she'd invented a new after-school club, bringing it to life on Hemdale stationery and inventing a series of email addresses that all routed to her, to buy this time from Julian's parents. This semester it was an illuminating class, and each time they had a session, Julian carried home one of the curlicued and ornamented letters that she herself had made as a teenager, replete with peering monks and lazy serpents. She scissored her initials out of the corner of each piece and he wrote his in. They were up to *J*: a boiling pot rounding out the lower curve of the letter with a pair of martyrs being turned into faithful soup inside it, twining their arms together around the rising trunk. Karen was refreshing the gold leaf, always the first to flake off, when Julian broke the silent rule and called through the glass door.

"What if, just saying, what if we let someone else see what we're working on? Like, a magazine, or even you could just show another one of the teachers?"

"You can show anyone you want to, but you can also keep the work private, and I think you should. Until you're really great. That's what no one told me, Jules. It's fine to wait."

"Don't call me that. It's girl-sounding."

"I don't think there's any risk of me thinking you're a girl, okay?"

"I just don't like it."

"Okay, let's agree that's not important and move on."

"What is important, though? I've written like two hundred of these saint entries and most of them are terrible, and you still haven't written one. You should be doing half if this is going to be any good."

"What I should be doing is encouraging and editing you. And that's what I am doing. You're going to be great, and I'm just going to be here, but that's okay. I'm okay with it."

Hallvard
15 May 2018

She's been out of jail for three years and the no-contact order has been repealed for two, but this is the first time he's gotten her to agree to meet him. Julian's in front of Ham and Tony's, which is still open but with a different owner, Mr. Rawley now living in Florida. The pavement's warm, and the blacktop under his sneakers is absolutely hot, having baked in hours of sun. Karen has the same Honda, she said on the phone, and he's waiting for that.

He can't remember how they'd gotten there in her car that first time, but he remembers Karen showing him how to shape his lips for a kiss, the right kind of non-familial kiss, and watching him while he did it, looking at his mouth and then his eyes, waiting for him to lean in and start it. Julian had told the cops about that moment after an hour of questioning, when they threw in Chris Latham's testimony about the kiss and fondling that he'd supposedly witnessed. Julian finally told them that Latham must have been lying, that they'd barely ever kissed in public after the first time. Then he told them the rest, a nice female officer who was only a little older than Ms. Rawley encouraging all the details forward, promising that Ms. Rawley wouldn't have to know that it was him who gave them, unless there was a trial.

"If she's as decent as you think she is, in the way you think she is, there won't be a trial," the cop said. And Karen did confess everything that night. Julian forgets the cop's name, the way he's been forgetting more about the past both distant and recent since he stopped going to school and writing and doing much of anything other than sitting on his parents' couch and telling them that he's almost made a decision.

Karen had hidden the pages of the *New Dictionary of Saints* they'd made, printing them off and smashing the laptop before the cops made their first visit. Her last text had been to tell him so, that the pages were safe. The phone call the school had gotten was enough for her to make that move. The pages were hidden somewhere now, a relic, lost like those books had been in the Hemdale supply room, before Ms. Rawley resurrected them by passing a box cutter through the tape that held their imprisoning flaps down. If he could get the pages back and talk to Karen, just talk, he could figure out what to do next. Maybe tell the cops that he'd lied to them, that Karen Rawley had gone to jail to protect him, somehow, that she was the real innocent. That she'd been helping him.

The car, Julian thinks it's the right one, turns into the parking lot and starts angling toward him. Maybe the pages are in the trunk. Julian starts to stand but waits, because she might want him to stay sitting at first.

California Underwater

CASON SHARPE

I work at a big movie theatre downtown where everyone is a teenager except for me. At first it was fun but now I just feel pathetic and creepy. It was supposed to be a temporary thing—I had just finished school and had no money and needed a job immediately etc.—but then somehow it became a not temporary thing. Somehow it has been over a year. I work six days a week and sometimes doubles: from the first screening straight through to the last. I am not even the manager. Kevin is the manager and also a freshman at U of T.

*

Teresa and some of the other girls who work at the theatre ask me to pick up alcohol for them one evening. They want to let loose because it's summer vacation but they keep getting carded and the guy at the LCBO won't accept Teresa's ID even though she borrowed it from her older sister. I agree and they hand me a wad of bills and a list of their requests written on the back of a discarded ticket stub: a couple coolers and few mickeys of Smirnoff. In the liquor store, the cashier looks disapprovingly at my purchases which makes me feel silly but when I bring the alcohol back to the girls they are so excited and grateful that I feel pretty pleased with myself. I'm ashamed by how earnestly I want to impress a group of seventeen-year-olds, just like the closet case I was back in high school.

The next day Kevin asks to speak with me privately. Earlier that morning someone found one of the storage rooms littered with empty liquor bottles, cigarettes butts, and a slick pile of puke. Kevin gives me a lecture about buying alcohol for minors.

"Do whatever you want on your own time," he says. "But keep it out of the theatre."

Kevin is a twerp but also what the fuck Teresa? I direct my embarrassment and anger nowhere in particular so it spills out everywhere untamed and clumsy. I hand back the wrong change a number of times and I snap at a customer when they ask me for directions to the bathroom.

*

After work I meet up with Kelly at a bar on Dundas. Kelly just got back from LA where he recently had a show. I am happy for him but he's already selling out. He's cuffed his Levi's. He wears a worn baseball cap and white T-shirt like he's a tradesman and not a painter whose parents happen to be two of the most celebrated architects in the city. I ask him how he liked LA.

"It was trippy," he says. There's a water shortage throughout California but rich people and celebrities still power wash their sidewalks. He met a Belgian curator who said he couldn't wait for the tsunami to come and submerge the entire state. Only the worthy will survive. True artists will be granted gills to attend aquatic openings. Kelly asks me how my practice is going.

"What practice?" I say, laughing. I haven't so much as touched a paintbrush in over six months. We chat about people from art school— this person has a residency and that person got a write-up in *Canadian Art* and so-and-so insulted whoever-the-fuck on Instagram. When everything is underwater none of this will matter. Buoyed by this thought, plus a few more beers, I am peaceful enough that when I get home I fall easily into bed and sleep like a baby.

*

The next day at work, Teresa and Eric get into this massive fight in front of everyone in the theatre including all of the customers. It starts off small and gets louder and louder until everyone is frozen watching them go at it behind the concession stand. Eric calls Teresa a stupid bitch.

Teresa says, "So what, you're just some dumb faggot." She dumps a cup full of Coke on his head. Someone has called Kevin in at this point. He breaks the two apart and apologizes to the customers. Everyone is buzzing from the drama. Who started it? She's so angry all the time. Eric is such a kiss-ass. I know that this is going to lead to some big team meeting about appropriate work behaviour and giving the customer the experience they paid for and blah blah blah.

I sneak outside for a cigarette break. Teresa is sitting on the front steps leading up to the theatre having a smoke. She waves.

"Hey," I say.

"Hey," she says. "Kevin sent me home for the day." I sit down next to her and we smoke in silence for a little while, staring at the street in front of us.

"Look," she says. "I'm sorry. I didn't mean—like, I'm not homophobic or whatever."

I laugh. "Don't worry about it. No big deal."

"Sometimes I just get so angry," she says. "And I don't know what to do so I end up saying all this stupid shit."

"I totally get it," I say. I do.

"He sucks. You know he's the one that ratted us out the other night in the storage room? Kevin put me on probation. I'm probably going to get fired now."

"Yeah, fuck Eric. I always thought he was a little prick."

"I don't want to get fired," she says. "I like it here. And I need the money."

"If Kevin fires you I'll quit in protest."

Teresa smiles. We talk about life for a bit. Teresa wants to go to school in Montreal after she graduates next year, maybe study psychology at McGill. Or maybe she'll stay here and get a job at Aritzia. Her sister Carmen works there and they might be hiring soon. I tell her about Kelly and the Belgian curator and California underwater.

"You really think that'll happen?" she asks.

"I don't know," I say. "Maybe."

The following evening I meet Teresa and Carmen in Christie Pits to drink a few beers in the crater of the park. Carmen is the same age as me. I can tell that at first she's like what the fuck why are you hanging out with my younger sister? I act really swishy until she figures out that I'm not trying to hit on Teresa and then she softens. Turns out she knows Kelly and a bunch of other people I know but that's not surprising. Everyone who grew up downtown in my age bracket kind of knows one another.

"So Kelly's like some big artist now?" Carmen asks.

"I guess so," I say. "He just had a show in LA."

"Mikey says that California's gonna be underwater any day now," says Teresa. Carmen glances at me sidelong.

"There's supposed to be this big tsunami coming on the west coast," I say, by way of explanation. "Like the one that happened in Japan in 2011 or whatever but on the other side of the Pacific. They say it'll hit the Alaskan coast and then go all the way down BC to California. It's been predicted for years now but it still hasn't come."

"Shit," says Carmen. "Florida's supposed to be fucked too 'cause of rising sea levels and shit."

We drink more beer and Carmen rolls a joint. We talk about normal, boring stuff: movies we like, what TV shows we're watching, how irritating our co-workers and managers can be. Carmen is the manager at Aritzia so she tells us about it from the other side. The more we talk the more I realize I haven't been around people my own age who aren't pretentious art school kids or people from my high school in a really long time. I make a mental note to ask Carmen for her number at the end of the evening. When I stand up to go pee in the bushes, a head rush tells me that I am very very fucked up.

When I get back from peeing Teresa's like, "Hey, do you want to go swimming?"

*

Carmen and Teresa Tasmanian Devil it right the fuck over the chain-link fence, toss their clothes on the deck, and cannonball into the water. Too headstrong and embarrassed to ask for a boost, I watch the two of them splash around while I shimmy and grunt my way up the fence. When I finally get to the other side, I trip on a pant leg while trying to slip it off. I fall into the water as though into a hug, laughing.

"This is so chill!" I say once my head bobs to the surface. "Isn't this so chill?"

Carmen and Teresa laugh. It really is so chill though! Teresa goes down the waterslide. She lands with a tremendous splash. I go under again and swim around with my eyes open. Everything is wiggly greens and whites.

Maybe I should go to LA. Maybe the tsunami won't be so bad. Maybe I would be granted gills. They'll need movie theatres underwater, right? And what good will painting be after we are all submerged? Every canvas will be wiped clean anyway. The only skill that will matter is how you can stay afloat.

I pull myself out of the water. Carmen's like, "Hey, is everything cool?"

I'm like, "Yeah, yeah. I'm gonna call Kelly. Kelly should come! I'm gonna call Kelly." Then I grab my phone out of my jeans and call Kelly.

*

I wake up the next morning two and a half hours late for work. My head is throbbing and everything feels like shit. I have five missed calls: one from the National Student Loan Centre, one from Teresa, two from Kevin, one from Kelly. They can wait till later. They can wait til never. Until after we're all submerged. I walk to the Loblaws down the street from my apartment to get Advil and orange juice. I wander through the aisles for what feels like forever like a fish paddling laps in its bowl.

Going Toward Gadd

JOHN ELIZABETH STINTZI

There Are No Oceans

In the world of Sacalia, there are no oceans. Water—in the wider universe—is asylumed to its own plane, a plane where there are no skies, or sea floor, or any creatures at all: just fresh, lifeless water. Water is the only element that does not naturally occur in Sacalia, while also being completely integral to the world's survival.

You wake up with the band of smugglers you've been with since abandoning the burning city of Candoma. You're on the cliffs overlooking the city of Abario. The rough sand you've been crossing for weeks looks like glass in the morning light. The aqueducts of Abario—old as life—glitter below, slowly circulating fresh water from the ocean plane. You're the first one to wake.

What do you do?

Hir Skeleton

There's a skeleton in the back of hir car as ze parks at the twenty-four-hour grocery store in Westport. It's past midnight, in July, and the Kansas City heat is still killer. Ze gets out of the car, an old hybrid, and opens the trunk to pull the skeleton out. Sweat hops onto hir skin. The skeleton is wearing an American flag bandana. The skeleton is wearing costume jewellery bought off Craigslist and Letgo. The skeleton is wearing a chest binder and a low-necked tank top and faded jeans as ze hoists them over hir shoulder.

Several bodies move in and out of cars on the dim-lit lot, carrying bags of 2:00 a.m. groceries, bags of 2:00 a.m. gin and vermouth and condoms. They don't bat an eye at hir, muscling dressed up bones out of hir car. It's hir night off, and when the automatic doors open to the near-empty store, ze gets blasted by the blessing of AC. Ze carries the skeleton past the sleepy security guard stationed near the door towards the produce section.

Ze cuts straight over to the assortment of peppers, props and poses the skeleton to look like they're inspecting the spicy dried red peppers, sticking one between the skeleton's teeth, to be held by the spring-shut jaw. Ze takes out hir phone and takes a picture, making sure the arm that ze's using to prop the skeleton up can be cropped out.

Ze takes a few photos, as many as ze can before the security guard ambles over, eyes baggy, and asks hir to "please, again, just—please leave."

The Fountains of Sacalia

In the material plane of Sacalia, there are nineteen fountains of infinite flow, around which the many civilizations grow. That's how this water-needing world survives. The complex network of aqueducts are used to move water around from the fountains' sources to the nearby sections of the plane, irrigating non-desert oases between the founts, sustaining cities and farmland and towns.

You have been told that the fountains are gates to the ocean plane. Mages, practised in interplanar spells, say that the output of water from these gates is at every moment moving the maximum volume of matter, so—theoretically—you wouldn't be able to cross through the gates to the ocean plane, making them effectively one-way. At least until the infinite ocean dries up.

Hu

Hir skeleton's name is Hu. Hu was purchased from a retired public school teacher living in Shawnee. Ze picked Hu up with hir roommate Sunny, but when they got to the house ze had Sunny go in without hir because ze started having an anxiety attack. Ze sat in the car, drowsy yet panicking at being awake and in those suburbs in the daytime, while Sunny went in and haggled the teacher down from $130 to $85. Sunny came out triumphant with the naked skeleton—*Hu*—lounged across her arms like Superman bearing Lois Lane. Hu was in good condition, besides missing the third finger bone—"Phalange," the teacher'd told Sunny—on their left hand.

"You made the right choice, kid," she said to hir when she got into the car. "The guy was pushing seventy at least, and there were Jesus faces everywhere—like, on every wall."

The Aqueducts

It's not known where Sacalia's aqueducts came from. The popular theory is that they were built by sandstone golems summoned by the gods to make the world hospitable to elves, dwarves, human, dragonborn—all the heartbeating things. The aqueducts are explained by a teleological understanding of the universe as something *designed*, something bubbling back to a first intent of a prime mover.

The fountains of Sacalia are rumoured to be the vertices of a magic sigil that, when connected correctly—using the proper reagents—will open a massive portal to the ocean plane. It's rumoured that this is how all life on Sacalia will end—these two planes merging, a suspension of dirt in flood. Some Sacalians believe this, but many don't. Others are trying to make it happen.

Welcome to Kansas

For the first few weeks after getting hir job at the University of Kansas Medical Center—a janitorial gig, working the graveyard shift—ze used Google Maps to navigate the ten-minute drive from hir and Sunny's apartment in midtown. Ze used Google Maps to get to work so ze wouldn't have to waste much attention on knowing where hir car was going. Every time ze was a minute or so away from work, hir phone announced: "Welcome to Kansas" over the car's speakers.

Eventually, when ze finally stopped using Google Maps to get to work—because ze knew the drive blindfolded—ze started to whisper that line to hirself whenever ze crossed the intersection at State Line Road. A quiet whisper to the bumping of—most often—Adult Mom or Worriers or sometimes Lou Reed:

"Welcome to Kansas," possibly the only sentence ze ever says five times a week, besides "I check for traps," and "I hate you" in the bathroom mirror.

Current Demographics of "Known Races" in Sacalia

Race*	Percentage of Population**	Life Expectancy (in Years)
Dragonborn	33.1%	321 Years
Elves	18.8%	193 Years
Mixed	18.4%	(Varies)
Dwarves	9.2%	93 Years
Orcs	9.1%	72 Years
Gnomes	5.3%	120 Years
Infernal	4.3%	78 Years
Tieflings	1.7%	237 Years
Humans	0.1%	23 Years

*Includes subspecies of races, such as, for elves: avariel, dark elves, drow, etc.
The current (recorded) population on of Sacalia is approximately 1.1 million*
***Of those 1.1 million Sacalians, at least 8% publicly self-identify as members of The Cult of the Water-Bringers.

@skelly.hu

Hu the skeleton—*@skelly.hu*—is relatively well-known on Instagram with just over 40k followers. *@skelly.hu* was inspired by the account *@omgliterallydead*, but instead of having a hipster-ish, white-girl kind of aesthetic, *@skelly.hu* strives for queer-punk and tries to post at least once a week. Their bio on Instagram reads: *"they/them/theirs. queerest bones ever tbh. #KCMO #TransBonesMatter"*

Feeling Rails in Abario

You and your companions make it to the base of the cliffs, through the sprawling towns skirting the walls, and to Abario's gate. There, through the checkpoint, you and your companions pass papers to whichever dragonborn guard is asking for them. Every paper the group passes is a counterfeit: none of you are who you claim to be. Your band's loose leader, Hienan—a high-elf and an unrivalled saboteur and intelligence agent—goes through first, and his getting through makes the rest of you optimistic. If he can make it, as a high-profile fugitive in Sacalia, you'll be able to make it through—yet again—against the odds. And then you'll all be that much closer to pilfering the riches of Abario.

One of your dwarven companions—Bengus—gets hassled about the portrait drawing on her papers but makes it through. Then her husband does. And finally, you do—as Faeroni the dark elf. The dragonborn doesn't frisk you, doesn't closely inspect your pointed ears, doesn't consider your eyes or your complexion or your bones. You get lucky because dragonborn can hardly stand the idea of looking at elves like you.

Once you've all made it into the main citadel of Abario, you head to a tavern near the outside of the rich quarter's walls. You get the sense, going there—attempting to be perceptive, to catch who might be looking at you and who might think they *see* something—that you're going exactly where you're designed to go. This is not a safe place for your sort, there are no safe places. You feel a confrontation brewing. You get the idea of running but don't run. You wonder if you even could.

Nobody really knows exactly who anyone else is. The band sticks together—mostly—by not being too curious about one anothers' lives. Respect, fear: words for proximity without intimacy.

Hu(s)

Ze goes by "Hu" in hir head, and in hir *Dungeons & Dragons* campaign. Ze plays *D&D* every Tuesday night with a guy ze met online. His name is Liam, and he ran away to Kansas City when he was fifteen, which was only about two or three years ago. He works at a game store in Overland Park, lives in a basement in Leawood, and spends most of his free time as a Dungeon Master. When they talk, they mostly talk about *D&D*, about hir playing *Pathfinder* with hir brothers when they were little, without the various sided dice necessary and getting by on tweaked rules, coin tosses, and two six-sided dice from *Monopoly*.

Ze and Liam have been playing for a while, but don't really know each other at all. They see each other three or four hours a week, but don't spend time together outside the game. Outside of Sacalia.

Liam does not call hir "Hu." Liam uses hir outside name, what ze thinks of as hir *zombie* name, at least until the whiteboard is set on the table between them and the dice are warming in their palms. In *D&D*, Hu is a human rogue. Hu uses a rapier and has focused most of their skill points into tumbling, lock-picking, search, and disguise.

When they met for coffee the second time, once Liam decided that Hu would fit well into his campaign—and after they determined Hu's ability scores and backstory in Sacalia—Liam asked, "What's Hu afraid of?" Ze didn't know how to answer that question, ze hadn't thought about that at all, so ze said, simply, "Bodies of water."

Liam drank down the sugared ends of his coffee. "Then Hu is lucky. In the world of Sacalia, there are no oceans."

The Cult of the Water-Bringers

In Sacalia, there are many reasons for a human like Hu to be afraid, particularly of water and cities, the biggest reason being the radical religious sect attempting to open this "doomsday gate" to the ocean plane: *The Cult of the Water-Bringers.* They're a relatively new extremist group—having existed only for the past three or four decades—who worship the evil demigod of drowning, Yeathan. The cult was started by a diaspora of infernal in Irrun, a town on the outskirts of Gadd— the largest Sacalian city—at a time when the infernal were by far the minority in Sacalia. The cult has since expanded, converting a sizable number of disenfranchised dragonborn, tieflings, mixed race, and orcs.

The cult is trying to create the portal to the ocean plane so that every Sacalian will be drowned. They see it as the only way to purify the sick world. A majority of Sacalians don't fear the cult, don't believe that what it is trying to do is possible, and don't bother to stop it.

This is all because most Sacalians are not human.

Hir Social Media

Ze doesn't have a personal Instagram, or a Facebook (anymore). Hir handle on Twitter—since ze started it, after moving to KC—changes every year, depending on hir age. This year it's *@RollOneD23.* Last year, it was *@RollOneD22.* Ze doesn't have hir name on hir Twitter and doesn't have hir account linked to hir phone number or an email that anyone knows. Hir photo is a picture of an egg with a small crack in it. Ze has 104 followers, and hir location is set as Perth, Australia. Occasionally, ze will retweet photos of water or news taken from *#Perth.* Ze hasn't ever uttered—on Twitter—a single word of hir own. Ze just lurks.

Humans in Sacalia

Humans, in Sacalia, are an endangered race because *The Cult of the Water-Bringers* preys on them. The cult believes that the key reagent in Yeathan's doomsday spell is present nowhere else but within human bodies. Since humans were the first, impure creatures created by the gods to inhabit Sacalia, they are believed to be the key to rewinding the clock to the purity of lifelessness. The cult believes the key is in the hormones produced by the adrenal and pituitary glands—as well as the ovaries and gonads—namely the human growth hormone, testosterone, estrogen, and progesterone. The cult believes that these hormones are the key to transforming the world into what they want it to be.

Yeathan's spell is barbaric, requiring such volumes of the believed-to-be-human-exclusive hormones that living humans must be "farmed" for them. Which consists of binding spells and horrible extraction techniques done on living human bodies over extended periods of time, squeezing them until the organs and glands fail.

They (Ze) / Them (Hir) / Theirs (Hirs)

Hu the skeleton's pronouns are *they/them/theirs* because ze wanted Hu to defy the binary in a simple way, in a way ze knew the majority of queer people would be able to relate to while not being excessively foreign to others who might stumble upon Hu's presence online. Those pronouns felt *polite*. "They" felt accommodating to the other as well as to the same. "They" felt *clear*.

But, for hirself, in hir head, ze didn't take this pronoun because hir relationship to hirself is based less on certainty and clarity than on tripping and murk, more on inaccessibility, unease. *Ze* and *hir* feel indefinite and suggestive of either end of the binary and are so difficult to train the tongue to utter. Ze wanted to feel like a trick question, an uphill battle between nuclear powers.

After a few preliminary sessions in Sacalia—as Hu joined up with the band of smugglers while fleeing Candoma (the small but prosperous elven city to the east) as it went up in flames (from the conquests of the greedy, red dragon Dyviassiel), the same band with whom Hu'd just fought off a small wave of a lamia's jackalwere on their retreat across the treacherous desert toward the valley city of Abario—Liam confessed that Hu wasn't the only player character in Sacalia.

"There are others," he told hir, after offering hir an energy drink at 10:45 p.m., just before they finished off that Tuesday's session. The family he lived under were arguing, stomping, fuming. "There are other *protagonists*. Most of them are in other parts of Sacalia—other cities—taking actions, sending ripples your way. I actually do at least seven different sessions a week, including you."

Ze was surprised when Liam said this. Ze'd believed that Hu was the only player character there, the only one that *really* mattered. Ze believed that hir character's importance was why the lamia didn't succeed in finishing Hu off when they fell unconscious after Hu was charmed into the tip of her quick dagger. But no, the dominoes of fate were scattered. In other places in Sacalia, other cities, characters of various levels of goodness or evil—characters whom ze hadn't thought existed at all—were spying or protecting, saving or plundering, progressing along their self-drawn paths. Ze couldn't express how this made hir feel. Ze pictured other bodies in hir seat, nodded hir head, and spaced out to the books on Liam's shelf: a wide collection of epic fantasy, science writing, and almost every single novel by Toni Morrison.

"Anyway," Liam said. His words felt extraplanar. "Hu, are you going to help pay for a room at the public house for you and your companions, or are you going to camp again on the outskirts of town?"

"We're going to the outskirts," ze says. "And while we go, I'm keeping an eye out for people following."

Ze rolls one d20 for perception but doesn't roll very well—a four. Hu doesn't see anyone.

Fear of Water

Hu isn't afraid of bodies of water insomuch as Hu's afraid of *space*, of the possibilties of space, of the mystery of what could be found or happen in it. Hu is afraid of bodies of water because of their mystery, their opacity, because of water's ability to reflect without revealing, because of water's ability to invade through any gap, no matter the shape. It's for the same reason Hu's afraid of the crowds, of the suburbs, of the sprawling similarities betraying the reality of a granular chaos. Hu is afraid of all the people Hu doesn't know, and most people Hu does know, because if life has taught Hu anything it's how easy it is to keep things hidden, submerged, and how unwilling people can be to truly reveal themselves.

Attack!

You wake up to the high death-cry of Bengus the dwarf, wake up to the sun teasing the west, to metal flying in glints. You wake up to Hienan impaling a dragonborn of Abario's police, wake up tumbling and drawing your rapier, aiming at Bengus's murderer but rolling too low to hit. There are fifteen of them surrounding ten of you—half not yet upright from their sleep. Magic begins to fly, concussive bursts shaking brains, magic missiles. Hienan throws you a look. You tumble, again, to flank an officer, and get a sneak attack bonus on a critical hit as you stab through lungs, through one of their two hearts. Score three points under Massive Damage.

You're all up now, clanging, being hit, hurt, dying. You take a crossbow bolt in the back of your calf and take a penalty to your dexterity-based skills. You try to tumble your way to Hienan's side without provoking an attack of opportunity and fail. A falchion skips along your ribs. Eight of the fifteen dragonborn are dead, but this is not going well. Hienan takes up Bengus's dagger and dual wields—at a disadvantage—but succeeds. Every enemy near him is dead.

You help, and a fight that takes about forty seconds in game time takes you about an hour and a half of rolling and being on the edge of your seat. When the smoke settles, you're alive—haggard but alive. Only three of your companions have died.

The Riding Floor-Scrubber

When ze is at work, ze works alone: mop cart, Windex, earbuds, half-lit halls on the riding floor-scrubber. Check-up rooms, men's bathrooms, lecture halls with naked skeletons like Hu hanging from bolts on their heads, women's bathrooms, waiting rooms, single-occupancy bathrooms. Ze has a set routine that ze follows every week.

Most days, ze gets up around 11:20 p.m., eats and dresses, then drives to work unshowered to start at midnight. On Tuesdays, ever since ze started doing D&D with Liam, ze wakes up early—around 6:00 p.m.—and goes over to Liam's, before heading to work, for hir weekly session: 7 to 11:30. It's the only day worth showering for.

"This is the life," ze sometimes thinks to hirself, grumbling alone around campus, dragging the mop cart or zooming along on the scrubber. Ze thinks about everything while ze works: hir very few (and mostly online) friends, hir family, Sacalia. Over the years working here, following the same map every week, ze has gotten so good at operating the scrubber that ze can do it without even looking up from hir phone.

All through hir shift, whenever ze is operating the scrubber, or doing anything else one-handed, ze mostly lurks on Reddit (r/trans, r/KCMO, r/nonbinary, r/aww) and Twitter. Queer Twitter, where queer people—comic artists, activists, chefs, journalists—from across the spectrum rally against capitalism and TERFs, subtweet one another, post selfies, and talk hormones and music and dysphoria and video games. Ze doesn't post anything, ze doesn't retweet any queer tweets, ze just reads and follows and—very rarely—likes. Ze exists silent among the chatter. A fly drowning in the stream of them.

Ze would like to say things but feels like hir identity is a fraud. Ze isn't out, ze is still questioning hirself, doesn't feel ze has anything to say that's worth listening to, despite the fact that in hir head ze knows everything exactly, has known it all for a while.

Ze also knows that most of the accounts ze follows and likes best are public alt-accounts, that there's a *secret* and *private* queer Twitter beyond the visible one, that waves of DMs synapse between so many of these humans ze looks up to. Ze reads along always knowing there are echelons of community that ze cannot access, but which ze believes hold the answers ze needs to become more honestly and loudly hirself.

When ze feels this way, catch-22'd from this world, while scrubbing the lonely halls, ze logs onto Instagram and basks in the queer-centred acceptance that hir *@skelly.hu* affords. The most beloved queer skeleton on the internet.

Hienan's Plan

You think you know why this attack happened: someone was suspicious of your group, recognized one of you, and ratted you out. Bengus's husband thinks the authorities in Abario are simply corrupt —*racist*—and want non-dragonborn like you to stop coming into their city. You believe that someone probably caught Hienan looking up from under his hood at the rich quarter's walls—where the dragonborn elite live in a lazy effulgence—and cross-referenced his elven characteristics against wanted posters and whispers that the last place he'd been seen was only ninety miles away, at the multicultural oasis of Bradgoth.

You want to leave Abario, leave the hiding spot you're in, but Hienan is furious and wants revenge. Everyone else—hurt and tired and angry—wants to stick to the plan too, because Hienan claims to have figured out the way over the walls and into the inner citadel, through a glitch in the guard cycle. They know how easy it will be to get rich once they're in. They're convincing. You feel rails telling your cart which direction to take.

You say okay, you're in. You are not.

Just Water

Ze obsessively stalks the accounts of people undergoing transition, watches from afar as HRT and surgeries shift the shape of the human body. Ze cannot get over the beauty of watching science turn a binary on its head, watching it overthrow the way a body is read. Ze doesn't believe there is anything more arresting than watching someone topple biology with biology to seem closer to who they've always been.

Hu the skeleton is hir key to the private sphere of queer Instagram. Hu follows thousands of accounts and likes basically every photo posted, gets messages about how validating those double taps are. Ze reads all these messages but replies only in hearts and hashtags: *#TransBonesMatter, #NonbinaryBonesMatter, #HerBonesMatter*, whichever seems best to apply. Hu sends back hearts and hashtags but doesn't converse. Hu's bones are marrowed with an indiscriminate yet aloof love of queerness, but through their own photos it's clear that Hu can't quite get their bones to feel right. Hu's presentation fluctuates, and sometimes even falters—occasionally posting a photo without them in it, noting that they're not happy with how they look.

There is a subtext between the overflow of pride and humour and love that Hu the skeleton can't quite get themselves to be who they want to be. That there's no stable identity inside them to try to present. That there probably never will be. That it's all just water.

Going Toward Gadd

Just after your watch ends, the night before you're meant to strike Abario back, you go inside and wake Bengus's husband. He's not the next on watch, but you know how long it takes him to get lucid after waking, so you nudge him up then run. You leave your wounded, furious companions and slip into the desert, south, toward the biggest city in the world: *Gadd*. You had no intention of ever going to Gadd. You know how dangerous Gadd would be, that the farther you stay away from population density—and particularly Gadd's—the better.

But you've been thinking: Gadd is the largest city in Sacalia, so whom could you find there?

Thursday? Sunday?

Same Time Next Week

Before ze leaves Liam's basement apartment, all hir dice and character sheets packed up, Liam asks:

"Same time next week?"

Meet Hu at the Shuttlecock

A fair number of *@skelly.hu*'s followers are from KC and often ask Hu to meet up with them. Ze has never had the guts to do it hirself, though one Monday afternoon—this past June—Hu did have a local meet-up at the Nelson-Atkins Museum of Art, beside one of the big shuttlecocks in the sculpture garden. Ze had Sunny take Hu there and send hir a photo of them posed against the sculpture—for hir to use to inform Hu's followers. Sunny pretended to be the first of the attendees. "Hu was alone when I got here!" she said to the first visitors to come by.

The whole time, ze wanted to go, or walk past, or at least watch from the distance, but couldn't bring hirself to. Ze sat in hir car a few blocks away, windows cracked to the breeze, getting texts from Sunny—"Come on! ppl are so diggin Hu"—and felt so unreflected in the world, spineless.

Ze wanted to disappear, ooze through the cracks in hir reality. Instagram notifications pinged, telling hir that Hu was being tagged in photos. Ze never brought hirself to look at them, but Hu liked them blindly.

Tuesday

On Tuesday, ze heads over to Liam's and parks hir hybrid far down the street because most of the spots in Liam's neighbourhood are taken. Ze goes, thinking of Gadd, walks with hir hands in hir pockets, trying to not be seen. Ze walks past a kid—probably thirteen—sitting on a longboard on the sidewalk, facing away from the street, playing *Pokémon Go* on his phone. He's cursing. Ze notices that he's trying to catch a Haunter—in a different layer of reality—that keeps breaking free.

When ze gets to Liam's ze goes inside and gets situated: takes out hir dice, Hu's character sheet, hir notes. The family above has the TV loud, spewing news about politics and war. Liam is already prepared at the other end of the table as ze picks up hir d20, readying to make Hu's first moves.

Possibility City

You start making your way toward the walls of Gadd. The desert has been rough, days of limping away from Hienan and your companions in Abario, each of which you expect is either dead or rich. You're not rich, but you're alive, having dodged the war parties of a Mummy Lord in The Crush—the seven-mile-wide strip of desert abandoned by law and populated by chaotic evil. Your bolt-stuck calf ached and dragged but you made it. You moved silently, and against all odds, you're here, outside Gadd.

Possibility City.

You start to make your way to the city's gate through the northern suburbs. Gadd's aqueducts weep in the high midday sun. The walls stretch twice as high as any you've seen before. One out of every ten Sacalians lives here, living off the swells of Fountain 7. You don't know what you will find inside those walls, but you believe it will be important. That it will somehow hold the key to changing the course of your life.

Death Threats

Sometimes, sometimes often, Hu gets death threats. Awful words fly, in direct messages or comments on pictures of them messily enjoying some extremely blue ice cream—Cookie Monster flavour—from the Westport Ice Cream Bakery. In comments, Hu's followers descend to defend them, but when they come as direct messages ze is terrified. Sometimes ze is brave and tells them that Hu is clearly already dead. Mostly ze blocks and reports them, and takes their advice: putting hir phone away and wrapping hir arms around hirself to try not to exist for awhile.

Friday

"When you're about four hundred feet from the walls, you hear a noise," Liam says, eventually, after rolling a dice. "From an alley beside you a robed figure is casting." Liam rolls. "Roll a Will save."

Ze rolls. "Eleven."

Liam looks down at an open player's handbook, then picks up his phone and sends a text.

"You're paralyzed, weakened, and dazed," he says. As he does, the door to his basement opens.

The boy with the longboard comes down, puts his phone on the table, and pulls up a chair. He doesn't look at hir.

"The character failed the Will save," Liam tells him, not looking at hir. "They are paralyzed, weakened, and dazed. What do you do?"

The kid looks at the map drawn on the dry-erase tabletop, the huge circle representing Gadd. "I go up to the character and inspect them, to make sure that they are human."

"They are human."

"I use my silk rope and bind them." The kid takes a handful of dice from his cargo shorts and rolls. "Twenty-two. Once bound, I take the human into the alley and meet up with my crew and we go to Irrun. When I get there, I put them under."

Liam notes all of this and looks up at hir, across the table. Ze says nothing, is looking at the numbers and words of Hu's character sheet.

"You wake up and you can't move. You can feel tubes going into your body. You can only move your eyes. You're not alone. Friday here is attending to pulling the hormones from your body. You hear others talking Draconic about how close they think they are to having enough reagents to complete the spell, how they have enough humans— almost spitting when coming to the word for human, *munthrek*. You can't move, or speak, but you feel extreme pain. You get the sense that there are other human bodies next to you that you can't see."

SAD Drow

Since ze started playing *D&D* with Liam, while working nights at the university, ze began to jokingly identify, in hir head, as drow: a subterranean elven race. Since ze started working the graveyard shift, ze mostly sees the sun when ze gets out of work. Ze spends most of hir days after sunset, and when ze comes home from work, ze retreats into the dark of hir room. Hu, hir skeleton, waits in the other half of hir double bed. Ze lies beside them and narrates the positive comments on their Instagram.

Hir graveyard shifts, ze's convinced, give hir a sort of seasonal affective disorder. For weeks at a time, sometimes, ze can barely get out of bed to go to work, and at work can barely function, and can barely make it home after. Sometimes, ze thrashes around in hir room, terrified of hirself. Ze feels so old, so densely packed in with sensations ze is numb to, so close to expiration. When tears come, they don't help. They don't release anything.

And it feels to hir that when ze is feeling like this—SAD, suicidal—that ze is falling precisely into the same narrative that all queer, all questioning, all gender-fucked people find themselves: inside a sort of validating, inclusive, yet depersonalized sadness. Ze feels like another body muttering a culturally tedious refrain.

And yet, even in this pain ze feels completely isolated from the community. Ze blames the sun, the moon, and hir confusion—believes hirself to be a fraud, dying out and invisible and alone on the fringe.

Friday, Friday, Friday

That Tuesday's session ends early, because ze can progress only so long in the timeline before needing to allow the rest of the concurrent player characters to make their moves in Sacalia. Ze didn't realize, before, how Hu was only ever able to go so far forward in time. Liam never let on.

Ze leaves Liam's without speaking. Ze goes to work early, wanders around the halls with hir earbuds in like a ghost, dragging hir mop from bathroom to bathroom. Liam texts hir later, asking if ze can start coming in on Friday evenings for a while, at least while Hu is in this predicament. "It works best for Max." Ze doesn't respond for a while—a day—until writing back, "sure."

Ze starts sleeping in on Tuesdays and going to Liam's on Fridays. Usually, the sessions last about an hour for Hu. Hu wakes up, is talked to by cultists, overhears them talk about their plans to place the hormones into the waters very soon, that they finally might have enough. Hu tries to move but can't, and then, eventually, Hu passes out and Liam rolls some dice privately and then tells hir it's probably fine for hir to leave.

"See you next week!"

Max doesn't look at hir, doesn't really look at anything but the map and the dots and circles or painted figures that represent people. Max parts his oily hair to the right, blocking hir from seeing his eyes. Max's sessions seem to consist mostly of discussing logistics, power dynamics, and who should go to which fountain with which amount of the reagents.

Hu's sessions were only ever about moving and staying alive.

Hu's Brand

Ze knows that the best way to make Hu popular and keep Hu popular is to keep them on brand, to deliver to Hu's followers exactly what is expected of them.

What's expected of Hu: satire, whimsy, sarcasm, denim jackets, and a low-key but constant struggle with dysphoria. What is expected of Hu is that they'll never find home in their bones, that they'll always try to hide behind deprecative humour. That sometimes—sometimes often—they will fail.

The first photo ze ever posted of Hu was a photo of Hu huddled up in hir closet, naked arm bones wrapped around naked leg bones. The caption of the photo—which has only about six hundred likes—ran "I'm Hu and I'll always be the questioning skeleton in your closet."

Bringing Yeathan's Water

Another Friday comes, and ze goes over to Liam's again. Ze isn't sure why ze is coming anymore, besides because ze has grown attached to Hu and doesn't want them to be harmed. That ze feels responsible for their life reaching this point.

But this Friday is different. "When you wake up, Hu, you aren't in the cult's den. You, among other scarred humans, wake up on a roof on the outskirts of Gadd. The emerald shimmer of the fountain waters glimmers over the edges of the aqueducts. The wind is cool. The cultists surround the edge of the roof, but the tubes in your brain and in your abdomen seem to have been removed. You can move. You don't trust that you should, but you can. You look around."

At the edge of the roof, fifteen feet away, a telepath shares messages from the cult's agents across Sacalia with the neutral-evil tiefling cleric Shalyre—played by Max. They're all in position, have secured access to each of the nineteen gates to the ocean plane.

You want to jump up and try to kill him, but you're weak. The other humans around you are only weaker, having been there longer. There are maybe sixty of you in total. Before speaking, Shalyre looks over at your lot.

When Shalyre tells the telepath to send the message "Do it," you think that is going to be the last sentence you'll ever hear. You feel relief, for a second, that life and torment will be over. A minute passes. Two minutes pass. Five. Nothing happens at all.

Fists bang a table, though there's no table on the roof. "What do you *mean* nothing happens?" a kid's voice rings. "What the fuck have we been doing all this shit for if nothing is going to happen? We've been playing at this for two fucking years. What the fuck?"

Shalyre is paused on the roof. Nobody is moving. You look around and everything is static, drawn. The world is neither dying nor alive. Yelling comes from beyond, Max yelling, the muffled yelling of the family above, and Liam speaks up and says: "Settle down, Max. Come on. It's just a game: this is all just part of the plot."

But the voice doesn't settle. It curses. A chair falls. A door slams. The TV of the family above starts to blare, to drown out the rage, and then things begin to move again. Shalyre looks over at you, Hu, with different eyes. You and the rest of the humans suddenly notice that the cultists have taken off their swords and left them near your crowd. "You all, suddenly, feel enlivened," Liam's voice says, after a minute of quiet. "The other humans go and grab the swords and toss you one as they start to take a surprise round on the cultists. You outnumber them three to one. They're all unarmed. Shalyre is closest to you, Hu, and is looking ready to cast. What do you do?"

What do you do? You do what you believe you're meant: You humans slaughter them all.

Routine

After the humans cut off the head of the cult, Hu's sessions move back to Tuesdays. Hu gets into Gadd and hears about a group of daring mercenaries who want to try to tame The Crush, where the rest of the cultists are said to have escaped into. Hu joined them because it seemed like the thing to do.

But ze doesn't want to wake up early on Tuesdays, doesn't want to go back at all. Ze has forgotten why ze ever wanted to be in that world in the first place, wondered why ze thought it was all that different, why ze thought ze had any agency there. But Hu, there, just keeps falling into new traps: fresh but equally devised regions of a set story.

There's no escaping the rails, no matter how hard Hu tries.

Ze spends the days between sessions waking up in the daylight to take Hu the skeleton to all sorts of places in the city, buying them

T-shirts in Waldo, buying them barbecue in the Crossroads, buying them donuts and coffee and pizza downtown. Hashtagging photos for Instagram.

Carrying their bones into and out of the car, showing off whatever spunk is left in their bones, working in variations on their long-tired theme.

Flash Flood Warning

On Tuesday, ze wakes up around noon to hir phone going nuts with an alert. *Flash Flood Warning in effect for Jackson County.* Ze reads it, silences it, and goes back to sleep. The storm is shuddering the sky outside. When ze wakes up again and leaves hir room, around 6:00 p.m., Sunny is pulling out candles in case they lose power. The weather outside is biblical, loud. Ze puts on hir shoes and grabs hir keys and tells Sunny that ze's going to go drive down to Liam's.

"You're insane, kid!" Sunny tells hir, and so ze goes into hir room and hoists Hu up, grabs hir bag of dice, hir character sheet, umbrella, and carries Hu outside—into the deluge—belting them into the passenger seat of hir car.

The lightning shatters sky, breaking holes that water pours through. Ze can barely see fifteen feet ahead as they drive south together, trying to avoid Westport and the other easy-flooding areas. Ze looks out the window for headlights but mostly navigates by their dot on Google Maps, slowly moving along the white lines of the streets. Ze needs to get to Liam's. To tell him that ze can't do it anymore.

As ze gets near Liam's neighbourhood, ze starts driving through inches of water and stops only when ze notices a truck a block ahead—during a clear lull in the rain—driving through an intersection with water to its hips. Ze can see the unread messages on hir phone but doesn't read them. Ze knows that in this weather, Liam's apartment is likely flooding, has decided that this means Sacalia has drowned.

Ze stops in the middle of an empty intersection. Ze imagines the water never ending, the sound of the wipers an eternal squeak. Ze opens hir door and steps out into the water, hood up, hir *D&D* bag under hir coat, leaving Hu in the car. Ze walks out until the water is halfway to the knee. Ze doesn't want to stop but does, because ze can't bring hirself not to. Ze pulls Hu's scrawled character sheet from the bag, the sheet covered in eraser smudges from the changes, from levelling up and growing over the years, and slips it onto the rain-stippled flood water. It floats away. Ze pulls out the bag of dice and pours them out at hir feet then turns back to hir waiting car.

?????

When ze gets back in the car, ze takes Hu's phalange-missing hand in hirs and turns the car away from their destination, toward the least likely direction they should go.

Together, ze and Hu speed toward it, headlong.

Beelzebub's Kiss

GAVIN THOMSON

When my son was but a tot, he wouldn't stop acting like a dog. Maybe he believed he was in fact a dog. I couldn't tell, and my psychiatrist wouldn't weigh in. This is because I had stopped seeing my psychiatrist.

On the car ride in my wife's white sedan from our apartment in Prospect Heights, Brooklyn, to my grandmother's bungalow upstate I asked my son if he was hungry and he said, "Woof." So I asked him if he needed medical attention—same response; and so on.

It had been cute at first, his identity crisis. Then it got annoying. Then worrying.

It was two days after Thanksgiving, a Saturday. Leaves died, fell, stank—and did these things very prettily. My son and I were on our way to my grandmother's house because I thought she was dead. On Thanksgiving, her latest husband, Camael, had phoned me to say she was dead and her funeral would be held on Sunday.

As my son and I would soon find out, however, my grandmother was very much alive. Had Camael played a joke at our expense? No: Camael had dementia. I couldn't blame him. But I could, and did, blame my grandmother. Not for anything in particular, though. I guess I blamed her for being who she was.

Besides the fact that she would end up bequeathing me a decent inheritance—perhaps because I showed up at what I thought would be her funeral—my grandmother, Lamia, was the worst.

My son and I arrived at her bungalow around dinnertime, and the first thing she said to us when she opened her front door was, "Why are you here?"

Lamia was tall and slim and carried herself with perfect posture, and was physically perfect, and wore tiny glasses on the bridge of her nose that she tilted her head back to see through. That was her go-to face, her default way of being. A portrait of dignity. When she titled her head back to see me through her glasses she pursed her lips and scrunched her nose and appeared to be disgusted by a stench. Did I smell? I had forgotten to shower that morning, as well as the morning before, and my natural body scent was not ideal. Neither was my body.

Lamia's yappy small white dog ran into the foyer and sniffed my son and me, and my son got on all fours and sniffed back.

"This is my son," I said, and I picked him up and held him in my arms like a baby.

"A bit of a misfit, eh?" Lamia said. She did not make to touch him.

I said, "Camael said you were dead."

She said, "He must've made a mistake due to his retardation."

The dog woofed; my son woofed.

"Is your son also retarded?"

"My son is four."

Then my uncle, who had recently gotten a divorce and quit his job and moved into Lamia's bungalow—and who, according to my mother, diddled dogs—waddled toward me from the kitchen, huffing and puffing, as fat men do, and we exchanged gruff pleasantries, and I didn't like how he looked at my son when he woofed. I thought, *How thin is the line between a man who diddles dogs and a man who diddles boys who believe they're dogs?* Then I thought, *Shut the fuck up you fuck and kill yourself.* That thought was directed at me; it was a Dybbuk thought. But I told myself it was just a regular thought. A problem I was having in those days was that I was trying to convince myself that I was not, contrary to what my psychiatrist had said, sick in the head with Beelzebub's Kiss.

Or I was trying to make myself even sicker in the head so that my wife would pity and therefore love me the way she used to.

Either way, I had been off my meds for two months and was feeling good, not too good but still good, and I kept telling myself I no longer needed my meds, had never needed my meds, which by the way made me slow in mind and big in body—not unlike my uncle, who for the record I feel bad for, maybe.

Anyway, one thing on my mind at the time was divorce, as my wife possibly wanted one.

My wife was still my wife, legally speaking, and I loved her so much I teared up when I bench-pressed in our storage closet, remembering how I used to bench-press her in bed, and each night I slept on the pull-out couch in the living room—I told my son I slept there because I snored, which I did—while she slept in our marital bed. We fought a lot. The sad thing is I don't remember what we fought about.

The interior of Lamia's bungalow was arranged from left to right thusly: bathroom, master bedroom, little bedroom, TV den, kitchen, and dining room. Below was the basement. The walls and ceilings were forest green and migraine brown. All but the kitchen and bathroom floors were carpeted. Even the toilet seat cover was carpeted. The toilet seat cover was frilly and pink, like a little girl's earmuffs.

I found Camael on the recliner in the carpeted TV den, poking his thigh through his corduroy pants with a butter knife. His beard was manly; also very white. He would have looked hale and profound, or at least fun to be around, had he not been poking his thigh through his pants with a butter knife. When he saw me he said, "Hello, Sir Gawain. The funeral will cost more than she was worth."

My dumbass fatass uncle said to me, "Ever heard of Pavlov's dogs?" He bopped Camael on the nose with a rolled-up newspaper, which he kept inside his waistband like a gun, and said, "Stop being retarded."

"You're not supposed to say that word anymore," I said.

"Woof," said my son, who was following me around on all fours in his tiny black suit.

Lamia said, "I microwaved some meatloaf men."

Why, given that Lamia was alive, didn't I drive back home with my son?

I wanted him to understand how much his great-grandmother sucked. I believed, at the time, that children needed not only role models but also the opposite of role models. Otherwise, my thinking went, children would take their role models for granted. My mother, who died when I was twenty-eight—the same year I met my wife—is still my role model. But when I was a child, a single child, I thought all mothers were like her. A part of me doesn't want to share this information for fear of sounding self-pitying but when I was a kid I was quite sick. From ages seven to twelve I was often sick with all sorts of symptoms: two-day migraines, facial swelling, fevers and vomiting, out-of-body field trips, daytime visits from ghosts. Doctors never agreed on a diagnosis. Chronic fatigue syndrome? Mono that had morphed into chronic Epstein-Barr virus? Blah blah blah. Someone blamed a vaccine. Another told me I had to think happier thoughts. I really was quite sick but sometimes I malingered so that I could stay home from school and have my mother hold a damp cloth to my forehead and stroke my hair.

My mother gave up her promising though mostly unpaid career as a pianist and theatre director to care for me. I didn't comprehend the gravity of her sacrifice. I didn't comprehend how hard she had worked to be unlike her own mother, Lamia. I took my mother for granted. I took her love for granted. (My father, still alive, thank God, is a good man too.) I never wanted my son to take my love, or for that matter his mother's love, for granted. Therefore, I wanted him to spend enough time with Lamia to get a good sense of how fundamentally different she was from his mother and me.

His parents: good.

His great-grandmother: bad.

Good dog. Bad dog.

A simple enough lesson for a small boy to learn, no?

In Lamia's dining room, which overlooked the muddy backyard and beyond it a brown pond infested by beavers—anyone who fell into the pond had a good chance of contracting beaver fever—Camael slept on a chair at the dinner table, the dog sat at his feet, Lamia looked dignified, and my uncle chewed cold meatloaf men with his mouth open and said to my son without swallowing, "Dog boy, when did you become a dog?"

"My son won't answer that in English," I said, "or will you, son?"

"Woof."

The forest-green ceiling had dots of black mould on it. The carpet was the same shade of brown as the beaver pond.

"Would your son like to play out back in the mud?" Lamia said. "That's where our dog plays—in the mud."

My uncle said, "I've got a big house."

"Is that so," I said.

"Down in Virginia," he said. He huffed, puffed, slapped the table. Camael woke up, said, "No," fell back asleep.

"Ol' Virginia, damn right," my uncle said. His knuckles were hairy, unlike his head. (At least I still had hair.) "Was working down there in the oil industry," my uncle said, "before the divorce." He coughed, wheezed, fanned his face with his hand, coughed again. "Man, lots of money in the oil industry," he said. "Considering buying a bigger house with a bigger backyard. Lots of room in my current backyard to play around, have a pool, a hot tub, and a bunch of dogs—but my wife got the house," he said, "and also my dogs." He pointed at me with his fork, then asked Lamia for another meatloaf man.

Camael woke up again and said, "She was impossible."

My uncle bopped him on the nose with a rolled-up newspaper.

To my son I whispered, "Do you miss home?"

He nodded.

Good, I thought. *Dogs don't nod.*

After dinner, Lamia and Camael retired to their bedroom, my uncle played fetch with Lamia's dog in the muddy backyard, and I washed the dishes in the kitchen sink with a sponge while in the carpeted TV den my son watched a cartoon about a talking underwater sponge and his best underwater friend, a likeable starfish and fool. My son and I were still wearing our black funeral suits; I had forgotten to pack a change of clothes. His suit was identical to mine but smaller. The window above the kitchen sink overlooked the muddy backyard and as I scrubbed cold meatloaf men off plates I watched my uncle play tug-of-war with the dog he might diddle.

Lamia's landline rang.

She stuck her head outside her bedroom, where for the past however many decades she had slept on a waterbed, and said, "How'd your wife get my number?"

I found the cordless home phone in the TV den and said, "She's not dead."

"You're not funny."

"I'm not joking."

"Let me speak to my son."

"Trouble in paradise, eh?" said another voice.

It was Lamia's.

"Christ," I said, "why are you still on the line?" and—foolishly—I hung up on my wife.

My plan for that night was that my son and I would sleep on the bunk bed in the little bedroom, which my mother and uncle had shared from babyhood through high school; however, my uncle told me he had dibs on the little bedroom, so my son and I had no choice but to sleep in the carpeted TV den on the pull-out couch and recliner, respectively, and before that we had to search Lamia's bungalow for linen.

We found the linen in the carpeted basement, in a closet beside the music room, where for decades Lamia had given piano lessons to children whose fingers she squeezed until they tingled. No pillows. There were enough sheets to cover the pull-out couch in the TV den but not the recliner. I reclined on the recliner, which smelled of Camael, and my son curled up on the pull-out couch and barked something that implied he wanted me to tell him a bedtime story, which I did most nights.

I kissed his downy hair and said, "Once upon a time, in a land far away, a knight and his son, a squire, rode a horse to a witch's funeral, at the witch's shack in the woods, because they wanted to celebrate her passing. But when the knight and the squire arrived, it turned out the witch was alive…" And so forth.

My son slept. I did not. Or did I? On his old bunk bed my uncle snored, due I think to sleep apnea, another thing we shared, and whenever Lamia or Camael turned in their sleep their waterbed sloshed like a big wet shoe.

Which reminds me that when my mother was nine and her brother six, when they still had a father—he was a chaplain who spoke six languages, took the LSAT and MCAT for fun, and legally disowned my mother and uncle when they were ten and seven, remarried, had a stroke, became kind and tried in vain for two years to be a father again, then had a second stroke and died—my mother could tell when her mother was having sex with her father because through the master bedroom door my mother heard their waterbed sloshing and her mother saying, "Ow, ow, ow."

Right before sunrise I felt briefly, briefly but vividly, that nothing was real, especially me. But I told myself that people without Beelzebub's Kiss also sometimes feel unreal, especially after sleeping poorly.

Or I was psyched that I seemed to be getting sick again.

I still don't fully know what my intentions were at that point in my life. What I do know is I regret them.

When my son woke we took Lamia's yappy little white dog for a walk. The wintry air smelled of spruce and pine and other scents I enjoy but can't name because I don't know nature. Wind blew this way and that, brown birds bobbed about and were happy or at least horny, squirrels chased other squirrels.

I should mention that when my mother was twelve and it was wintertime, she fell through the pond while ice-skating, climbed out of the pond, and hurried in her soaked skates home, where Lamia told her to stand outside until she got sick, because Lamia wanted to teach her a lesson about—about what?

My son and I took the dog for a walk in our funeral suits through the mud to the beaver pond, which wasn't yet frozen over, and I instructed my son to look at his reflection in the pond and told him the story of Narcissus.

"And that's how the beautiful boy died," I concluded.

My son made a doggish noise that sounded vaguely like "mommy."

"Do you want breakfast?" I said, and he made a doggish noise that meant yes.

But when we returned to Lamia's bungalow, she told us she had already served breakfast and because my son and I hadn't been there to eat it, she'd tossed it in the trash. All of it.

She descended into the basement to speed-walk on the treadmill beside the ping-pong table.

Camael and my uncle were in the TV den watching poker. Camael was on the recliner and my uncle was on the pull-out couch. Camael said, "I have wasted my life," and my uncle bopped him on the nose with a rolled-up newspaper and turned off the TV and fed the yappy white dog a spoonful of apple butter and said to me, "Walk time, that's what I call it. I call it walk time."

When I was kid I thought the neighbour's dog was a robot made by God to spy on me, by the way.

I said, "We just took her for a walk."

"Dog can't get too many walk times in a day," my uncle said. "Impossible. I've enough room in my backyard, I mean my wife's backyard—I mean my ex-wife's backyard—for lots of dogs, so many dogs. Thinking of starting a dog farm after I get my job back and then retire, which I could do at any time. But I enjoy my line of work, you know? You ever think about working in the oil industry? You could work your way up from the bottom, unlike I did, for thou art not an engineer whereas by comparison me? Touché."

He shook my hand and waddled outside with the dog.

Camael was watching the blank TV and, in the basement, Lamia was speed-walking on the treadmill. She was loud. She breathed in through her nose and out through her mouth.

I think that's how people breathe in the military.

It's also how the nurses told my wife to breathe when she was giving birth to our son.

In the kitchen my son got on all fours and I said, "Bad boy." He stood up and said, "What's great-grandma doing?"

Wahoo, I thought. *He speaks.*

This was a major breakthrough. I was excited to tell my wife.

"She's doing her best to remain alive," I said.

"She's not a ghost?"

"This whole time you thought she was a ghost?"

"Do you love great-grandma?"

"Do you love her?"

"She said, 'Go play in the mud.' That was mean."

"Correct," I said, giddy, and I searched the kitchen for eatable breakfast food but found only cold meatloaf men, apple butter, pickles, and ranch dressing.

"Yum," said my son.

I said, "If you don't eat proper food, you'll start crying, and if I don't eat proper food, I might also"—but I stopped myself.

Nowhere do I claim to be a good father. Nowhere do I claim to be bad.

I told my son we'd go for a car ride, and he got on all fours and regressed. C'est la vie.

But I couldn't find my key chain with my car and house keys in my coat in the foyer.

I descended into the mouldy basement with my son in my arms and asked Lamia if she had seen my keys.

"No," she said.

Die you demon fuck you, you stupid piece of shit ass bitch, I thought. This was a Dybbuk thought directed at me, not her.

Or it wasn't.

My son followed me on all fours in his tiny suit through Lamia's bungalow in search of my keys. Afterward, because why not, I showed my son the garage, where Lamia hoarded things: chewed tennis balls, broken musty sofas, cracked ping-pong balls, hundreds of newspapers, juggler's balls, a man-sized cardboard cut-out of Gumby. "Scary," my son said, and then we searched the muddy woods out back for my uncle. We found him by the beaver pond. He hid behind a pine. The dog peed on the pine. My uncle jumped out from behind the pine, holding a red canister of gasoline, and said, "April Fools."

I said, "It's November."

I said, "Have you seen my keys?"

"I know a lot about cars," he said. "I know for example how to seal your gasoline."

"Where are my keys?"

My uncle laughed until he death rattled. "I forget."

Kill him, I thought.

Definitely not a Dybbuk thought. Definitely not directed at me.

I said, "Would you please trace your steps from the moment you stole my gasoline to the moment you lost my keys?"

"What's in it for me?"

Anyone who's looked up BB's Kiss on the internet knows that it's incurable and tough to live with. But I don't think it's as tough as working in a coal mine—although people with BB's Kiss are more likely to kill themselves than men who work in coal mines (about one in six of us)—although people who work in coal mines kill themselves just by working in coal mines. What I'm trying to say is that in that moment it took my entire shallow reservoir of psychic strength not to push my uncle into the beaver pond and thereby possibly give him beaver feaver. Instead I channelled my inner good person and said, "Would you please be so kind as to let me borrow your car?"

"No can do," he said. "That car's my baby, my sweet Caddy baby, four-wheel drive, SUV."

"Would you please drive us in your Caddy baby to a place where the three of us can eat breakfast?"

"I like pancakes."

"Would you please drive us in your Caddy baby to a place where the three of us can eat pancakes?"

"Great idea," my uncle said. "I love pancakes. Just give me half an hour to finish walking this little cutie pie."

On the drive toward pancakes I sat in the passenger seat of my uncle's SUV and tried to remember what being slim and not stupid had been like. Meanwhile, in the back seat, my son sat beside a wooden baseball bat and quietly woofed to himself. He was without his child seat. His child seat was in my car, technically my wife's car. (We split the insurance, but she'd bought it before meeting me.) While my uncle talked on and on about his achievements as a high school baseball player and how much better he had been at his job than his colleagues and boss, I remembered the last night my wife and I had shared a bed. I remember that she had said, "You believe you are only lovable when sick."

"Pardon?" I said.

"Growing up," my wife said to the ceiling—she was on her back with her hands crossed on her chest like a corpse in a casket—"your mother paid the most attention to you when you were sick, right?"

"Right."

"So you grew up equating being sick with being pitied, and being pitied with being loved, and being loved with being sick."

"Whoa."

"Now let us follow this logic to its conclusion," my wife said. "You and me, it'll be a team effort. It'll be fun. More fun than I've had in months."

"Months?"

"Months."

"What about San Francisco?"

"Months."

"This is a lot to take in," I said.

"You want to be loved," my wife said, "and yet, in your mind, to be loved is to be sick, to be sick is to be loved. So in your mind it follows that if you were to get better—if, for example, you were to go back to your psychiatrist and start taking your meds again—you would no longer be loved."

I said nothing.

"Therefore," my wife said, and finally she looked at me, "I'm offering you an ultimatum: you do those things, and I stay; you don't, I don't."

"Mommy?" our son said, in the doorframe.

We had forgotten to shut our door.

He must've heard his parents fighting, or something like fighting. My wife and I had made it a rule to never fight in front of him. Her parents had fought in front of her. She would never.

Our son held his stuffed monkey, Ape Boo, to his chest. "Why?"

My wife said, "Did you know that humans evolved from monkeys?"

"I'm a monkey?"

"You're not a monkey," I said. "You're most certainly a human. But long, long ago, in a land far away, humans were monkeys, before they evolved into humans."

"Friendly monkeys," my wife said.

"But I don't want to be a monkey," our son said. "I want to be a human." And he threw Ape Boo on the floor and said, "Or maybe a dog?"

Hence his metamorphosis, as it were.

"We're here," my uncle said. He parked his SUV outside a diner beside a gas station and honked his horn and said, "Honk honk."

I said, "Beep beep."

"Man oh man," he said, "are the pancakes here ever buttery. Used to come here all the time as a teen. Used to come here when I was hungover. These pancakes cure the worst hangovers and let me tell you, I could drink the lights out when I was a teen. I had a nickname with regards to my epic drinking. My nickname was The Drinker. I also had a nickname with regards to my baseball playing. My nickname was The Home Runner. My wife named me that. We were prom king and queen. Every guy in town wanted to have sex with me. I mean her. But she only ever had sex with me. Put that in your pipe and smoke it."

He gave me a high-five.

The diner's wood-panelled walls were covered in cross-country skis and black-and-white photos of malnourished men with handsomely gaunt cheekbones building useful things such as roads. The diner was empty; nonetheless, the only waitress led us to the table nearest the bathroom, where it smelled like a bathroom. On our table was a candle inside a mason jar. (This was before candles in mason jars were hip.) I focused on the flame. The flame was panicking. Also, it had nothing to do with me. Everything had nothing to do with me. The table was not a table but rather a gritty VCR recording of a table—or no, it wasn't even a recording, it was a recording of a recording—it was, in fact, a simulation; it was a simulation of—of what?—and the waitress, a tired teen who appeared to be experimenting with eyeshadow, was also a simulation; and so too were my uncle and son; and if I observed the simulation carefully enough I would maybe spot a blip. My nose smelled canned corn. My ears heard a song. Did other people hear it? It was an autotuned R&B song about a sixteen-year-old boy persuading an older woman at a club to dance with him while her boyfriend is elsewhere, being a lesser man. The vocal track was one thing; the instrumental track was another. The two tracks didn't belong together: I had found a blip. And now my arms were not arms but rather globs of meat, not unlike uncooked pork sausage, which moved when I thought, "Move," but which were limited in their range of motion. I tried to separate the uncooked pork sausages from my torso, which was also an uncooked pork sausage, but the rules governing the simulation prevented me from doing so. The blip, the song, kept going. La la la. Was the simulation using the song to antagonize me? But then it occurred to me that there was no me to antagonize: my thoughts were also simulated, they were not governed by me, they were governed by whatever logic governed the simulation, and so too was my very sense of self—it was a simulation. I myself was a simulation. If "I" acted, then and only then, "I" could escape. How? Suicide, of course. I would hurry toward the kitchen and chug a bottle of bleach. So I hurried toward the kitchen to chug a bottle of bleach. But no, I was still at our table. "Move," I told my legs, two uncooked pork sausages, but they didn't move. And now some mouth was mouthing something. Some mouth was mouthing, "Daddy, daddy, daddy."

"Bleach," I said.

"Who is great-grandma?"

I was me again.

My uncle said, "I didn't know the boy could habla Inglés."

He said, "Father abandoned us but mom did not."

"Hm," I said.

"It's thanks to your great-grandmother, dog boy," my uncle said, "that I'm basically a genius with numbers. She used to test me with matches! Watch this: tell me a number, any number, then tell me to divide by another number, any number, and I can do all of it in my head."

The waitress said, "Coffee?"

Despite my rapid and possibly irregular heartbeat I said yes please.

To my uncle I said, "We'd rather you tell us stories about what your mother did to you when you were a child, such as, how did she test you with matches?"

"Mom used to drive me to my baseball games," he said. "I was very big back then, and super strong."

"Did you ever play sports with your mother?"

"She's very good at ping-pong. She's even better than the Orientals, and also the Chinese."

"Did she play with you nicely?"

"By age twelve," my uncle said, "I could compete with her. Started almost winning by sixteen. You should have seen my hair at sixteen."

The tired teenage waitress returned with two coffees and asked if we were ready to order. I told my son he could order whatever he so desired.

Then I said, "But please don't stain your suit."

"Cute," the waitress said.

There was something about being inside my uncle's SUV that made me have emotional memories. On the drive back to Lamia's bungalow I could not help but remember the night I first met my wife. I met her at a Halloween party at a penthouse in Chelsea; the host, a friend of a friend, or maybe a friend of a friend of a friend, had a relative who had invented the Michelin Man. At least a quarter of the people at the party were coked out. I was not. Neither was my wife-to-be. This was nine months after my mother had passed due to sickness. She was dead and would never come back. My wife-to-be was twenty-seven at the time and in grad school for social work. I was slim and smelled good. I could bench my body weight. I was dressed as a tax return. She was dressed as a big purple grape. Both of us despised the host, as well as rich people in general, though we'd learn that later. We would learn early in our relationship that we agreed on the important things. One thing that we agreed was important was fun. Both of us were at the party to have fun. Both of us did not know the host. My first impression of my wife-to-be was that she was well-adjusted, mentally stable, a good person but not in a scary way, and not grieving—in these ways, my opposite. She was one inch taller than me but I could get used to that. She tugged at me. She didn't know it, she didn't even seem to notice me, I saw her before she did me, but she was a leash tied to my guts, or no, not a leash but a ribbon, a blue and perfumed ribbon, so easy to cut; and every time a man spoke to her, every time a man leaned in close so he could hear what she said, the ribbon tightened and loosened, loosened and tightened again. I needed her. I couldn't face her. A crowd formed in the kitchen, as they always do at fun parties, even penthouse parties, and I found myself standing back-to-back with her. She spoke to one cluster of drunk and/or drugged people while I spoke to another. I didn't know what anyone, including me, was saying. I pressed my back against hers. She didn't move away. I felt her shape, so this was her shape, this was her shape beneath her grape costume, here she was pressing her back against mine, and still against mine, and still.

"Home run," my uncle said. He pulled into Lamia's driveway and parked beside my wife's car, which was beside Lamia's station wagon. (Her garage was too cluttered with junk to fit a car.) My son and I found her in the living room eating white bread with margarine and a pickle. Camael was still on the recliner in the carpeted TV den. I asked Lamia if she would play ping-pong in the basement with my son and she said, "Don't interrupt me when I'm eating."

So I waited until she finished eating and she said, "Can he hold a rally?"

But she didn't rally with my son.

"One nothing," she said to him. "Two nothing. Three nothing. You're terrible. Five nothing. It's nice having you here, Sir Gawain."

"What?"

"Six nothing. Seven. This is a joke." And she left the basement. My son cried.

It hurt me to see him cry.

"Repeat after me," I said. "My great-grandma is evil."

"My great-grandma is evil."

"Mom and dad are good."

"Mom and dad are good."

"Correct," I said. "Now would you like to go home?"

My son nodded. I wiped the tears from his face and adjusted his tiny tie.

"First, though, your dad must find the phone book."

I found the phone book in the carpeted TV den, where Camael was watching the TV, which was off.

"Please listen to me," he said.

"I'm listening."

"I'm lucid."

"I'm all ears."

"It's hell for me here," he said. "I worked my whole life as a dental assistant in Buffalo. I know Buffalo. I know mouths. I know hell. And this is hell. They treat me like the dog. Or no, they treat me worse than the dog, because they play with the dog, and feed it."

He closed his eyes and fell asleep.

On the cordless home phone in the TV den I called the town's only mechanic. The phone rang and rang. No voicemail. Again I searched the bungalow for my car keys. My son followed. My left leg started involuntarily kicking. "Stay back, son."

We entered the cluttered garage. It smelled of mice and must. I faced the life-sized cardboard cut-out of Gumby.

"Who's that big green man?"

"Great-grandma's friend."

"I hate him."

I punched Gumby in the face.

Gumby fell.

"I love daddy."

Ah, how I miss hearing that.

My son and I searched Lamia's basement for my car keys, and when we entered the music room we saw what any omniscient being knew we would see.

We saw the dog. We saw my uncle.

My uncle looked at us. We looked at him. The dog looked at us looking at him.

I saw the jar of apple butter.

I do not feel bad about the things I did next. Nor do I blame them on BB's Kiss. First, I kicked my uncle in the shin, called him what he was, and with one arm picked up the traumatized dog and with the other arm picked up my traumatized son and carried them upstairs like two footballs. Lamia was in the muddy backyard, juggling. Camael was still asleep in the TV den. I stole my uncle's car keys from his jacket in the foyer, opened the back door of his SUV, placed the dog on the backseat, got my uncle's wooden baseball bat, closed the door, used the baseball bat to break open the back window of my wife's sedan, took out the child seat, installed the child seat in my uncle's SUV, sat my son down in the child seat, made sure the dog was beside him, and sped away—with both my son and the dog— in my uncle's SUV. Then I did a U-turn and sped back to Lamia's bungalow, locked my son and the dog inside my uncle's SUV, opened the bungalow door, found Camael sleeping on the recliner in the TV den, picked him up, piggy-backed him toward my uncle's SUV, sat him in the passenger seat, buckled him up, got into the driver's seat, buckled myself up, made sure my son was still buckled up in his child seat, made sure the dog was still beside him, and sped away again, this time for good.

I worried about getting home without committing a murder-suicide. It was nighttime. The moon was pixelated and pickled. The dark purple sky was a screensaver on a cosmic computer that cared nothing for me. I huffed and puffed and was too conscious of my body fat. Camael slept. The dog slept. My son said nothing. My shaking hands kept involuntarily honking the horn, and other drivers kept voluntarily flipping me off.

Eventually my son, in his child seat, said, "I don't want to be a dog. I want mommy."

I dialled his mom on the car phone and handed the phone to him.

He whispered something. He whispered something else. "Daddy?"

"Yes?"

"Phone."

I took the car phone and my wife said to me, "You fucked up."

"I didn't know he was actually a pervert."

"Your mother told you he was actually a pervert."

"I thought she was exaggerating."

Camael grabbed the car phone and said, "Police? I've been kidnapped."

I took back the car phone and said, "I love you."

"I'm leaving."

"Please don't."

And that's when I hit the doe.

People say time slows down. Incorrect. It's more like time breaks apart into a series of pulsating instants; between each piece is nothing—the void between quarks. I hit the doe. Void. I was standing above the doe. Void. I was off the road, in a dark forest, and the doe's back legs were flattened, immobile, not even bleeding, and its neck was flailing like a loose hose. Void. I was holding a rock in my hand. Void. I was bashing and bashing the doe's head until it died.

Until that moment the biggest creature I had ever killed was a worm.

In that moment my life was so real it felt fake.

My son, who couldn't see the doe or me, said, "Is the deer okay?" I had forgotten about my son. Also Camael. Also the dog.

The dog wasn't dead. Neither was Camael. His nose bled onto his beard. "Ow," he said. My son was intact. Crying, and by now doubly traumatized, but intact. His child seat had saved him. I unbuckled my son from his child seat and held him to my heart and kissed his head.

The rest of the way home I drove very carefully, as though stoned, but also way over the speed limit, given that I needed to get home before my wife left me. I did not want that to happen. On our third date, at a bar, she arrived late and surprised me by jumping on my back, and her hair fell over my face, and I smelled whatever shampoo she was wearing, and I wanted everyone in the bar to see her on my back. I never tired of being seen with her in public. I wished my mother had been alive to meet her. She would have been proud, I know.

To stop my son from sobbing, I told him another educational fairy tale about knights and squires and so forth.

The fairy tale didn't help.

So I settled on telling him that everything was okay.

But nothing was okay.

When finally we did arrive at our apartment, rather late at night, I needed to figure out how to parallel park my uncle's SUV.

There was an empty parking spot on our side of the street, between a silver hatchback and a red sedan. With three cars behind me, plus a U-Haul, I tried to align the front of my uncle's SUV with the back door of the silver hatchback; then I put my uncle's SUV in reverse, wrapped my right arm around Camael's head, and with my left hand palmed the steering wheel rightward until the front of my uncle's SUV inched into the opposite lane—cars there stopped—and I backed up slowly, very slowly, until the SUV's front tires straightened out and I was at a 90-degree angle from the curb. "Am I going to hit the red sedan behind us?" I asked Camael. He was asleep. I accelerated out of the parking spot, into my lane, until the front of my uncle's SUV was again aligned with the back door of the silver hatchback. *Go die slut*, I thought. This was a Dybukk thought. I turned on the SUV's hazards. Behind me, the driver of the U-Haul flashed his high beams. I rolled down my window and waved for him to pass—he couldn't, however, because the vehicles in the opposite lane were now stuck behind a parked UPS truck. I turned and reversed my uncle's SUV until its front bumper nearly bumped the driver-side door of the car in the opposite lane; its driver rolled down his window and told me to suck a nut. The SUV's back right tire rolled onto the curb. I turned the steering wheel as far leftward as possible and backed up. The back right tire was still on the curb. The driver of the U-Haul behind me started honking, and the driver in the opposite lane, the one who'd told me to suck a nut, started filming me with a camcorder. I inched forward, into my lane, until the front of my uncle's SUV was about two feet in front of the silver hatchback's front bumper—another mistake—and, placing both hands on the wheel, I backed up while examining my progress in the rear-view mirror. A bicyclist slalomed past the *passenger* side of my uncle's SUV. "My ears hurt," my son said. Lamia's diddled dog licked my right elbow. Camael, whose beard was red with blood, and who'd spent most of the ride asleep and possibly concussed, woke up and said, "The life I could have lived but did not is more real to me than the life I did live, which I regret." The cars behind me now filled the entire block, while in the other lane, the cars were still stuck behind the parked UPS truck. The intersections at both ends were clogged with cars. It was bumper to bumper. *Kill yourself you piece of fuck*, I thought. The driver of the U-Haul behind me started tapping his horn: bip, bip, bip, bip—4/4. At least he had a sense of rhythm. "The thing about mouths," Camael was saying. I turned the steering wheel as far leftward as possible. Or as far rightward as possible. I couldn't tell. I inched forward. I straightened the wheel and backed up. "When you stare into a mouth," Camael was saying. I was still too far away from the curb. The cars behind me still had no room to pass by. My son, now sobbing again, said, "I hate this dog." "Yip yip," said the dog. "Oh, I once had dreams," said Camael. My left calf clenched. My hands were uncooked pork sausages. They slid slowly down the wheel, onto my thighs, which were also uncooked pork sausages. "Move," I told the hand sausages. The hand sausages didn't move. "Move," I said again, and still the hand sausages didn't move. I couldn't move. "Yip yip," said the dog. "Bip, bip, bip, bip." *Suck a nut and kill yourself you fucking shit of fuck shut up.*

The driver's door—my door—was opened. Void. The seatbelt—my seatbelt—was unbuckled. Void. I was on the concrete. Void. Concrete. Void.

Then I was me again, and a small man, the man from the U-Haul truck, was at the wheel of my uncle's SUV.

"My son," I shouted, or thought.

I rescued my son from his child seat and held him to my heart in the middle of the street.

The small man parallel parked my uncle's SUV.

Camael was still inside the SUV.

So too was the dog.

I abandoned them there and, holding my son under my arm like a football, ran toward my apartment and pressed the intercom because I did not have my keys. Through the intercom I told my wife she was right. I was not. I was sorry.

Through the intercom I said, "Are you still there?"

Creaturæ

CHRISTIANE VADNAIS
translated by Pablo Strauss

D on't swim in the evening. Don't wash clothes after dusk. Don't travel over water to visit your friends.

When lanterns fat as jellyfish burn above the boathome doors, and candles flicker in rows along sagging railings, the insects flitting around in the heat are bewitched by the light. Drawn by the glimmer of their bodies around the window, the birds of the sky and the nocturnal fish begin circling these dwellings built right on the water. The carnivores emerge; their predators soon follow.

Don't swim in the evening, the villagers say. The lights dancing like a bonfire are far too alluring, drawing the lake monsters from all sides.

It's a windless evening, a perfect night to be out on the water. Flames from the brazier rise up toward the stars, twisting between faces half hidden by shadows. Hours have passed since the town stopped pitching and rolling, though Thomas hasn't noticed. His neighbours are earthsick. He twirls a skewer between two fingers. An eel is impaled on the tip. His heart is elsewhere.

Thomas's gleanings decorate the wharf: seashells and glass bottles and pennants cover the stains and knots in the wood. In the shimmering festive light, it's an almost elegant scene, a welcome worthy of Thomas's sister, who is back from the Coast for a few days, with a friend. Every chair Thomas could borrow from neighbouring cabins has been set out for dining al fresco, and a nearby table has been laid with grilled fruits, fried larvae, and other delicacies. *I did my best*, he thinks, *but it's still not enough.*

At the wharf's edge, the whole village makes toasts to the prodigal daughter and to Laura, her friend from away. The pair have travelled a great distance from their school on the dryland to holiday here. From their clothing to their smiles to the coronæ of flies above their perfumed hair, everything about these women proclaims their foreignness.

To Laura, say the villagers in chorus, raising their glasses. The newcomer lifts her cup, like a ship hoisting its standard before setting sail.

To Laura, Thomas says breathily, as his heart brims over.

The village has been cobbled together from old barges and sailboats, boards salvaged from yachts, whatever odds and ends the lake tossed up. From the sails of the ships that once plied these waters, the villagers have fashioned tents complete with living rooms and sleeping chambers. There is even a bar selling local grain alcohol alongside liquors imported from the Coast. Looking out from these dwellings, when the heat has broken and the mist has cleared, you can almost see the dryland, at the confluence of water and sky.

To people from away, the village looks like a squat, sprawling oil rig. Nothing could be further from the truth.

Walking the boardwalks reveals a world of bleached wood, rusty metal, and perpetually damp canvas. Precarious housing stands alongside gardenbarges where vegetables grow under broken-window mosaics. The decks are connected by treacherous rope walkways along which the village kids grapple, screeching like monkeys, on their way to school. On the west side are small craft of more recent manufacture, pleasure boats moored for the celebration. Discordant music emerges in bursts.

On a deck Thomas has painted a thousand times, only to see his work peel away under the waves and squalls, friends and family have gathered. Glasses shatter; laughter clashes; all around, people chatter and hum. Laura sits next to Thomas. She's smiling and frightfully relaxed. An earthy smell emanates from her hair. Girls like her—outlanders unfamiliar with their ways—rarely visit the village. The natural flow goes in the opposite direction, the one Thomas's sister chose. Not many stay here. The ones with rheumy eyes; the ones whose hips lurch no matter what they do, the ones whose dank toes harbour colonies of fungus.

Thomas lowers his eyes.

She'd never want to be with a local like him. If she could read his thoughts, she'd never take him sailing down the waterways to the Coast, to the cities, to that whole other world that doesn't pitch or yaw. Tormented by this thought, he completely forgets his eel. She reminds him. With slightly trembling hands, he breaks apart the blackened, crispy flesh and hands her a morsel that immediately disappears between beguiling lips.

Throughout the evening, Thomas introduces Laura to the guests pouring over from neighbouring decks. Cousin-this, friend-that. Without hesitation she kisses and hugs and explains. She's here for research. She goes to school with Thomas's sister. She's from the North. She has travelled several days to reach the shore of this vast lake, to find herself on this deck surrounded by rare birds and endemic species.

At these words, glasses clink, mouths laugh and speak in an unbroken stream. They sing the village's praises and comment on its habits of thought, wax lyrical on the art of grilling. The deck begins shaking from the music in a concert of foot-tapping and savage yelps.

On the makeshift dance floor, Thomas shows Laura the basics: how to wriggle your arms like twin catfish; how to trundle-step like a fiend. With sweat steaming from her skin, she leaps, and laughs, and scrunches up her face. Performed by Laura, these awkward steps transcend mere local custom and are transfigured into the nuptial parade of some rare bird, the promise of another world shining in the black village night. She wriggles her arms like twin catfish; she trundle-steps like a delirious fiend. A world can be seen radiating out from her yellow eyes and narrow hips, a sweat-drenched world along her chest where mosquitoes alight.

With generous swigs of rum, Thomas had hoped to screw up his courage for a slow dance. He manages only to orbit Laura, adrift in her exotic scent. He'd give anything to be worthy of this woman, to surrender to his unchecked desire to flee this village and discover the splendours of the dryland. But his embarrassment over his permanently moist skin and his uncertain footsteps thwarts Thomas's attempts to move closer.

Surrounded by marine and avian life, the village at the centre of the lake is a nest of writhing appetites. On the deck, shoes clack on cracked boards, mouths sputter and pant, hips sway. It's as if the villagers' stomachs are bottomless pits, their legs spring-loaded dancing machines. You could almost believe that the moths whose flight captivates Laura are not insects but fairy godmothers sparkling in the oil-black night. It seems that this party will never end, that the villagers will remain forever in motion, spinning and jolting and waiting for a dawn that never deigns to show its red nose.

Only when a neighbour extends a hand toward the stranger, hoping to show her some new steps, does Thomas finally find it in himself to lead his partner off the dance floor.

The pair sit on the bench. Cigar smoke rises in curls above them. Nearby, card players are staking their honour, and losing. Fists pound the table. Two boys cling to the railing. Their game is to gobble down anything and everything the universe puts in their path: scrambled liquids, writhing insects, wormwood twigs they gnaw with gusto.

Side by side, with their noses in their drinks, Laura and Thomas feel like they're the only people in the world. Laura gazes at Thomas, eyes shiny from alcohol. He'd like to get down on his knees, travel up the byways of her body, tilt her head back and release a cry from her depths. But he's petrified. He asks about her job. She describes her lab and research missions, aquariums and graphs, petitions and campaigns. With extravagant hand gestures she talks and talks and talks some more, and he does his best not to hear. He never should have unleashed this torrent of ideas from her mouth. He knows villagers who have almost lost legs to the jaws of a freshwater shark, and others forced to fend off the birds to protect their catch of fish at the end of the day. It's not the pernicious intelligence of animals that needs protection but the people who dwell on this vast lake. It is he, Thomas: he needs Laura to take him away from this teetering existence, far away from his breeding pond; to hold him to her heart and take him away like a specimen fished from the water.

Rum-drunk, Laura suggests a swim. *We can't do that.* He reminds her in a whisper that the fish-filled waters surrounding the village are full of sharks. She's so new to this world. Sweeping away his warning with the back of her hand, she mutters something about old wives' tales. In the joyful glow of the lantern, she takes off her clothes.

Thomas finds a dark corner and does the same.

Their bodies tumble like deep-sea divers; they plunge into the black water, then rise to the surface, coming together halfway up. He pursues her past boathouses and shell-laden docks, swims between gardenbarges and fishing nets. Shadow puppets on tent walls gently light up the night and their path through the water. She dives as effortlessly as a sea snake, and at regular intervals the water's surface is broken first by her shiny head of wet hair, then by the smooth, firm curve of her ass.

She stops in front of him and treads water. Laura's face now wears the very expression he has been dreaming of, but Thomas can't supress a wince when he feels the viscous side of a fish against his thigh. *Don't wreck this moment.* There she is, slowly paddling her arms to keep her shoulders and neck above water level, her face like a buoy. Small fears snap and pop in every muscle in Thomas's body. There are sparks in his fingers and legs, but he moves forward, unsure whether he most fears the menacing calmness of this water or the daunting proximity of such beauty.

Laura makes the first move. She brings her lips to his. Her kiss contains the chill of snow in the tropical heat, an immaculate wind awakening in him the desire to leave this place behind. They breathe as one. Their hands touch; their feet locate the improbable crest of a shoal. Underwater, she seeks out his thighs and hips and ass. Astounded by the texture of her skin, its purity in this murky water, he tries without success to lead her into the shadow of the platform, near the hulls. She finds her footing on the slick algae that populates the lake floor, as if it were the most mundane substrate, and clings to him, setting the pace, imposing her movements and rhythms and desires.

Her fingers slide under water, over his flank.

Though her face can't conceal her surprise, Laura's hand holds fast. Curiosity makes her linger over the hard, scaly skin, a patch that grows larger by the day, increasing Thomas's likeness to the other lake creatures. She palpates and then releases it, exploring its relief. A crease of concentration lines her forehead. She dives and stays under long enough to glimpse the silvery lustre of this patch of skin, then resurfaces. For a second her nail digs into his flesh—as if to take a sample—but the movement shifts into a caress. She runs her palm down the mark, measuring its size and shape, studying its form and sensitivity.

She draws him even closer, gives him a bright smile.

Don't swim in the evening. Don't wash clothes after dusk. Don't travel over water to visit your friends.

Under the boathomes, hungry fish lie in wait. Others leap up to snap at the prey flitting above the water; a few enjoy the luxury of deep, dreamless sleep. All this nocturnal fauna blends together in a fog of pleasure and need. In the shadow of the dock, a shark undulating to the music of a faraway concert band slowly circles an embracing couple. The man shoots phosphorescent semen into the water, then waltzes his partner around. In spite or because of the foreignness of these customs, she feels her whole body quake as she cries out.

The shark listens, feverishly arches its back, and continues its rapturous encircling.

Deep underwater, dark ribbons of seaweed sway back and forth, and the party's cast-off scraps swirl like confetti.

Jean Marc Ah-Sen is the author of *Grand Menteur* and *In the Beggarly Style of Imitation*, and is one of the participants in the collaborative omnibus novel *Disintegration in Four Parts*. His writing has appeared in *Hazlitt*, the *Literary Review of Canada*, *Maisonneuve*, and elsewhere. He lives in Toronto with his wife and two sons.

Ryan Avanzado is a Filipino-Canadian-American author, born and raised in Toronto. He attended the MFA program in Writing at Columbia University, where he taught undergraduate fiction and served as Director of Columbia Artist/Teachers. He currently resides in Brooklyn, New York.

Carleigh Baker is an author and teacher of nêhiyaw âpihtawikosisân and European descent. Her debut story collection, *Bad Endings*, won the City of Vancouver Book Award and was a finalist for the Rogers Writers' Trust Fiction Prize, and the Emerging Indigenous Voices Award for fiction.

Tom Thor Buchanan is a writer from Dryden, Ontario, living and working in Toronto. His work has appeared in *Hazlitt*, *The Baffler*, and *Best Canadian Stories 2018*.

Paige Cooper's debut collection of short stories, *Zolitude*, was longlisted for the Scotiabank Giller Prize and shortlisted for the Governor General's Literary Award. The CBC, *The Walrus*, *The Globe and Mail*, *Toronto Star*, and *Quill & Quire* listed it among their best books of 2018.

Marcus Creaghan is a writer whose work has been featured in *Literary Hub*, *Vox*, *Catapult*, and *Augur,* among other places.

Paola Ferrante's debut poetry collection, *What to Wear When Surviving a Lion Attack*, was shortlisted for the Gerald Lampert Memorial Prize. She was longlisted for the 2020 Journey Prize and anthologized in *The Journey Prize Stories 32* along with *The Master's Review Anthology IX* (2021). She won *The New Quarterly*'s 2019 Fiction Award and *Room Magazine*'s 2018 Fiction Award, and received an Honorable Mention for *North American Review*'s 2019 Kurt Vonnegut Prize for Fiction. She is the Poetry Editor of *Minola Review* and lives in Toronto.

Camilla Grudova lives in Edinburgh, where she works as a bartender. *The Doll's Alphabet* was published in 2017, and her debut novel is forthcoming in 2022.

David Huebert is a settler writer, educator, and critic from K'jipuktuk (Halifax). His fiction debut, *Peninsula Sinking*, won the Jim Connors Dartmouth Book Award, was shortlisted for the Alistair MacLeod Short Fiction Prize, and was runner-up for the Danuta Gleed Literary Award. His poetry collection, *Humanimus*, was shortlisted for the J. M. Abraham Atlantic Poetry Award. David's second book of fiction, *Chemical Valley*, appeared in fall 2021. David teaches literature and creative writing at the University of New Brunswick.

Jessica Johns is a Nehiyaw aunty with English-Irish ancestry and a member of Sucker Creek First Nation in Treaty 8 territory in Northern Alberta. Her short story "Bad Cree" won the 2020 Writers' Trust Journey Prize, and her novel of the same name will be released in January 2023.

Cody Klippenstein's short stories have won the *Zoetrope: All-Story* short fiction competition and *The Fiddlehead* short fiction contest. Other work has appeared in *Epoch*, *The Malahat Review*, *Room*, and elsewhere. She holds an MFA from Cornell University.

Michael LaPointe published *The Creep*, a novel, in 2021. He has written for *The Atlantic*, *The New Yorker*, and *The Times Literary Supplement*, and he was a columnist with *The Paris Review*. He lives in Toronto.

Julie Mannell is an author of poetry, fiction, and creative nonfiction. She is a professor of creative writing at George Brown College and was the 2020 Visiting Writer at the University of Nebraska at Omaha's MFA Program. She was the recipient of the Lionel Shapiro Award for Excellency in Creative Writing, the Mona Adilman Poetry Prize and the 2020 Doris McCarthy Artist-in-Residence Program. She holds an MFA from the University of Guelph, where she was awarded the HarperCollins and Constance Rooke scholarships. She lives on a fruit farm in Welland, Ontario.

Sofia Mostaghimi is a Toronto-based fiction writer, editor, and educator. Her fiction has appeared in *Joyland Magazine*, *The Fiddlehead*, and *The Puritan*, among others, and has been longlisted for the Journey Prize. Her novel *Desperada* is forthcoming in spring 2023.

Téa Mutonji is an Afro-Canadian writer from Scarborough currently based in Manhattan. Her first collection of short stories, *Shup Up You're Pretty*, was shortlisted for the Atwood Gibson Writers' Trust Fiction Prize and won the Edmund White Award and the Trillium Book Award. She is a recipient of the Jill Davis Fellowship at New York University, where she is completing her master's in fiction.

Fawn Parker is the author of *Set-Point, Dumb-Show,* and *What We Both Know.*

Casey Plett is the author of *A Dream of a Woman, Little Fish,* and *A Safe Girl to Love.* She co-edited *Meanwhile, Elsewhere: Science Fiction and Fantasy from Transgender Writers,* which won the ALA Stonewall Book Award for Literature. She is a winner of the Amazon First Novel Award and the Firecracker Award for Fiction and is a two-time winner of theLambda Literary Award. She is also the Publisher of LittlePuss Press.

Rudrapriya Rathore writes fiction and nonfiction. Her work has appeared in *Brick, Hazlitt, Joyland, This Magazine, Humber Literary Review,* and *The Walrus.* In 2021, she was nominated for a National Magazine Award. She lives in Toronto.

Eliza Robertson's debut story collection, *Wallflowers,* was shortlisted for the East Anglian Book Award and the Danuta Gleed Literary Award and was selected as a *New York Times* Editor's Choice. Her critically acclaimed first novel, *Demi-Gods,* was a *Globe and Mail* and *National Post* book of the year and the winner of the 2018 QWF Paragraphe Hugh MacLennan Prize. Originally from Vancouver Island, Eliza lives in Montreal.

Naben Ruthnum lives in Toronto and is the author of *Curry: Eating, Reading, and Race* and *A Hero of Our Time.* As Nathan Ripley, he is the author of two thrillers, *Find You In the Dark* and *Your Life Is Mine.* He also writes for film and television.

Cason Sharpe is a writer currently based in Toronto. His first collection of stories, *Our Lady of Perpetual Realness,* was published in 2017.

John Elizabeth Stintzi is a nonbinary writer and artist who grew up on a cattle farm in northwestern Ontario. Their work has been awarded the 2019 RBC Bronwen Wallace Award for Emerging Writers, *The*

Malahat Review's 2019 Long Poem Prize, and the Sator New Works Award, and has been shortlisted for the Amazon Canada First Novel Award and the Raymond Souster Award. John Stintzi is the author of the novels *My Volcano* and *Vanishing Monuments* as well as the poetry collection *Junebat*. They live and work with their wife in Kansas City.

Pablo Strauss is a three-time finalist for the Governor General's Literary Award for Translation with *The Country Will Bring Us No Peace* (2020), *Synapses* (2019), and *The Longest Year* (2017). His shorter translations, reviews, and essays have appeared in *Granta*, *Geist*, and the *Montreal Review of Books*. He lives in Quebec City.

Gavin Thomson has an MFA (Fiction) from Columbia University, where he was a Felipe P. De Alba Fellow. He lives in Vancouver and is at work on his first novel.

Christiane Vadnais was born in 1986 in Quebec City. Her first novel, *Fauna*, won the Horizons Imaginaires speculative fiction award, the CALQ Award for an emerging artist in the Capitale-Nationale, and the City of Quebec book award.

ACKNOWLEDGMENTS

For permission to reprint previously published material, grateful acknowledgment is made to the following:

Jean-Marc Ah Sen: "Swiddenworld: Selected Correspondence with Tabatha Gotlieb-Ryder" from *In the Beggarly Style of Imitation* (Nightwood Editions, 2020) by Jean-Marc Ah Sen, reprinted by permission of the publisher; Carleigh Baker: "Baby Boomer" from *Bad Endings* (Anvil Press, 2017) by Carleigh Baker, reprinted by permission of the publisher; Tom Thor Buchanan: "Jamaica," originally published in *OMEGA Metatron*, reprinted by permission of the magazine; Paige Cooper: "Record of Working" from *Zolitude* (Biblioasis, 2018) by Paige Cooper, reprinted by permission of the publisher; Paola Ferrante: "Underside of a Wing," originally published in *The New Quarterly* (Fall 2019), reprinted by permission of the magazine; Camilla Grudova: "Madame Flora's," originally published in *The Puritan* (Spring 2019), reprinted by permission of the magazine; David Huebert: "Chemical Valley" from *Chemical Valley* (Biblioasis, 2021) by David Huebert, reprinted by permission of the publisher; Jessica Johns: "Good Bones," originally published in *Cosmonauts Avenue* (2018), reprinted by permission of the author; Cody Klippenstein: "Minor Aberrations in Geologic Time," originally published in *Little Fiction* (January 2015), reprinted by permission of the author; Michael LaPointe: "The Stunt," originally published in *Hazlitt* (September 10, 2018), reprinted by permission of the author; Julie Mannell: "Today Is Cool," originally published in *Joyland* (November 20, 2021), reprinted by permission of the author; Sofia Mostaghimi: "Roxane and Julieta," originally published in *The Fiddlehead* (November 2020), reprinted by permission of the author; Téa Mutonji: "Property of Neil," originally published in *Joyland* (November 2021), reprinted by permission of the author; Fawn Parker: "WunderHorse II," originally published in *Concordia University Magazine* (September 19, 2017), reprinted by permission of the magazine; Casey Plett: "Portland, Oregon," from *A Safe Girl to Love* (Topside Press, 2014) by Casey Plett, reprinted by permission of the author; Rudrapriya Rathore: "Girls Who Come in Threes," originally published in *The Humber Literary Review* (Winter 2019/20), reprinted by permission of the author; Eliza Robertson: "The Aquanauts," originally published in *carte blanche* (Spring 2019), reprinted by permission of the author; Naben Ruthnum: "Eight Saints and a Demon," originally published in *Hazlitt* (December 9, 2016), reprinted by permission of the author; Cason Sharpe: "California Underwater," originally published in *Bad Nudes*, reprinted by permission of the author; Christiane Vadnais: "Creaturæ," from *Fauna* (trans. Pablo Strauss, Coach House, 2020) by Christiane Vadnais, reprinted by permission of the publisher.

Véhicule Press